THE BRICKWORKS

PRAISE FOR THE BRICKWORKS

"Lucy E.M. Black's affection for her characters shines through on every page. The intricacies of friendship and love are beautifully woven throughout. *The Brickworks* is a charming journey into the turn of the twentieth century, with unexpected twists that will leave you with a smile on your face and an insatiable craving for pie."

~ Crystal Fletcher, author of *Beauty Beneath the Banyan*

"Immersive and masterfully written, *The Brickworks* by Lucy E.M. Black opens a portal to a past that thrums with immediacy. Black's attention to detail is exquisite. She deftly envelops us in the lives of Alistair and Brodie, two Scotsmen who find themselves in Canada at the turn of the twentieth century and are brought together by their resolve to forge their own paths in a world determined to keep people in their place. A stunning, riveting read!"

~ Hollay Ghadery, author of *Fuse* and *Rebellion Box*

"Lucy E.M. Black's beautifully crafted prose and rich historical detail vividly transport you to Canada at the turn of the twentieth century, engulfing you in the struggles of two pioneering Scottish immigrants. The pair rely on gumption and each other as they rise above their tumultuous pasts to embark on the difficult and dangerous venture of establishing a brickworks in an isolated community. Encompassing love and loss, hope and despair, friendship and betrayal, *The Brickworks* takes you on an unforgettable journey."

~ H&A Christensen, authors of *Stealing John Hancock*

"Lucy E. M. Black's *The Brickworks* is an engaging, enlightening, impeccably researched look at turn-of-the-twentieth-century industrial craftsmanship. With crisp dialogue and a sharp eye for historical detail at the personal, human level, Black has created a compelling world of ambitions and setbacks, tragedies and redemptions, and the sustaining power of community."

~ K. R. Wilson, author of *An Idea About My Dead Uncle* and *Call Me Stan: A Tragedy in Three Millennia*

THE BRICKWORKS

A Novel

LUCY E.M. BLACK

[N₁ [O₂ [N₁
CANADA

*Publisher's note: This book is a work of fiction. Names, characters, places and
incidents are either the product of the author's imagination or are used fictitiously,
and any resemblance to actual persons living or dead is entirely coincidental.*

Library and Archives Canada Cataloguing in Publication

Title: The brickworks : a novel / Lucy E.M. Black.

Names: Black, Lucy E. M., 1957- author.

Identifiers: Canadiana (print) 20230446620 | Canadiana (ebook) 20230446647 |
ISBN 9781989689547 (softcover) | ISBN 9781989689585 (EPUB)

Classification: LCC PS8603.L2555 B75 2023 | DDC C813/.6—dc23

Printed and bound in Canada on 100% recycled paper.

Now Or Never Publishing
901, 163 Street
Surrey, British Columbia
Canada V4A 9T8

nonpublishing.com
Fighting Words.

We gratefully acknowledge the support of the Canada Council for the Arts
and the British Columbia Arts Council for our publishing program.

In memory of Dr. James Gilbert Black,
his sense of adventure and view of the world.

And can it be that in a world so full and busy, the loss of one weak creature makes a void in any heart, so wide and deep that nothing but the width and depth of vast eternity can fill it up.

—Charles Dickens

Chapter One: The Bridge
Dundee, Scotland ~ December 28, 1879

The throng was impatient. Strangers had begun to confer with one another, crowded together as they were on the wooden platform. The winter wind howled as it swept up the steep bank of the Tay and along the frozen landscape to the train station. Buffeted by the icy gales, its timbers cracked as the roof lifted slightly in its struggle against the force.

Ladies wrapped tightly in shawls and heavy capes huddled anxiously against their male companions. Many kept a hand to their hats, concerned lest a gust of wind rip them from carefully pinned hair. Clusters of men, two and three at the start, merged with other groupings and walked short spans together, faces to the weather, straining for a glimpse of the expected train. Most had already waited an hour or more.

It must be the weather, they agreed. *The wind has blown summit on the tracks and they're working to clear the way.*

Ayes were heard as the men nodded in agreement. Returning to their wives and daughters, they spread the message and assured the women that the wait would not be much longer.

There's plenty o' men aboard to help wi' the work, they said. *It willnae be long now.*

Thus consoled, the women smiled and resumed waiting. A small stove was lit in the reception room inside the station and the ladies took turns indoors, warming their feet and hands, while the men continued to brave the elements.

After a second hour had passed, the men conferred once more. One young man, not long past twenty, volunteered to walk the tracks—to cross the long iron bridge so that he might seek a sighting of the train or any obstacle in its way. He would come back to report, he promised, and call for help if it were needed. A group of men walked with him off the platform and towards the long sloping curve of the bridge. The group bent into the wind, the snow covering them quickly while they walked.

A few hung back from the steep embankment. *This is daft,* said one.

Turn aroun' if you need, shouted another.

I'll be fine, if the Almighty intends... said the young man, the rest of his message drowned out by another gust of the strong, biting wind. The men walked a few paces alongside as he set his foot upon the bridge and stepped carefully forward. After a dozen footsteps they saw him buckle slowly and clasp the tracks with his gloved hands. He fell to his knees and began to creep ahead. They watched silently until he was obscured by the dense snow and they could no longer make out his huddled form crawling steadily onwards.

January 9, 1880

At first light the men assembled solemnly at the pier. Before boarding their launches they decided who was to cover which section of the estuary. Each craft had several men stationed as lookouts, and all were equipped with ropes and long-handled grappling hooks. As in their earlier searches—and in the searches to come—there was none of the customary bantering. It was a sombre group that took to the water.

Thaur! shouted one man, standing and pointing. Two boats advanced in the direction indicated, pulling up on either side of a floating body. At first only the torso was visible, a dark coat billowing above his back. As they manoeuvred closer they saw that the man was facing downwards, his arms and legs trailing below the surface. Then, when they pulled him onboard, they saw that he was missing a boot; a foot was exposed. It seemed unbearably intimate to witness such nakedness. They covered him tenderly with a canvas tarp, murmuring quietly to one another as they arranged him on the deck.

March 4, 1880

Margaret Hamilton stood stoically in line at the grocer. Although she'd nodded at the three women ahead of her, not one had returned the courtesy. The public shunning wounded her afresh. Janet Blair had been a friend in school, and Aileen MacKay lived but two doors down. Margaret waited patiently while the customers departed with their purchases. When it was her turn, she lifted the small wicker hamper onto the counter and smiled stiffly at the proprietor. The woman turned her back and busied herself straightening tins on the shelf behind her. Margaret continued to wait. The woman continued to fuss with the display in an exaggerated show of particular attention and care.

After some long minutes, Margaret cleared her throat. The proprietor remained facing away and did not turn.

Is yersel na willin' te tak ma coin?

Dinna ye ken? Yer coin isnae welcome here.

Margaret stepped sharply back from the counter. Stiffening her shoulders and holding herself purposefully erect, she left the little shop and walked out onto the high street. Without pausing, she navigated the cobbles swiftly, striding deliberately away from the long row of shops and home to her son.

September 10, 1884

On this, his third day of school, Brodie Hamilton was seated in his usual place in the classroom. As the other children came piling in, he smiled at the prospect of seeing his new friends. He shared a desk with Donald Ballantyne, and had done so since they started together. He turned to watch Donald unexpectedly take the seat next to Bryan Fordyce. Brodie tried to catch Donald's attention by waving and calling out to him but his friend seemed not to notice. Only yesterday the two had sat together in class, kicked a ball in the field behind the schoolhouse and shared their lunches.

Partway through the morning Brodie felt a light projectile of sorts hit him in the back of his neck. He looked down at the floor and quickly scooped up the crumpled ball of newsprint. Surreptitiously, he slid it onto his thigh and carefully smoothed it flat. The fragment was ripped from a newspaper article condemning those involved in the Tay Bridge Disaster.

His mother had told him the story of the winter storm, the collapsing bridge, how his own father had died while bravely trying to drive the train to safety through the worst of the weather. Brodie could not make out all the text, but he saw his father's name and the last part of a line that read *and the engine driver is to be blamed for taking the bridge too fast.*

It was enough. Brodie had a sudden sick feeling deep down inside. His face burned red. He felt that he could easily cry. *Murtherer* was whispered loudly from somewhere at the back of the room.

Chapter Two: The Art Gallery
Buffalo, New York ~ May 1, 1909

Alistair Lamont had anticipated this day with secret pleasure. It was the first Saturday in May and he was treating himself to a half day's holiday. He would soon be leaving on another bridge assembly and would be away for at least four months, so it might be some long time before he again had the luxury of such an outing.

He approached the new building eagerly, skirting the little lake and striding directly to the white marble columns at the front entrance. His eye detected something distractingly amiss with the placement. He paced out the distance between them. Even accounting for an inconsistency in his steps, he could tell that the columns were unevenly positioned. What was more, there was a lean to some of them, as if they were buckling under the weight they supported. He placed his hand discreetly alongside one of the columns, pushing his shoulder into the bulk of it, testing it for movement. Satisfied that it was yet stable, he straightened himself and walked purposefully through the heavy entrance doors and into the impressive marble foyer.

Alistair navigated his way to the central sculpture gallery. He did not stop to admire the marble forms but rather kept his gaze ceilingward as he took in the light-filled rooms, the transepts, the workmanship in the entablatures. He moved quickly through antechambers and elegant doorways, noting the carved details in the crown moulding, the exquisite finishing of joints, the fine polish of surfaces. It was the gallery's construction that had drawn him, after all, and not the paintings that hung on its walls. Clusters of visitors were grouped politely around the artwork. This suited him; he was easily able to slip past and continue his private survey of the rooms.

In his tweed suit, woollen tie, and thick-soled brogues, Alistair looked every bit a Scot. Red hair, cut in short waves framed his face. His eyes were bright blue and merry and his complexion ruddy, suggesting much time spent out of doors. He was a man accustomed to hard work but also a man with some small degree of refinement. He strode confidently through the spaces, intently focused on his studies. He did not notice those in the gallery who glanced at him curiously, taking his measure: a handsome man in good clothes and with strong, roughened hands held easily at his side.

A pair of wrought-iron screens having drawn his attention, Alistair moved towards the set of doors leading to an outside porch. As he approached, he observed a young woman on a little stool close by, absorbed in replicating a painting. She was bent over her palette and studiously mixing a pale shade of pink. Embarrassed to have trespassed so closely, he tipped his head in her direction. *Pardon my intrusion,* he said.

The girl looked up at him and smiled. *No matter, I was making of a mess of it.*

And then she laughed, a light, musical sound. Alistair was struck by the delicacy of her, the earnestness with which she worked, the light-hearted manner in which she had excused him. He took in her fine features and long, paint-smeared fingers.

Excuse me, he said again, taking a step away, feeling flushed and not a little clumsy.

There's no need to leave. She stood and extended her dainty hand. *I'm Violet Lewis.*

Alistair moved forward and bowed, touching her hand lightly. *Alistair Lamont. At your service.*

I'm so glad, she laughed. *Perhaps you can help me with this. What do you think it needs?*

Needs? Alistair looked at her canvas. She was painting an exact copy of the piece on the wall. *It looks a replica. Very good, I'm sure.*

She laughed again. *You are too kind. It is nothing near as good. Mine is clumsy and badly coloured. Look how softly he has mixed the skin tones.* She stepped more closely to the painting on the wall and pointed to the faces of the little girls playing on a grassy slope.

It looks well to me, Alistair suggested hopefully, *but I dinna profess to know anything about art.*

Why of course not. That is why you are here, is it not? To learn more. That's why we all come.

Well, Alistair countered. *I am here to study the building. I am interested in the construction.*

Really? How perfectly lovely. I think it simply beautiful. I come here to paint and to study the collection. I feel as though we are in a Greek temple!

He hesitated, unsure how to respond politely. Good manners would surely dictate he excuse himself, but he was thoroughly charmed and wished to delay, as much as possible, his withdrawal. Alistair was struck by her open yet intimate tone. She was dressed in a long navy skirt of some heavy fabric, her white shirtwaist high collared and trimmed with lace. Her sleeves rolled up to the elbow, a straw hat abandoned beside her on the floor. Dark brown hair was casually pinned up in a loose arrangement, with many tendrils having escaped the attempt at order.

Are you from Buffalo? she continued.

No. From Scotland. I came for the Exposition and decided to stay. I work now as an agent for a steel mill but am a brickmaker. I learned my craft at home and thought as there might be need of my skills in a growing country.

Alistair, conscious of her scrutiny, was immediately mortified by his personal disclosures. He saw her looking at his brogues, his suit, his sharply knotted tie. She glanced at his hands. They were not gentleman's hands, but neither were they uncared for. An effort had been made to apply ointment and trim and clean the nails. He felt tempted to hold them out for inspection, as he had often done as a child for his grandmother. He flushed further at the thought, aware of her steady assessment.

Brickmaking sounds perfectly fascinating. It must be tremendously interesting.

It can be. There's science to it, and some luck involved. You need all the right ingredients to make them come out well. And patience. It can be a keen disappointment when the kiln does no heat right and after six weeks' labour the bricks are ruined and all you have left are clinkers.

A clinker?

Alistair smiled to hear her ask. She made the word sound lyrical.

Och aye, a clinker is a ruined brick. It's good for naught but garden walls or paths.

Oh, I see. It sounds entirely delightful. And then she laughed again pleasantly, a light tinkling burst of melody.

Alistair was captivated. He could not bring himself to leave the gallery. He stood awkwardly, hands now in his pockets and staring at the floor, hoping she would further engage him in conversation. He waited a long moment. *I should leave you to your work. Excuse me.*

Violet reached out to shake his hand once more. *It was lovely to meet you, Mr. Lamont. I do hope you enjoy your visit.*

Alistair bowed, turned, and left the room, the wrought-iron screens forgotten. He was aware that his neck and face were deeply reddened. He dried the palms of his hands on the sides of his jacket and hurried self-consciously through to another gallery. The architectural details suddenly seemed far less absorbing. More of the same opulence and expensive finishing, he thought. Utterly unaffordable for most buildings. Brooding, he prowled its circumference, eyeing the artwork with skepticism.

What was it, he wondered, *that made these pieces so extraordinary? Why did people pay large sums for them? Some were attractive, admittedly, especially the thunderous stormy landscapes that looked a little like Peeblesshire, but why erect a costly building to warehouse nothing but pictures?*

While he indulged in such private reflections, Alistair continued to amble through the galleries, returning by chance every now and then to the central sculpture gallery filled with marbles. There the human form was represented in a collection that mostly he found he could not study. The partially clothed female figures, with their rounded breasts and full hips, discomfited him; he had to walk away quickly.

Deep in thought, Alistair finally left the building and began to walk around its garden, viewing the structure from its diverse aspects. Altogether, it really did resemble a temple, he thought. He found a bench beneath a tree and sat down to study the front portico once more.

There you are, he heard. *I wondered where you had gone.*

He looked up to see Miss Lewis walking towards him, wheeling a bicycle while awkwardly balancing her wooden stool, paint kit, and canvas on its seat. Her hat was now in place, long waves of hair curling out from underneath. She looked charming—and entirely incapable of travelling any distance without mishap. Alistair got to his feet and rushed to her side. *Allow me to assist you?* He reached for the stool and paint kit.

She handed these to him casually. *What were you looking at so intently?*

The front columns. I wondered why, when all else was so carefully done, that the columns were unevenly placed. Also, they look as though they're no straight and are bending under the weight of things.

By way of response, she laughed: that lovely sound he'd heard earlier. *How clever of you to notice. It was intentional, you see. The architect designed a classical temple, recreating all the details perfectly. Even the spacing and shape of the columns, and the lean of them. It was a brilliant thing to do.*

You seem to know a great deal about it.

My father was one of the subscribers. We have all heard a great deal about it for a very long time. I do, though, take an interest in such things. She smiled at him, inviting a response.

Alistair hesitated. His own interest in the building went only so far. *I would no wish to delay your departure by asking to know more,* he finally muttered.

How very proper you are.

Alistair felt himself colour once more. He felt that his ears, especially, had grown hot.

Are you much occupied in learning new things, Mr. Lamont? You sound as if you enjoy the cultivation of your mind.

Alistair realized that he could not stop looking at Miss Lewis. He startled, realizing now that she'd finished saying something and was pointedly waiting for a response. He began to sputter out a reply, but as he spoke he gradually became more assured.

I have no the benefit of a formal education, but I take it as necessary to learn what I can about the things that surround me. Fine paintings— he gestured towards the gallery—*may escape my understanding, but I am interested in the finishing of buildings, and also in a great many innovations in machinery and scientific discovery.*

I myself, said Violet, *am interested in learning about new ventures, Mr. Lamont. Of late, I have been reading a great deal about about the Ottoman Empire for instance, although I do not profess to understand all that I read. I will tell you anything you care to know about the building if you will help me fasten this stool and paint box to my bicycle. Herbert fastens it so beautifully for me in the mornings when I set out, but I am afraid that I cannot manage the knots and make a muddle.*

Have you any rope?

Violet set the wooden paint box on the grass and opened it. Inside were some short lengths of twine which she passed to him. He studied the bicycle and the paint box and stool for a moment. *Where does he put the canvas?* he inquired.

Inside the paint box. But it's dry in the morning and wet now so I think I shall have to leave it out.

Does he fasten these things to your basket or to the back fender?

The basket. He's tremendously clever with knots. She laughed again, and Alistair smiled to hear her.

Is Herbert your husband? Alistair waited for her response, his fingers poised to perform their service.

Herbert? Oh no! Violet broke into a spate of gay laughter. *Heavens no! Herbert is our butler. He must be one hundred and two and has been with us forever.*

Alistair looped the twine through the wicker basket and fastened the stool and paint box tightly to its top. Gingerly he lifted the wet canvas and tucked the top edge under a twist of cord. *That should do,* he said, *but you will need to exercise caution. I have no secured it overtight.*

How perfectly splendid! Thank you. I don't know what I would have done had we not met.

Alistair bowed stiffly. *My pleasure, I'm sure.*

Violet prepared to mount her bike. With one hand she gathered her skirt and straddled the crossbar. Alistair had a flash of layered petticoats and a peek of black stocking above her neat leather boot.

Be careful, he cautioned, *or the painting might shift itself.*

I know, she smiled, *and become airborne and sail across Lake Erie like a bird and then I shan't have to struggle again with the skin tones.* She laughed at her small fancy. *Goodbye, Mr. Lamont.*

Alistair bowed as she wheeled away. He'd considered asking if he might walk with her, but that seemed entirely too forward. Besides which, he was a man building his fortunes. He could not afford to be distracted.

Callaghan's Steel was not the largest mill in Buffalo, but it was the most prestigious. The main building, of buff-coloured stone construction, nestled into the banks of the Niagara River. No expense had been spared; its copper roof alone proclaimed its importance. Upon approach, one could see further evidence of its distinction. At the top of the marble steps stood wide, double glass doors trimmed in brass relief, and fifty feet above them soared a great window bordered by ornate metal fretwork. Once inside the rotunda, one could look up to see a sunburst glass ceiling three storeys above. Descending from the glass skylight was a spectacular mosaic made from thousands of sheets of Venetian glass, cut into millions of tiny squares. A group of skilled workers had laboured for a full year to install it. The sparkling gold, rust, and bronze tiles formed a geometric border with a simple biblical quotation: *That all men may know His work.* The men joked that this could refer to the Almighty or to Callaghan equally.

Across the rotunda and opposite its doors wound a gleaming metal staircase, beckoning to be climbed aloft. The balustrade was highly ornamented with polished copper, brass, and steel detailing. The balusters themselves were ornate metal screens, the steps thick slabs of black marble. With fan-shaped light fixtures affixed to the walls, the general effect was of an interior sparkling with bright golden light. And despite the building's abutment onto a working steel mill, and the small army of craftsmen labouring in its south wing, one felt a soft hush. It magnified the sound of shoes, of polite coughing, of any sound at all, reverberating disquiet and creating a bold echoing in the hall.

It wasn't simply the building that evoked awe but also the reputation of the firm's owner, Daniel Callaghan, who was known to *grow his own men* and promote from within the company. His treatment of workers inspired a loyalty uncommon in the often fractious industry. Frick's Mill, not a mile away, had laid off three hundred men and brought in scab workers to break a union. Callaghan had no need to resort to such measures, as his men felt they were well compensated for their twelve-hour days, six days a week. Half-holidays were granted for weddings, births, and funerals, not a usual practice in the other mills.

Callaghan had been among the first to adopt a premium incentive plan, paying a basic wage with a sliding scale based on piecework, tonnage rates, and market prices. For exceptional jobs, a bonus piece rate often paid as much as a dollar an hour for extraordinary production. In this way he ensured that important delivery dates were met and that his men stayed with him long enough to transfer their craft from the old to the young. And he was able to retain not only craftsmen aplenty but also unskilled workers who would load the skips, feed the blast furnaces, work the cradles, run the coal fills, and engage in the hot, hard labour of managing the molten liquids and moulds.

Daniel Callaghan was the man behind the mill, but he had several silent partners who received a quarterly interest on their investment. He counted these men as friends—they had supported him during the lean times, and used their influence to help him secure lucrative contracts for bridges, along with steel for the burgeoning railways. Among them were Gibson Lewis, Trevelyan Cooper, and Otis Haig, men who'd partnered on a number of smaller ventures, and who were well established in society. Their wives and daughters were social intimates and active supporters of the amateur theatrical association, the horticultural society, and the newly opened art gallery. Their sons were all young men headed to good colleges, groomed to take over their fathers' business interests. Fathers and sons often took time away from their endeavours to visit hunt camps and embark on fishing expeditions.

Alistair Lamont felt fortunate to work at Callaghan's. A morning did not go by when he did not count his blessings as he walked the road to work and drew close to his place of employment. He had come to Buffalo, as he'd told Violet, for the Pan-American Exposition in 1901 and had been so taken by its wonders that he had determined to stay—to seek his future here among these men who had dared to envision a city filled with such modern marvels. A fellow boarder in his rooming house had directed him to Callaghan's.

It were the best of the worst places to work, the boarder had said, *but an honest man would do well there.*

Testimonials folded neatly in his wallet, Alistair had approached in his good coat and trousers, hoping for an interview with a foreman. Instead he found himself invited up the splendid staircase to a panelled office where the great man himself sat, insisting that he meet everyone who came looking for work. Although Alistair's experience lay in brickmaking, and that in another country, Callaghan read the letters carefully before refolding and passing them back.

I've no work with bricks here. But it sounds as if you are an honest man and hardworking. I need an agent for my bridge business and wonder if that would be something you could take to. I'd start you in the factory, watching the men and learning the jobs. You would see them take a plan and work the steel until they build the bridge and set it up inside the warehouse. Then you will help to take it apart, pack it and travel with it until it is delivered and reassembled. It will mean being gone for three months or more at a time but I'm guessing you are unmarried and there's no one waiting for you? Having ended with a question, Daniel Callaghan now eyed Alistair carefully, waiting for his answer.

It was easy for Alistair to declare that he was indeed yet unmarried, and to readily accept the terms. He had been eight years now in Callaghan's employ. Having lived simply at Mrs. Beswick's rooming house, he had amassed savings enough as to make him think about investing wisely.

Callaghan's Steel was in the midst of completing a swing bridge intended to span a large river in Welland, a town across the border in Canada. It was Alistair's twelfth bridge, but the first swing construction the company had attempted. The crew worked in a roughly built wooden warehouse with heat provided by the barrels they kept filled with burning scrap and soft coal. The men all wore heavy leather gloves. In the winter, these kept their skin from adhering to the cold steel, and at all other times protected them from the heat the steel could hold. Alistair had learned how to meticulously inventory the parts of a bridge. He helped trace out the patterns for cutting, and drew the necessary sketches for the complicated assembly instructions. He worked with the men to heave the trusses into place and to hold them there while others shimmied along the girders and slipped the rivets into holes without securing them. Callaghan favoured the Warren truss and Alistair was constantly amazed by the way in which a simple triangle could support so much weight.

To Alistair, the sight of a bridge fully assembled, sitting on logs laid out on the dirt floor of the warehouse presented a study in contrary conditions. The symmetry of the bridge seemed to him a magnificent thing. The soaring lines and elegant patterning of its trusses struck Alistair as works of great design and ingenuity. But the poverty of its surroundings, and the knowledge of what went into its construction, were also present for him. He could not look at a finished bridge without measuring it against the toll it had taken: the red-hot rod that slipped from its tongs and shot through Samuel Adam's leg, severing and cauterizing the lower limb with only a piercing scream before Adam crumpled to the floor; the rip across Gerald Smythe's chest from a rough burr of steel, necessitating an elaborate quilting of stitches; the countless burns and the smell of scorched flesh that came from dropped rivets straight from the small fires; the time that a tunnel collapsed on Little Percy Hobson as he emptied ash from beneath the hot furnaces, smothering him in fine powder and dirt as the men scrabbled through the burning earth to extricate his body. And always there were the rats that seemed to fatten with the heat and were constantly underfoot.

Alistair had begun to long for another life, despite the opportunities he'd been given and the respect he held for Callaghan. It was brickmaking he loved and to which he wanted to return. There was satisfaction to be had in creating something solid and useful from a handful of earth, and the tactile aspect of that was gratifying in itself. He dreamt about his father's brickworks, about the primitive compound that kept employed ten men and several donkeys. Alistair had long pondered those simple arrangements, and had devised for himself a scheme for an improved and modern operation.

It would involve several components:

~ Clay source
~ Storage shed for clay, shale, coal, and wood
~ Sorting, crushing, grinding, and pugging shed
~ Dry press shed
~ Drying shed for green bricks
~ Kiln and chimney
~ Storage shed for fired bricks
~ Easy road or rail access to market

Additionally:
~ Office (sales and accounts)
~ Machine shop
~ Carpenter shop
~ Chemical laboratory

From his father's workforce of ten men, Alistair dreamed of a new crew that would be thirty men strong, with eight kilns and four chimneys.

Full Crew:
Carpenters/Welders – 6
Engineer – 1
Setters/Tossers – 4
Wheelers – 2
Firemen – 2
Machinists – 2
Pugmill workers – 4
Secretary – 1
Labourers (digging, excavating, lumbering) – 8
Accounts/Sales – Alistair

And so Alistair arranged that when this last bridge had been installed, he would take his two-week holiday with a view to seeking out some other venture that might bring him closer to his dream of a brickworks of his own. He wanted an opportunity to put his skills and training into practice, and a chance to carve out for himself a life that would one day perhaps include a family. He would teach his sons brickmaking and fly fishing and a little rugger.

Alistair's father, James Lamont, had been among the finest examples of a gentle and kindly man. His small brickworks in Peeblesshire was where Alistair had first learned to walk, and where he later learned the trade. It had been James's plan to rename the Lamont Brickworks the Lamont & Sons Brickworks, but when his wife died in childbirth and the baby also, he left the brickworks sign as it was and did the best he could to be father and mother both to four-year-old Alistair.

Alistair could not remember a day in his young life when his kindly Da had not placed his oversized hands upon Alistair's shoulders and gently drawn him near to solemnly kiss him on the forehead and wish him *Guid morning!* when their day began, or *Guid nicht an sweit dreams!* when they retired for the evening. Alistair's youthful days had thus been bracketed by a sure and steady expression of his father's love. But at the age of fourteen, Alistair was shocked to learn that, without warning, a massive heart attack could kill a man, and later that a house and brickworks you had assumed would always envelop you could be mortgaged heavily and sold at auction.

When Alistair arrived in Welland, he discovered that the crew working on the bridge was an experienced and hardworking one. Among them were an engineer, responsible solely for the massive gears and turnings of the apparatus; his apprentices, who worked specifically on the mechanical aspects of the bridge; and several masons, who had constructed the footings and the three giant piers that would support the bridge, and who would remain to make any adjustments as might be needed. Also on site were twelve general labourers to do most of the heavy lifting and the backbreaking assembly work. Finally, there were two four-man teams responsible for the important riveting work, each team comprised of a riveter, a rivet-heater, a holder-up, and a rivet-set holder. Tens of thousands of rivets had been fabricated for this bridge, and the men were using Gustave Eiffel's hot-riveting method for fastening them. It was precise, repetitive, dangerous work, often resulting in falls from the trusses or burns from the portable furnaces. In addition to all these men was an engineer, also from Callaghan's, to supervise the work and ensure that the bridge was entirely safe. This man was another Scot, Brodie Smith.

Brodie had met Alistair Lamont twice before at Callaghan's, although they'd never worked together. His initial impression was that Alistair was a stickler for detail, as he kept meticulous notes with endless lists that he frequently checked. Looking over his shoulder one day, Brodie saw that the lists included crude sketches of bridge components and how it was they were married together. These sketches intrigued Brodie. As far as he knew, Alistair was untrained, yet his line drawings, simple as they were, indicated a fair hand and an understanding of the complexity of the assembly as well as the importance of each component part.

One night, Brodie approached Alistair and asked whether he fancied going upriver for a bit of fishing. Several boats had been commandeered for the installation of the bridge, and Brodie had brought with him his tackle box and fishing gear with just such an eventuality in mind. Alistair readily agreed and the men arranged to meet early on Sunday.

A light rain was falling that morning, but they set out as planned. Brodie led the way down the banks of the river to the impromptu dock that had been hastily assembled for the flotilla of watercraft required for the construction. Selecting a rowboat, the men deposited their gear and stepped down into the little vessel. They rowed against the current, heading inland in search of reed-filled shallows. Once they sighted a spot that looked promising, they pivoted towards it and began casting. It wasn't long before some nicely-sized bass had been acquired.

When they returned to the work site they were welcomed by the men, some of whom set to cleaning the fish in preparation for a meal. Alistair and Brodie meanwhile sat down with hot tea and began to reminisce about the fresh salmon of their youth, caught while fly fishing in the Tweed and Tay rivers back home.

I know where there's good salmon to be found for fishing, said one of the group. Brodie and Alistair both looked at him, all attention. *Farther into Canada, but not that far. You take the CPR train to Braemor, and it's a short walk to the Brae River. Packed full of fish. I was there last summer.*

Alistair nodded in thanks and returned his attention to Brodie. *What do you think? I have some time when the bridge is complete.*

I have a bridge on the Buffalo River next, Brodie said, *but I'm no expected there for some time yet. If we finish shortly, I could go.*

The men grinned at each other. The thought of fishing was deeply pleasing to Alistair. The hot, pounding toil of the steel mill and the hard, tedious assembly had made him hunger for time to walk through the countryside freed of responsibility. Although he was anxious to keep an eye out for a business opportunity, the chance to enjoy some sport with good companionship was also welcome.

Alistair, unwilling to be idle during the installations, would often assist the riveters in their labour, spelling them off for short breaks. The repetitive work was taxing for the men, who welcomed his offer to hold the bucking bar as they took turns hammering the furnace-hot tail of the rivet until it formed a second head, securing the rivet tightly in place. Although he wasn't expected to work on the assembly, Alistair was the face of Callaghan's and it was up to him to ensure that everything went back together as planned. If there was a shortage of pieces or if his drawings were unclear, he was the one called upon to rectify the matter. Fortunately, the careful process used to pre-assemble the bridge before packing meant that serious issues seldom arose. Inevitably, however, human error being what it was, tensions sometimes built and tempers detonated. The idea of a respite, then, was a welcome one.

Meanwhile, the installation and assembly of the bridge was proceeding well. Brodie was pleased with the crew responsible for the gears. They seemed competent and were working steadily to ensure the project was done carefully and efficiently. He was able to concentrate his time on the finishing details, and in this he had Alistair's help. Alistair seemed every bit as invested in performing his duties well, conferring frequently with Brodie as to the sequencing and finishing of the final tasks. It was now certain that the bridge would be completed on time and within the monies that had been allotted.

Brodie had also been pleased to see the interest with which Alistair approached the enterprise while yet maintaining excellent relations with the crew. This combination was, Brodie recognized, a highly unusual one. He had often seen good masters who valued their relations with the men above the quality of the work and let things slip, or, by contrast, hard taskmasters who drove their underlings cruelly and were so hated that the men kept important information from them, teasing and testing their overseer to see what faults he could or could not discover. Brodie found that Alistair's approach—cautious, careful, respectful—combined those values that he himself valued.

Dundee, Scotland ~ November 1, 1892

Brodie sat his leaving exams at fourteen, eager to exchange the drudgery of school for the paid drudgery of employment. His classes had often bored him. The curriculum consisted of prayer and psalmody, elements of Latin, religious and moral instruction, English writing and reading, geography, arithmetic, and mathematics. There was no sport, and no science. Fully one half of each day was spent in religious instruction: Mondays were Old Testament, Tuesdays the Gospels or Acts of the Apostles, Wednesdays Catechism, Thursdays Psalms and Proverbs or the Prophets, Friday the Epistles. Saturdays meant being thoroughly examined on the entire week's instructions, then being subject to a penetrating review of each boy's personal grasp of the articles of the Westminster Confession.

As a scholarship student, Brodie had felt set apart from the boys whose families paid tuition. The reputation of his father was not unknown and occasional reference was made in the cruel way that boys often find. Brodie felt ashamed of his father, while yet sustaining a keen sense of injustice.

Once he found work, Brodie planned to turn over his salary to his mother, who laboured at laundry and mending for others. Her hands—often swollen and cracked from scrubbing with lye soap—would bleed when she turned to her sewing. Blood drips on the linens were a constant worry. Brodie would comfort her as she wept over a stained underskirt, her fingers too thickened and sore to manage the fine repair.

Chapter Four: Fishing in the Brae

Braemor, Ontario ~ August 30, 1909

It wasn't hard for Brodie and Alistair to find the river. Sitting in the train had left them both feeling stiff, but after dropping off their belongings at the small clapboard station, the two set off at a good pace to explore. They strode through the village, past the hotel, the mercantile and the church, and then beyond to a stretch of country that dipped and swelled in steep rises. From there, they found themselves in an area of lush greenery and hurried forward, eager to investigate. It wasn't long before they heard rushing water. Following the sound of it across a field of corn and down a sharp embankment, they stood at the edge of a river, perhaps eighty feet across and at least eight feet deep, with a current that moved with some urgency. The men smiled at each other and walked along the bank, scanning for potential fishing spots. It was not unlike rivers either had fished before, and there was a freshness to the air that made them both feel at ease.

Brodie pulled out his pipe and sat down on a large rock to fill it. While Brodie carefully tamped the bowl with his thumb, Alistair gazed around. The shallows, he noticed, had good clay. He bent over and clawed some between his fingers and then squeezed his hand closed to see that the lump it formed held its shape. This was fine brickmaking clay. He walked on, checking the banks for continued evidence of primary clay deposits. The river seemed to be bordered by it. He glanced farther along and saw what looked like shale. Walking near, he reached for a piece and smashed it on adjacent rocks to watch it shatter.

There's clay here, Alistair called out to Brodie.

So I see.

Good for brickmaking.

There seems a quantity.

Bricks take a quantity. And shale—there's enough here to crush and mix with clay. Together they'd produce a fine brick.

Brodie watched as Alistair dashed from one section of the riverbank to the next. Alistair was an affable, earnest fellow, smart and keenly interested in detail, despite his lack of formal training. Brodie thought that in some ways Alistair was a reflection of who he might have been were it not for his kindly uncle's intervention. Only a few minutes before, Alistair had been holding up a handful of clay and proclaiming its virtues for brickmaking. Now he was shouting about the presence of shale with equal enthusiasm. It was always an adventure with this man. He was more daring than Brodie was, and was willing to challenge himself. A man could do worse, thought Brodie, than spend time with such a friend.

Kicking some loose shale with his boot, Brodie bent down and examined both sides of an oddly-shaped shard. On bridge sites he was accustomed to finding bits of fossil, or broken pottery, or even the occasional arrowhead. He would pocket them all for closer examination later in his tent. They held a fascination for him that he could not readily explain. It seemed somehow mysterious that the earth itself could house such evidence of previous lives. That the soil would envelop these traces, and years later surrender them to those who disturbed the ground, felt akin to having been given a rare gift.

I will furrow into your depths, Brodie had thought on more than one occasion, *and you will reveal to me a sign that someone or something has been here before me. And I will build a superb structure so beautiful and strong that you will embrace its footings and keep it steady and stalwart for generations to come. And someday, long after I've passed, the bridge will fall and you will reveal to a seeker that a man was once here, and that he had a vision and left a mark.*

Shaking his head at this fanciful pondering, Brodie pocketed the shard. He walked over to join Alistair. *What is it ye ken?*

I'm thinking there is everything needed for brickmaking. Water and clay and shale. I would no require much else to start.

Brodie looked at him closely. *What about Callaghan's?*

I have dreams.

As do I. Brodie paused. *Settled wi' no more of the travelling and making shrift in canvas tents.*

What would you do to live?

Farm. Nothing grand.

Sounds a fine plan.

It's only a dream.

Why no make a start?

I need land, and for land I need a stake.

Would you miss the bridges?

Brodie hesitated briefly. *I had summit to prove once but that is long past.*

Alistair turned to study his companion, who was once again tamping his pipe with great precision. Brodie continued. *My Da died on a train bridge when I was a lad. Seventy souls were lost that day. I grew up wanting to prove it wisna my Da's fault. People ken what they want. That's the truth of it. There was a winter storm to blame, and footings not sunk in bedrock, and steel no well tempered, and supports too high, and all of it worked together to cause the bridge to fail. But there's many that yet blame my Da who was the driver.*

Alistair took this in. *How did you come to Buffalo?*

I trained in civil engineering and went to M.I.T. for two years. Callaghan hired me from there. And you?

I came by ship when my grandparents passed. I worked in New York digging tunnels for a subway at the first. Then I took a job burying gas pipes. I had a head for numbers and the foreman gave me his books to balance. He paid me cash to do it in secret and I saved enough to travel to Buffalo for the Exposition.

Brodie nodded. *Callaghan's is a good job, but the responsibility weighs heavy. I would no be sorry to leave it behind.*

Do you have some saved?

Yes.

As do I. Alistair paused for a long moment. *What if we combine our savings and buy some land? We could start both a small brickworks and farm.*

Brickworks and farm together?

Aye. I have long thought of my plans for a brickworks.

Brodie clapped Alistair on the back. *Let's away to our rooms, and perhaps you will tell me further what you propose.* Once they booked into the hotel, both men climbed the stairs to Alistair's room. Ushering Brodie inside, Alistair took out his notebook and began to explain the brick manufacturing process and the schedule he had long since established for an entirely modern operation.

Year One (6–8 men)

✓ Build medium kiln (beehive style) and 1 chimney—use purchased bricks

✓ Build one small shed for tools and donkey

✓ Order a pugmill (or fabricate) and make wooden moulds for bricks

✓ Begin brickmaking

Year Two (10–16 men)

✓ Construct manufacturing building large enough to house many processes

✓ Construct drying shed, connected to kiln for heat extraction

✓ Construct a materials building for warehousing purposes

✓ Build a second kiln and connect to first chimney

Year Three (15–30 men)

✓ Construct carpentry shop for forms and moulds

✓ Build small chemical laboratory

✓ Build an office

✓ Construct two additional kilns and a second chimney

✓ Construct a storage building for finished bricks, ready for market

✓ Lay steel tracks for all carts, barrows

Brodie had many questions about the brick business, but Alistair's experience and enthusiasm soon won him over. Both men were taken with things technical and happily discussed the various pieces of equipment that could be purchased should funds become available. The beauty of this particular endeavour was that it could begin inexpensively and then expand, using purchased equipment as they could afford it. To Brodie, Alistair's three-year plan seemed well thought out, needing only some land, water, clay, shale and a modest infusion of cash.

Alistair and Brodie met early the next morning to return to the Brae, this time with their rods and tackle boxes. They easily found a spot to establish themselves. Brodie waded into the river first, casting beautifully so that his line rose above the water in a long graceful loop before slowly settling downwards towards the glinting surface. Alistair watched appreciatively and then walked farther upstream until he was at some distance away. Sorting through his tackle box, he carefully chose a hand-tied fly and fixed it in place. When he stepped into the river he smiled at the feel of the chilly water rushing against his legs and soaking his trousers. It was a familiar sensation, one that made him sigh contentedly. This was a land he could grow to love, he thought, the first such place since Peeblesshire.

Returning to the hotel mid-morning, both men carried freshly caught salmon, giving these to the staff with the request that one of the fish be cooked for their breakfast. After changing into dry clothes, Alistair and Brodie met in the dining room where they were served their salmon along with poached eggs, warm biscuits, and fried potatoes. They ate heartily, savouring not only the meal but also the attentions of a pleasant waitress. Although not in the first flush of youth, the woman was not yet thirty and had an energy about her that was compelling. She'd been shy at first, but continued to offer the men more tea and more potatoes. They ate and drank until each felt he might burst a button.

May I ask, where would you gentlemen be from?
Peeblesshire.
And Edinburgh.
You're a long way from home.
Och aye, so we are.
Are you on business or a pleasure holiday?
We're looking for some land to buy.

What sort of land?

Good farming land close to the river.

Well then, it's Mr. Colbert at the bank you should be talking to. Over in Boltyn. He's the one to know.

It wasn't long before Alistair and Brodie were studying the modest bill, each counting out the coins needed to cover his share. They each left an additional coin for the woman. *Shall we?* said Alistair, standing up from the table.

Moving towards the door, it was Brodie who said it. *I wonder how best to get to Boltyn?*

A gentleman standing outside the hotel gave them directions. Although the country was hilly and uneven underfoot, they were both accustomed to walking and had on stout boots. The trees were dense in places where tall pines and wide bushy cedars grew thickly together. Further along, maple, birch, ironwood and elm grew in abundance. The greens were still vibrant, although not so bright as they would have been in spring. The men admired the fields of wheat and tall corn they passed, speculating that the heat had been good for the crops. They followed a second river at one point, and later came upon a little waterfall. Occasionally they spied a small farm, situated beautifully in the luxuriant expanse. Both men began to wonder if they were viewing the landscape of their futures.

Brodie had made it a point to put aside at least half his pay every month. By living modestly he'd saved a significant amount, and it was his intention to continue in this way until he'd amassed enough to purchase a farm in Scotland. Something in the Highlands, perhaps, suitable for sheep. He liked sheep, he thought. They seemed docile creatures and would not require much in the way of looking after. Or so he imagined. The farm should have large sweeps of country, good grazing pastures, a tidy homestead big enough for a family, a picturesque stream or small river, and a shelter of sorts for the livestock. Nothing more. He would return home once he had sufficient savings but before he was too old to start a family. His wife would need to be younger, of course, and still bonnie.

Alistair's proposal had astonished him. A brickworks and a farm together? And here, in Canada, where they knew no-one and were so far from home? It seemed preposterous. But then, upon reflection, there was much to credit. Alistair had experience with brickmaking, and there was a need for bricks here. He also had detailed, comprehensive plans, in keeping with his approach to such things. Land might be affordable besides, and a new country was welcoming to men with a very little coin but with some skill and big dreams. It was a risk, of course, but he was sorely tempted. It was possible, Brodie considered, that the two of them together might forge a partnership that would allow each to realize his ambitions.

Chapter Five: The Garden Party

Buffalo, New York ~ September 9, 1909

When Alistair returned to the steel mill early in September, he carried signed receipts accepting delivery of the bridge and documentation that all had gone smoothly with the installation and assembly. A further letter from Welland's town clerk was profuse in its praise for Alistair's contributions, declaring that he had been an excellent representative of his employer and had provided exemplary service.

Well, Alistair, Daniel Callaghan said, patting him on the back in greeting, *come upstairs and tell me all about it. Were they truly pleased? I want to know all about those gears.*

After guiding Alistair up the metal staircase with occasional pats on his arm, Callaghan ushered him into his office and the two sat down in oversized leather armchairs. Callaghan reached for the cigar resting in a vast glass ashtray and settled in comfortably, puffing on it from time to time.

Now, tell me about the trusses first of all. Was the web striking?

Once assured that the bridge looked attractive and that tests demonstrated it moved as planned, the older gentleman relaxed somewhat but continued to pepper Alistair with technical questions.

The shafts from the bottom cords—were they strong enough? The mechanical house—does it look a sight or is it well integrated? Were the gears at the southwest end of the bridge operating smoothly? The centre gears were between the floor beams—was there enough clearance to grease them? They were putting bearings in the northeast end of the gear works—how did those look? What size were they again? Tell me about the drive shaft—does it swing out of the way or retract when the bridge opens? Is the top cord sturdy?

No aspect of the bridge escaped his interest. Although he had given another company the contract for the working parts, Callaghan felt that the bridge was *his* bridge, that *his* company had manufactured it, and he therefore desired the satisfaction of knowing that all had fit together seamlessly and was working as intended. He was delighted with the report his agent brought him, and read the papers carefully.

It says here as how you represented us well, Alistair. A good job, I say. Well done. And did you manage some fishing after, as I think you planned?

I did, sir. Caught some largemouth bass in the Welland and later some beautiful salmon in a river over in Braemor.

Braemor, eh? Is that in Canada?

It is, indeed. And beautiful country too. Alistair hesitated. *It happened that Brodie Smith and I purchased a parcel of three hundred acres. The river runs across the bottom and it sits convenient to a rail line.*

Callaghan looked momentarily taken aback. Then he seemed to recover himself. *Good for you! Now that's wonderful news, son. Shows initiative. Brodie is a fine engineer. Damned clever. What are you planning? It's a distance from here.*

I'm hoping to set up a brickworks someday, and Brodie wants to farm.

Ahh, I remember now. You told me that when I hired you. You're a brickmaker. But I had no need of bricks.

That's correct, but you gave me this opportunity and I have learned a great deal in your service.

That's all right then. Callaghan gazed out the wide clear window. *I will be sorry to lose you both.* Now he looked directly into Alistair's eyes. *Have you the funds in place, or do you need some backing?*

Alistair hadn't expected such consideration, let alone a question of such intimacy. He flushed slightly. Callaghan kept his eyes on him, and quickly ascertained the answer. *There's no one who doesn't need a little help starting out, Alistair. Tell you what I propose. I'm due at Lewis's for a garden party the ladies are having. It's a benefit for one of their many charities. The house is on Delaware, number eight hundred and eighty-eight. You come by around five o'clock and stay for a drink. I will introduce you to a couple of gentlemen who might be in a position to help.*

Alistair stood and bowed slightly. *Thank you, sir. It is good of you to take such an interest.*

Callaghan stood at this also, and walked over to the front of his desk. *Nonsense. If there's money to be made, it will be an opportunity for us all.*

Alistair bowed again, and left the office. Pattering down the stairs, there was a slight bounce to his step. He and Brodie had anticipated working for several years more before they would have the capital required to begin their venture. Most of their funds had gone into buying the property. Backers would mean an earlier start. The invitation from Callaghan was extraordinary.

Alistair's duties kept him at the mill until late that afternoon, leaving him without enough time to return to his lodging. He had intended to change into his good suit before making his way to the Lewis house. It was a long, brisk walk, but the day was pleasant with a warm September sun.

The houses on Delaware Avenue were a little daunting. Each residence seemed to proclaim the success and affluence of its owners, and eight hundred and eighty-eight was no exception. It was clear that Alistair had arrived at the correct address: the drive was choked with parked buggies and quite a number of automobiles; he eyed the latter with interest as he navigated around them. He approached the sprawling, three-storey clay brick house, registering its sharply pitched slate roof and copper gutters. Clusters of tall cement pillars stood sentry across its front, with narrow balconies jutting out from the second level. All manner of ornate coining and finishes had been integrated into the construction. As he drew near, Alistair saw that the bricks were finely finished; he rubbed his thumb along one of the edges appreciatively. A Flemish Bond pattern, he noted, with herringbone details on the chimney and dormers.

Now he could see that a massive canvas awning had been erected behind the house, with crowds of people milling about. Bracing himself, Alistair swallowed hard, straightened his tie, and walked towards them. The gathering, he noted, was largely female. Dozens of women dressed in ruffled, softly coloured dresses with tremendous hats were clustered in groups, talking and laughing. He stood at the edge of the throng, looking for any gentlemen. As he did so, his eye was drawn to a young woman sashaying around the assembly carrying a tiny basket filled with some sort of favour. She seemed quite merry and the others responded to her in kind. He saw women reach into the basket to remove little pieces of paper which they exclaimed over with enthusiasm. Intrigued, he continued to watch the proceedings in an effort to determine what was happening. There was something about the woman that seemed familiar. He held still, waiting for a glimpse of her face.

A voice he knew called out to him. *Alistair. You've arrived! Did you get yourself a drink? Come join us in the study.* Alistair turned to see Daniel Callaghan eagerly gesturing towards the house. Two or three other men stood with him. Alistair nodded, and as he moved in their direction the young woman with the basket rushed up to the group of men.

You must take a ticket too, Father, she called out. *We shall play a game of charades after dark and I want you to set a good example.*

She presented the basket to a gentleman, who smiled and withdrew a scrap of paper. He eyed it quickly before tucking it carefully into his coat pocket. *Very well, dear, if you insist. It's for a good cause, I know.*

At first Alistair could see only strands of dark hair escaping from beneath a wide-brimmed hat, but when she turned he recognized at once the young woman from the art gallery. *Miss Lewis?* he said, bowing in her direction.

Violet looked up and coloured delicately. *Mr. Lamont, how very surprising.*

You know my daughter? inquired the gentleman in the heavy woollen suiting.

Yes, sir. We met briefly at the art gallery.

The father's face relaxed. *Yes, she's always there, copying the paintings. Are you an art lover, Mr. Lamont?*

I confess, sir, that I am no. I sought merely to view the building.

I told him it was like a Greek temple, and he helped to tie my paint box to my bicycle. Alistair glanced at Miss Lewis as she spoke. He was grateful for her explanation, not wanting the others to think he had approached or been in any way impertinent.

Mr. Lewis considered his daughter's face and then looked at Alistair, scrutinizing his appearance. *We should join the others,* he said firmly. *They've gone inside already.*

A group of five gentlemen stood waiting in the study and Callaghan began the introductions. Alistair felt like an interloper. He was conscious of the cracked leather of his shoes and the coarse tweed of his jacket. He did not belong in this room or in this house. These men were among the most influential in Buffalo—they could crush him with only a word. He felt foolish for having accepted the invitation.

Now, Callaghan began, smiling encouragement, *tell us what the plan is for your brickworks, son. I know you have purchased land; is it free and clear?*

Yes, sir, responded Alistair promptly. *We have title for the acreage. The land includes a river bordered by clay banks that are suitable for brickmaking. There is also an abundance of shale—we have no dug down, but there was much of it on the surface—and it too will be needed for brickmaking. The parcel is a walk from the Braemor train station and not twenty minutes from the village. Our plan is to approach the railway and pay for a spur line to pick up our brick shipments. We can transport them affordably that way, and easily make back the cost of the rails. There is a farmhouse on the property, a small barn, and a pair of out-buildings. My partner, Brodie Smith, will establish a farming operation while I work on the kiln and sheds. We intend to live in the house and use it for our base, as we are yet unmarried men.*

Brickmaking was something Alistair loved, and so without willing it he had become more assured and animated as he spoke. The men responded to his passion and confidence, asking intelligent questions and expressing genuine interest in his plans. Mr. Lewis eyed him carefully throughout. At one point Callaghan began pouring drinks and handed Alistair a tumbler of good whisky. Although Alistair did not often indulge in alcohol, he enjoyed his drink. He saw the men glancing at each other before Mr. Lewis spoke.

Well, young Mr. Lamont, you have set before us an… interesting proposal. We will need some time to consider. May I suggest that you join the ladies outside and have some further refreshment? Someone will find you when we have completed deliberations. The men stood at this, and Alistair thanked them for their time.

Alistair was filled with self-doubt when he returned to the garden. Mr. Lewis had not sounded particularly warm. He remembered things he should have said and cringed at some of the things he had expressed poorly. The ladies were all seated under the protection of the awning now; he didn't want to intrude, so he walked further into the garden, stopping only to study a decorative pond situated adjacent to a sweeping border. A bench had been placed there and he sat down, reviewing his impromptu presentation and wondering about the response he might receive. He hadn't been there long when he heard Miss Lewis's voice in the near distance. *May I join you?*

He stood at once and saw that she had left the company of the other ladies and was approaching him. Smiling widely, she bowed her head. *May I join you for a moment?*

Of course. He stepped further back so that her dress would not brush against him. Sitting down, she patted the seat beside her. *Please do not let me disturb you.* Alistair positioned himself near the far end of the bench, remaining on his feet in order to maintain a respectable distance.

What a splendid day we have had, she began. *We raised a prodigious amount for the Orphans' Society and have had such good fun in the doing of it. And are you enjoying yourself?* She looked at Alistair expectantly.

I am invited here on business only. I am sorry to have intruded on your party.

It must be very important business. Father doesn't believe in mixing business with pleasure. That is one of his sayings. He is always saying such things.

It was Mr. Callaghan who invited me. He is my employer at present.

Well, just the same, I'm sure it was tremendously important.

Important to me but likely no to them.

Mr. Lamont, you must absolutely tell me about this business. I am most curious. I think you will discover that I am a careful listener.

I would no want to bore you, Miss Lewis.

I assure you that I am never bored, Mr. Lamont. I would be thoroughly charmed, I'm sure.

But am I no keeping you from your guests? Will it be proper?

Please tell me. Miss Lewis laid her hands on her lap and clasped them together encouragingly.

Alistair was struck again by the small delicate fingers, gloved and not visibly paint-smeared today. Her gown was of fine material, in a soft blue that suited her. He swallowed. *Very well then. I have a proposition and am hoping to interest backers. I have bought land with a partner in Canada, and we are proposing to build a brickworks there. Mr. Callaghan suggested that he and some of his acquaintance might be agreeable to my scheme; I am waiting while they deliberate. I am certain, however, that I have misjudged their interest in such a venture.*

And why did you choose that location?

It is fine country. We happened across it by chance. I felt at once as if we were in Scotland; the hills and the gores and the fresh river… there's much to recommend it. And it has everything needful to start a brickworks.

And what about the wildlife? I have heard that grizzly bears and wolves and all manner of beasts roam freely.

Alistair smiled. *If we keep to our business, I am sure they will keep to theirs. I've no intention of becoming dinner.*

You must be very brave, Mr. Lamont, to begin a venture in the wilds.

I'll no be alone, Miss Lewis. I have my good friend Brodie Smith and my Remington besides. A man could no do better.

Miss Lewis was quiet for a moment, then stood up and leaned towards Alistair slightly. She reached over, and patted his arm so gently that he couldn't feel her hand even as he watched it move. His face and neck felt suddenly reddened and hot. He discovered that he could not look down at her face; instead, he studied the delicate hand that rested briefly on his forearm. The cuff of her sleeve was embroidered with tiny flowers in the palest of pinks and greens. The work was so fine that he couldn't imagine how it was done. He stepped backwards abruptly, carefully reintroducing the space between them.

But tell me, she said, *will you not miss female companionship?*

Alistair looked at her to see if she was mocking him. There was no flirtation there, no mockery, but only a genuine concern for two presumably incompetent fellows. He laughed then. Gently so as not to offend. The laughter provided a release also for the tension he was feeling.

There's no lady alive who would muck in with us. There will be naught but hard work from first light to dark. It will be some years before we have established ourselves.

But what then, Mr. Lamont? You will not always want to live with Mr. Smith, surely?

No, Miss. Lewis, I expect the time will come when that will no longer be desirable.

Well, I do hope you will communicate that eventuality to me, Mr. Lamont. I'm sure that I have many among my acquaintance who would welcome an adventure such as the one you describe.

You are very kind, Miss Lewis, but I canna believe that young ladies would relish such a life. What of the grizzly bears and wolves?

And now Mr. Lamont you are teasing me. And I only meant to be helpful. She withdrew her hand at this. Although Alistair had not felt the weight of it on his arm, he missed the intimacy of the gesture and wished its return. Without hesitation and without thought as to appearances, he reached across and reclaimed her hand, cupping it tenderly.

Dundee, Scotland ~ March, 1894

He had a bowl of thin oatmeal for breakfast; there was a cold potato for his noon break. The tea canister had long since been empty. Brodie put the potato in his jacket pocket and tied his bootlaces tight. They had been his father's boots, and although two sizes overlarge were carefully lined with folded newspaper to help keep out the cold. Brodie had filled the kettles with water and put them to boil so his mother could start the laundry. He checked to make sure she had enough wood for the stove, enough to do the boil for the water leastways.

It was coming up on seven, already time for him to leave. The walk to the Works would not take long but he needed to be sharp or risk losing his place. He wrapped the knit muffler over his head and around his ears before knotting it at the neck. His mother pulled up the collar of his coat over the scarf. He saw that her hands were already cracked and bleeding, a thin strip of cotton wound around one palm. The knuckles were swollen with arthritis. The pain of them, he knew, made her work grim.

As he walked to the mill he determined that one day he would earn enough to keep her in tea and sugar and flour, and to save her hands from the labour that worsened them. He was sixteen and young and sure.

Chapter Six: The Academy of Music
Buffalo, New York ~ September 16, 1909

Daniel Callaghan had arranged for Alistair and Brodie to join his friends and family at the Academy of Music. There was to be a much-anticipated performance of Beethoven sonatas, one for which he had purchased a block of tickets. Over the years, Callaghan had taken quite a liking to both men, and felt that a social evening was just the way to celebrate their newly formed partnership. Not having sons of his own, he was delighted to live vicariously through their youthful enterprise and took pleasure in the details of their preparations.

The lobby was tightly packed when Alistair and Brodie arrived, the throng waiting for the ushers to open the concert hall doors and guide patrons to their seats. Pressed closely together were the most prominent men of Buffalo society, wearing their finest apparel. The women in the crowd gave off intricate flowery scents that wafted through the air with a commingling of honeyed fragrances. The fabric of their fine gowns caught the light; their jewellery and hair ornaments sparkled brilliantly. It was an animated grouping, filled with music lovers and those simply welcoming an opportunity to parade in all their splendour.

Alistair surveyed the crowd for Callaghan's party. He and Brodie would have to navigate quickly if they were to join them before the doors opened. Grabbing Brodie's arm, Alistair was halfway across the lobby, excusing himself every few seconds, when he spied Miss Lewis. She was smoothing her elbow-length gloves and fidgeting with her hair. The thick tresses had been pinned up in a mass of waves and studded delicately with tiny sprays of white flowers. Her ivory dress, although modest, was scooped low in the front and generously trimmed with lace as fine as gossamer. Had she not been tugging at her gloves and patting at her hair with such fervour she would have epitomized feminine grace. As it was, he smiled and waved at her across the crush.

By way of response, he heard her welcoming laughter. *Why, Mr. Lamont, you look as though you are positively swimming through the crowd. I think it's a version of the front crawl, is it not?* She smiled as he approached, holding out her gloved hand first to Brodie and then to him. He dared to hold it a moment longer than politeness dictated and noted that she did not withdraw it. This filled him with a deep sense of satisfaction.

I'm delighted to see you again, Miss Lewis. Are you with the Callaghan party?

I am. And I'm pleased to see that you and Mr. Smith have made time for some of Buffalo's finest entertainment. My father says you are both determined upon leaving shortly for Canada.

We are indeed, replied Brodie, *and this will be our last evening of pleasure for some long months. Then it's off to Braemor in two days' time. Our provisions are packed and we're mostly equipped.*

The ushers swept open the doors and the crowd surged forward. Alistair offered Miss Lewis his arm. She clung to him as the swarm moved past, and Alistair wondered if she was clinging somewhat more tightly than was necessary. He looked down at her merry face and saw that she was playing at being a fragile thing, blown about by those around them. He pulled his arm in closer to his chest and guided her down the carpeted aisle. Callaghan had secured tickets in the centre of the front row. Alistair felt strangely protective of his charge, proud to be escorting her, if only for a short distance. Somehow, as they congregated in front of their seats, Miss Lewis managed to link arms with Brodie as well. The three of them chose seats together, with Miss Lewis in the middle.

Alistair bent down to hold the seat for her while she adjusted the short train of her gown. She perched on the edge of the chair and then looked up at him, laughing. *Now isn't this delightful. I cannot imagine a more perfect situation.*

Brodie caught Alistair's eye and lifted an eyebrow. Alistair felt a deep flush moving up his neck. He seemed to himself to have been exposed, as though both Brodie and Miss Lewis had somehow discovered his feelings. But just then the lights dimmed and an expectant hush filled the theatre. Alistair adjusted his legs to avoid grazing Violet's gown; she, in turn, shifted slightly, moving closer to him within the confines of the plush chair. He felt rather than saw her sheer loveliness. It was a heady sensation. In that delicate dress she looked more a woman and less a spirited girl. He glanced to his right and saw the curve of her neck, the sweep of her hair, the gentle mound of her bosom. The lace sleeve of her gown was floating almost imperceptibly above her arm. He watched it flutter for a moment before it settled against the pale skin. He resisted the urge to look at her again, concentrating intently on the programme he held.

Are you a lover of music, Mr. Lamont? she whispered. *I already know that you do not love art. Will you redeem yourself this evening?*

Alistair coughed slightly. *Would you think better of me, Miss Lewis, if I pretended to love music simply to please, or would you prefer me to be bold and state the truth plainly?*

She laughed softly. And then, in the lowest of whispers, *I think I must take it upon myself to educate you in the fine arts, Mr. Lamont.* After a pause she added, *I do enjoy a challenge, however, and I especially find that those who undertake the practice of learning new things are among my favourite sorts of people.*

A single spotlight was turned on and a violinist, carrying his instrument tucked under his arm, walked out with a grand air and made the slightest of bows. Polite applause followed. A second spotlight illuminated a tall thin man who strode across the stage and seated himself at the piano. He flipped his coat tails out over the bench with great ceremony and raised his hands above the keys where they hovered expectantly. A second bout of polite applause followed and then, immediately, a profound stillness descended as the entire assembly held their breath.

The pianist began with a few solo notes, and then the gentle singing of the violin joined in. At first there was sadness, a deep sorrow and pain pouring out in passionate weeping; then the movement changed and slow, sweet love crept into the notes, followed by bursts of joy and light. Alistair was entranced. He felt that he had never heard anything so lovely in his life. He leaned forward in his seat and stared at the two performers, trying to follow their every movement. It was as though they were performing solely for him. He forgot where he was; the music mesmerized him entirely. He was startled by the deafening applause and realized that both performers were now bowing. He had been so enraptured that it took a few moments for him to realize the performance was over. He jumped to stand with the rest of the audience.

Alistair cleared his throat and looked at his two companions. *Did you enjoy it, Miss Lewis?*

She smiled at this, then reached into her little bag, drew out a lacy handkerchief, and passed it to him. *I do believe, Mr. Lamont, that despite yourself the music has affected you.*

Alistair put his hand to his face and realized that both cheeks were moist with involuntary tears. He duly mopped his face with his own handkerchief. *Och aye, I apologize.*

Not at all, I assure you. I am glad to know you are not so insensitive to such things, despite your affinity for bears and wolves.

Alistair could yet hear the music replaying in snatches in his mind and wanted desperately to be still, to let the music come to him once more. The sonatas had been played right through without an intermission; now the guests were assembling in small groups, discussing their plans for the remainder of the evening.

Callaghan's guests remained at the front of the theatre, waiting for the crowds to thin. Alistair noticed a woman he believed to be Mrs. Lewis; she was holding on to her husband's arm and speaking animatedly about melodic shapes and harmony and the effect of chords and keys on the relationship of wind to string instrumentation.

She was an attractive woman, and had the look of her daughter about the eyes and mouth. Although expensively dressed—Alistair could see flashing rings and brooches—there was something soft and kind about her smile. The others were listening to her attentively and nodding at appropriate intervals. It was obvious that she was a favourite in the group.

Father, Miss Lewis said suddenly, *Mr. Lamont has offered to walk me home. Isn't that splendid!* Alistair tried not to look shocked, focusing instead on gauging Mrs. Lewis's reaction. Amused, it seemed, but not displeased. He dared not look to Mr. Lewis.

Mr. Lewis spoke first. *That is kind of you, Mr. Lamont, but we have a car waiting and would not wish to inconvenience you.*

Och… it would no be a trouble, sir. It would be my pleasure. He quickly added, *if you have no objection.* Alistair hated himself for the way his voice quavered when he spoke.

Father, I've been in the house all the day long and am just longing for some exercise. Please don't be a troublesome dear. And with that, Miss Lewis draped herself on her father's arm and looked up at him with a pleading expression.

Alistair, mortified by the situation in which he found himself, stood stock still.

You must hook your train, my dear, said Mrs. Lewis. *That fabric is too delicate for a long walk out of doors.*

She ran her hand along the skirt of her daughter's gown and pinched a small fold of fabric in her fingers. *Now, take this, Violet, and borrow my wrap. Yours is much too thin.*

Mrs. Lewis bustled around her daughter, covering her tightly with a thick paisley shawl. *There,* she pronounced when satisfied. *That will do.* She nodded authoritatively.

Alistair extended his arm towards his charge. *Are you joining us?* he asked Brodie.

No, I have some packing yet. Brodie smiled. *I'll see you in the morning.*

The group nodded courteously as Alistair escorted Miss Lewis outside. As soon as the door closed behind them, she began to laugh.

Are you very cross with me?

Should I be?

You look dreadfully anxious.

I am at your service and grateful for the privilege.

Miss Lewis looked at him and laughed again. *Are you always so correct and proper, Mr. Lamont?*

I try to be. The right of it is no always clear. Alistair walked on silently, unsure of how to continue their conversation. A gentle tugging on his arm made him look down at her.

I was certain, you see, that you had something important to say to me last week in the garden.

I had something important to say?

Yes, I'm sure of it. You were holding my hand like this—she placed her gloved hand in his—*when Father came charging towards us like a storm cloud, and you returned abruptly back to the house with him. I have a woman's intuition, you see, and I am certain you intended to say something momentous. You had already begun.*

Alistair was not a little confused. *Perhaps you could help me to recall?*

Miss Lewis stopped walking and stood facing him, still holding his hand. She was smiling but there was a look of sheer mischief in her expression. *You were saying…*

I was saying…

That you felt a sympathy between us.

That I felt a sympathy between us.

And that it was quite unlike anything you had experienced.

And it is quite unlike anything I have experienced.

Exactly! she proclaimed.

Exactly?

Exactly that!

And then what?

Must I tell you everything you intended to say, Mr. Lamont? She put her free hand on her hip and cocked her head at him. *And then you said that you intended to say that you would be sorry to part from me for three long months.*

I intended to say all that? smiled Alistair, retaining her small hand and stepping rather more closely.

Yes, of course, she nodded. *That is exactly what you intended to say.*

Alistair moved imperceptibly forward again, closer yet, and reached for her other hand. She dropped the train of her skirt and clasped his hand tightly. He looked into her eyes and saw a tenderness sparkling there that assailed his chest. *And am I to know how this story ends?* Spoken so softly that she could barely make out the words.

She broke free of his hands and rehooked her train. *What ending would you choose?*

Alistair waited for a moment, considering his response carefully. *With you, if you will have me.*

She threw her arms about his shoulders. He kissed the top of her hair. *You're shivering*, he said.

It's the damp, she agreed.

Alistair removed his coat. *Take off your shawl.* He helped slide her arms into his coat and did up the buttons. Then he wrapped her tightly in the paisley shawl as he had seen her mother do.

Now you will become cold.

That is far better than you catching a chill.

You must write my father while you are away.

And what am I to say? I am in no position to make you an offer.

You shall thank him for his patronage, and tell him how fares the brickworks. And you will enclose an open letter for me, and ask him to pass it on. In it, you will remark upon the pleasure of having made my acquaintance and ask if you may call upon me when you return in December.

And am I to return in December?

Yes, certainly! But first I will consult with Mother, who will help me write you a reply that is correct. And both my parents will then know that you are coming back to court me.

So it is settled?

Unless you are eaten by bears or wolves.

CHAPTER SEVEN: THE FOUNDATIONS

Braemor, Ontario ~ September 27, 1909

Alistair had given much thought to the pugging—the soften-ing—of clay. He'd ordered generous amounts of lime for the purpose, but before it arrived he would need to build a little roundhouse in which to place the pugmill.

That machine functioned as a heavy mixer, breaking down the clay and removing potentially disastrous air pockets. Mechanized pugmills were available for order, but Alistair had yet to establish a reliable power source, and in any case their cost was prohibitive. For now, the primitive approach—the one used at his father's brickworks—would suffice. It involved filling a large steel barrel with buckets of water and clay and stirring it with a centre shaft hosting multiple paddles. The shaft was turned with a gigantic wheel that could be powered by two men or one donkey walking in circles around the barrel. The need to con-struct a roundhouse for the machine was pressing. Alistair had already felled two trees and was preparing the upright posts for the circular, open-sided building. The timber planks could be purchased in nearby Glen Mor.

After some hard labour he took a short respite, and removed a letter from his coat pocket, unfolding it carefully. Written on thick ivory stationery and still lightly scented, it read:

Dear Mr. Lamont,
Thank you for your solicitous inquiry regarding my well-being. As always, I am in fine spirits. I would be pleased to renew our acquaintance upon your return to Buffalo. You may call at the house on any afternoon.
Sincerely yours,
Violet Lewis

Her response had been prompt. He'd posted his letter not two weeks before, on the day he and Brodie had arrived in Braemor. Written on the train, his had been a clumsy attempt to follow her very explicit instructions.

Dear Mr. Lewis,
Let me take this opportunity to thank you again for your kind patronage. Mr. Smith and I are deeply obliged to you, and your associates, for the interest you have taken in our venture. I will write you directly with a report as to our progress.
Might I also ask you to be so kind as to share the enclosed with your daughter, Miss Violet Lewis.
With thanks, I remain yours truly,
Alistair Lamont

And also:

Dear Miss Lewis,
I am writing to ask whether you developed an illness after our walk home from the Academy. I am fearful that the chill air might have done you a harm. I wonder if I might call upon you when I next return to Buffalo. I would like to assure myself that you are well.
Yours very truly,
Alistair Lamont

He wasn't at all sure that this was the sort of communication Violet had been anticipating, but he was a novice in these matters, and Brodie had proven to be of no assistance. Alistair was just now rereading her letter for any nuances that he might have missed. He and Brodie had recently bought a good-sized wagon, a donkey, and two horses. Brodie was at the blacksmith's having the horses reshod.

The men had decided to fence off a pasture for the sheep once the roundhouse was complete—for without the sheep operation up and running before winter, there would be no spring lambs, and no meat or fleece to sell. Brodie had already arranged to sell the fleece to a nearby woollen mill once the shearing was done. They had also made arrangements with a couple of locals who would come to their farm to pre-wash the wool and crock the lanolin in small pots.

Once the fencing was erected, Brodie intended to enlarge the shed that was already on the property so that it could shelter seventy-five sheep at night. Neither he nor Alistair had seen a wolf or coyote but they had certainly heard them howling and yipping. The sounds carried across the fields in such a way that they could never be sure how far off the predators actually were. Not wanting to take any chances, Brodie had proposed an interim measure, and so it was that he and Alistair walked around the outbuildings, passing water on the ground and walls. Brodie had assured him that their scent would keep the wild animals away.

With the sheep due to be delivered the following week, they had very few days to complete preparations. Brodie had chosen Suffolks, as he felt the breed would do well in a harsh winter climate. Alistair didn't know much about sheep but he did fancy the little black faces and could imagine, in some future letter, describing them sweetly to Miss Lewis. Brodie had told him that although Suffolks were heavy feeders, they would provide excellent economic returns. They had only afforded one ram in the group and had made arrangements to borrow another. Apparently they would need to keep the two males apart.

Alistair was looking forward to the delivery, and more specifically, to completing all of the sheep-based preparations. He was anxious to begin work on the clay kiln, the final step in the brickmaking process. Just that morning he had posted a notice at the hotel.

Wanted
Strong, able-bodied men
wanting to learn the trade of brickmaking.
Fair wages guaranteed.
Apply directly,
Alistair Lamont & Brodie Smith

Thanks to their financial backing, the men were in a position to hire hands so that they could quickly establish the brickworks and begin production before the worst of winter set in. The locals delighted in telling them stories of snow ten feet deep and temperatures forty degrees below freezing. Although they didn't quite credit the stories, they weren't so foolish as to entirely dismiss them.

Two days later, just after five o'clock in the morning, Alistair finished pumping fresh water for the horses as Brodie stood indoors at the woodstove stirring oatmeal and toasting thick slices of bread. Alistair was carrying the water buckets through to the barn when he saw three men walking towards him.

Good morning, he called. *What is it you're after?*

The tallest man in the group stepped forward and removed his cap. *Good mornin', we be lookin' fer Alistair Lamont or Brodie Smith. We come 'bout te sign posted by te 'otel. We be t'ree steady men, lookin' fer 'onest work.*

Alistair sized them up quickly: they appeared to be in their thirties, all of them outfitted in thick-soled boots and warm coats. They seemed hardy enough. *Well then,* he replied, *we best discuss terms. Let me get these to the horses first.* He turned towards the barn, but one of the men stepped forward and took the buckets.

Give 'em 'ere.

Alistair stood aside and let the man pass into the barn. *I'm Alistair Lamont,* he said, addressing the other two.

Sean Maguire, sir.

Patrick Lynch, and in yer barn is Thomas Jobson.

Come to the house and meet my partner, Brodie Smith.

The men followed Alistair to the kitchen door and scraped their boots carefully on a log before entering. When Brodie saw the newcomers, he reached over and took down three more bowls. *Come away in, there's plenty here.*

Alistair made the introductions. *Have any of you worked with bricks before?*

I 'ave, said Thomas, who had now joined them. *I worked in Manchester before coming 'ere. I was fireman to the kilns.*

Were they downdrafts? asked Alistair.

Yes, there was talk of a tunnel kiln being built but I dint ever see it.

And sheep? asked Brodie. *Are any of you used to sheep?*

It was Patrick's turn now. *Aye. We 'ad sheep at 'ome, like. Galways. Stubborn as tey come. Beautiful wool, soft and tick.*

Well, sheep is like that, said Brodie. *Did you shear? Dock their tails?*

Yes, sir. An dipped 'em. Te keep mites away an sickness. An helped wi' lambing. I reckon I can do most tings needing doing, like.

Brodie looked over at Alistair and grinned. Alistair nodded back. This was a good start.

Well, said Brodie, *we work from six to six, six days a week.*

With half holidays for births, weddings, and deaths, added Alistair.

Unless it's your own death, said Brodie. *We'll no be paying you to die.* The group laughed heartily at this. By now all five men had finished their meal and they stood to pile their bowls by the dry sink.

We'll pay you fair on the last workday of the month, said Brodie. *And take on any men you recommend. We've the kiln to build and clay and shale to dig for the brickmaking. We're also in need of farm buildings when there's time to spare. There's no shortage of work before winter.*

Well, Thomas said, *are we to make a start?*

The men divided themselves into two groups: Brodie and Patrick were to continue the preparations for the sheep; Alistair, Thomas, and Sean were to begin the kiln. The newcomers set off eagerly, glad for the chance to engage in steady work.

Alistair's group made good progress on their first day. Not an hour into their labour and they were joined by a new man, Kyran Meacham, who was also after signing on. Alistair sized him up quickly as well, scanning his calloused hands. The others stood silently by while Alistair asked questions, but in no time at all Kyran had stripped off his coat and put his back into the heavy work of mixing the mortar for the bricks. He did so cheerfully, whistling and from time to time shouting out his thoughts. *Like makin' a mess a porridge but no need te worry about burnin' et.*

Alistair had already prepared the site for the kiln. Eight external fireboxes for the fuel would be needed, he had decided. The stacking area for the bricks would be circular, and connected by underground vented channels to the chimney; to create a good draft, the chimney would need to be several feet away. Alistair had calculated his requirements carefully. To get them started, he had already ordered bricks from Milton to build the kiln itself— an expensive way to begin, but it was important to get the operation going soon. They needed the income.

By late afternoon they had mostly completed the fireboxes and had even run—laid—the first several courses of brick for the kiln itself. They were stopping for a drink when a boy of nine or ten approached them.

Is the master here? he enquired.

I am Alistair Lamont; what's your business?

I have come for work, sir. I am strong and wanting to learn about the making of bricks. The boy was not tall but he stood erect and proud, tipping his chin upwards as he spoke.

Alistair walked over to him. *Show me your hands, lad.*

The boy held them out for inspection, and Alistair turned them over gently. *These hands are yet too small to do a man's work.* This was kindly said, with no intention to ridicule.

They will grow, sir, as will I.

Alistair was much struck by the boy's earnestness and pluck. The other men were silent, watching the exchange carefully.

Are you no supposed to be in school?

I was there today but all we did was mathematics and English grammar. I would just as soon work and help out my Ma.

And does your Ma know you're here, lad, looking for work?

She does not. The boy hung his head at this.

I see. Alistair thought for a moment. *Well, I have no wish to upset your Ma who has sent you to school. I tell you what I propose: I will take a chance on you on certain conditions.*

The boy looked up brightly, smiling broadly at him. *You will?*

I will so. But only if you do as your Ma says and go to school first. You can come here when your book learning is finished to look after the horses and do some sweeping up and other jobs when the sheep arrive. But only if your Ma agrees. Understood?

Yes, sir. The boy reached out his hand to shake Alistair's.

Alistair bent down slightly and shook the boy's hand solemnly. *What is your name, lad?*

Johnny Gowan, sir.

Pleased to meet you, Johnny Gowan. Now you go off to the barn, and check on the water and hay for the horses, and muck out the stalls. After that, both horses will need a good brushing. Everything is there. And after that, you go home and speak to your Ma.

Yes, sir.

As Johnny turned and ran across the fields towards the outbuildings, Alistair smiled at the look of their newest crew member.

What do you think? he asked the men, gesturing at Johnny's small figure.

He's a good lad, dat. His Ma was widowed. Dicky Gowan died in a farm accident maybe four years past. He was fixin' a wheel on his wagon when te bracin' gave way an et rolled. Crushed him. Charley found him when he didna come for supper. Twas past time te do a ting fer him. Dead as a stone.

And who is Charley?

His wife, Charlotte. She goes by Charley. Takes in washin' now and works at te hotel. Johnny's a good un.

You done the family a kindness.

Dicky was a worker. His lad will be te same, added Kyran. *Never a bad ting said about him and there's plenty to be said about te rest of us.*

Dundee, Scotland ~ April, 1894

The girls were already clustered around inside. They wore long dark cotton skirts and shirtwaists with sleeves rolled up over the elbows. Some had on coarse striped aprons but most had forgone the bother, the fabric on their clothes already too far worn to merit such precautions. Some were barefoot, others wore the rough clogs of the poor, still others had on shoes however thin the soles. They looked unwashed, and tired, hungry, and cold before their day's work had even begun. Ten hours they would spend bent over the jute, retting the stalks, washing and breaking down the long fibrous ribbons in deep concrete baths.

This was the lower mill, the filthiest and most disreputable of workplaces. Only the uneducated and the poorest laboured here, in the grimiest of conditions. Mill fever, from which no one ever fully recovered, caused in part by the inhalation of dust and dirt and chemicals from the emulsion, and also by the dank conditions, the lack of heat and cold, struck suddenly. The mill was often thin in numbers, many workers having fallen ill without having been replaced. On those days, Brodie's work was multiplied.

The bales were received at the large doors riverside; it was Brodie's job to cut into and sift through them quickly, eliminating unsuitable stalks. Then he'd carry armfuls to the bays where the girls waited. They would submerge the goods in emulsion baths and work at them under the water, picking apart the useful fibres and setting them aside for breaking and drying. When they were short-handed, Brodie would run two or three of the bathing stations by himself. He kept these filled and retted, ready for the drying and spinning.

At twelve-thirty and five-thirty, a gong was sounded ominously by the overseer, Angus Thomson, who stood on a tall wood platform overhead, scowling at them as they began to dry their hands on their skirts and petticoats, arching their backs as they straightened themselves in exaggerated postures. Brodie and the others were conscious of Thomson's oversight as he regularly prowled the floor, examining the baths, or peered down at them from the catwalk while they worked. Some of the girls tittered nervously when he was anywhere near, given his predilection for pushing himself up against them. He'd grin nastily if anyone protested, exposing his badly tended teeth and licking his lips. Brodie knew that the girls were dead frightened of Thomson. There were whispers of his having taken unwanted liberties: overpowering girls, forcing them to endure his groping and grasping.

May, 1894

The gong had long since sounded. Brodie had swept the bays and was after tidying the receiving area when he heard someone cry out. Hurrying through the mill, he followed the sound until he saw Thomson holding one of the younger girls against a brick column, one hand down her shirtwaist and the other pulling at her skirts. Brodie flung himself at Thomson's back. He clung to his neck with one arm, pummelling his face, kicking him, screaming for him to let her go.

Thomson released the girl and turned his attention to Brodie. Quickly, neatly, he peeled him from his back and deposited him in an emulsion tank. When Brodie attempted to climb out Thomson pushed him back under the water and held him there. Brodie struggled against the pressure but felt his face being crushed by the man's massive paw.

Then the weight was abruptly released. When Brodie climbed out from the bath, dripping in the oily solution, he saw that Thomson lay on the floor. One of the older women had come back for the girl, seen what was happening, and hit Thomson soundly on the head with a wrench, stunning him. The girl stood shivering, looking from the cruel giant on the floor to Brodie and finally to her Ma, standing by with the wrench yet in her hand.

Is he kilt?

I daursay the deevil will nae be kilt. But ye, lad, need hie away afore e wakes.

Brodie ran home, told all to his distraught Ma, and began walking towards Perth that very night.

Perth, Scotland ~ May, 1894

Dear Ma,
This letter is to sae I am employed at the dyeworks in Perth. You have heard tell of it. They make many fine colours especially a mauveine. I stir the fabric in the vat with a large pole. Other colours are purple and red and yellow and brown. The masters are very kind. I will send monie.
Your son, Brodie

Perth, Scotland ~May, 1894

Dear Ma,
A baud thing is the owner has died. Some lads and I have
decided upon walking suin to Stirling where we micht find
work. I will write again.
Your son, Brodie

Stirling, Scotland ~ June, 1894

Dear Ma,
We have found lodging and work at the Saddlery. There are
many horses here and cab drivers. The town is brawlike.
Your son, Brodie

Stirling, Scotland ~ June, 1894

It was said of Ol' Willie, one of the regular drivers at the
Saddlery, that he could *talk to the deevil hisself.* People often avoided him, particularly if they were pressed for time, though he was
well liked for all that. He was taking a particularly cumbersome
load of provisions to a colliery outside of Motherwell and had
asked for a lad to sit on top of the cartage to ensure that nothing
dropped off. Brodie, always keen for adventure, had volunteered.

Brodie noticed the stains when he walked past the wagon to
the rear of the load. All around the front bench and down its sides
were streaks of dark brown tinged at the edges with a golden yellow. The streaks intrigued him. He hadn't noticed such a pattern
before, and wondered what could have made them. Ol' Willie soon
made his appearance, swathed in a thick greyish greatcoat with cuffs
and collar waxed against the weather. Brodie eyed the coat respectfully, as it was yet a dreich day with a fine drizzle. Brodie's own
short jacket had been cut down from one of his father's; its weave
was of a thick wool but the lining was thin and he was often chilled.

Ol' Willie waved at Brodie before climbing aboard. *Hang*
fast, lad, he bellowed, *as the road is rough and I'll not want ye to drop*
off wi' part o' the load.

The novelty of this undertaking was a little exciting to Brodie, who looked around eagerly as the wagon pulled away from town and headed south. He clung to one of the ropes fastened across the crates, vigorously jostled as he was by the progress of their heavy dray.

They had been two hours or more on the road when Willie pulled up alongside a stream and climbed down to unfasten an empty pail. He brought this to Brodie and bid him fill it for the horses. Climbing back aboard, Willie added, *An there's this 'ere to wet our whistles,* drawing out a flask from one of his many pockets and grinning at the boy.

The whisky made Brodie cough at first, and burned unexpectedly as it went down. After the second taste of it, though, he decided that it had a warming power and that he no longer felt the chill damp.

Ol' Willie was as talkative as his reputation. *Tell me, lad, wot ye be doin' ridin' the dray wi' me. Wot's yer aim?*

Brodie was startled by the question. No one had ever asked him such a thing. *To make a little monie for my Ma,* he stammered.

Yer a guid lad, I can sae et. But yer Ma will no be wantin' ye te ride dray for always. While speaking thus, Willie dipped into his pocket and withdrew a small tin of chewing tobacco. He opened the tin carefully and pinched out a goodly amount, which he put inside his left cheek.

Brodie nodded in agreement. *We've nae monie and I mean to provide.*

Ye need to aim fer summit more, lad, summit more than a roof and a meal. At this Ol' Willie spit a stream of coloured sputum down the side of the wagon, leaving a small fresh trail of stain and an answer to Brodie's earlier puzzlement. *Were ye clever wi' books at school?*

Brodie nodded again.

Can ye manage to booklearn and work altogether? Is there someone who could help wi' booklearnin'?

I have an uncle in Edinburgh who is well taught.

That's the right of et! exclaimed Ol' Willie. *Seek out yer uncle and ask fer his help.* Willie spat again, but this time his aim wasn't as sure and he managed instead to mark the front of his coat with the stream. It was not the first of such stains but was pronounced nonetheless. Willie seemed unconcerned, however, and patted his knee with enthusiasm, having solved to his own satisfaction the fate of the lad he had only just met.

Brodie was silently absorbing what Ol' Willie had suggested. He loathed the school system he'd just left. Yet he was curious about many things he encountered and saw, was eager to learn more about the world, and was not unhappy to read a book when given the chance to do so.

The dray was entering Motherwell when a sense of excitement seemed to come to the horses. Brodie saw that their ears were perked. Ol' Willie, too, seemed more alert to his surroundings and ceased his conversational torrent. Brodie adjusted his grip on the rope and turned himself carefully so that he could look forward.

Willie veered the wagon away from what looked to be a main thoroughfare and drove instead towards the colliery on the outskirts of the town. As they pulled into the yard, Brodie saw that a sizable crowd had gathered, with much shouting and running back and forth. Willie pulled the lever on the brake and climbed down. *Stay 'ere, lad, and I will see wot's wot.*

Willie was gone a good while; Brodie had grown impatient and was about to slip down from his roost when Willie finally returned. He was grim, and tears slid down the good man's face.

Ach… a melancholy occurance, he said, *a melancholy thing has happened. Fire damp has caught light and exploded and three men expired wi' another two terrible hurt. Their women have just come.* He pointed in the direction of the crowd. Only now could Brodie make out the pitiable sound of women weeping. Willie swiped away the wet on his face with a much used handkerchief balled up discreetly in his palm, secreting it away again in one of many deep pockets.

Did you know these men? asked Brodie.

No lad, it's no fer meself I greet.

Brodie waited for him to continue.

It's fer the mothers who will miss their boys and husbands. I sae et before at Motherwell when the choke damp kilt a group o' miners. The women live wi' fear all the time. They sit waiting for their men every afternoon, each o' them counting time on the clock and listening fer the whistle, and them never recovering when summit terrible occurs.

Motherwell, Scotland ~ June, 1894

When they finished unloading the dray, or rather when Brodie finished unloading the dray to Ol' Willie's satisfaction, and after he had ferried small crates and boxes to the colliery offices while Ol' Willie coiled the ropes and pointed him towards the various directions for their delivery, Ol' Willie suggested they *drive into Motherwell proper and have a bowl of summit hot.* Brodie readily agreed, particularly as he'd never seen the industrial town before.

They were seated at their meal when Ol' Willie asked once again about Brodie's plans. *Have ye no thought at all as to yer future?*

Brodie shrugged apologetically. *If I could, I should like to build bridges. Large ones that are strong. But I have nae the training or experience.*

Ol' Willie nodded thoughtfully while he considered the matter. Finally he looked up and spoke with conviction. *Booklearnin' is wot you need. It comes down to booklearnin,' lad. Now this is wot we will do. It's two days on the road to the Fair City. I have a langin' fer a new look at et. We will on the road together and when we reach et you will look out yer uncle.*

Aware that Ol' Willie was going far out of his way to assist him, and conscious of the man's generosity, Brodie agreed. In truth, his mother had long since provided him with his uncle's address, which was folded up neatly in the bottom of his boot, along with the insulating layers of paper. She'd foisted the address upon him before he left home but he had given it no further thought. Although he did not remember meeting his uncle—Hamish Smith was his name—he did know that his uncle sent a monthly allowance to help with their living expenses. He had done so since the death of Brodie's father. His mother had always spoken lovingly of her older brother and his kind and giving nature.

Chapter Eight: The Hotel

Braemor, Ontario ~ September 29, 1909

It was past seven when Alistair finally left off laying brick. The men had stopped at six but he'd kept at it, intent on finishing the top course on the final wall so the site would be ready for the roof, a full day's job on its own. The men had proven to be strong, quick workers. Thomas had a natural affinity for bricks and Sean was especially strong; he'd taken on the heavy job of mixing the mortar and keeping the materials at hand, moving skids of bricks with the help of a sturdy chain and one horse. Alistair was pleased with all they had accomplished.

He was still standing on site when Brodie approached, hands in his pockets, whistling an old tune. *Al, are you done?*

Just finished.

How did it go?

Have a look. We have just the roof tomorrow.

Brodie walked around the kiln's walls and whistled approvingly. *You got to it, I'd say. It looks well. How will you enclose the roof?*

Alistair was about to respond when he remembered Johnny. *Have you been to the barn? I hired a wee man to muck out stalls. Was he there when you were at the house?*

I didna see him.

We better look. I hope he has no wearied himself.

The men walked together across the fields discussing the progress of the paddock, Patrick's knowledge of pen construction, the sheep themselves, and several other matters of ongoing concern. They called to Johnny as they approached the barn but no response came. Once inside they saw that the floor had been neatly swept, the horse stalls mucked out tidily. A pile of straw and dung had been freshly deposited a sufficient distance away. The horses had fresh hay and fresh water.

Alistair smiled. *It looks as if he's finished his chores and gone home to his Ma.*

How old is the lad?

About nine or ten, may be. I'm no certain. No bigger than a sack of potatoes, but looks like he wants to work.

It's been a good day overall, then.

It has. Shall we drive to the hotel and have a hot meal?

That's a grand idea. And see if they will sell us more bread while we're there.

Shall we save the horses and walk?

Save the horses. Let me wash.

As Brodie waited in their little kitchen he called to Alistair. *Have you figured how to set the roof?*

It will be a tricky business staggering the brick and getting it to hold while the mortar sets. I'll need to make a wooden frame in the morning for support. I've seen it done but havena done it myself. I thought to set Sean and Kyran on preparing the trench to the chimney site while Thomas and I work on the roof. Alistair came out of his room still buttoning a clean shirt.

It will be the devil's own job, said Brodie. *Do you want me to lend a hand? I can leave Patrick.*

We need more help. There may be more men in town who would take on work with us.

As they walked across the fields and out to the road, they looked around with a sense of pride. They were making a start. And it seemed that all of nature was in harmony: geese were flocking overhead in the lavender-streaked sky, a gentle wind was stirring the fields of corn and wheat, the current in the river was pushing forward and the fragrant smell of good earth seemed to fill the air.

Laughter was sounding as they entered the hotel. Groups of men conversed amiably at the bar while others sat at tables finishing their dinner. Brodie led the way to a table by the window. The waitress came to them at once.

Is it too late for a meal?

The kitchen is open yet. There's beef barley soup and stew and chops.

Brodie ordered first. *I'll have the soup and chops with any kind of pie.*

Same please, said Alistair, *and are there spare loaves of bread we could buy to take home?*

The waitress hesitated before nodding at them and moving off.

She's pretty, said Brodie.

I didna notice.

Well she is.

Alistair twisted around in his seat to look. She had a trim figure, with jet black hair pulled back in a tight knot at the nape of her neck. He couldn't see her face but did remember her bright green eyes. She moved efficiently around the dining room, gliding quickly and gracefully from table to table. She did not waste time or motion, he thought, but seemed effortlessly fluid. He turned back to look at Brodie and saw that he was still watching her.

He raised an eyebrow in Brodie's direction. *You're staring.*

I am no.

Aye. Now tell me. When will the sheep come?

Any day.

The waitress soon rejoined them, carrying two loaves of bread which she placed on the table. *Fresh this morning.*

Thank you, said Alistair.

Do I remember you gentlemen?

Yes, replied Alistair, *we bought the old Kerr place and are setting up a brickworks and farm.*

She smiled at them. *Would you be the men that hired my son? Johnny?*

Yes, he told me about your kindness.

Alistair broke into a broad smile. *He's quite a wee man. Determined to do man's work and not yet out of school. He did a fine job for us.*

She bobbed down in a half curtsey and then excused herself.

Alistair looked at Brodie and raised his eyebrow again. *Has cat got your tongue?*

Brodie flushed. *Why do you say that?*

A minute ago you were saying as how pretty she was, and then when she's standing here you go silent as a kirkyard.

She's married.

The men told me her husband died in a farm accident. She's a widow.

Och. We've no time for women, Alistair. There's no time for us to mess about with courting. We've real work to do. Even if she does have fine eyes.

Mrs. Gowan returned just then with two bowls of soup that she put down before them. She must have heard: her cheeks were flushed a delicate rose and her hands were slightly unsteady. She excused herself and hastened away.

Oh, bugger it, said Brodie quietly.

They wolfed down their meal without further conversation. Then they spoke to the men at the bar, asking that anyone looking for work come out their way. Alistair and Brodie left the hotel in a far greater hurry than they had entered it, and walked home briskly in the chill evening air.

Chapter Nine: The Kiln

The roof of the kiln proved to be a trial. It was to be a beehive design, similar to the kilns Alistair grew up with. The men had constructed wooden forms and tried to prop them up with rough timbers and logs, but the timbers kept slipping out of place; the staggered brick courses collapsing time after time. Alistair was in a black mood and kept losing patience with Thomas and Sean. At bottom he was frustrated with the process itself and sorry to look a fool in front of the men.

After their last attempt came crashing down, Brodie suggested they let it rest and turn their attention to the chimney stack. It would take several days to get the height needed, he reasoned, and during that time they could all think about the roof problem. Alistair wasn't keen on giving up, but as he had no better plan, he agreed that they'd all start on the chimney in the morning. There was no joking or bantering that afternoon; the men respected Alistair's mood and were not for provoking him. Alistair, for his part, could think only of the waste of wages the setback was costing, and was as dour as could be. The only smile he cracked came later in the day when Johnny was seen running across the fields from the direction of the school. He stopped to shout hello and to catch his breath before running the next distance to the barn.

The following afternoon Alistair looked away from the chimney and said, *Here he comes, right on time.*

But e's not running, tat can't be 'im.

He's the right size and it's the right time.

It ain't Johnny.

They all looked to scan the field and identify the dark figure approaching. As the figure got closer, they saw that the man was pacing with a distinct limp and was using a cane for support.

Ah, that's Admiral Sterling Barnes, said Sean.

Who's he?

An Englishman. He owns the mercantile.

'e fought wi' te Brits over in Russia, Thomas put in. *Claims 'e sailed te Black Sea an te White Sea an te Baltic an te North Pacific in te one ship. Fought Tsar Nicholas an destroyed 'is fleet. 'e was pensioned off after a piece of planking sliced 'is leg wide open. 'e's been 'ere a good tirty years or more.*

To be sure, added Kyran, *He's all that and te tales lose nothing in te tellin', eh lads?*

I wonder what he's about?

Looking for work?

Not likely.

Hello there, called the Admiral. *I've come to inspect your progress.*

Welcome, replied Brodie. *And if you have any engineering skill, we would be glad of your thoughts.*

Alistair coloured at this, and the other men looked away from his discomfort.

After Thomas had performed the introductions, Brodie walked the man around their site and explained their processes. The open kiln roof was examined.

Have you extra bricks lying about? asked the Admiral.

Not many, answered Thomas, *a tousand maybe. Need te make sure we 'ave enough te seal te opening once we're done and finish te chimney.*

Are there enough bricks to build two sturdy columns inside the kiln?

Alistair counted the courses forming the height of a wall and calculated carefully. *There could be...*

Why not build two strong supports within the kiln, said the Admiral, *to hold the forms firmly in place while the bricks over the roof are setting? If you go a third of the way in on each side, the weight will be evenly distributed. It would be stronger than using timber and logs to hold the weight of it.*

As the other men exclaimed over the proposal, Thomas walked into the kiln and began to pace out distances, marking the measures with the heel of his boot. Brodie looked inquiringly at Alistair.

Let's do it, said Alistair finally. *Thank you, Admiral. I believe you have just saved us from another cock-up.*

He turned to Thomas and Sean, directing them to start on the supports as Patrick resumed work on the stack. Kyran, meanwhile, was dragging the toe of his boot in the dirt, making crude lines. *Go on, go on, go on,* he muttered to himself impatiently while the men spoke. *Eh lads,* he finally added, *that Sassenach has his notions.*

Alistair was smarting a little, unnerved that Barnes—surely not a man acquainted with brickmaking—had proffered such an uncomplicated solution. Still, not wanting to convey an ounce of this in his manner, he offered the Admiral a tour of the property.

The Admiral readily agreed. They set off across the field towards the outbuildings and beyond that, to the river. *You'll want to see the clay beds and shale we've located,* said Alistair. *They're on the far side but will provide everything we need to make good bricks.*

And how will you transport it from the river?

By wagon. We have a pair of strong horses.

The men walked on in silence. Alistair was resenting the time away from his work but knew the situation required him to be companionable. He was aware that his foul mood had made him unpleasant company.

I wonder, began the Admiral. *Have you ever seen an aerial ropeway in operation?*

Alistair paused. *No sir, I dinna believe I have.*

Well, it may just be the thing you need. An aerial ropeway could be set up the whole length of your land, without much expense. You need strong metal towers and ropes and buckets big enough to hold the clay and shale. The buckets would be filled at the river and transferred along the ropeway to the area where you prepare the bricks. From there you slip the bricks into your kiln—and you've not driven back and forth a dozen times a day.

Alistair stopped walking and looked at the Admiral with a dawning sense of the possibility suggested. *Why, that could be a help for certain, but I've no experience with such a thing and wouldna know how to construct it. We've had enough ballyhoo with the roof, as you have seen yourself.*

Ah, yes, well, I'm no engineer, replied the Admiral, *but I've seen one at work in a colliery. I think it might do you a service here.*

Alistair began to feel some excitement. *If we had paper, would you draw it? Show me what it needs?*

I can do better than that. I will send a letter to an old friend in Wales. I'll ask him for the particulars. This winter, when we're both snowbound, we can talk again. I wouldn't mind helping you boys with a project like this one.

The two shook hands at the river, the Admiral saying he'd sit awhile there—*Water's calming for an old man,* he said—before returning to the mercantile.

Alistair got back in time to see Sean and Thomas finishing a top course of brick on the two columns. They had been careful not to use all the bricks; the columns were not as thick as Alistair had envisioned, yet rose a good foot higher than the side walls. He saw at once the wisdom of their decision.

Well done! he shouted. *That will do the job!*

The men grinned. They were pleased with their work and pleased to see Alistair once more restored to better humour. It was well past six when they finished, but all felt the satisfaction of a job well done.

Come, said Brodie, smacking Alistair on the back. *Let us check on Johnny and see if we can't hitch up the wagon and drive him home. We can eat at the hotel.*

CHAPTER TEN: THE WHITE CHURCH
Braemor, Ontario ~ October 3, 1909

After discussing the matter on Saturday night, Alistair and Brodie had resolved to attend a church service. On the outskirts of the village stood a white clapboard church, quite without distinguishing features. It was a Methodist congregation with an itinerant preacher and the only Protestant church in the community. The Catholics in town attended mass in nearby Boltyn.

Both men had been raised in the Presbyterian tradition and were not themselves religious, although Brodie was particularly well schooled in all things scriptural and doctrinal. At his uncle's home, a more practical approach to faith, emphasizing the importance of kindness and good works rather than strict adherence to formalized religion, had been gently instilled. Alistair, for his part, found the vengeful God of the Old Testament distasteful but had made it his custom to read the Psalms and Shakespearean sonnets on a regular basis. These had then become his oft-quoted moral compass.

Brodie took some trouble with his appearance in the morning, shaving carefully and knotting his tie with particular attention. *You clean up well,* remarked Alistair. *Is there anyone that you are hoping to impress?*

Brodie elbowed him on his way outside to harness the horses. Alistair followed, chuckling to himself. *Tell me,* he said, climbing onto the wagon seat, *do you suppose Mrs. Gowan and Johnny will be attending divine service?*

Och. Can a man no take an hour to reflect on his good fortune wi' out having his motives maligned?

People had begun to gather outside the church by the time the men pulled up, and so after tying their horses out of the wind, they walked over to join them. They were greeted warmly by those they knew and introduced to some new acquaintances. Admiral Barnes was in attendance, as was Patrick Lynch and his young wife, as well as Thomas Jobson, his wife and small son. Alistair smiled as he watched Brodie scanning the crowd.

As the congregants began to enter the church, Brodie and Alistair hung back, and were nearly the last to join them, sliding into the closest pew and trying to be inconspicuous. Alistair looked around, noting that the plain, decent clapboard structure would hold sixty people at most. Its walls were whitewashed, its window glass clear, and the pews plain pine, as was the boxlike pulpit and small communion table. The only ornamentation was a wide looping ribbon at the front of the church with the words *The Truth Shall Set You Free* painted in blue and gold.

Brodie continued to search the congregation for someone he could not see. *There are forty-three people here,* he whispered to Alistair.

The call to worship was a hymn, "O for a Thousand Tongues to Sing." There was no piano or organ, but the minister had a booming voice and the congregation responded with gusto. Brodie and Alistair stood with the others and began to sing the familiar words. Alistair was surprised by Brodie's deep, rich baritone.

The itinerant preacher blasted out a sermon on the "Parable of the Workers in the Vineyard." Alistair listened carefully as he outlined the goodness of God in offering to His people the fruits of His vineyard and in giving all equal access to His Kingdom, irrespective of how long they had laboured and been faithful. This was a sensitive topic for Alistair. The men had just been paid, depleting their account significantly. Alistair found that he could not much concentrate on the sermon, preoccupied as he was by the topic of payroll. He ran columns of numbers in his head, trying to forecast when he might have the first firing of bricks ready for sale.

The exhorter followed next; when he shared his story as a struggling sinner, urging his listeners to be faithful, his words elicited enthusiasm in the congregation. Alistair and Brodie slumped down uncomfortably in their pew. Yet when they stood again, this time to belt out "Love Divine, All Loves Excelling," Alistair found himself a little moved by such a thunderous rendition. Beside him, Brodie sang lustily and with conviction. When Brodie nudged him as the collection plate was passed, Alistair reached into his coat pocket to find an offering.

Then came prayers, and a final hymn to end the service. Afterwards, people visited inside the church, and no one seemed in any particular hurry to leave. Alistair and Brodie were introduced to a few more townspeople who conveyed their hope that the men would feel welcome to return.

Brodie was fidgety and signalled to Alistair that he was leaving. Alistair followed him outside to the horses. *Why the hurry?*

I thought we might have a meal at the hotel.

Aahh, and there may be a waitress there to see you in your finery?

Brodie shook his head, but they both laughed. Alistair continued in this vein during the short ride to the hotel. *Shall we ask Mrs. Gowan why she's working and no at divine service where we might have admired her singing?*

Brodie snorted derisively.

Or perhaps we should say that as we have been to morning service and she hasna, we would welcome an opportunity to discuss the sermon? Once inside the hotel, they were surprised to see that it was Johnny handing out the menus and acting as waiter.

Where is your mother, lad?

Ma has taken sick with a fever, and I told her that I would do her work until she's recovered, he said as he flew past them on the way to the kitchen.

The men looked at each other a little sombrely. *He's young for that kind of responsibility*, said Brodie. *And too young no to have a father looking out for him.*

There's others who will.

Johnny came back to take their order, returning once again smartly with a basket of sliced bread to start their meal. Their luncheon was a hearty one—chops and beans and stewed cabbage. Brodie, when paying his share of the bill, left a twenty-cent tip for Johnny. Alistair, although surprised by the amount, matched it. *That was an expensive morning,* he joked as they got into the wagon.

Brodie nodded. *We can eat more potatoes and oatmeal this week. We need eggs.*

I wish we didna have the bother wi' shopping and all such, said Brodie.

Are you thinking of a housekeeper?

We'd save time if we didna always have to be scraping a meal together and remembering to drop off our washing.

Still, said Alistair, *I imagine there's a drawback. Besides the coin which we canna afford, we may find a woman in the house creates expectations. I dinna suppose our bachelor ways would suit most. We might find ourselves in a difficulty.*

Brodie considered this. *The trick will be to find the right sort of woman. Someone eager to fit in with things as they are and no wanting to change us.*

Have you been giving this some thought?

No, but I think only a certain sort could adapt to our ways. Someone with experience working hard and accustomed to looking after herself.

Alistair looked at him. *So, it's Miss Lewis you're ruling out?*

Listen, Al, I didna mean a slight to her but Miss Lewis is a lady, born and bred. She is accustomed to fine clothes, good society and she is spoiled. She is no the sort of girl who could muck in here and be happy.

Alistair clenched and unclenched his fists. The anger rose up from his chest and neck and spread across his face until he was streaked with red blotches of rage. He said not a word in response. Brodie saw that he had upset his friend. It had not been his intention. The point of the conversation was actually to introduce the idea of his courting Charlotte Gowan. He cleared his throat awkwardly. *Mrs. Gowan, now, she is the sort who might put up wi' us.*

Alistair remained quiet, controlling his temper for fear of saying something in wrath.

And little Johnny would be well looked after in the bargain. He's a good lad and could use a man to watch out for him.

Alistair pulled on the reins to stop the horses, then jumped down from the wagon. *I'll walk the rest o' the way. I have a need of exercise.*

Brodie knew better than to cajole. He hesitated for a moment, then snapped the reins and drove off. This was the first serious disagreement the two of them had shared, and it was significant. There was no easy way of predicting how they would resolve it.

Chapter Eleven: The First Firing
Braemor, Ontario ~ October 4, 1909

B rodie woke at four in the morning and walked to the river with his pipe and fishing rod. It was the end of the salmon run, the current growing icy cold, and he was sure of catching some fine fish for breakfast. But when he waded out, he saw that Alistair had also risen early and was casting upstream. The two hadn't spoken since their wagon ride, and Brodie was unsure of his reception. So when Alistair raised his hand silently greeting Brodie returned the wave with some relief.

Once he'd caught three good sized salmon and one trout, Brodie decided to return to the house. Alistair was walking towards him carrying his own catch. *If we put mine in the ice chest,* Alistair said by way of greeting, *we can send them home wi' Johnny.*

He may no come if his mother still has fever.

If he comes, there they will be.

Brodie nodded. *What's on the schedule today?*

We should finish the roof. If you have no need o' Patrick, we can set him to digging clay and collecting shale.

Brodie nodded again. He was scanning his friend's face carefully for any residual signs of anger or resentment. *I didna mean to offend, Alistair.*

That's all right then, Brodie. Friends should speak truth to one another. You were correct. This is no place for a lady. I was foolish to think it. Alistair clapped his friend on the back, quoting as he sometimes did from the Psalms, *how good and how pleasant it is for brethren to dwell together in unity.*

Did you leave her with expectations?

Yes. I will have to extricate myself.

When they checked the kiln that morning, the men saw that the brick columns had set nicely and easily supported the wooden forms created for the roof. The crew set to work quickly, following the forms by staggering the bricks inwards, leaving some few unmortared for ready extraction, slowly forming a softly rounded dome. The work was finally completed by midday, with everyone pleased to see it holding in place.

The forms, or moulds, for the bricks themselves had been made by a carpenter in Boltyn; what remained was to prepare the clay mixture and fill the first of them. The pugging of the clay would be a laborious process. Brodie had completed the roundhouse, but many buckets of water needed to be gathered there in preparation for the work. For just this purpose the men had bought a second, older donkey from a local farmer. Brodie had named him Horace after a particularly morose individual from their time at Callaghan's.

Thomas and Alistair showed the men how things were to be done. They all joined in the work: finely pounding the shale, mixing it with the clay and water, dusting the forms with a fine layer of water and sand in preparation for scraping in the kneaded clay mixture. Thomas demonstrated how to shape the mixture into rolls, then how to cut off sections to fill the moulds. The filled forms were then lined up outside the kiln to dry. Tarps were placed nearby in the event that the weather changed and it was necessary to cover them. When the roof was set, in three days' time, they'd need to remove the wooden forms before stoking the fireboxes and preparing for the first firing.

In the late afternoon, just before quitting time, a wagon filled with lambs appeared, leading a widespread flock of sheep across country. They heard the yelping of the dogs and the indignant bleating of the flock before they saw them. Brodie directed the shepherds towards the paddock and then ran across the fields with Patrick to ensure that things were properly prepared. Alistair and the remaining men tidied their site and followed after Brodie to watch the unloading.

The sheep looked to be sorely stressed by their travels; the ruckus they were sending forth seemed a clear indication of their feelings. They ran from one end of the paddock to the other, bumping into one another, almost trampling the smallest ones. Alistair stood at the fence with the others, chuckling at the carryings on, while Brodie, in the thick of them, was continually buffeted by their panic. Then the ram was unloaded and, taking an instant dislike to Brodie, he charged straight for him, almost knocking him down.

Hey! shouted a small voice, *be careful!* The men looked around to see that Johnny had joined them and was gesticulating wildly at the sheep.

They're just trying to settle, son, Alistair said. *They mean no harm. They've had a long journey.*

That one tried to knock Mr. Brodie over!

Rams do that sort o' thing. It's their job to be charging after one thing or another. Now tell me, how is your Ma?

She says she's feeling better and Mrs. Carruthers, our near neighbour, is looking in on her. I was permitted to miss school and help out at the hotel today. Johnny looked very proud of this. *And Ma says I'm to thank you for your generosity.*

Alistair messed the boy's hair and smiled. *You're welcome, lad. There's fresh fish in the icebox when you're ready for home.*

Thank you. Without another word, Johnny ran off to begin his evening chores.

Once the wagon driver and the two shepherds had finished herding and unloading their delivery, they pulled away with a vigorous wave. Alistair joined Brodie in the sheep pen, and they set about trying to guide the frightened animals into the shed. Patrick was of the opinion that the tight space would help make them feel secure, and so calm them.

Later, when Brodie went to check that the horses were in their stalls, he saw that Johnny had fallen asleep on a pile of hay in the corner. Scooping him easily in his arms, he carried the boy out of the barn and into the house, where he laid him down gently on the settle. Returning to the paddock, he helped Patrick drive the rest of the sheep indoors and secured the door tightly, rolling a heavy rock in front of it for extra measure.

I'm going to take one of the horses out, Brodie told Alistair. *The boy is asleep and I carried him into the house. I'll wake him and give him a ride home.*

Dinna forget the fish.

I'll check on his Ma and see if she needs anything.

Alistair nodded. *You wake the boy and I'll saddle a horse.*

Brodie was glad that equanimity had been restored. They were so much together that it would be miserable otherwise. Women, he thought ruefully, were a complicating factor.

Alistair, for his part, returned to his own musings once Brodie had cantered off with his young charge. He'd long ago learned most aspects of brickmaking, but this was the first kiln he'd built himself and was anxious to see whether it would work efficiently. Each kiln had its own nature, he knew, and it typically took several firings to learn how to handle its particularities. The trick was to first control the damper—the metal flap designed to maintain proper pressure within the kiln—and then to actually control the heat during the firing stages.

They were close now to their very first firing. He could feel how unsure he was, yet how eagerly he anticipated the prospect of success. Inevitably his thoughts turned to the finances of the thing, and the pressing need to be able to pay the men. If they could manage to successfully fire thirty or forty thousand bricks in each firing, and sell them for ten dollars per thousand, he and Brodie would easily cover payroll and overhead, with half the amount left to reinvest in the business. It might just work. It would have to work.

Three days later the men congregated at the kiln. First they stacked the air-dried bricks inside, setting them ready while one of the men removed the temporary forms from the domed roof. These came down easily, and were put aside for re-use. Alistair and Thomas carefully set firing cones in place so they could measure the heat by the melting of the cones; a little viewing hole had been left in the kiln wall expressly for this purpose. Next they stuffed the fireboxes with a mixture of soft coal and wood. Finally they bricked the kiln door closed and sealed it with a thin skim of plaster across its surface.

When all was finished, the fires were lit. Alistair fussed with the damper, opening it wide to make sure the resulting draft would draw the heat into the kiln. The men circled the kiln protectively, touching its walls, listening carefully for any sounds of explosion within. They continued to feed the fireboxes, working hard to ensure that the temperature rose steadily.

At noon Alistair called a halt to their nursing and fussing, and they broke for their midday meal. Then, once they'd finished eating, he showed them the plans for a large shed he'd designed to warehouse the coal, clay, and shale. During the cold months it would also serve as a mixing area and as a workspace in which to fill the forms. The men scrutinized the plans with interest, making suggestions about where to situate the building, the number of doors needed, and the necessity of strong storage racks.

It would be twelve days at least before they could open the kiln and check the bricks. In the interim, Alaistair set the men to preparing a building site, ordering the lumber required from the sawmill in Glen Mor, and excavating and stockpiling clay and shale. Patrick was excluded from this work, as he'd become solely responsible for the sheep and all manner of farm-related jobs. Thomas and Alistair had taken on the feeding of the fireboxes, mindful that too much heat would fuse the bricks and too little would produce only clinkers.

In the evenings, Alistair and Brodie had been discussing a suitable name for the brickworks. It was high time they had one; in their efforts to drum up business they'd been hard put to answer when asked what their fledgling venture was actually called. Alistair had favoured Peeblesshire Brickworks, or something like it that hailed from Scotland, but Brodie was leaning towards combining their names, suggesting SMONT as one possibility, or perhaps L&S. Finally they resolved the matter. Alistair had since sent a letter to Daniel Callaghan requesting an order for sheets of thick metal stamps that they would place within the moulds. In this way, before firing, every brick they produced would have LAMITH deeply imprinted.

Alistair had arranged to return to Buffalo to collect these stamps once they'd been prepared. He determined that after the kiln was opened and the results of the first firing examined, he would take one brick with him on his travels to show their investors. While he was away, Thomas could oversee the next stacking and firing. For now, however, they just needed to wait.

When day twelve arrived, Brodie and Alistair led the men to the kiln at first light in the morning. Alistair placed a ladder along the outside wall and shimmied along the edge of the rounded roof. Feeling his way carefully with his hands, he removed some of the bricks that had been left without mortar and tossed these down, avoiding the men below. Brodie passed him a long iron hook that had been especially forged at the blacksmith's. After some careful manoeuvring, Alistair withdrew the hook from the kiln… and the men saw a brick dangling from its end. Once Alistair had stepped down from the ladder, Thomas passed him a thick pair of gloves with which to unhook the hot brick and lay it down tenderly on the ground. The colour was even on all sides. Then Thomas handed him a small hammer and Alistair tapped the brick tentatively, listening carefully. The men were silent, waiting and watching.

It is sound! declared Alistair. *Open the entrance!*

The men disassembled the sealed opening. This seemed to take only seconds, for in their eagerness they ripped at the wall with picks and shovels. They stepped away when the opening was revealed, standing aside respectfully while the first rush of heat escaped.

Alistair, Brodie, and then Thomas entered the kiln. Excited yelps were heard from within. The men re-emerged carrying two bricks each; they clapped these together over their heads. *We did it, men! They're sound and hard!* Whooping and shouts and the enthusiastic smacking of bricks resounded in the chill morning air as the men marvelled at what they'd accomplished. The hot bricks were passed from man to man, each declaring that *finer bricks could not be found.*

Brodie produced a silver flask from his jacket pocket; this too was passed around the group. Each man held the flask aloft, intoning *To Lamith Bricks!* before taking a swallow and handing the flask to his neighbour. It was a solemn and emotional moment after much hard work and uncertainty. Brodie and Alistair pumped the men's hands energetically, thanking each for his efforts. Then the partners clapped each other across the shoulders and grinned with a deep sense of satisfaction.

Edinburgh, Scotland ~ September 16, 1894

Hamish Smith, a lecturer in the School of Divinity, lived near St. Giles Cathedral in Advocates Close —and it was there, on his doorstep, that Brodie had appeared one rainy night in July. Hamish had welcomed the lad without hesitation, ushering him indoors, and hurrying to find him a plate of dinner.

Brodie had been living with his uncle for a few months now, and had since found work in an Edinburgh dyeworks. Hamish had been taken by the boy's intelligence, his work ethic and his dedication to his mother. He was overall deeply pleased with him. And so, calling Brodie to his study one Sunday evening, he presented him with a startling proposal.

My dear boy, you have worked diligently and demonstrated in every way filial devotion and respect. I fear, however, that you are wasted in your current employ and so I wish to make you an offer. I have named you as my heir—you will inherit all that is worldly that I hold. But I desire to give you something else. It is my plan that I should give you my name. Your father's name, God rest his soul, has been tarnished. You carry with you that misfortune. I have been in prayer and it is my conviction that this is the way forward. If you agree, you will take my name and study at the University. You have within you great gifts and talents and these must not be wasted. For unto whomsoever much is given, of him shall be much required.

April 30, 1895

Brodie's courses included math, physics, chemistry, engineering science, mechanics, thermodynamics, drawing and drafting, machine construction and manufacturing, lab testing materials, machine tolerances, design of machines, collection and investigation of artifacts, engineering research, hydraulics, and materials science. There was nothing in the curriculum that did not come easily to his analytical mind. The practical nature of the coursework suited him, and he found the professors instructive, patient, and clever. He enjoyed the problems put before him, taking delight in puzzling through solutions and testing his responses. His ability to visualize things spatially proved helpful, too. He would often sketch little pictures for his classmates so that they could more readily understand what it was their professors described.

He brought with him at all times a small leatherbound diary that held the specifics of the Tay Bridge construction. He had transcribed the details from a file he found in the Fairweather Library and had meticulously copied the illustrations and plans. As to the disaster, Brodie focused only on the subsequent inquiry, deliberately setting aside the newspaper clippings of the actual event.

Writing in fine pencil in the margins of his diary, he had added his own calculations, his own notes on tolerances. He listed calculations for tensile strength, compressive strength, sheer, and torsion alongside columns of numbers and various formulae. One day, he hoped, he would compile these notes into a manual for bridge building. Several pages were dedicated to cables, particularly the cable system used by Roebling for the Brooklyn Bridge. The strength of these cables, along with the fastening system devised to secure them, was infinitely interesting to Brodie. He felt certain that such innovations would enhance bridge safety. He kept this diary out of sight, and showed it to no one.

Brodie was in the kitchen when Alistair emerged from his room, packed bag in hand. *We'll take the wagon to the train, Al. I have time to walk.*

I'll enjoy the drive and may have tea at the hotel.

Alistair nodded, then set to cutting himself thick slabs of bread that he wrapped in a clean piece of brown paper. This bulky package he slipped into his jacket pocket, along with a couple of apples from their cold room. *And may be see if Charley is feeling better.*

May be. Brodie grinned and punched him softly in the stomach.

I've taken two bricks. Alistair held up his bag. *I'll leave them with Callaghan and his friends and then pick up the stamps. Is there anything else?*

Brodie nodded, *A more unpleasant errand, perhaps?*

Should I call on her?

You said you would.

Would it be better if I didna call?

You need to be clear.

It may be awkward.

It may.

The men looked at each other sombrely. *There's no other way of managing, is there?*

You will be doing her a kindness.

Let's away then.

On the drive to the station, Alistair was preoccupied with the difficulty of his social errand while Brodie, although sympathetic, was fixated on a more imminent and decidedly more pleasant one.

I wish you were coming, Brodie.

I have to keep an eye on things here.

And an eye on someone else, too, I suppose?

They both laughed. *There's no time for that, Al. We've discussed it. Besides, it would hardly be fair. One of us canna make plans wi' out hurting the other. Charley is a fine woman, but there's no reason to believe she'd have me, say I was in a position to think about such things.*

A half hour later, Brodie, having left Alistair at the station, seated himself at his accustomed table by the window of the hotel's dining room. The tablecloth was checkered in a fresh blue and white fabric, and someone had set a little glass filled with yellow flowers in its centre. This small touch affected Brodie. He played with the glass, twisting it absentmindedly as he studied it. Such feminine touches weren't something he'd been particularly aware of missing, but now it made him acutely conscious of the unadorned life he and Alistair had been leading. He felt some remorse, too, for the course he had encouraged his friend to take. Miss Lewis was a lovely creature. He knew that Al was smitten. And there would be tears, he thought, on the one side at least, if not on both.

You are deep in thought, Mr. Smith.

He looked up sheepishly. *Good morning, Charley.*

Tea?

Please.

She brought him a steaming cup along with a little sugar bowl. *Three, I believe?*

He nodded. She leaned over him, counted out the teaspoons of sugar, then passed him the cup and saucer. *You're an early one today.*

Yes, I was for dropping Al at the train. It comes early.

Where is Mr. Alistair going?

Back to Buffalo. To see our investors and pick up an order.

It's a nice day for a journey. I'm sure he'll have a pleasant trip.

No likely.

Charley looked at him inquisitively. *Why? Is there something amiss with your brickworks?*

The bricks are fine. Hard and solid. Our first firing was a resounding success.

Is it the sheep?

The sheep are sheep. Brodie was practically squirming by now, not having intended to discuss such matters.

Well then, Mr. Smith, why are you so pensive and glum? This was said a little playfully, but she was smiling encouragingly, and reached out across the table to tap his arm.

Brodie paused. *I've set him a personal errand, and it's no one he has much appetite for.*

I see. She continued to watch Brodie. It was clear that she couldn't entirely follow his meaning, but was trying to understand. *Have you quarrelled then?*

Brodie sat up straight and shook his head. *We're partners in all things, and close as brothers.* His unease was palpable now.

Have I made you uncomfortable? Charley stood leaning against the back of a chair.

Brodie smiled at her awkwardly. *No. I'm broodish about summit altogether different.*

She pulled out the chair and sat down, perched uneasily at the edge of the seat. *Tell me. Let me see if I can perhaps help. Sometimes the telling of a worry can ease it.*

Brodie scratched the back of his head and hesitated. What he wanted most in the world right then was to keep her by him at the table, to talk to her until his heart was emptied and there was naught else left to say. He wanted to tell her about the sheep and the bricks and his friendship with Al, and about his family in Scotland, and his ambitions, and the farm, and their hopes and plans for the partnership.

He looked at her carefully. Her starched white apron, the dark cotton dress done up primly at the collar and cuffs. The white cotton cap concealing most of her hair. The small, unadorned hands, her clear complexion, her smiling face. He felt he could drown in the brightness of her look and the warmth of her. She coloured a soft pink under his scrutiny; he was suddenly aware that he'd been staring.

I apologize. He looked down.

No matter. This was spoken softly.

Now Brodie found that she, in turn, was inventorying him. She took in his grey waterproof covert coat lined in brown corduroy, his worsted vest, cassimere flannel twill shirt, woollen tie, and his hands, large and calloused with clean trimmed nails and a slight sheen of lanolin. His neck above the softly worn collar was brown and weathered from the sun, as was his face and forehead. His hair was shaggy but clean and neatly combed, his face recently shaven, accentuating a deep cleft in his chin. His dark blue eyes looked at her timidly and she saw, in an instant, her own power. She met his gaze and did not lower her eyes.

Alistair has gone to break off wi' his sweetheart, he blurted. *Our farm is no place for a lady. I have encouraged him in this.* Brodie watched her carefully while he spoke.

And will his sweetheart be very disappointed?

She had expectations.

And was there also an obligation? Charley leaned forward in her chair.

I believe so.

Was there much affection in the matter?

On his part for certain. And, I believe, on hers.

Their eyes were still locked; neither had lowered their gaze. Had anyone passed by just then they would have been unnerved to have witnessed such intimacy. *Then I think it a great shame, Mr. Brodie.* He warmed to hear how she said his name, her gentle rolling of the *r*.

He willna, for some long time, be in a position to marry. He's doing her a kindness. She should be free to find someone else.

And what if she doesn't want someone else? What if her choice is to wait until he's in a position to marry? Does a woman have no say in the matter?

She is yet a girl. She'll find someone better suited. And it will spare him the pain of trying to provide a life to match what she's known.

So you've chosen for them both? Charley lowered her eyes. *Then I'm sorry for you all.* She stood and excused herself, disappearing quickly into the kitchen.

Brodie felt strangely indicted and ashamed. But he was also exhilarated; the unexpected intimacy of the moment had filled him with an overwhelming sense of bonhomie. The morning seemed positively glorious, good fortune just within his grasp. There was a niggling sense that he had, perhaps, somehow offended Charley, but that would come to rights in time, he decided.

Leaving a few coins for his tea, he left the hotel and walked outside in time to see the train pulling away from the station. He raised his arm in a farewell salute, silently wishing his friend godspeed.

Edinburgh, Scotland ~ June 30, 1896

Over time, Brodie's diary grew to include what he hoped was a comprehensive checklist of those things he felt important to a well-constructed bridge.

<u>Bridges must be:</u>
+Functional and <u>entirely safe</u> and give all appearance of being so.

+Attractive if not beautiful or striking or handsome.

+Well-proportioned and elegant.

+Respectful of the prospect lest the bridge ruin the outlook.

+Well-placed so as to provide efficiencies without disrupting the surroundings.

+Carefully balanced with regard to amplitude and resonance when the bridge is load-bearing.

+Well-constructed of superior materials that are durable to the weather.

He was mightily pleased with his list, referring to it whenever he evaluated any new bridge he encountered in his studies or travels. The list, he felt, would be of seminal importance to the book he planned to write.

Brodie had written a second list, too, intended for the benefit of those responsible for maintenance and upkeep.

Upon Completion:
+Thorough and regular maintenance and inspections required annually, if not more frequently;

+Nothing shall be hidden or concealed. Linking mechanisms in particular to be always visible for safety checks;

+Load tests to be conducted at regular intervals and in differing weather conditions.

Queensferry, Scotland ~ July 5, 1896

His preoccupation with the Tay Bridge, which had led Brodie from the disaster itself to a means of preventing harm, now brought him to a fascination with the beauty of bridges themselves.

He studied Baker's work at the Forth Bridge in Queensferry, devoting many hours to sketching its complex web of ties and struts and braces. Three double-cantilevered structures rose high above their piers, their arms reaching out to each side and linked by suspended girders. One of the towers had been built on a little island, two more on either side of the Firth of Forth. Adding to all the complication was its colour: as a means of preventing surface rust, the steel had been painted, and someone had chosen a brilliant red.

The Forth Bridge seemed to Brodie to be overbuilt, inelegant—and yet, for all that, somehow gracious. The aesthetic revealed itself to him gradually. He came to appreciate that its proportions were balanced, its symmetry satisfying. The basic truss structure reassured with its sturdy grounding; somehow its additional braces did not detract from this. Even the colour, Brodie had to concede, was more pleasing than a solid black might have been, scarring the landscape as it would with dark lines. And so again and again he returned to the bridge, watching the trains cross its span, each time coming away with a stronger appreciation of its mastery.

Edinburgh, Scotland ~ March 6, 1897

There was a little tea shop in Grassmarket where Brodie liked to take refreshment upon occasion. Although the allowance from his uncle was liberal, after many years of poverty Brodie did not wish to alter his frugal habits overmuch; he couldn't bear frivolous waste or expenditure. But tea and a toasted bap no more than once a week was a minor extravagance that he allowed himself.

Mrs. McGary ran the shop with her daughter Jeanie. They spread the sweet butter generously before toasting and would sometimes add a slice of bacon or a runny egg to the inside before serving him. These rich floury treats provided an indulgence for the young man that was conveniently coupled with Jeanie's personal attractions. She was a spirited, hardworking lass with a quick wit and a sharp tongue. Brodie was smitten with her but could not bring himself to ask her out walking—not until he was in all ways independent.

Chapter Thirteen: Buffalo Visit

Buffalo, New York ~ October 14, 1909

Callaghan's was Alistair's first stop. He took a carriage there directly from the station, eager to show him the bricks and to see what the stamps looked like—he would worry about paying calls later. The reception lobby gleamed, as always, in all its glamour, and Alistair smiled at the familiar feel of the place. The men downstairs patted him convivially about the back. It was good to see some of his old friends; he remained with them a good half hour before making his way to the second floor.

The railing was cool and comfortable under the curve of his hand, the marble steps smooth and substantial as he sprang up the winding stairway. When the aroma of Callaghan's cigar hit him at the top landing, in an unexpected and funny way Alistair felt as though he'd come home.

Callaghan was effusive in his welcome. *Come in, Alistair, come in. We've been expecting you.*

Good to see you, sir.

Good to see you, Alistair, good to see you. Your letters were well received. How was your journey?

It was a pleasant ride, sir. And I have something to show you. Alistair unfastened his bag and withdrew a brick. He placed it upon the desk. Callaghan picked it up immediately, smacked it against the heel of his shoe, then turned it over in his hands and weighed the heft of it.

Good job, son. Good job. Are you pleased?

Yes sir, that was the first firing. We cleared thirty-five thousand bricks. They'll sell for ten dollars per thousand. We have orders lined up. There's a hotel in Boltyn that alone has requested forty thousand.

Ah, that's very good news. And how is Brodie Smith?

He is well, sir. Sixty sheep in place already and a small crew of reliable men.

We should celebrate with a drink, I'd say. But first... Callaghan opened a desk drawer, withdrew a metal stamp, and held it out to Alistair. LAMITH was emblazoned on its surface.

Oh! Alistair exclaimed, taking the proffered stamp and gazing at it with some awe. *Och, this is splendid. My thanks, sir.*

Callaghan smiled. *I've got a few crates of them for you, ready to go. It does look fine, doesn't it?* He reached into another desk drawer, and now withdrew two crystal tumblers and a decanter of whisky. *To the brickworks!* He poured a finger of the golden liquid into each glass.

The men toasted each other and their mutual success.

Where are you staying?

I havena arranged for a room yet. I should excuse myself and book in before it becomes too late.

You do that. And tomorrow you should come by again in the morning. We'll talk some more business and you'll come to the house for dinner.

They shook hands and parted, whereupon Alistair booked a modest hotel down the avenue. Although the city was teeming with life, he was weary from travelling and so retired to his room to contemplate his circumstances. He and Brodie had done very well. Their business associates were supportive; they had ample funds to begin their venture; their crew were loyal, steady, and hardworking men. Orders had begun to come in, and now they'd be able to fulfill them with bricks bearing their name. They were managing to keep operating costs down. It was all promising. And yet Alistair felt strangely dispirited.

The prospect of a call to the Lewis establishment filled him with anxiety. He believed he had no right to lead Miss Lewis on; he had no immediate hope of providing for a wife, let alone someone so accustomed to refinement. But at the very thought of Violet—her merry manner and her openness, her lovely face and soft hair, her womanly form at the Academy in that delicate dress—a longing he had tried to set aside swept over him.

Alistair walked over to the little desk, sat down, and wrote.

Dear Miss Lewis,
I hope this note finds you in good health. I have
returned to Buffalo for a brief visit on a matter of business. I will call upon you tomorrow afternoon and hope
to find you at home.
Sincerely, Alistair Lamont

He sealed the note, addressed it, and carried it downstairs to
the porter, who arranged for a messenger boy to deliver it later
that evening.

In the morning Alistair breakfasted at the hotel and then
walked to the steelworks. He would meet with Callaghan and
thereafter make his round of calls to the other investors. Late
afternoon he would visit the Lewis household. He would not stay
long. All in all, it would be a satisfactory day; he would get much
accomplished. The matter most pressing to him, extricating himself from the attractions of Miss Lewis, must be treated as a matter
of business, and he was determined to do so expediently and efficiently. He would be distant, matter-of-fact. He would feign
surprise at any suggested intimacy. He would articulate the need
to remain focused on expanding the brickworks. He would, of
course, be as delicate as possible, and then remove himself at the
earliest occasion. He was resolved.

The remainder of the morning and early afternoon were spent
in a series of pleasant business encounters. The investors were
mightily pleased with his report and congratulated him, and also
Brodie, although absent, upon their early success. It was an auspi-
cious beginning. Callaghan was particularly enthusiastic, reminding
Alistair that he was expected at dinner at seven o'clock.

A small party, he remarked, *something put together quickly, in
your honour.*

Thanking his benefactor, Alistair excused himself and hailed
a carriage. He directed the driver to stop at a florist's shop. A
modest nosegay of tiny pink roses with silk violets and a ribbon
would do. The saleswoman bound it together quickly under his
direction.

Do you think— Alistair paused. *Do you think this is suitable for a young lady?*

It depends, smiled the woman. *Is she your sweetheart?*

He flushed at this. *No. I am simply paying a call.*

Perhaps then you might also take her mother flowers?

Ah. What do you suggest?

Perhaps these? The woman pointed to a large arrangement featuring feathers and exotic-looking greenery that Alistair did not recognize.

Yes.

Two bunches of wrapped flowers in hand, Alistair returned to the waiting carriage and was driven to the Lewis house. He got down rather slowly, feeling nervous and unsure of himself. He studied the brick as he drew near and once more admired the excellent pointing on the masonry work. He did not relish the idea of inflicting disappointment. Still, it was possible, he told himself, that Violet had been trifling with him, and that it would not be the letdown he feared it might be.

He strode to the door and raised his hand to grasp the knocker. Before he could do so, the door swung open and Miss Lewis, rather than the butler, stood before him smiling widely. *Mr. Lamont, I thought you would never arrive! Please come in. Mother is in the parlour and we have tea ready.*

Alistair coloured deeply. He extended the smaller of the two paper-wrapped flower parcels in her direction.

Oh, Mr. Lamont, I'm so glad to see you. Miss Lewis beamed at him. *I can't wait to hear about your adventures and business successes. And I've also been improving myself. I've set myself the task of understanding how it is that Mr. Ford—my father and his colleagues speak of him often you see—how it is that Mr. Ford is revolutionizing the manufacturing process.*

Alistair followed her into the parlour, where he greeted Mrs. Lewis and handed her the second bouquet.

Why, thank you, Mr. Lamont. Let me put these in water. Violet, will you please pour our guest some tea? Mrs. Lewis smiled at the young couple as she left the room.

Violet sat down behind the tea table and picked up the pot.

Will you have some tea, Mr. Lamont?

Yes, thank you. He noticed that her hand was trembling as she held the saucer. He was interested in this, and studied her. She looked nervous. This surprised him. He walked over to the table and took the proffered cup. *Are you in good health, Miss Lewis?*

Yes, Mr. Lamont. I am. Thank you.

He regarded her carefully while she spoke and saw that she was slightly flushed. He noted too, for the first time, how elegantly she was dressed, in a tightly fitted jacket and matching skirt of the palest grey. She looked older than her years, her hair neatly pinned up and smoothed into place. A lace collar sat high on her throat; matching bits of lace peeked from the jacket sleeves. Yet she retained a delicate air, and seemed in fact, almost tremulous. Having tried to convince himself of an either aloof or indifferent reception, this sudden turn disquieted him.

Father says that you and Mr. Smith have had a productive first quarter.

Things are going to plan. This was his chance. Alistair plunged on. *But it will be a long time before either of us will be independent. Able to start out on our own, for instance, or have families. But we're managing well.* He studied the pattern on the tea cup. Brightly painted in red and yellow, it was. Flourishes of gold leaf. He found it infinitely fascinating.

Mrs. Lewis came back into the room just then, carrying an immense vase filled with his flowers and feathers. Alistair stood.

Thank you, Mr. Lamont, this is quite stunning.

I am pleased you like it.

Isn't it lovely, Violet?

They both looked at her. She had her head down and was also studying her tea. *Yes, Mother.*

And your flowers, Violet, you have not opened them?

No. Excuse me. Violet seized the bouquet and rushed from the room.

Are things quite all right, Mr. Lamont?

Alistair coloured deeply once more. *I was telling your daughter, ma'am, that our first quarter has been prosperous but that it will be many years before either Mr. Smith or myself will be in any way independent. That is all.*

Mrs. Lewis gazed at him intently. *I understand.* She sat down and poured herself some tea.

Yes. The business must be well and truly established before either of us thinks of engaging in any other endeavour.

And by this I believe you mean matrimony, Mr. Lamont?

Alistair bowed his head. *I am in no position to make an offer of any kind.*

Mrs. Lewis fixed him with a steady gaze. *I believe you have been clear, Mr. Lamont, and I commend you for your business acumen. I am sure Mr. Lewis will be pleased to hear it.*

I should perhaps excuse myself.

Now Mrs. Lewis stood and extended her hand to Alistair. *My daughter, Mr. Lamont, will be sorry to hear that you've taken your leave.* She smiled at him kindly, he thought, and for just a moment he saw a flash of Violet's sweet features in her face.

Thank you, Mrs. Lewis. Please extend my apologies. I am expected elsewhere.

Of course.

It was all Alistair could do not to run from the house. He was aware of how flushed he was, how entirely mortified. It would not have been possible, he thought, for things to have gone more horribly.

Returning to the hotel, Alistair changed for dinner and had the porter send for an overlarge box of candied fruits. He could not bring himself to visit the florist again. At a few minutes to seven he flagged down a carriage and made his way to the Callaghan house. The drive was choked with motorcars and carriages, lights blazing out from all the windows. The brickwork was laid in English bond, he noted despite himself, but many of the bricks had rough edges. They weren't what Alistair would call a fine finishing brick.

He took a deep breath. *Tonight,* he thought, *will be just the thing I need.*

A butler ushered him into the study where a group of men were smoking cigars and drinking whisky. Alistair knew many among the company; he was soon surrounded by his investors and their friends. Callaghan was again effusive in his praise for the young entrepreneurs. The evening had begun well. Alistair could feel himself relaxing.

When the dinner gong sounded at eight o'clock the men obediently put down their drinks and followed their host to the dining room. A group of ladies in evening dress awaited them; Mrs. Callaghan partnered off her guests, two by two, and guided them to the table. When Alistair's turn came she took his arm and led him to a woman he hadn't noticed, standing in the shadows in a deep pink evening gown, soft dark curls falling loose about her shoulders and back. She turned to be introduced. Unlike the other ladies in the room she wore no jewels or hairpiece, only a nosegay of soft pink roses and silk violets fastened to the front her low-cut dress. The flowers—his flowers—were clearly intended to be the key feature in her adornment.

Mr. Lamont, I believe you know Miss Lewis?

Yes, of course. Delighted to see you again. Alistair took her hand and bowed deeply. His face, he knew, was scarlet. He led her to their seats and held out her chair. When he sat down beside her he found himself entirely without speech.

You left without saying goodbye, she whispered.

Yes.

Are you displeased with me?

He shook his head imperceptibly. *No.*

I had waited for you with great anticipation.

It was wrong o' me to encourage you.

I thought we had an understanding.

I apologize. But such a thing is no viable.

An attendant interrupted with his serving of the soup. Alistair concentrated upon it, shifting slightly in his seat so that he looked to the left, away from Miss Lewis on his right. He entered into general conversation at the table, every aspect of his body on heightened alert to the figure beside him. He picked out the tones of her voice in surrounding exchanges, once in knowledgeable response to a conversation about assembly lines and production schedules. He heard her slight laugh, and imagined he could inhale the fragrance of the flowers at her bosom. At one point (he was certain of this), he felt her deliberately kick him under the table.

Following the main course—prime rib and stuffed pork tenderloin with an array of brightly coloured vegetables—Mrs. Callaghan announced that dessert would be served after the dancing. Alistair's heart sank at once. The men stood and led their partners through to the vast living room, now cleared of its furniture and carpets. A six-piece orchestra had begun playing in one corner; the Callaghans led the dancing. Couple after couple entered the room and began to sway together. Alistair led Miss Lewis onto the dance floor and assumed the position, holding her stiffly. She smiled at him mischievously. *Is this entirely viable, Mr. Lamont?*

He began to lead her around the room while she, in turn, clasped firmly in his arms, dipped and swayed to the music, responding to the pressure of his hand on the small of her back. Alistair hadn't danced for some time, but the feel of her in his grasp, the fragrance of her perfume, the lightness of her movements were captivating. Her soft curls floated around her face as they moved; he felt the desperate urge to seize one and hold it close to his lips. She danced well, making even his stiff overtures seem natural and effortless.

The second dance was much slower. Alistair found that he could not avoid it. She stepped towards him and he felt the warmth of her as she pressed close. He led her sedately, taking the smallest of steps, aware of her proximity, feeling her breath upon his throat. It was unbearably exquisite. He closed his eyes briefly, savouring the moment of sheer bliss.

What about now, Mr. Lamont. Am I viable now? came the enticing whisper mouthed close to his heart.

He opened his eyes and looked down to see her looking up at him. He stopped dancing suddenly but remained holding her close.

Alistair spoke quietly into her hair. *Please excuse me.*

He walked away from her abruptly and left the room. He found Daniel Callaghan smoking a cigar, surrounded by a few friends in the study. Alistair remained there for the briefest of moments. After thanking his host, he made his exit. Then he made his way back to the hotel, striding furiously, his face burning.

Chapter Fourteen: Return to Braemor
Braemor, Ontario ~ October 20, 1909

The train ride back to Braemor was bleak. Alistair had equipped himself with a couple of newspapers and settled into the upholstered seat, preparing to read for the trip's duration. His quiet was disturbed by a young couple who sat opposite him, holding hands discreetly and whispering to each other. Having established that Alistair posed no threat, the man introduced himself and his wife, proudly announcing that they were commencing a honeymoon tour. Alistair wished them much happiness and retreated once more behind his newspaper.

He found himself staring out the window as the landscape slipped slowly by. The look of Violet's face replayed itself repeatedly. He could not help but conjure the memory of dancing with her, savouring the fragrance of her hair, the colour of her gown, the lightness of her dancing, the feel of her breath upon his neck. But also, each time, came her fateful teasing words, *What about now, Mr. Lamont, am I viable now?* An essence of combined longing and self-loathing knotted into a lump that lodged itself in the middle of his chest and caused great discomfort.

For part of the journey he had cursed Brodie silently for his insistence that neither of them should yet consider matrimony. Now, though, as he neared Braemor, he looked forward to catching up with him. He was anxious to hear the news, to discover how the second firing was progressing and whether all the bricks had been delivered. Deliberately, he filled his thoughts with a myriad of other details and clung to these practical worries.

He saw the wagon waiting for him at the station and knew that Brodie would not be far away. Alistair gathered his bag, directed the porter to load the crates with the brick stamps onto the wagon, and gave him some coin for his trouble. Then he headed for the hotel, where he felt sure Brodie would be enjoying a late meal. And as he approached, there was Brodie smoking his pipe by the window. When he walked into the dining room and Brodie stood up to give him a mock salute, Alistair felt a surge of relief to be back in this familiar, comfortable place. Things were much simpler here. It was good to be home.

Brodie, how are things?

Couldna be better. How was Buffalo?

Productive. Busy.

Was Callaghan happy wi' the report?

Completely.

The second firing is set.

Bricks delivered?

Yes. And paid in full.

And the men are well?

Hale and hearty. Working hard.

How's the new building coming?

Almost finished the walls.

That's great progress. And the sheep?

All's well there. Have you any news?

Nothing really.

Did you see Miss Lewis?

Alistair flushed a deep magenta.

Hello, Alistair, greeted Charley as she approached their table. *Welcome back. How was Buffalo?*

Very fine, thank you.

What can I get you? Oxtail soup is good today.

A bowl of soup would be just the thing.

And you, Mr. Smith, will you be wanting anything?

Brodie looked up at her, startled by her formality. *Stew would be good.*

I'll just be a moment.

Why is she calling you Mr. Smith?

I'm no certain. Things were fine a couple of days ago.

Did something happen with Johnny?

Of course no. Dinna be daft.

Charley came back carrying a tray with their soup and stew, along with cutlery, napkins, and a basket with bread and butter. She arranged these things with delicacy on Alistair's side of the table and all but slammed them down on Brodie's. Alistair observed carefully but said nothing. They spoke little after that, each concentrating on his meal. Just as they were finishing, Charley returned.

Will that be all for now, Alistair? There's a slice of peach pie I've been saving for you.

Yes, pie would be nice. Thank you.

Oh yes, enthused Brodie, *peach pie is my favourite!*

There's only the one slice left. You can have apple if you want, or none at all. With that Charley stomped off to the kitchen.

Alistair shook his head and then laughed outright. *I dinna ken much about women, Brodie, but I tell you this, that woman is seriously scunnered.*

Och, well, women are a mystery.

Perhaps, chimed in Charley—who'd returned with Alistair's pie, a piece so generous it could have easily been divided into three—*perhaps people should know when to leave well enough alone and not meddle in others' affairs. There's no apple either,* she added pointedly before walking away.

You've gone and done summit.

Brodie eyed the dessert. *All I said was that you might be calling on Miss Lewis.*

Why did you say that?

Just that we'd agreed we wouldna be in a position to marry for some long time.

And how did that come up?

She wondered why you were off to Buffalo wi' out me and I filled her in.

And shared my personal business? Thank you very much.

No, it was a general remark about the both of us needing to remain bachelors. It didna seem important.

Well, whatever you said gave offence. You have no pie!

Brodie sat back in his chair and pondered. *Well, I did say as how I encouraged you to break wi' your sweetheart. She didna like that.*

She said as how women should also be allowed to have a say in such matters. I thought it was just twaddle.

I'm guessing she didna. This pie is delicious.

I'll check the horses and get the wagon. You can pay. Brodie stood up and left the dining room abruptly. Alistair devoured the last of his pie before knocking on the kitchen door. Charley was busy washing dishes.

The pie was wonderful. Thank you.

I'm glad you enjoyed it.

After leaving a pile of coin on the table and a tip besides, he went outside and climbed up beside his friend.

So, home?

Did she say anything?

Just the amount.

I dinna understand what's got her in a lather. Brodie sounded much aggrieved.

You've put your foot wrong.

And how did you make out wi' Miss Lewis?

I dinna want to talk about it now.

Brodie was respectfully silent for several minutes. Then: *It was the right thing to do.*

Alistair didn't want to blame Brodie, but neither did he want to let him off the hook for his share in the misery. Not wishing to quarrel, he kept his own counsel.

Chapter Fifteen: The Harvest Dance

Braemor, Ontario ~ October 20, 1909

Alistair was eager to inspect the work done during his short time away. The men, in turn, were proud of their efforts and gladly showed off their progress on the new building and the substantial stores of shale and clay they had amassed. Impressed by Thomas's leadership in his absence, Alistair clapped him on the back repeatedly, saying, *Well done, Thom, well done!*

His obvious pleasure was infectious; the men genially doffed their caps with *'appy to see you back, Mr. Alistair* and *How's about you?*

Kyran was, as usual, full of chat, regaling the men with a story of his prowess as a logger one summer. *Te cuttin' down an trimmin' te trees was hard work but I could handle meself an cut as many or more den most—but den te mad bastards unload te wagon besides te river, an she's runnin' fierce as te Shannon wi' a devil of a current, and tey says to me to jump on a log an I'm thinkin' deys funnin' wi' me, but den te others jump on te logs and te logs keep spinnin' and te lads keep steppin' and te mess of it moves on down the river, I swear by all dats holy.*

The crates were pried open and the men gathered around to admire the LAMITH stamps that had been prepared. After Alistair exhibited how these were to be inserted in the bottom of the brick forms, he and Kyran set about to do so. Much of the day was spent carefully removing the wooden partitions, layering in the metal patterns upside down, then replacing the partitions and securing them with little nails.

While they worked, Kyran kept up a spirited monologue. He was pleased to fill Alistair in on all the news and events that had lately come to his attention. It was in this way that Alistair learned there was to be a Harvest Dance over in Glen Mor on Saturday night. Fiddlers from as far away as Barrie were coming, and the ladies were baking cakes and pies. This was a local tradition, according to Kyran, who added in a quiet undertone, *Dem Beatty boys will bring their shine and I'm sayin' dat you doan want te be tryin' et, as et will burn goin' down and hit ye like a hammer.* Kyran demonstrated by hitting himself lightly in the head and then falling down flat on the ground.

Alistair laughed appreciatively.

Wot's up wi' you? called Thomas from across the yard, *'ave ya had a taste o' Beatty's shine?!*

Kyran sat up and said triumphantly, *See, what I tell ye? Everyone knows te hammer.*

That evening, while Alistair and Brodie were frying up some onions with a couple of tins of corned beef and some slices of leftover potato, they reviewed the events of the day.

There's to be a Harvest Dance in Glen Mor on Saturday. I think we should go.

We'll have to leave off work early if we do.

We should let the men off early. We can go later.

Such a dance willna be like those society ones in Buffalo.

I havena been dancing overmuch, Brodie, as you know. But I think it's good to show the men we're community-minded.

Well, we've no had many entertainments, that's certain. Is everyone going?

Sounds like. Kyran warned me about the drink Beatty brothers distill. Apparently it's deadly.

That Kyran is a talker. Did you get a breath in?

No many. He fills the air, does our Kyran. But we got all the stamps inset in the forms. He's a careful worker for all that.

Brodie carried the frying pan over to the table and put it down between their two plates.

Elegant service, commented Alistair wryly.

Now you're sounding as crabbit as Charley.

Have you thought about what set her off?

It's no my concern if she wants to be tetchy.

Brodie served Alistair a heaping portion and then served himself before sitting down. The men concentrated on their dinner for a few minutes. Finally Alistair leaned back in his chair and winked at his friend. *A piece of peach pie sure would be a nice way to finish this meal.*

Brodie stood up indignantly. *Rubbing salt in a wound?*

Just having a bit of fun. There's to be pies at the dance, I heard.

You're bent on going, then?

The next few days were cold and rainy ones. Alistair tried to set the men to working on the new shed's roof, but nothing could be done in such weather. Reluctantly, Alistair sent the crew home and asked them to return when the skies cleared. He and Brodie were both feeling irritable, with nothing to turn to.

Saturday's sky was at last clear, although a damp chill had set in. The men showed up at six and worked furiously on cladding and roofing the building—knowing time was precious, they were all of them anxious to have a place to work when the snow came. At noon, Brodie announced it was time to leave off for the day. The men put down their tools and tidied the site quickly. There were no polite demurrals.

When Brodie and Alistair went to check on the livestock, Johnny was just finishing his chores.

Are you going to the dance, lad? asked Brodie.

Yes, sir. Everyone goes.

So, your mother is going wi' you then?

Yes, she's been baking pies and cakes and I don't know what else. She has a new dress. The Carruthers are collecting us on their way.

Well, that's good then. We'll see you this evening. Brodie reached over and tousled Johnny's hair.

Alistair smiled to himself as Brodie led the way into the house, whistling a merry jig.

The dance was being held at the Glen Mor school; lanterns had been hung from nails and rough board benches lined up along the sides. Brodie and Alistair could see the lights and hear the music wafting across the fields a distance away. Once they arrived, they tied their horses up with the rest and approached the throng. A group of men had gathered around a bonfire behind the schoolhouse, apparently having their own party.

Brodie strode through the open doors, scanning the crowd impatiently.

Do you fancy a turn, Brodie? Alistair asked when he'd caught up. *It's a circle dance and we could join in.*

Later.

Alistair nodded sanguinely, hands in pockets, and watched the dancers whirling around the floor. It was a lively tune and they were flushed with the rapid stepping. He was pleased to see Thomas and Patrick and Sean and Kyran in the mix, obviously having good fun. He looked over at Brodie, who seemed perturbed, and jostled him slightly.

Shall we have a look at the pies and see who's serving them?

The men stepped around the dancers and walked over to the front platform where the teacher's desk normally stood. Long tables with baked goods had been set out, with large bowls of punch. Groups of ladies were standing about, chatting and laughing softly. Cornucopias of gourds and pumpkins had been arranged on the tables, with bunches of dried cornstalks propped up along the walls, festooned with ribbons. It was a lovely sight.

Brodie was once more scanning this part of the crowd.

She's over there, whispered Alistair, *talking in the corner by the door.*

Brodie walked straight over. Alistair followed at a more leisurely pace, hands in his pockets again.

A fine evening, ladies, began Brodie.

Yes, they agreed. *So lovely,* enthused a couple of others.

A fine evening for dancing, he continued. *You're all enjoying the festivities?* He looked pointedly at Charley when he spoke. She was standing, hands on her hips, with the rest. Her hair was down, noticed Alistair, and she looked very fine in a tightly fitted blue dress. The ladies tittered at Brodie's words but no one responded to him directly. Alistair was enjoying the scene, eager to watch his friend's attempt at charm.

Would one o' you honour me wi' a turn? asked Brodie, looking directly at Charley and extending his hand towards her.

I've no intention of dancing, Mr. Smith, she said tartly. Brodie flushed but recovered quickly and turned to the other ladies. When one of them accepted he led a rather plain, dumpy woman toward the floor.

A polka was being danced with some intensity, and then a reel, and a jig. When Alistair's own partner said she needed to rest he escorted her to the benches and went in search of Brodie. He found him glowering, arms folded across his chest, standing near the fiddlers.

What's got to you? Was your partner no a good dancer?

Look at her, Brodie motioned discreetly in Charley's direction with his thumb. *She says as she's no intention of dancing, and the next thing she's out there doing a two-step wi' some other bloke.*

Alistair looked over at the man Charley was dancing with; it wasn't someone he recognized. The fellow was holding Charley fairly close, the two apparently enjoying themselves—Charley was laughing and the man was smiling at her and they were moving about deftly and in time to the music. Charley's brightly coloured dress could be followed around the floor in flashes of blue.

Brodie continued to sulk.

Perhaps you could cut in?

She said no. I'll no ask again. With that Brodie turned and walked in the direction of the door.

When the dance was over, Alistair looked across the circle and saw that Charley was smiling and flushed. She said something to her partner and went as if to walk away. Alistair was surprised to see the man grab at Charley's elbow and pull her into his arms. She protested briefly but then danced the next reel with him. Alistair watched for her carefully in the throng. She was no longer laughing; in fact she looked a little anxious, as though she was trying to break free from him. Alistair strode directly towards them and quickly cut in.

Are you all right? he asked as he whisked Charley across the floor.

Thank you, he was overly familiar.

I thought you were no for dancing this evening?

Charley smiled at him. *It's a woman's right to change her mind, is it not?*

Charley, can I ask, has my friend Brodie done summit to upset you?

Before Charley could answer, the man she'd been dancing with put his hand on Alistair's shoulder and tried to pry him away.

Hey, that's my partner you're with, he slurred.

Alistair lifted the man's hands off him and stepped closer to the intruder. He spoke directly to his face. *The lady has chosen to change her partner, sir.*

Doan you sir me, I ain't gotta take that.

The man swung at Alistair's face but Alistair, who could be quick on his feet, stepped to the side. The man lost his balance and staggered about the floor until he regained his footing. Then he turned and came back towards Alistair, who had taken on a boxing stance and was ready for him. Around them, dancing had stopped as people were quietly watching the small drama unfold. The man swung again; Alistair again neatly sidestepped the swing; people laughed.

Perhaps you might consider sitting this one out? suggested Alistair, playing to the crowd.

I ain't doin' what you say. Now face me proper and doan be running off.

Alistair sighed and waited for the man to have another run at him, but this time he held his ground and punched the fellow on the side of his face, knocking him to the ground. He reached down to help lift the aggrieved party to his feet, but the man appeared to be too drunk to stand. A group of his friends came and dragged him from the dance floor.

I apologize, said Alistair to the crowd. He bowed and made to excuse himself. Several people patted him on the back. Charley seemed to have left the dance floor—he didn't see where she'd gone—and so he made his way to the back of the school, where he found Brodie sitting with the others, drinking Beatty's shine.

Brodie, I warned you no to drink that. It will poison you for sure.

No worries, Al, said Brodie. *It makes you shoogly, is all.*

Well. Enough for now. Let's get some tea into you.

Brodie stood up and promptly sat back down. *A bit too fast. Lemme try again.* He stood a second time and walked over to Alistair slowly. *Tea would be good.*

They walked into the schoolhouse, where Alistair directed Brodie to sit down on one of the benches. He went to the woman pouring tea and asked for two cups. These he doctored with many spoons of sugar and carried them back to Brodie, who had since slumped over. *I've the start of something banging around inside my head,* he said, *and it feels wicked vile.*

Drink this.

Brodie drank both cups in rapid succession.

As Alistair stood over him, he spotted Charley walking in. She came straight over. *Thank you, Alistair, for your service. I only met that gentleman this evening.*

It was my pleasure, Charley, but he was no gentleman.

What's this about? asked Brodie, perking up.

No a thing to fret yourself with, said Alistair. *Only a man who was taking liberties with Charley.*

Taking liberties, was he? roared Brodie, standing up unsteadily. *Show him to me and I'll deal wi' him.*

There's no need, Brodie, the matter has been dealt with. Sit down and I'll get you more tea.

Have you been at Beatty's shine? asked Charley.

I'm as right as the rain, Mrs. Gowan. There is naught the matter wi' me. Brodie was, however, holding his head in a pitiable manner, which undermined the sentiment somewhat. A commotion was heard at the door just then—a group of men entering. Charley's former dance partner was among them, seeming even worse for wear.

There's my girl! exclaimed the drunk, pointing at Charley and advancing towards her. *I've come for another dance, sweetheart!* He put his arm around her waist and boldly kissed her on the cheek.

Charley pushed at him, trying to free herself, but the man was holding her tightly. Brodie rose angrily and in one swift motion grabbed the man away from Charley and swung him around, flinging him into a table laden with cakes and pies. The table collapsed as Brodie dove after the man, cuffing him soundly. The two rolled around on the floor, punching at each other, until Alistair was able to pull them apart. Then he seized the man and dragged him to the front door, where he threw rather than pushed him outside. He returned to help Brodie, but before he could, two men jumped on his back and started another brawl. Brodie came to his friend's assistance, as did several others besides.

While the women and children watched in astonishment, the group of wrestling men rolled about in the desserts, punching and kicking at one another. Finally, Alistair and Brodie were able to extricate themselves and stood up, looking at the ruined tables with embarrassment. Several drunken men lay on the floor, making no effort to comport themselves. Alistair and Brodie were both of them covered with the remains of the smashed and splattered desserts.

Charley observed the display with disgust. *I suppose you think you're defending my honour or something like? Well, look at the mess you've made! And you're bleeding besides.* She walked up to Brodie and touched the gash on his brow. *This is split wide open and will need stitching.*

A group of women began to put the room to rights while Brodie and Alistair stood sheepishly by. Brodie looked down at his jacket and used a finger to absentmindedly taste the whipped cream smeared across the front.

Have you brought the wagon? asked Charley.

Alistair nodded.

Well, harness the horses; you can drive us to my farm. I have a sewing kit there and can stitch up your friend. Johnny will come home with the Carruthers.

Alistair did as he was told. By now Brodie's wound was bleeding heavily and had soaked through several cloths. Charley sat between them on the wagon bench, checking on the bleeding from time to time. She was not particularly gentle in her ministrations, making it clear how severely put out she was with both her male companions.

When they reached her house the two followed Charley docilely into the kitchen, conscious that they were trailing bits of cake and pie filling on the floor. She bathed the wound with soap and water, then poured some whisky on it. Brodie made a little joke about preferring to drink the whisky, but Charley only smacked him on the arm and told him to be quiet. Then she left the room briefly and returned wearing an apron over her dress and carrying her sewing basket. She passed a needle to Alistair, telling him to sterilize it with a match flame. Alistair followed her instructions then watched as she threaded the needle with thick black thread and leaned over towards Brodie's cut.

Hold him in the chair and don't let him move, she said. Charley pinched together the wound and began to sew the edges together. She counted the stitches as she completed them. *One, two, three, four, five, six, seven, eight, nine, ten, eleven, twelve, thirteen.*

She grimaced as she worked and the men marvelled inwardly at her stamina but did not dare, either of them, to speak. When she was done, she bathed the area in whisky again then poured water from a pitcher into a bowl and washed her hands. Brodie saw that she'd gotten blood on the sleeves of her fine blue dress. He was trying to think of something to say but his head thrummed and he could not think clearly.

Finally Charley stood up and disappeared into a little larder off the kitchen. She returned carrying a berry pie, the top crust of which had the appearance of a crisp candied layer. Without a word, she cut three generous slices and then sat down between the two men.

Brodie and Alistair thanked her profusely, but both were feeling shamefaced about the fight and didn't particularly want to prolong their embarrassment by receiving a scolding. It was an awkward exchange. They hurried their pie down, eager to leave. Charley, for her part, had no intention of making things easier. They were as foolish and impetuous as any men, and she was not pleased with either of them for having ruined the dance.

CHAPTER SIXTEEN: THE AFTERMATH

Alistair and Brodie did not rouse until mid-morning. Brodie was the worse of the two, but both were overall tender from the brawl. They stepped slowly, with premeditated movements.

We missed church this morning, said Alistair.

Just as well.

Alistair nodded rather than attempt speech again. That single nod caused him extreme discomfort, however, and he sat down abruptly to recover, moaning ever so slightly.

Al?

Aye.

It's a shame about all those pies.

You are a daft lummox.

I think we may have compromised ourselves.

You may be should have thought about that before you dove head-first into the pastries.

I was trying to make a gesture.

Well, that you did.

It was meant as a grand gesture, to impress Charley.

You have impressed her, for sure. As a blundering git who fights like a schoolboy.

Och, Alistair, was it so bad?

Let me see: you dropped bits of pie and cake over the whole of her kitchen floor, you bled on her gown, and you whimpered like a wee bairn when she stitched you. But no, no so bad if that was your intention.

Brodie groaned and rested his head in both hands. *It was so?*

It was.

The men were silent for several minutes. Each of them musing quietly. Alistair stood up slowly and reached for his coat.

Where are you off to?

A swim.

There was a skiff of ice on the river the other day.

No matter. It will be bracing.

You're barmy.

Come with me.

As expected, the river was ice cold. It was only late October but the air was crisp and most of the trees had lost their leaves. The men stripped off and plunged in, exclaiming loudly as they did. Their clay and shale excavations had created a hole deep enough for swimming; they tread water for less than a minute in the shocking cold before they began to shiver with chattering teeth. Waving their arms about them in energetic circles, they climbed out and made their way up the bank. They dressed quickly, fastening their coats closed and pulling their collars up high.

I've lost all sense of feeling, said Brodie.

Maybe it's gone chasing after your common sense.

I've made a fool of myself.

Och, aye.

I need a way to impress her.

You tried that, Brodie. We ended up rolling in cakes and meringues.

What shall I do?

No a thing for now.

No?

No. You said yourself there was no time for courting.

Have I been a fool?

Yes. We both looked fools.

Do you blame me for Miss Lewis?

Alistair was quiet a moment. *No. I blame myself. I know she'll soon be with someone else. But Brodie, if I ever do see her again, and if she is yet unattached, I'll make her an offer and beg her to accept. There is no another woman for me and I canna forget her.*

Brodie was thoughtful. *Then so be it. We'll let things happen as they do.*

And what of your grand gesture?

We will worry about that when the pounding in my head stops.

The next morning was an early wakening; they had much to prepare. Both left for the work site before six. Their men had already assembled, each with his head heavily bandaged above the brow and carrying a hammer. Alistair and Brodie squinted, trying to discern the meaning of this strange presentation. As the partners drew near, the men lifted their hammers silently and tapped their heads with them.

Good morning, did ye enjoy Beatty's shine?

We tried te warn ye.

How's the head, Master Brodie?

'ave you any cakes left for our morning tea?

Did Charley stitch some fancy work on yer brow or were it a plain job?

And on they went, each making a remark in turn, smirking at their masters and continuing to lightly touch the hammers to their heads. Alistair and Brodie had the good sense to enjoy the joke, even though it was at their expense.

All right, we deserved that, said Brodie, grinning.

Thank you, said Alistair, *we have learned a lesson.*

We missed you in church, added one last voice.

Edinburgh, Scotland ~ April 11, 1897

After some gentle deliberations, Margaret Hamilton had moved to Edinburgh to join Hamish and Brodie. She had protested at first, even declining the modest housekeeper's wage Hamish offered, but was soon won over by her persistent brother.

If ye'll stop yer haver noo and say nae more, she told him, *I'm after takin' haf the amoont.*

She was now managing the household, relieving Hamish from the worry of all things mundane. For Hamish this proved a relief, for he did not particularly want a housekeeper fussing and meddling. For Margaret the move was welcome, as Dundee had not forgotten Tay Bridge. The town wore its grief like a heavy cloak; it could not disremember the night when so many of them lost those whom they loved. And so the three, Hamish,

Margaret, and Brodie, settled into a domestic harmony no less precious for being unexpected.

December 29, 1899

Brodie had completed his degree and was once more a working man; although, as an apprentice engineer now, he had advanced in the world. Still, he was young yet, and so was left to copy out letters and plans and to run errands like a schoolboy. His good nature was such that he did not view these things as beneath him. The work was mindless and the hours long, but it did allow for some small use of his education and training.

After work, he'd taken to reading and writing notes in the Edinburgh Central Library. Opened five years before, it had quickly become a local hub, a place where anyone might freely enter, peruse the shelves, and borrow books without cost. Andrew Carnegie's vision—that everyone, regardless of status or income, should have available to them the knowledge found in books—appealed to Brodie. It helped shape his own developing view of the opportunities that must be available in America. The library itself, with its light-filled rooms, gleaming wooden tables, and brass railings and fittings, enveloped visitors with its inviting mixture of grandeur, elucidation, and optimism.

One night he'd managed to slip away early, before the *Edinburgh Evening News'* offices were closed. At its entrance he dusted off his jacket, straightened his cap, stamped the mud off his boots, and opened the door. Inside was a phalanx of desks, with two or three men still at their work.

Good evening, he said to the room in general. *I've come wi' a story for publishing.*

One of the gentlemen at the back popped up his head and waved Brodie to come closer.

Brodie stepped forward eagerly, drawing out from his jacket pocket the sheaf of papers he had carefully prepared.

These papers here, he began, *show the faults present in the design of the bridge afore the train came and ran into the wet of the Tay.*

An what makes you think there's a story here?

The people should know twarn't the engineer's fault, he who was driving it, but the fault o' the bridge and how it was put together. I've done the research and checked the facts.

An' why would you care what people think about this now, so many years after?

To clear the name of them that's been held to fault.

The inquiry was put to rest, along with the souls lost, and no one wants to be reminded.

But people dinna ken all the facts.

Yer wastin' time, lad. There's no story left to tell.

May 15, 1900

It had been another wearying day at the firm. Brodie had spent the whole of the morning, a long five hours, meticulously copying by hand the drawings for a plumbing install in a great house outside the city. The owners had purchased a Ferguslie pedestal washout from Royal Doulton and were having it built into a small closet. Brodie had been appointed to first transcribe the plans and then prepare the required materials list. The plumbing schematics were, however, complicated. An indoor convenience of this type was not in common application; Brodie was unsure of the requirements. He'd attempted to consult with the chief engineer but had been dismissed with a cursory and unsatisfactory explanation.

Dispirited, Brodie had taken his leave at midday to visit the university library, seeking clarification on the importance of gravity and water pressure for such work. An American monograph provided the insight required; Brodie returned to the office, confident that either a realignment of the piping and or the relocation of the unit to another part of the house would save the owners a great sum of money. He shared these ideas with an associate. He was warned to keep his ideas to himself until they were wanted.

June 9, 1900

Brodie was now, with his uncle's blessing and his mother's encouragement, contemplating further study in America. He'd written to several universities and had included for their review handwritten copies of his diary pages. He wanted to design bridges. He felt that although he had much still to learn, he also had something to contribute.

He was eager, in particular, to visit New York and walk across the Brooklyn Bridge. Roebling had long been of much interest to Brodie; he felt that his use of cables was an act of brilliant engineering. Brodie was confident that cables would have further application in bridge making. He wanted very much to explore the possibility.

On this particular day Brodie was sipping his tea with greater delicacy than usual, summoning the courage to speak, at the last, to Jeanie. She came to his table with a fresh pot and exchanged it for the one he had emptied.

You are long at your tea today, Mr. Smith.

Yes, I feel to enjoy it, as it may well be my last.

Your last cup of tea?

My last here wi' you.

Are you away then? Jeanie seemed surprised, and hesitated at the table. One hand rested on a chair back, the other held the cool teapot away from her body.

I'm away to America. To study in Cambridge, at the Massachusetts Institute of Technology. He tried to keep the excitement out of his voice.

Jeanie seemed not to notice either way. *I reckoned your studying was all done 'ere in Edinburgh.*

I'm to take a second degree.

And you'll no be back?

Nae for some long while. I have much to learn. I will return to visit my mother and uncle when I can.

It's a long way, to be sure.

I shall miss these fine baps of your'n.

And we shall miss havin' you 'ere enjoying them.

Jeanie curtsied at this and excused herself, leaving for the kitchen with the empty teapot. Brodie sat awhile, waiting for her to come back, imagining some pretty words he might say, but she did not return. And so, his romantic fantasies extinguished before having had a chance to ignite, he prepared to leave Scotland a single man with no promises to keep.

As the weeks went on, the crew made concerted efforts to complete the winter work shed and to stockpile as much clay and shale as possible. Alistair and Brodie would often arrive at the site at half past five in the morning to discover a handful of men already labouring. And come six o'clock in the evening, their traditional quitting time, the men would lag behind, completing some small task or staying late to help one of their mates finish a job. In this way, before the first hard frost had come, the shed was prepared and stocked for the winter months. The kiln had been carefully strengthened, its exterior now encircled by sturdy iron bands equipped with clamps for adjusting when the bricks expanded or contracted. Great stores of coal and wood were covered with heavy tarps, kept ready for the fireboxes.

Alistair and Brodie spoke often of the men's commitment and how it might be rewarded. In the end, they decided upon a Christmas bonus and a festive dinner. Brodie quickly volunteered to make the catering arrangements at the hotel. Ever since the Harvest Dance they had mostly avoided the broader community—creeping into the back pew at church and not lingering afterwards; driving into the village for mail and supplies but forgoing any drinks or meals there. In this way they hoped to put some distance between the embarrassing events of the dance and re-establish themselves as serious men of business.

The brickworks, meanwhile, was continuing to expand. Alistair had secured a contract with the railway, which had agreed to run a spur line through to the bottom of the worksite. Once constructed the following spring, they would be able to transport their bricks effortlessly to waiting customers. Alistair had committed to both paying for the rails and supplying the labour. The line would be laid at no inconvenience or cost to the railway but would have to meet its exacting specifications. It was a mutually satisfactory arrangement: Lamith Bricks was assured of a timely construction while the railway was assured of additional shipping revenue. Alistair and Brodie were mightily pleased, and both men eagerly anticipated the passing of winter and the first thaw.

On Saturday night, after Johnny and the men had left, Alistair entered the house to find Brodie in the kitchen, bathing in the giant galvanized tub they'd purchased some weeks before. *It's early yet for our baths. What are you about?*

I thought as I should go to the hotel and speak to Charley about the Christmas party for the men, Brodie said cheerfully as he rubbed the soap bar up and down his arms. *Consult her, and such. We discussed it already, you and me.*

The kettle was on the stove and Alistair checked to see that it had been refilled and was hotting up more water. *I see. And the reason you're bathing first is simply to review the menu with her?*

Och, Alistair. Dinna be such a galoot. I smell like sheep.

Aye, that you do. Alistair grinned. *I'll make shift for myself then. Do you want summit to eat?*

I thought I might eat at the hotel tonight.

Am I invited or would you prefer going on your own?

On my own tonight, Alistair. I know you have the accounts to do.

Ah yes, the accounts. I see. It's no my company you're wanting then?

Brodie stood up and let the water run from his body while he reached for a towel. *I feel to do this on my own.*

If the accounts show a surplus, Brodie, then we might think about a trip to Toronto to view the Parkhill Martin brick machines.

Aye, in time. Let's see if there's coin to do it.

Alistair began to boil some potatoes for his dinner while Brodie went upstairs to dress. Alistair did have the accounts to do, but it was a tedious job and he would have welcomed a more sociable evening. Brodie came down the stairs with his hair neatly combed and wearing his good tweed suit.

Alistair arched an eyebrow. *Dinna worry about me, Brodie. I have a pot o' potatoes here and some fresh bread, and hours of work ahead of me. Just ye go and have a nice hot meal and dinna give me another thought.*

Brodie punched him lightly in the stomach and took his leave. Only a few minutes later, Alistair saw him through the window riding across country. He must have saddled the horse before he came indoors to bathe. Alistair smiled to himself and sat down to his dinner. Inevitably, it seemed, his thoughts returned to the brick machines. The spur line would undoubtedly help them expand. Yet Alistair knew that for Lamith Bricks to be a truly profitable undertaking they would have to do more—to raise their production even higher—and that mechanizing was the only means of doing so. But the expense! Figures jangled in his head.

Patience, he thought. After Christmas, he told himself. While the weather isn't much good for excavating clay and shale. Come January, perhaps a visit to Toronto then.

As he rode, Brodie rehearsed two alternative speeches. *Charley,* began the first, *I meant to make mention o' my appreciation for the service you did me. When I was last in town I bought this small token to express my gratitude.* The second was less serious: *Charley, in the event that I have need o' your fine stitching again, I thought as to buy you something for your hands.* Her mood when he arrived would determine his approach. But at the end of either speech he would present her with the little parcel in his suit jacket pocket: a pair of rabbit-lined gloves.

He'd stood in the shop feeling awkward and out of place for some minutes before a kindly saleswoman had taken pity on him. *I need a small gift for a lady,* he had begun, *but no too personal or showy. I dinna want to give offence by being too familiar.* The woman had nodded and directed him to the glove counter. First she pulled out elbow-length kid-skin gloves, but Brodie thought them too fine and couldn't imagine when Charley would ever wear them. Lace gloves were next on offer; these he thought too frivolous. The rabbit-lined ones he greeted enthusiastically, carefully selecting a dark pair that looked warm and well made. These, he calculated, would please her very much. He paid an extra few pennies to have them gift-wrapped in gilt paper.

Brodie had kept the parcel for several weeks. He had intended to send it home with Johnny but had reconsidered, deciding that was too impersonal and might be misunderstood. But since the dance he had not felt able to face Charley, studiously avoiding her at church and during his short forays into the village. He knew this was cowardly but could not puzzle out how to manage it, and so he'd done nothing. The longer he left things, the more awkward they became and the more difficult it all seemed.

The dining room was full when Brodie arrived. He sat down at an available table and casually scanned the room, nodding at those he knew and greeting a few more who passed by. Johnny was waiting on tables this evening, as was the hotel owner, Mr. Justus Ketchum. At length, Justus came to take his order.

Well, said Brodie, *it's no often we're waited upon by the hotel royalty his self.*

Hello Brodie, it's been a good while since we've seen you here. Are you fully recovered?

Brodie reddened uncomfortably. *I am, sir. Thank you. But where are your regular staff this evening?*

Cook is sick and Mrs. Gowan has undertaken to manage the kitchen entirely. I've been pressed into service in her stead, with Mrs. Ketchum managing the front desk.

That is unfortunate.

Yes, Cook has been off these three weeks now with a septic leg and is not likely to return soon.

I am sorry to hear it.

And what news do you boys have at the brickworks? We hear from the men that you're continually expanding the operation.

Yes. It goes well. We're to run a spur line in the spring.

Justus nodded pleasantly. *That is a bold move. You must have great plans. What will you have for your supper? There is colcannon, chicken pie, or smoked tongue.*

Chicken pie, if you please.

Justus nodded and excused himself, walking directly to the kitchen. Johnny, meanwhile, had also passed by Brodie's table with a friendly greeting. Brodie attempted to relax, patting the small parcel in his jacket pocket for comfort. He did not yet know how he would manage to deliver it to Charley. With a sinking feeling, he realized that his practised speeches might be for naught.

Justus delivered the chicken pie along with a generous helping of mashed potatoes and pickled beets. As Brodie poked at the top crust with his fork a wisp of hot steam escaped, carrying with it the pleasant fragrance of the warm cream sauce generously spiced with black pepper and parsley. The meal was delicious, far finer than anything he and Alistair could manage for themselves. It had been a long while since he'd eaten anything beyond their hastily thrown together mashes and fry-ups. Brodie was feeling very satisfied now, and somewhat more expansive. He summoned Johnny to his table and asked what was on offer for dessert.

There's fruit cobbler with whipped cream.

Any pie?

No pie, Mr. Smith. My Ma is doing the cooking and she had no time to do pies today.

I see. Well, I'll have some cobbler then, and a cup of tea.

With whipped cream, sir?

Yes, Johnny, plenty of whipped cream.

Johnny ran off to the kitchen and returned promptly with a meagre serving of cobbler in a bowl without whipped cream. He shifted from one foot to the other. *My Ma says to tell you that too many sweets will make you fat.*

And was this message for me particularly, asked Brodie, reddening again, *or is it a general message for all the patrons?*

For you, in particular. I told her as how the cobbler was for you and needed lots of whipped cream. And she said to give you her message.

I see. After Johnny had ducked his head awkwardly and moved off to another table, Brodie sat there puzzling out what next to do. He knew he wasn't fat. He and Alistair worked hard six days a week, and were solid and muscled from their labours. They put on good suits only occasionally, but when they did he knew they both looked trim and strong. It was a curious message to convey and he sat there stymied, wondering at the meaning.

He thought he once saw the kitchen door open only slightly and imagined he saw a face there peeking out at him.

Leaving the money on the table to cover his bill and a tip besides, Brodie stood and began to put on his coat. He had resolved to retreat to the farm, where he could consider the significance of her words. He was just about to go when Johnny came rushing up to him.

Are you leaving, Mr. Brodie?

Yes, I should get back to Alistair and help him wi' the accounts.

Will you not stay and visit awhile? We are almost for closing up.

No, lad, I dinna think it. No tonight.

My Ma will want to know if you enjoyed the chicken pie. What shall I tell her?

Tell her it was very fine, and thank her for me.

Johnny hesitated. *You could tell her yourself, if you wanted, sir. She's in the kitchen and she asked me if I thought you had enjoyed it.*

Did she now? Brodie smiled broadly.

She did.

Well then, Johnny, in that case, tell her I choked it down, despite it being too salty.

Johnny's eyes grew wide at this. *Really?* he asked in a thin, worried voice.

Really. I could barely finish it. Now, go tell her, lad, and I will wait for her answer.

Brodie stood with his coat on as Johnny rushed into the kitchen. He waited for only a moment before Charley came storming out in a long apron, her hair tucked into a white cotton cap. Her sleeves were folded up to the elbows, she had a tea towel in her hand, and she looked flushed and indignant. As she approached he saw that her fine eyes were snapping.

He smiled at her. *Hello, Charley, how are you this evening?*

Don't you be saying Hello Charley to me, Mr. Smith. You have some nerve. First you make a drunken spectacle of yourself destroying the pie table, bleeding all over my kitchen, dropping mess everywhere you walk, and then you hadn't the decency to show yourself till now and all you have to say is that the chicken pie was salty and you could barely choke it down!

Brodie hung his head while Charley gave him a telling. He was entirely tickled by her indignation. He couldn't remember a time when he'd seen a woman look more fired up or beautiful. He knew that if he didn't keep his eyes on the floor he'd be in far more trouble.

Mrs. Gowan?

Yes?

I apologize for my behaviour. All of it. I came here this evening wi' the express purpose of apologizing.

Well, you certainly have a fine way of doing that, Mr. Smith.

I brought you this as a token of my appreciation. Brodie held out the gilt-wrapped gift. She took it from him, looking abashed.

I know my conduct was unforgivable, but I was hoping we might discuss a matter of business regarding my men. I dinna rightly know how to make amends. I was hoping you'd be generous enough to forgive me.

And the remarks on my chicken pot pie? Am I to I forgive you for that as well? Charley, still holding the package in her hands, put her fists to her waist and stamped her foot.

I was only funning you, Charley—

Mrs. Gowan.

I was only funning you, Mrs. Gowan. I didna intend to hurt your feelings. It was the best meal I've eaten in weeks. Honestly. Alistair is no a cook and we've missed having a good meal.

And why have you stayed away for such a time?

We've been very busy and I've been very ashamed. I didna know how to make amends.

Charley began to look mollified. Her posture softened; she became less warrior-like in her stance. She turned the parcel over in her hands and looked uncomfortable.

Please open it and see if they suit.

Charley shook her head. *You should not be giving me presents, Mr. Smith. It's not seemly.* She passed the parcel back to him.

Brodie took it from her and immediately slipped it into her apron pocket. *Open it later, then, and know that a friend chose them for you wi' particular care. I bid you good evening.*

Brodie bowed, excusing himself quickly. He swung out the door and then stood outside on the boardwalk, the cold air

welcome on his flushed face. It hadn't been an entirely unsatisfactory exchange after all. Her temper had deeply amused him. A
woman with such a disposition, he speculated, might likewise be
passionate in other ways. This made him smile. He walked
towards the stables, whistling thoughtfully as he filled his pipe.

Braemor, Ontario ~ November 30, 1909

Charlotte Gowan was such a wonder to Brodie. He felt,
when he was with her, that he'd somehow come home. It wasn't
so much that she reminded him of either his mother or his uncle
as the comfortable feeling he had in her presence. He sensed that
he could be entirely himself with her—that he could tell her all
his thoughts and dreams, his worries and even his past hurts, and
she wouldn't mock or dismiss him but would listen silently in her
serene way and swallow them down whole. And somehow all
those emotions and longings would in this way also become hers
and they would share in them together. And perhaps in time he,
in turn, could become home for her.

Chapter Eighteen: A Dinner to Plan
Braemor, Ontario ~ December 5, 1909

It had become Alistair and Brodie's habit to attend church services whenever possible. They believed that it set a good example. Most of the village showed up for services, and in this way their neighbours, who lived spread out across the county, connected socially. Tea was served afterwards; a great hubbub of chatter prevailed as everyone mixed in together, children and adults, and shared bits of news and gossip. And so on this morning, without talking much about it, Alistair and Brodie readied themselves for the service and hurried out the door.

Shall we take the wagon or the horses? asked Alistair.

Horses maybe.

Once they'd reached the church's open driving shed, they tied up their animals inside with the others. In the autumn months they'd just looped the reins around a tree branch and let them graze on the bushes and weeds, but a bitter wind was blowing from the east and Alistair was fussy about keeping them out of the gale. Brodie patted a few of the horses appreciatively before trailing after Alistair towards the church.

The men took their customary seats near the back. Brodie liked to survey the congregation from this vantage point while Alistair joked about making a quick exit should things became uncomfortable. Brodie hadn't shared details with Alistair about his recent encounter with Charley. He kept this entirely to himself, savouring it privately.

The sermon seemed long and ponderous to Brodie; he found himself studying people's backs, trying to locate Charley and Johnny in the crowd. He thought he spied them in the front right corner of the church and strained to make sure. Alistair noticed his undignified manoeuvres and looked at him quizzically. Brodie slumped back down in the pew and comported himself.

Over the last several weeks, they'd continued to slink out at the end of the service, in an attempt to re-establish some dignity. Today, however, right after the benediction, Brodie headed to the front of the church, joining the group waiting to walk through to the tiny hall. Alistair shrugged and followed somewhat reluctantly.

Brodie, he saw, was engaged in conversation with Charley and Johnny, the former busy wrapping the latter in a long knitted muffler.

Good morning, Alistair, she said. *It's nice to see you're both feeling convivial once more. We had all wondered at your long absence from our tea.*

Good morning, Charley. Are you leaving already?

Yes, the Carruthers are driving us home. It's biting cold for walking.

Has Brodie made the arrangements for our Christmas party with you?

Charley looked at Brodie inquiringly.

We wondered, he said, *if we could ask your advice about a dinner for the men? At the hotel one night, if Justus approves.*

We must go now, as the Carruthers are in some small hurry this morning. Perhaps the two of you would join us this afternoon at the house? We can discuss the details then. Charley put her hand out to pat Brodie on the arm. Alistair noticed that she was wearing a very fine pair of winter gloves.

The men took their coats down from the hooks and hurried out to the horses. A light snow had begun to fall, with deep grey clouds overhead holding more to come. The sky seemed particularly ominous as they headed home.

I'm no certain we should go out again, said Alistair when they had arrived back at the farm and were busily brushing the horses down. *Foul storm coming.*

Brodie was quiet. *The Gowans are expecting us, Al. We need to make the plans. Christmas is in three weeks.*

It's as black as the Earl of Hell's waistcoat!

Dinna fuss yourself.

As Alistair built a fire in the kitchen stove Brodie dumped a couple of tins of beans in a saucepan. *Should I go on my own and leave you here to tend things?*

Alistair looked at him.

Then I could make the arrangements, Brodie continued airily, *and you wouldna need to go out again.*

Alistair nodded. *It's good of you to be so thoughtful, Brodie, but this weather is no fit for man nor beast. I dinna think either of us should be out in it. We've both heard of the winter storms here. It's a short ride in good weather; there's no knowing what might happen if the snow sets in deep.*

Brodie stood at the window, looking out at the thick white flakes that were now falling and blowing around in a dense storm. The snow was accumulating so quickly that everything had been covered and had taken on the look of shapeless white mounds.

It's no so bad, Al.

You're daft.

Brodie left the window and served the beans. Alistair had already set the table with cutlery and water and bread. They each of them tucked in without speaking.

Alistair carefully wiped the inside of his bowl with a slice of bread. *Brodie, if you've a mind to go, I'll no try to stop you. But it's madness in this weather.*

Brodie nodded at him.

I need to speak plain, Brodie, as I expect you would do also. Charley is a widow with a good lad for a son. People will no take it kindly if your intentions towards her are no serious. You have to decide that you want to marry her or you have to leave off. I've seen the way you look at her and I'll no be the only one. Tongues will wag soon and the talk of it will do us harm. Unless you're serious.

Brodie had started pacing around the little kitchen and continued to pace, hands in his pockets, after Alistair fell quiet. He knew his friend was right. But he felt a pull towards Charley he couldn't ignore. He'd never met a woman with such an appealing disposition. He found her outspokenness and practical nature entirely charming. She was beautiful besides—and never as beautiful as the day she'd scolded him for insulting her cooking. She could be good company, and a deal of fun. But marriage?

We have said, Brodie finally replied, *that this is no the time for courtship and that we have time only for our business.*

Yes. But we neither of us wants to live out our days together as miserable bachelors. It may be our plans need revising.

Brodie sat back down at the table. *What are you saying?*

I'm saying that she's a fine woman and she's no spoken for. And if you wait too long some other might turn up to court her. How would you feel if that were to happen?

Damned miserable.

Then maybe that is your answer.

What would you think about that? After you broke with Miss Lewis?

I'd think that some things are meant to be, and that if she'll have you, which is no certain, then things are unfolding as they should.

You dinna think she would have me?

She's been a wife, Brodie. You may no measure up to a man long since passed.

Do you think it?

I've heard that her husband was a fine man and a good farmer.

Look, the snowfall has lessened. Both men stood up and walked to the window. They nodded at each other.

By the time Brodie was ready to leave, the clouds overhead were still a dark grey. He knew more snow was yet to come but felt enlivened by Alistair's encouragement and eager to visit the Gowan homestead. The ride, normally a short, gentle one, was far longer, the horse picking its way through the deep drifts. Brodie was anxious not to push him too hard. He rode straight to the Gowans' barn, slid open the door to let himself in, then guided his horse into an empty stall and quickly rubbed him down before walking to the house. The wind had picked up again; he felt his face tingling with windburn and his eyelashes caked in ice. He knocked loudly.

Johnny opened the door, struggling to hold it in position. Brodie stepped inside and looked to see what the matter was, taking the weight of it in his gloved hands. *The top pin has come out of the hinge,* he said to Charley, who had appeared at the end of the hallway. *Did you manage to save it?*

No, it's been that way for ever so long. I don't know where the pin has got to. We mostly use the kitchen door. Is Alistair not with you?

He had the accounts to tally. Have you any nails about?

In the cellar. My husband's tools are down there.

Shall I see if I can fix it?

You look frozen. Perhaps you should warm by the fire and have a cup of tea first.

Na when there is work to do.

Johnny, will you please show Mr. Smith where your father's tools are. There may be something he can use.

Brodie stepped out of his boots and left them by the door. Then, after he'd handed Charley his coat and gloves, she passed him an oil lamp. He followed Johnny down the dark narrow stairs, carrying the lamp carefully before him as he surveyed the deep cellar, its rubble-stone walls glistening when the light touched them. In a corner of the room, its legs set upon rough planks across the packed earthen floor, was a table with tools strewn about its surface as if someone had just walked away for a moment. He stood before the array, taking in its significance. He could practically feel Dick Gowan's presence here. Perhaps that was why it had remained so untouched. Charley had barely spoken of her late husband, yet how she must have grieved; how she must miss him still. Brodie bowed his head. Then he tipped out a mason jar that held an assortment of screws and nails. After picking out a couple that he thought might work, he and Johnny went back up the stairs.

Charley had managed to wedge the door shut, and so Brodie was easily able to slip a nail through the hinge, securing the two pieces together. He opened and shut the door a couple of times to ensure that the nail was doing its job. *I could come back sometime with a proper pin,* he said, *but this will hold for now.*

Johnny led Brodie to the kitchen where the pot-bellied stove was blazing a hot fire. Brodie saw that Charley had laid out his coat on a chair nearby so that it would dry in the heat. He removed his hat and laid it also nearby. Charley moved about the room, preparing a pot of tea and pulling out a pan of fresh biscuits from the woodstove. She set out three bowls, placing a biscuit in each one, then brought down a large tin of maple syrup and poured a generous amount over them.

The three of them sat down together. Charley seemed unaccountably shy; Brodie was likewise feeling a little uncertain. Johnny carried the conversation. *We didn't think you would come, Mr. Smith, with the snow and all. But Ma made biscuits just in case. Aren't these the best you ever ate?*

Indeed, said Brodie, *they are very fine biscuits.*

Not too salty? asked Charley wryly.

Perfect. Brodie looked at her and smiled. Charley would not meet his eyes; instead she got up and started tidying things in the kitchen.

This maple syrup is from Carruthers' farm, said Johnny. *I helped them tap last spring.*

It's very good syrup.

Ma uses it for special only.

Well, I am honoured then.

She said as how you might like it, given that you have such a sweet tooth and all.

I do have to be careful, said Brodie, *else I'm told I'll get fat.*

When Charley laughed at this, Johnny looked from his mother to his employer trying to understand the humour.

Do you have schoolwork to be finishing? asked Charley.

Only my reading.

Well, I'd like you to do your reading in the parlour. Mr. Smith and I have business to discuss. After Johnny had duly picked up one of the lamps and walked carefully down the hall with it, Brodie sat back comfortably in his chair and watched Charley. She was wearing a very fine dress he hadn't seen before. A little cameo had been pinned at the neckline and her hair was twisted up in a tight arrangement of some kind. She looked demure and a little uncomfortable.

Now then, she said, bringing a pad of paper and pencil to the table, *would you like to tell me what you have in mind?*

Brodie knew she meant the Christmas dinner, but his talk with Alistair was still fresh in his memory and he found himself colouring. He could think of no way of broaching the subject.

Goose, he blurted out. *And all the trimmings. Black buns. Potatoes. Vegetables. Gravy. Everything to make it special. Our crew has worked hard, and we want to show our appreciation.* The thought of the men gave Brodie courage, and he found himself able to then discuss the details of the dinner with some equanimity.

At length, he reached across the table and put his hand on Charley's arm. *And do you mind organizing this for us? I know it's an amount of extra work.*

It's no trouble, Mr. Smith. The men will enjoy it, I'm sure.

Mr. Smith again, is it?

Charley blushed slightly. *Brodie.*

Brodie smiled at her. *I should be heading home now. I've kept you a long while.* He stood as though to leave.

Charley glanced out the window. *Not now, look.*

Brodie went to the window and saw what she was seeing: dark grey clouds had slowly rolled overhead, and the room, he realized only now, had become darker even than before. With the snow swirling so thickly, he couldn't even see the barn or the road.

It's likely no so bad once you're outside, said Brodie hopefully.

Charley shook her head. *I don't think so. Stop awhile and wait for it to lessen.*

Alistair had said there was more coming.

Well, he was right. It was unwise to set out.

I said I would come. We had the dinner to plan.

It could have waited.

Brodie hesitated. *It could have done, but I couldna.*

Charley stood still, absorbing his words. Then she coloured a soft pink and looked at him wonderingly. Brodie took a small step closer, then stepped closer again. *I'll no pretend with you, Charley. I needed to see you this day and could not wait. I feel pulled towards you and desire to know if my attentions might ever be welcome. I have no experience wi' such things and don't rightly know how to manage.*

Charley had turned a deeper shade of rosy pink, and was looking down at her hands. *I think you are managing,* she finally stammered.

Brodie reached out to tip up her chin so that he could look in her eyes. *Do you think you could come to care for me?*

I think I might.

Brodie grinned broadly. *Well then! What do you know about that!* He was tremendously pleased but unsure of what next to do.

Charley was smiling at him and reached out her hand to lightly caress his face. *You are a one!* she said fondly.

Brooklyn, New York ~ August 23, 1900

The Brooklyn Bridge was every bit as striking as Brodie had imagined. He stood at its foot for some long time, admiring its situation in the cityscape and the tall granite towers from which the elegant cabling swung. He watched the crowds of pedestrians making their way across, effortlessly and without fear. He counted the number of vehicles that rumbled and jounced from one side to the other. And then he too joined the throngs of people on its span. Brodie luxuriated in the crossing, stopping to admire the Statue of Liberty and the skyline. He stood in the middle of the bridge and looked at the banks on both sides, trying to imprint the memory of it all, marvelling at the Gothic arches and the network of cables that conspired together to create such a breathtaking monument. He felt childlike in his wonder, diminutive in his importance. It seemed as if nothing he had learned, nothing he had read, nothing he had dreamt, had taught him anything of consequence. This bridge alone was to become his teacher and his ambition.

Cambridge, Massachusetts ~ September 5, 1900

It was difficult to watch young couples, arms linked decorously, walking out together along the Charles River. Brodie often felt lonely, oppressed by thoughts of what he'd missed. His determination to make his own way in the world meant that he often felt friendless and untethered. His rooming house could never provide the same intimacy and caring he'd known in his Uncle Hamish's house.

He wrote long letters home, detailing the interesting things he was learning, and spoke naught of his aloneness. Life would be rich, he sometimes thought, if his mother and uncle would transplant themselves from Edinburgh to Boston and bring with them the nurturing comforts of home. He felt guilty from time to time, knowing they were growing old and that he wasn't there to help them as they became frail. It all seemed a desperate situation. He resolved half a dozen times to quit his studies and return to Scotland.

Buffalo, New York ~ October 7, 1901

The Pan-American Exposition was unlike anything Brodie had ever imagined. He and two of his classmates—they had given themselves a five-day holiday—had travelled by train from Boston to view the fair, advertised as an event that would promote trade relations by showcasing American goods. Brodie was particularly fascinated by the Electric Tower, which he felt so vividly demonstrated innovative American technology. But spectacles of all types were to be seen all about the grounds: elephants, prosthetic limbs, microscopes, boat rides in constructed canals, elaborately decorated temples for music and entertainment.

Brodie and his friends patronized the free-lunch counters. Pickles and preserves, along with crackers, porridge, gingerbread, and candies, were freely dispensed to the crowds, and Brodie found that he could easily make out his meals by waiting patiently at the counter for whatever was on offer.

Brodie was impressed, too, by the city itself. Buffalo, he thought, more so than Boston or Cambridge, might prove to be the type of place that would foster a young man's vision for bridge-making.

August 18, 1902

Dearest Mother and Uncle Hamish,
I write to you from Buffalo where I have now found myself living and am employed. Callaghan's is a large steel manufacturer; I have been hired to supervise the installation of the railway bridges they construct. The bridges are of the truss type, assembled using hot rivets, a most practical approach. I enjoy the work very much. I have been on only one site to date, but I know the work will prove interesting and will make good use of my training.

Mr. Callaghan is well known in this business. He sought advice on hiring from one of my professors; I was highly recommended and so received a letter from him offering employment with a small advance for my travelling expense. He is a generous employer, and although he has firmly established opinions about what is to be done, he has been fair in all things.

I received your parcel including a jumper and thick socks. While there is nae need for such things at present, I know the time will soon come when we prepare for the cold. Thanking you for your kind remembrances.

Is everyone at home in good health and good spirits? Has Senga reconciled herself to the coal stove as yet? Is her bread still blackened? I expect to hear that you have taken to making your fine soda bread in the iron skillet once again.
God bless you always, your Brodie.

Buffalo, New York ~ October 3, 1902

My Brodie,
Hamish and I were delichted te hear news o' ye. Hamish said he heard o' Buffalo and showt it me on a bigg map. We are sair hearted te think on ye so far frae hame.

Yer work soonds braw. I unnerstaun it is a guid chance fer ye. Ye were always after wanting te work on bridges an such. Glad a'm that ye be working fer a guid man. A bless him.

A'm sairy to say, Senga took herself off home after burning o' bread once more. But our Hamish is pleised te cut off the black and haet hisself.

Sairie nae te have more te say.

A'm yer mother who loue ye and prays fer ye always.

Chapter Nineteen: Two Bachelors
Braemor, Ontario ~ December 6, 1909

The first real winter storm had shrouded the country in deep white snow. It was heavy and wet and muffled the landscape with its sparkling mantle. Brodie arrived home from the Gowans at just past midnight, cold and tired from his long ride. Alistair had waited up for him, with oil lamps burning in the windows, fearful he might lose his way. They did not talk long that evening, enough only to establish that all was well.

Alistair went upstairs first proclaiming, *Weary with toil, I haste me to my bed*, while Brodie sat by the kitchen stove warming his hands and feet. He looked around the room with a critical eye, wondering how someone like Charley would view its arrangements. There were no curtains and no bits of pretty china or crockery—he and Alistair had managed with the barest of essentials, and had not worried themselves with anything fine. It was fairly bleak, he realized. Not likely to meet with a woman's approval. This might pose a difficulty.

Meanwhile, Alistair was lying upstairs, reflecting on the sudden turn in events. If Brodie and Charley were to marry, would they move Charley and Johnny into this house and rent out Charley's farm, or would Brodie repair to the Gowans and leave Alistair alone here? Each situation would have its advantages and disadvantages, but in each one Alistair felt he might be in the way. He had no desire to live with newlyweds, but neither did he wish to live a solitary life. He rolled over heavily, pulling the covers up against the cold air, and groaned. He should never have encouraged Brodie to pursue Charley, he thought. Things were about to change, and Alistair was a little sorry.

Life with Brodie had been among the most comfortable and stable arrangements he had known. His adolescence had been uneasy and filled with change. He'd lived for a time with his paternal grandparents, but they had passed when Alistair was fifteen. He sold their meagre bits of furniture and clothing and used the money to buy passage to America. Peebleshire had come to represent only loss—his loving father, his grandparents, the brickworks, his childhood home—and so he had turned his back on Scotland and prepared to make his fortune in a new land filled with promise and opportunity.

Morning brought further snow; it would be foolhardy, Alistair and Brodie decided, to tramp through to the brickworks in such weather. They did not believe their men would come until the winds abated. Brodie went to feed the animals while Alistair set to making oatmeal, toasting bread, and frying sausages and potatoes. Finally, they sat down together to eat.

Did you plan the dinner for the men?

Yes, nodded Brodie, *goose and cider, and pies. Charley will confer with Justus and let us know the cost.*

The men will enjoy a fat goose, I think.

I agree.

And was anything else decided?

Brodie carefully put down his porridge spoon. *I fixed a broken hinge on the front door. We talked.*

Are things decided between you, then?

No entirely. She said as how she would welcome my attentions. She made biscuits for tea and had on a bonnie dress. I think she is overall receptive to the idea.

So what happens next?

Brodie groaned. *Damned if I know.*

Alistair spooned his oatmeal. *Well, we've puzzled out how to build bridges and start our own brickworks. Surely we can puzzle out how you are to proceed.* He couldn't help smiling at his friend's predicament. *There may be someone we can ask advice of? Kyran is married, and Thomas and Patrick. Maybe they can suggest summit. It's no as though you can ask her father or mother for permission to court.*

I'll no be asking Kyran or Thomas or Patrick for advice, thanking you just the same!

Alistair continued to ponder their dilemma. *Well I'm still no certain she'll have you, but if she does, it would be a favour to me that she take you off my hands. You're one jaggie bastard from time to time.*

A jaggie bastard?

And you dinna appreciate my cooking or my needlework.

You dinna say?

It's true, Brodie. She would be in the way of helping me. Both men laughed.

You're a good friend, Al. We've had a fine time.

We have indeed. But although some things will need to change, many will remain the same.

Will you stay on here at the house?

If you go to the Gowan farm. Or I could take a room at the hotel. And what of Miss Lewis—are you quite recovered?

Alistair was silent for a moment. *I am no. I am still set to throw caution to the wind and offer my hand should we ever again happen to meet. You were right to warn me against raising her hopes but I was wrong-headed and proud in the way of breaking with her. If she willna have me, then it will be a long while before I will think on anyone else.*

Well then, we are two bachelors about to embark on unfamiliar territory.

Unknown adventures again, then!

Buffalo, New York ~ December 2, 1902

A letter from his uncle Hamish had alarmed him. His mother had suffered a stroke, and although she was yet at home, she was no longer able to speak or care for herself. His uncle had retained the services of a neighbour to bathe and dress and feed her, and another woman to help Senga with the meals and laundry and housework. He assured Brodie that they were managing very well and that she wanted for nothing.

Brodie was of two minds: he could return to Scotland, having accomplished only his degree and not yet having completed a single bridge, or he could build one bridge for Callaghan, be paid, and return home with some coin in his pocket. Whether it was his pride that made him choose the latter, or perhaps his youthful eagerness to astonish the world by making an innovative contribution, he chose to remain.

This was a decision he came to regret. His first bridge was not yet finished—it stood in the wide wooden warehouse, only partly assembled—when the next letter arrived in his uncle's spidery script. The envelope was bordered in black ink, signalling before opening that his mother had passed.

He could not afterwards look at his first bridge, a source until then of great pride, without feeling its cost. The guilt taunted him. For weeks he despised himself and the bridge alike, and took no joy in seeing the men at work on it.

Callaghan encouraged him to return to Scotland for a visit. Yet Brodie couldn't face admitting to his uncle the foolishness of his pride. His accomplishments seemed hollow; he abused himself for superficial ambitions. Instead he wrote his uncle, begging him to join him in Buffalo. He thought that in this way he might appease his guilt, and be all to his uncle that a loving son should be.

Uncle Hamish gently declined the invitation, assuring Brodie that he was well and that, as a man in his eighties, he had experienced all the adventure he required in one lifetime. He was content in his small routines at home and in time would himself be ready to embark on a final journey. Brodie, crestfallen, resolved to return to Scotland before the year had ended. He was making such arrangements some months hence when a further letter arrived in an unknown hand. It informed him that his uncle was now resting in the arms of his Lord and Saviour.

Brodie left for Scotland the next day. He arrived in time for the funeral, which had been stayed for him. The service was held in St. Giles Cathedral; all the deans and university faculty from New College were present in their formal robes and gowns. Brodie felt underdressed in his worn tweeds, but did not have time to have a new suit made. The service was unremarkable but for the many former students and associates who approached Brodie to extend their condolences. He found himself overwhelmed by the sheer number of those who'd held his uncle in high regard and expressed their affection for him in the most genuine of terms. Story after story was told—of his kindness, a sympathy expressed, a gentle encouragement, funds discreetly passed along—and how each gesture had made a difference in the life of the teller.

That evening, alone in the empty house, Brodie felt chagrined to realize that he had never thought of his uncle as someone who went out into the world and made his own contributions, touching the lives of others as he had touched Brodie's with such generosity and kindness.

When the solicitor arrived the next morning he brought with him a stack of papers, including the deed to the house, bank records, the will, and a letter addressed to Brodie. Later, once he was alone again, Brodie sat down to read the letter.

It had evidently been written shortly before his uncle's passing. The handwriting was frail, bordering on illegible. Hamish's voice came to him through the words, however, and Brodie sat in his chair and wept as he read his final thoughts. The first was his uncle's deep gratification and joy in knowing that Brodie had completed a fine education and was now striking out on his own. *Our purpose,* Hamish wrote, *is to make a contribution, however small, and thus to leave this world a better place than we found it.* The second was Hamish's eagerness to meet his Saviour and discover what worlds lay ahead. The third was his love for the Lord and the feeling of peace he'd been granted by having lived a life in His service.

The final sentences read,

> *My son, you who are the pride of my life, I bid you always to remember the great mystery and great promise of our faith. John 3:16: For God so loved the world that he gave his only begotten Son, that whosoever believeth in him should not perish, but have everlasting life. And I give thanks for the inexpressible joy I have had in watching you grow into a fine man. Go into the world knowing always that you are loved, however imperfectly, by this fallible, earthly parent, and oh so perfectly by our loving Father in Heaven.*

November 6, 1903

Messrs. Sorley & Still
Dalrey Lane
Edinburgh, SCOTLAND

Dear Sirs,

Thanking you for your recent correspondence upon the occasion of my uncle's passing, the Rev. Dr. Hamish Smith of Advocates Close, Edinburgh. As I am yet employed in Buffalo, New York, I request that the following arrangements be undertaken:

i) His collection of books and small library to be donated to the University of Edinburgh, and a generous scholarship established in his memory for a deserving student in financial need,

ii) His personal effects be crated waiting upon my return,

iii) His clothing and wardrobe to be distributed to the poor,

iv) His house and furniture to be let out at a rent you establish, to tenants who will take care of the premises, the term to be at least a twelve-month period but subject to severance at any time afterwards,

v) Senga Campbell, his devoted maid, to be pensioned at a modest rate you establish as fitting for someone in his service these past years,

vi) A fine headstone to be cut by a quality stone mason, inscribed with my uncle's name, his dates of birth/death, and the following verse of scripture:

1 John 4:16 God is love; and he that dwelleth in love dwelleth in God, and God in him.

I trust that these arrangements will be satisfactory and that I will hear from you confirming the details.

With appreciation, I remain, Brodie Smith

April 16, 1904

A letter from the barristers had arrived. Brodie swept it up off the boarding house hall table with an impatient gesture and jammed it into his coat pocket. Then he closed his eyes and tried to calm himself, aware of his clenched jaw and tight fists. Navigating the narrow hallway, he took in the plaid carpet, the wallpaper made dingy by years of passing figures, the fern in its stand on the landing, the polished railing worn smooth by many hands.

He unlocked the door to his room and entered thoughtfully. After removing his boots, he sat down upon the bed and retrieved from his coat the crumpled letter which he now smoothed upon his leg. Still, he did not open it. The light outside had shifted from a late afternoon sun to a menacing dark grey. As Brodie sat, the first few timid taps of rain pattered against the window. He listened to the clatter as the shower intensified and began a battery against the glass. He closed his eyes and inhaled the sound and the sudden smell of it coming through the open casement. He knew he should move quickly to close it but suddenly it was an April rain in Edinburgh splashing furiously on the cobbles, the damp of it held in the wool of his coat, seeping through the soles of his shoes, a fragrance of promise held in the wet. Brodie stood and savoured all of it before moving to the panes and pulling them tight against the weather. Rain had soaked the window ledge and the carpet beneath his feet.

I should ha' been there. Guilt. Guilt that he'd not been home for either his mother or his uncle. Guilt that he'd left the aftermath of death to Sorley & Still. Guilt that he'd intended, by now, to have accomplished far more, and to have earned sufficient funds so as to return to Scotland an independent man.

As Brodie stood upon the spongy carpet, he was overwhelmed by sorrow for the loss of what was and what now would never be. His family was gone. He was completely alone in the world. He would never bring a child into their house and see the joy brought by a young one flash in their faces. He would never bring a wife to meet the two people who had been his family.

He shuddered with the damp, and with new awareness of his circumstances. Stretching out upon the thin mattress of the iron bedstead, he allowed his emotions to overtake his usual control until, finally, he wept.

Chapter Twenty: A Gift for a Lady

Braemor, Ontario ~ December 20, 1909

The twenty-first of December was the date appointed for the men's Christmas dinner. Since Charley was making all the preparations with Justus, Brodie found it necessary to confer with her on many occasions. Alistair felt only a little wistful from time to time. He'd grown accustomed to their shared bachelors' existence; the many nights alone in the farmhouse seemed to him quiet and solitary. Still, he had no wish to intrude upon Brodie's courting, such as it was, and regularly declined offers to join him at the Gowans'.

The news of Brodie's courtship having reached the men, gentle, good-natured jibes had become the order of things. Although the comments were often lobbed in Brodie's direction, and within his easy hearing, remarks were also made to Alistair suggesting that he too should find a sweetheart. Alistair would reply that he'd need a lass as pretty as Charley and as good at pie-making and needlework, but one no so daft as to choose his friend. That always brought laughs from the group, along with half-hearted suggestions about someone's sister or cousin. Alistair was quick to counter that if she had the look of Kyran or Thomas or Patrick about her she'd be far too ugly to consider. And so it was that in the eyes of their crew, Alistair and Brodie gently crossed the threshold from purposeful bachelorhood to a middle ground where they were not yet family men but more than likely to become so. This gave them unexpected status in a way they found surprising.

And when the twenty-first finally arrived, for all the appreciation Alistair and Brodie expressed for the men at the raucous, joyful dinner they hosted that evening, the men repaid it several times over in a sequence of toasts—to the two of them, then to the brickworks itself, then to Charley, Johnny, and Justus, and finally, in a merry crescendo, to themselves and all other living creatures.

Alistair and Brodie awoke the next morning with fairly thick heads. Much cider and whisky had been consumed the night before, not only with the men at the party but also later at home while they discussed the evening. It was past two in the morning before either thought to take himself upstairs and away to bed.

Brodie went outside first to feed the livestock. Although the sun had only just risen in the winter sky, the light of it hit him like a hard blow. He staggered around while completing his chores, squinting with his eyes half shut. Moving indoors, he was gladdened to see that Alistair had hooked his jacket on a couple of nails above the kitchen window and was fixing their oatmeal in the dimmed room.

Damned bright outside, muttered Brodie.

It's the snow. Makes everything brighter.

Too bright for me this morning.

And me.

The men commiserated, trying proudly to refrain from resting their heads on their hands and closing their eyes entirely.

I havena felt this badly since Beatty's bloody shine.

Aye. But I have to go to the shops today, Al—to get Christmas gifts for Charley and Johnny. Will you come?

I'll come but I dinna ken what help I can offer.

Do we have any powders for aching heads?

Alistair made as if to stand but did so carefully, bracing himself on the edge of the table. *I'm thinking, Brodie, if you have no objection, that we might consider awhile, and close our eyes for another hour until the pounding stops.*

It was mid-morning when they reconvened in the kitchen, still feeling somewhat the worse for the previous evening's festivities but better all the same. Together, blinking in the sunlight, they set out for their little barn and saddled two horses.

I was thinking a good knife for Johnny, said Brodie.

Just the thing, agreed Alistair. *Have you thought o' something for Charley?*

No. It has to be right. Something personal but no so personal as to give offence.

Perfume?

That would say that I dinna like the scent of her. And I do, especially when she's baking.

So you would have her smelling like pie?

That's no what I mean.

Something for the house?

Too practical.

A gun?

A gun?! Alistair!

The men rode directly to the blacksmith's shop, left their horses there, then hurried to the train station where they joined a group of fellow travellers also bound south for town. The train arrived promptly and the men climbed aboard, still pondering the purchases they needed to make. The shops, they saw when they arrived, were decorated for the season. Alistair and Brodie contemplated carefully where to begin.

The general store will have pocket knives, said Alistair, *and I was thinking to buy Johnny a box of checkers. Meanwhile, you can look about and try to get an idea for Charley.*

That's a fair plan.

Alistair went off directly to the general store, where he also had in mind to purchase himself some new shirt collars and a necktie for Brodie's Christmas.

Brodie meanwhile was walking up and down the main street, looking in windows and hoping for inspiration. The millinery shop had a vast array of women's hats; he wondered whether Charley would appreciate one. Somewhat self-consciously, he entered and looked about awkwardly. When the clerk approached him he stammered out the purpose of his visit.

I need a gift for a lady, he began. *Nothing too fine but smart and o' good quality.*

I have just the thing. She smiled and drew Brodie over to a display of felt hats, showing him a black one. *This one is camel's hair felt,* she explained. *The silk cording is of the best quality. As you see, it's trimmed in black—conservative, but also versatile in that you can add a coloured ribbon to the trim and match it to any ensemble. The look is becoming to most women. Stylish, without seeming too grand.*

Brodie had relaxed as she spoke, finding himself nodding along sagely to her words. A hat might just be perfect. *It does no seem very warm,* he interjected.

Why sir, exclaimed the shopgirl, *that is because it is intended to be worn with a caperine. Will you permit me to show you?*

Brodie nodded, and the girl guided him towards a display of caperines and fancy shoulder scarves. These were made of fur and seemed very elegant. The girl showed him how the caperines were positioned above the collar of one's outer coat by deftly placing it around Brodie's own collar and tying the fur extensions tightly under his chin. The fur felt luxurious against his skin—he could readily believe that it would prove comforting in cold weather—but he was embarrassed to be adorned in this way and rapidly removed it.

Any lady would be delighted to receive the gift of a caperine and a smart black hat, enthused the girl.

Brodie considered only briefly and then selected a black Persian lamb caperine to match the hat. Charley would not appreciate the expense of sable or mink, he decided; she might suppose he was being reckless. The lamb seemed a practical choice.

Now he had one final stop before meeting Alistair. He had determined some time before to buy him a new copy of the collected works of William Shakespeare. He knew Alistair loved to read of an evening, and thought the plays would entertain him on those nights when he was alone at their farm. Brodie felt remorse for continually leaving his friend and thought by this means to compensate for his loss of company. The stationer's shop was not far. Brodie was able to find a leatherbound copy of the plays and sonnets. He was delighted with the gifts and felt filled with Christmas cheer.

Alistair wasn't hard to spot in the crowds, stationed as he was outside the general store. Brodie greeted him happily. *Are you done, Al?*

Yes—I've a knife for you to give Johnny. I chose one with a lock-back on it as I thought it safe. It's English, just over four inches long, and I spent seventy-five cents on it—I believed you would want the finest. I also purchased a box o' checkers and a harmonica.

Thank you, Al. I've bought Charley a fine black hat and a fur scarf. It will keep her warm and look smart.

I noticed a jewellery store around the corner. Shall we take a look? We have some time before the train.

Brodie shrugged and followed, finding himself looking dutifully at the selection of rings in the window. Alistair had apparently studied the selection already; he pointed out one with a violet stone.

It's the colour o' Miss Lewis's eyes, said Alistair.

The green rings are very smart, don't you think? Should we go in? Do you want to buy one?

I just want to look. There's no harm in a look.

Alistair and Brodie were greeted immediately by a Mr. Laslett, the proprietor of Laslett's Jewellers, a balding gentleman dressed formally in grey striped trousers, a bow tie, and tails. *Gentlemen,* he began, *I can see you that you are interested in only the finest of merchandise.*

Good afternoon, said Alistair. *We are no intending to importune you, sir. We only thought to take a closer look at the rings.*

Might I see the green ones? asked Brodie.

Of course. Emeralds from Colombia. Only the finest. He drew out a velvet tray studded with rows of emerald rings. *The hue is of the deepest green, sir, and my stones have no visible inclusions, ensuring that they are not prone to cracking or splitting. The gold is eighteen carat.*

Brodie looked over the selection and pointed to one that caught his eye.

Ah, sir, very discerning. Very discerning indeed. That is an oval-cut stone, surrounded on each side by a half-carat diamond. The diamonds are from a mine founded in Brazil in the late 1700s. This mine has produced some of the most beautiful diamonds in the world. Hold the ring to the light and you will see how the facets flash their own fire.

Brodie picked it up, pinching it carefully between his thumb and forefinger. *Look, Alistair,* he exclaimed, holding it aloft, *it really does flash fire.*

Alistair leaned closer to peer at the ring. *Are you certain she's prepared to accept you?*

This is a beautiful thing, and I could keep it at the ready. You said yourself that I should no raise expectations wi' out following through. I have only to convince her that I'm worthy of her affections.

And you, sir, Mr. Laslett said to Alistair, *did I not notice you admiring the amethyst rings in my window?*

No! said Alistair, a little too abruptly. *Brodie: I will wait upon you outside.* Alistair left the shop in a brusque fashion. Brodie completed his transaction and then joined him on the sidewalk, patting his coat pocket theatrically. Mr. Laslett stood in the doorway of his shop and merrily wished them both a very good holiday season.

Alistair, who felt suddenly in poor humour, decided that the previous night's entertainment was continuing to take a toll. Brodie, in his elation, paid him no mind. Their train ride home was silent, with Brodie gazing out happily at the passing landscape and Alistair leaning back in his seat, eyes shut, signalling an unwillingness to talk.

Buffalo, New York ~ May 8, 1905

Brodie was packing for yet another bridge job; this time he'd be on site for at least three months. He'd been careful to give his landlady notice and to pay in advance for his room so that it might be kept at the ready for his return. It wasn't an especially spacious or elegant accommodation but it was a convenient one, and Brodie found that he particularly enjoyed Mrs. Fairfields's cookery. She always had a pie resting under a starched linen towel on the kitchen counter and was never miserly about serving him large slices, with generous dollops of whipped cream.

Although Brodie suspected that she regularly snooped through his things and steamed open his letters, he felt that with nothing in particular to hide, the pie slices she served as penance more than compensated for the breaches in his privacy. He was quite fond of her, in a way, and would sometimes bring her a small remembrance when he returned from one of his installations.

On his last bridge assignment, in Orchard Park, he'd spied a simple pearl brooch in a shop window and later proffered it to her with thanks for keeping his room for him. She was delighted, and wore it pinned at her collar on all future occasions, patting it when she spoke as if assuring herself it was still securely fastened and in place. Brodie was touched by her obvious delight in such a little ornament.

December 25, 1906

Brodie had told Mrs. Fairfields that he was bidden to dinner at a friend's. As the only boarder left in the house, he didn't want to importune her with the bother of making him a meal. He knew she was anxious to visit with her daughter, to spend the day enjoying her grandchildren at their home in Polonia. Her son-in-law, Josef, owned a furniture store there; Mrs. Fairfields had informed Brodie, in strictest confidence, that he was struggling to manage, which was why they had to live behind the showroom.

It was a bleak day, and not one that held much significance for Brodie. Hogmanay had been the thing at home with his uncle and mother. She would first scrub the entire house from the cellar to the attic and then cook for days to prepare. Cock-a-leekie soup, black bun, tipsy laird with dollops of custard, steak pie, shortbread, haggis, cranachan—all appeared in the pantry to be served to friends and other assorted guests. His uncle would often bring home divinity students for an evening meal, and if they were black-haired so much the better, for it meant good luck if they were the first to cross the door in the new year. The bells at St. Giles always rang at midnight to sound in the year—and if you listened carefully you could pick out the bells of the surrounding churches in and around the city. As far as Brodie could determine, Christmas dinner here could not compare to the feasts at home. He smiled to recollect the fine meals they'd shared, whisky poured out in crystal tumblers, his mother bustling about in her lace cap and best dress.

Brodie did not like being deceitful with Mrs. Fairfields, and he knew she'd quiz him later about where he'd been and what had been served. Nonetheless he decided to spend the day walking about the city, specifically the east side, where there were synagogues and a Jewish library. He hoped in this way to be a little less conspicuous in his wanderings and perhaps find an open diner for a meal. As he wrapped a scarf about him and did up the buttons on his coat, he thought what a sorry thing it was to spend such a day alone and looking to make himself invisible.

Chapter Twenty-One: A Popcorn Box Surprise

Braemor, Ontario ~ December 23 and 24, 1909

You know, said Brodie, *I dinna think I have ever looked forward to Christmas in all my life.*

Aye, said Alistair. The two were on their way home, having dropped off a goose at the Gowans'; it was Alistair's contribution to Charley's upcoming dinner. *Hogmanay was always the time of real funning in my family. We visited friends and relatives, bringing gifts of black buns and salt, and in the evenings there were games in the town square. Everyone turned out.*

Yes, and we exchanged gifts then and no at Christmas. It was far different.

Just the same, I've a feeling this will be a rare fine occasion.

They arrived home to see that Patrick Lynch was waiting at the door. *Hullo,* shouted Brodie, *Merry Christmas.*

And to you, sirs. I've brought a raisin pie from my wife with our very best wishes for the season.

Will you come in and have a visit?

No, tanking you, I have other deliveries te make.

The men were not long inside when a knocking came at the door; Thomas Jobson stood there with a carefully wrapped plum pudding. And as the afternoon progressed, many of their men likewise stopped by with a festive offering. Some stayed for a dram; others rushed off to complete further errands. Brodie and Alistair found themselves with a larder filled with biscuits, and barmbrack, and several pies.

Brodie smiled happily, looking over their sudden inventory. *Now this is a nice tradition.*

I imagine they think we canna fend for ourselves.

We should sample a pie, Brodie said. He didn't trouble to wait for an answer; he was already busy cutting the pie into fat wedges. Alistair rolled his eyes comically and reached for a plate.

Christmas Eve day was bitter cold—Alistair had to scrape at the ice, thick on the inside of the windows, just to look out. But Brodie was full of nonsense; insisting that they decorate the sleigh, he set about sawing off fir branches and nailing them to the sides. Then he stood back to consider the effect. *What it needs are some sleigh bells.*

What it really needs, Alistair said, *is a fresh coat of paint and lacquer, but there's no time for that now.* They needed to set off for the church service, after which they were invited to the Gowans' for refreshments and gift giving, with the dinner itself to be held on Christmas Day proper.

The fir branches will make it look festive.

Why are you fussing?

I want it to look nice for Johnny.

*Ahh, for Johnny is it, and no his mother? Women do take notice of such things, but I think your Charley is more practical of nature—no one who'd countenance you freezing off your fingers while you—*he paused dramatically, waving his hands about the sleigh—*festoon.*

The little church was crowded when they arrived; all of Braemor seemed to have turned out, bringing everyone they knew with them. Each had been handed a tiny white candle with a tin holder when they were seated. The service was made up entirely of hymns and carol singing. Alistair and Brodie joined in, lustily singing the words to music familiar and dear.

At the end the minister took up a candle and intoned, *We share and celebrate the light of Christ, and take His love into the world.* Then he lit the candle. Those sitting nearest the oil lamps blew them out while everyone took turns lighting their individual candles. Soon the church was lit only by diminutive flames. A soft hush filled the sanctuary.

The men greeted many of their acquaintance after the service, but it was not until the crowd thinned and a number of people had left, that they could join the Gowans and move outdoors together.

Charley had prepared a big pot of mulled cider, still hot on the stove when they arrived at the farm. There was sliced Christmas cake besides, as well as mince tarts. Johnny carried things through to the parlour while Alistair and Brodie carefully lit the tiny candles on the Christmas tree. Once they'd taken their refreshments Johnny looked at his mother and asked whether it was yet time to open their stockings. Smiling at him indulgently, Charley nodded her consent.

Johnny retrieved the four long socks from the mantel and handed them out carefully. Stuffed in the top of each was a box of candied popcorn—each one proclaiming "a prize in every box." Brodie had brought these along with the goose the day before, remarking to Alistair that he'd first tasted their like in Buffalo and that they'd make a fine Christmas treat.

I'm going to eat mine now, said Brodie, *and see what the prize is.* Grinning, he scooped up a handful then held the box open and passed it around.

What's your prize? asked Johnny. *Can you see it?*

I'm still hunting.

Can I look? Johnny peered into the box.

Brodie hugged it to his chest. *You have your own. I predict this prize to be a valuable one, meant to be shared with one particular person.*

Alistair, sensing a game afoot, joined in. *Is it me then? We're partners after all.*

No you neither.

Will you share it with me? asked Charley.

Brodie stood and walked over to her chair. Silently he passed her the opened box. She looked down quizzically and withdrew a small leather jeweller's case. Alistair leaned back in his chair and smiled. Johnny moved in closer and watched as his mother open it.

Charley, perplexed, looked at Brodie. He had dropped down on one knee in front of her. *Charlotte Gowan, I am asking you to be my wife, and for Johnny to be my son, and for the three o' us to be family together.*

Charley sat quietly for a moment. Then she looked at Johnny, who was grinning happily at her and nodding his head.

She smiled at Brodie and leaned forward in her chair to embrace him. Soon the three of them stood and came over to Alistair, who was then wrapped up in a tangle of extended arms.

You're a fortunate man, Alistair said, *and I'm happy for you both. But I canna be certain Charley knows how much trouble she's just brought on herself.*

Well, she said, *there's not many women who can say they found their man in a box of candied corn, but that's what I'll tell people for sure. It seems fitting, knowing this a one.*

Johnny had entered into the occasion and contained his own Christmas excitement as well as any ten-year-old boy could do. He began to hop unceremoniously from one foot to the other, fidgeting with the cuffs of his sweater, pulling them down over his fingers and making mitten-like sleeves.

Charley understood his quiet antics. *Perhaps we should open our gifts now,* she proposed. *Give Alistair and Brodie mine first, Johnny.*

Johnny brought each of the men a soft, lumpy package tied together with yarn. Alistair, pulling out a knitted vest in deep green wool with brown buttons down the front, was delighted, and slipped it on immediately. *Thank you, Charley, it is very fine and will help keep me warm in this bitter weather.*

Brodie pulled out a matching vest, his a deep burgundy. He likewise was delighted, modelling it for the group.

The colour is so we can keep an eye on you, said Charley, *and see what you're up to.*

Next, Johnny opened his gifts from the men, including the knife and checkers which delighted him. Charley looked less excited about the knife, but kept her own counsel. At the last, Brodie gave Charley her presents. She was enchanted by the hat, but thought the caperine extravagant. *You should take it back,* she said, stroking its fur tenderly, *for it looks too fine for me.*

In response Brodie lifted it from the box and draped it around her shoulders. His hands lingered briefly and then grasped hold of the fur, pulling Charley towards him and kissing her full on the lips. *I think,* he said, grinning, *there's a special purpose to this fur; I think we should keep it. What do you think, Johnny?*

Yes, laughed Johnny in agreement. *Look at Ma now, she's gone all red!*

As Alistair and Brodie made their way home across the open country, the horses' hooves cracked little openings through the snow's sparkling crust. They had to pick their way carefully in spots lest the horses twist a leg or slide on the slippery surface. Brodie's mind was pleasantly preoccupied, but he was aware of the dangers and held the reins lightly, letting the horses find their footing.

Alistair was genuinely pleased for his friend: Charley's temperament was a good match for Brodie's, and he felt certain that although the two would continue to spar, theirs would be a steadfast union. If only, he thought, he might one day know such happiness.

He'd tried, but had found he couldn't stop thinking about Violet. The flutter of gauzy material against her arm. The look of her wrapped tightly in his jacket and her mother's shawl. His first glimpse of her at the art gallery, wisps of hair falling down around her face. The unmistakable sound of her laughter, the mischievous way she had of organizing things to suit herself. The hints of keen intelligence shown by her interest in classical music, Ford motor cars, the gallery's construction.

There had been a Christmas card from her some weeks back—he'd been only too aware of his excitement when he read the return address and saw the feminine penmanship. Then he'd read the handwritten note inside.

Wishing you a blessed Christmas with the hope that the
new year brings you continued health and happiness.
~ V. Lewis

It was an entirely proper greeting, he knew. And yet it was a generic one, likely sent to all of her acquaintance. She hadn't even signed her name as Violet.

Alistair had since found himself wondering whether he should send one in return. He decided that would be considered too forward without also sending one to her father—and if he sent one to Mr. Lewis, surely he should send one to the other investors? The entire situation seemed complicated, and so Alistair did what he often did in such circumstances: brood. Much thought went into his nonresponse, although this was not something Miss Lewis would ever know.

Chapter Twenty-Two: Smells Like Christmas
Braemor, Ontario ~ December 25, 1909

Christmas morning, after completing their farm chores and then a breakfast of donated pies and puddings, the two friends exchanged their gifts. Alistair, who'd bought Brodie two patterned silk neckties—*I thought as how you were courting, you should be a bit spruced up*—was much taken with the fine copy of *The Complete Works of William Shakespeare,* and the thoughtful words Brodie had inscribed on its frontispiece.

The drive to the Gowan farm was cold. A north wind was blowing hard against their backs, pushing them forward in the seat; the horses too felt the buffeting of the wind and moved carefully on the packed snow. They were all of them relieved to arrive at the shelter of the Gowan barn. Reaching into a canvas feedbag, Alistair held out a handful of oats. *Would you take a sweet bite?* The horses nuzzled his hand and whinnied their approval as Brodie brushed them down and covered them with blankets.

When Johnny opened the kitchen door to them they were hit by a wall of heat that made the exposed skin on their faces burn anew. The cooking stove was on, as was the furnace, and both Charley and Johnny were dressed in their Sunday-best outfits. Laughing at the sight of the men so carefully bundled against the weather, they helped them to remove the layers of sweaters and vests they'd worn on top of their good suits. Brodie had put on one of his new ties, much admired by Charley and Johnny.

Alistair breathed in deeply. *Good smells,* he said, grinning. *It smells like Christmas!*

When the tea was ready, Brodie carried the tray through to the parlour. Johnny, who had doctored his cup with several spoons of sugar and a great deal of milk, was finished first.

Brodie, would you like to play a game of checkers?

Well, yes, I would.

Brodie moved over to the dining room table where Johnny had already begun to set up the board.

Alistair watched as Brodie, sitting across from the boy, used his index finger to align the checkers in their starting position.

No cheating now, Mr. Smith, teased Charley.

Brodie looked a little flummoxed. *You're no thinking of changing your mind, are you?* He'd meant it to be light-hearted, they could all see that, but it came out sounding so worried that Charley and Alistair both laughed.

I am not, she smiled, *for I like a challenge.*

Alistair leaned back in his chair and laughed with them, enjoying the intimacy of the moment.

CHAPTER TWENTY-THREE:
ARRIVAL OF THE MACHINERY

Braemor and Toronto, Ontario ~ January 9, 1910

January came quickly, and with it an established set of routines. Brodie had taken to spending Saturday evenings with Charley and Johnny at the Gowan farm; on Sundays, Alistair was invited to join them after church for dinner and a quiet afternoon of reading and parlour games.

It was on one such afternoon that Alistair and Brodie pored over an *Illustrated Catalogue of the Latest and Best Improved Brick Machinery*. Alistair had sent for it in November and had since found himself thumbing through its pages with fervour whenever he had the opportunity. It was the brick press that interested him most: a machine that would do the work of first mixing the clay and then pressing it into moulds. Brodie, meanwhile, had been too preoccupied with his sundry improvements to the Gowan farm to take much notice.

There's a showroom in Toronto, said Alistair. *I think we should take the train to the city and have a look. We could improve our production tenfold if we mechanize.*

Och, aye. But will we be hurting the men by relieving them of their jobs?

No at all. We'll shorten our production and delivery times. There will be as much work or more with this.

But the cost of it, Al?

We must keep up. The spur line, once it's built, will mean inexpensive transportation. We should capitalize on that and increase our revenue.

Aye. But we would be increasing our debt as well as revenue, Al.

I'm no a proponent of mortgages and debts as you ken, Brodie. I saw my family home auctioned off and was left wi' out a shilling. I'm as unsettled by the proposition as you but there's families depending upon us and I canna see the way forward without taking some risk. Come with me to Toronto to look at the equipment. Then you can say if you think it's going to work. I know they're using such machines in Great Britain, but those are steam powered. This description says we can use horse power or steam.

Steam will be the way to go. Brodie rubbed his chin thoughtfully. *It's no so difficult to arrange. We'll need a boiler and water and a heat source, but coal or wood would do.*

Can I come? Johnny had been standing behind them, listening quietly. He moved closer to the table. *I've never been to Toronto.*

Alistair regarded him affectionately. *You would have to ask your mother, lad.*

Charley came into the dining room from the kitchen, wiping her damp hands on her apron. *What is it you three are scheming?*

Brodie pointed to the yellow catalogue. *We're going to Toronto to look at some machinery for the brickworks. Johnny has asked to come.*

He'd be welcome, said Alistair. *Every lad should enjoy a long train ride and a night from home.*

Charley hesitated briefly, *All right then. But mind you listen to them, Johnny, and I don't want to hear about any shenanigans.* This last was said with a menacing look at Brodie. *When are you leaving?*

Later this week?

I'll get one o' the men to do the animals, said Brodie.

And put Thomas in charge. We can speak to them tomorrow and be off in two days.

The men grinned at each other, and then looked to Charley for her approval. She nodded slowly, her face revealing her mixed feelings; she was pleased for her son but not entirely sure that she was ready to let him go. Patting Johnny on the back, she returned to the kitchen.

I'm going to tell the Carruthers! Johnny exclaimed.

The train for Toronto left Braemor at 10:12 in the morning. The three travellers were waiting on the platform, tickets in hand, at 9:30. Charley had wrapped up brown sugar sandwiches and tea biscuits. *This should satisfy your sweet tooth,* she told Brodie.

She'd kissed Johnny repeatedly until he pulled away, embarrassed by her attentions. Now she and Brodie stood close together, looking at each other intensely but not embracing. Meanwhile Alistair, anxious for the train to arrive, paced the short platform in long, impatient strides. He had with him the earmarked machinery catalogue and a bank draft carefully folded inside his vest pocket which he had pinned closed for extra measure.

It had snowed the night before, and was mercifully milder than it had been. The sun was out, a good omen. Johnny could not contain his excitement, and kept peering down the tracks for a glimpse of an approaching train.

The train, when it arrived exactly on time, whooshed into the station with much screeching of brakes and billowing of acrid smoke. Their being the only passengers getting on, the conductor wasted no time in helping them up the steep narrow steps and slamming the tiny door closed behind them. Johnny had hesitated at the bottom, but Brodie grabbed his arms and lifted him across the wide gap between the edge of the platform and the car. Charley stood waving as they pulled out, becoming smaller and smaller.

They were on the train's milk run, stopping at large farms and seemingly every little village and town along the way. Johnny peered out the window, fascinated by the changing views, while Brodie sketched plans for a new building to house the brick press. It would need to be two storeys high, Alistair had told him. The horses would pull the clay and shale up a ramp and dump it near the top of the press. Here the structure would need to be big enough for between two and four men, who would pour the clay and sand and water down into the machine. The press itself would be situated on the lower level, allowing gravity to do some of the work of feeding it. Around the machine there would have to be room for another four to six men—the tossers, the ones who would sling the pressed bricks onto special carts to be wheeled to the drying sheds. These sheds, Alistair said, should be close to the kiln, with connecting tunnels between them to capture excess heat.

Brodie then sketched a side view of the proposed building, illustrating the earthen ramps for the horses and a below-grade level for the press. *If we excavate and build down deep,* he said, *we can avoid building too high and can use a natural earthen ramp for the horses. It will save time and money, and will be guaranteed strong enough for the weight of the machine and the weight of the horses and men.*

Alistair studied the plan critically. *Aye. And if the ramp leading away from the machine is positioned opposite the one the horses use, we can build it up from below as well.*

Brodie nodded. *No too deep, then. Or the grade will be too steep to push the bricks up. We may need to think on that.*

A wee problem?

There will be a way to make it work, Al. We need to plan carefully. How long will it take to knock this together, do you think?

The digging will be the slow part. Six feet down maybe, and since the ground is still frozen we'll need pickaxes.

As deep as that?

At least. Brodie scratched his chin. *We have to measure the press and see what clearance is needed.*

The men looked over at Johnny and saw that he was slumped over, his head against the window glass, dozing. Brodie took off his overcoat and laid it tenderly across the sleeping boy. *Charley said he didna sleep a wink last night wi' excitement.*

Alistair smiled. *We'll be there shortly. I see the lake in the distance.*

Let him sleep until we pull into the station?

Aye.

Where shall we book in?

I've stayed at the Queen's Hotel before. It's a better place to take the lad than some.

The train began to slow, and as it did Johnny sat upright and rubbed his eyes. *Is that the lake? It looks like an ocean!*

Brodie reached over and lifted his coat from the boy. *It looks big enough from here, for sure. But no so wild as the sea.*

They collected their bags and stepped down from the train with a group of other passengers who pushed against them in their eagerness. Brodie clamped his hand on Johnny's neck to steer him through the crowd on Union Station's canopy-covered arrival platform. Johnny stared around open-mouthed, trying to take in all that he saw.

Over here, said Alistair, *to the overpass.*

A walkway above the train tracks connected their platform to a massive red-brick building, seven storeys tall, some distance off. The men led the way, with Brodie still clamped onto Johnny. After they'd climbed the stairs to the walkway, the three of them stood to admire the vista spread out before them. By craning their necks, they could see that buildings crowded the fringes of the harbour and that the lake itself was a clear blue, mirroring the cold sky. They ambled slowly towards the station itself, allowing Johnny time to gawk.

Once inside the opulent hall, they all looked instinctively first at the soaring ceiling and then at the rows of decorative wickets edging its walls. Long waxed benches with gleaming dark wood were lined up for travellers to rest. Close by a tiny news-stand stood shoeshine chairs, raised on wooden steps, where gentlemen sat while their shoes were cleaned by a couple of men dressed in long canvas jackets. Johnny stared at these men as Alistair and Brodie pushed him along. Other men, outfitted in dark uniforms with gold braid, rushed about sweeping floors and polishing the brass.

They swung through the gilded front doors, then walked slowly along Front Street to the hotel. Johnny peered in shop windows, twisting around to read the painted signs on the sides of buildings and posted on massive boards, and watched as black motorcars and carriages navigated amid the electric streetcars proceeding along metal tracks. The majestic-looking Queen's Hotel wasn't far from Union Station. Alistair noted with satisfaction that its brickwork was running bond; a suitable choice, he concluded. The hotel was fronted by a row of massive columns facing the street. They passed through these into the grand entrance, with its ornate flourishes and finishings, and on to the opulent reception desk. The men arranged for two rooms.

Could you bring up a cot for my son? asked Brodie.

Johnny beamed at this, and skipped a little as he followed the men along the patterned carpet, past fine parlours and oversized buffets and sideboards, and up the stairs to their rooms. The furnishings were lavish. Johnny had never seen such highly decorated tables and chairs and beds.

It's like a palace, Brodie. Are we really allowed to stay here?

It is costly. But for one night we can manage. Now let's find Alistair, and then we'll make our way to the showroom.

A twenty-minute walk west along Front Street brought the three to its doors. Alistair strode directly to the Parkhill Martin brick press, prominantly featured with little flags and bunting, and began to examine it carefully. He and Brodie were soon joined by the proprietor, Mr. Vales, a portly gentleman impeccably dressed in a suit of brown plaid, a necktie of deep red, and highly polished, toe-capped shoes with heavy stitching. His feet looked remarkably diminutive for a man of his proportions and Johnny watched him carefully, wondering if he would somehow topple over. His girth was particularly pronounced around his middle section, his vest and jacket struggling to cover him without an unwelcome ripping of fabric or liberation of buttons.

Mr. Vales, whatever his personal appearance, was passionate in his enthusiasms for the the brick press in question and punctuated his remarks with a clenched fist banged on the machine, on the barrows arrayed around the machine, and on the shoulders of Alistair and Brodie respectively.

His presentation ran thus: *This is the strongest brick press on the market, made of the best selected materials,* fist bang; *It's remarkably simple in its construction,* fist bang; *Skilled labour isn't required to operate it,* fist bang; *It's not liable to break down,* fist bang; *Adapted to every variety of clay, it makes good, merchantable brick,* fist bang; *It grinds and tempers its own clay by means of wrought-iron knives,* fist bang; *It moulds the clay very stiff, just the thing for pallet brick,* fist bang; *Every brick is turned out with sharp, clear-cut edges and smooth faces,* final fist bang.

After the first couple of bangs Brodie and Alistair had stepped away from Mr. Vales, but as they circled the machine he moved in closer towards them, reaching out with a clenched fist to reinforce his point. Johnny, still fascinated by Mr. Vales's tiny feet, studied the man's footwork as he stepped delicately around the equipment, looping his way around the shop floor in a staccato ballet.

The business was soon conducted and Alistair and Brodie retreated to the sales office, eager to put a desk between themselves and the pugilistic Mr. Vales. The delivery of the press was deemed a priority—the winter weather would make cartage far less difficult than spring's muddy conditions. The press would arrive from Britain to Quebec by steamship, whereupon it would be conveyed by train to Braemor; finally it would be transported by sledge to the brickworks.

Alistair turned to Brodie as they emerged from the office. *The site will no be ready.*

We can tarp it for now, and then build the shed.

Right on the site, then?

Aye. Keep it close so we willna have to move it far.

Johnny had since turned his attention to the range of barrows on display. Now he called the men over to look at one with heavy springs. *Why is it built this way, Mr. Alistair?*

It's to handle a load of pallets instead of just the one, Johnny. It's a good idea. If we're producing more bricks, we'll need to move more of them quickly. Brodie, have a look at this.

Brodie crossed the showroom floor. *It's a fine design, Al. Come here, Johnny.* With that, Brodie deposited Johnny on the barrow and easily manoeuvred the mechanism up and down and back and forth. Johnny swung his legs over the edge and whooped appreciatively. *We could no make one as well for the price. I think we should order two of these to start. If the men like them, we can order more later.*

Will you tell him? Alistair cocked his head towards Mr. Vales, who hovered by the office door, observing his customers from a distance.

I will, agreed Brodie, *but if he punches me again it will no go well.*

CHAPTER TWENTY-FOUR: THE EXPLOSION

Alistair and Brodie returned to find that the men had worked hard during their absence. Despite the light snow, they'd hollowed out a shallow cavern in the riverbank, and from within this space they'd been excavating the clay. They even had a fire burning in a barrel near the mouth of the chamber and took turns warming themselves over it. And now, having amassed a sizable amount of clay in two days, they were using a horse-pulled sledge to transport it across the snow and ice to the kiln.

Brodie examined the cavern walls, pushing his shoulder into the sides and pressing his body weight against them. *We need to be sure this is safe, Al,* he cautioned. *I wonder if it needs some shoring?*

Kyran, what do you think?

I tink it's solid. Et's froze hard an te pickaxe has to do ets work te get hold.

Well, be careful, said Brodie. *You could hit sand and find that things shift rapidly.*

I think we should get some boards and shore it, agreed Alistair. *I'd rather take the time to be sure. Kyran, will you stand down and take time to brace the sides?*

I will if ye says, Mr. Alistair, but et would be a shame to stop, et would.

Kyran, Brodie put in, *do as he says. The clay can wait.*

Alistair and Brodie turned away and walked back towards the house. Brodie had laid out a series of finished drawings for the two-storey manufacturing building, and they planned to calculate the materials needed and place their order at the mill. They hadn't walked far, when they heard a ferocious swhooshing sound, followed by the surprised shouts of the men. Turning quickly, they saw tall flames shooting high above the riverbank. The two tore off towards the fire, shouting the men's names, *Kyran! Thomas! Sean! Patrick!*

At the edge of the embankment a tremendous flame shot forty feet high above the barrel where the four men had been warming themselves. All four now stood waist deep in the frigid river, looking astonished and panic-stricken.

Jaysus, Mary, and Joseph, Sean shouted.

We doan know what happened, fer sure, added Kyran, *but te lads ran when te roarin' started.*

Te fire shot straight up like, called out Patrick.

Skirting the blaze, Alistair and Brodie climbed down the embankment, assuring themselves that no one was hurt. Brodie walked closer to the flames, now only ten or twelve feet high, stopping a good six feet away and sniffing. *Methane gas. It must be leaching from the riverbank. It will burn itself out.*

He walked back to join the men. *If there is methane here, we need to be careful. When this fire stops burning the gas will be gone and it will be safe enough to work. But we should drill some test holes to make sure there are no more pockets.*

How long will it take to burn out?

It depends how much gas there is.

I never seen such a ting, said Thomas.

Nor want te again, said Kyran, *saints preservin' us.*

Just the same, we'll have to be cautious, said Brodie. *I'll get some pipes. We can hammer them in deep and see if a faint smell comes up. If it does, we'll set it on fire and let it burn itself out. Just like this one.*

We're fortunate no one was hurt, said Alistair. *Come away to the house and get dry.*

Should someone stay here te watch? asked Kyran.

No, said Brodie, *it will take care o' itself.*

The men sloshed out of the river, shivering, and gingerly navigated past the flames still raging in the barrel, the blaze snapping and spiking, the smell of gas stronger than before. They followed Alistair and Brodie to the house, where they removed their boots and pants and long johns and stood close to the kitchen stove, trying to warm themselves. Brodie went upstairs and returned with several pairs of trousers and socks that the men shared out between them, dressing hurriedly. Alistair, meanwhile, was pouring out generous shots of whisky.

Warm yourself from the inside, he joked in a feeble attempt to lighten the mood.

Well, declared Kyran, *God's truth, I was wantin' a break from te damp.*

It gets in yer bones, agreed Patrick, *as cold as a nun's tit, like.*

Aye! agreed Thomas while the others nodded.

Alistair picked up the whisky bottle and once more made the rounds.

God's truth, said Kyran, *I thought as dat fire was goin' te consume us. I never saw such flame come from no where.*

Brodie looked thoughtful. *It was methane fire damp hitting the heat from the oil barrel,* he said slowly. *It does that when it gets near a flame. We have to be cautious in future. I didn't know there was any around, but I should have expected it. I saw the same thing happen once on a bridge build on the Buffalo River. We were digging down for the piers and hit a pocket. One of the men was smoking a pipe and he blew himself up before we knew what happened. There was no saving him it was so sudden.*

Ye never knows wen te Almighty will call us 'ome, offered Patrick solemnly.

I'd as soon he dint call fer me just yet, cracked Kyran. *I have a few calls of mine own to make first.*

Well, we know you done calling on Maggie, said Sean. *Te result is plain to see.*

Dat's my wife, Sean Maguire, ye watch yer mouth or I'll teach ye fecken manners. Kyran clenched his fists and changed his stance, bracing himself ready to throw a punch.

Easy, interjected Alistair. *He meant no harm, Kyran. He was just offering his congratulations, weren't you, Sean?* Alistair looked pointedly at Sean, who quickly concurred and slapped Kyran amiably on the back. Kyran relaxed and loosened his fists.

I meant no harm.

A drink then, said a relieved Alistair, *a drink to Mrs. Meacham and her expanding family. Slange var!*

And now, said Brodie after the toast, producing a second bottle, *you can all drink to my good fortune. Charlotte Gowan has agreed to marry me. The banns are to be read next Sunday.*

Brodie uncorked the bottle for the second toast.

Hear, hear, shouted Alistair, raising his glass, *to Charlotte Gowan's bad judgment and the good fortune o' my undeserving friend. To Brodie and Charley!*

To Brodie and Charley! echoed the men with a great cheer.

Now, said Brodie, *let's clear the table and we'll show you the machine we bought in Toronto and the plans I've drawn for a building to house it.*

The men dutifully removed the dishes and fry pan left on the table from breakfast, along with the untidy piles of books and newspapers that had accumulated over several weeks. Pulling up chairs, everyone sat down eagerly while Alistair and Brodie spread out the plans and passed the machinery catalogue around.

It will increase our production tenfold, said Alistair. *No more hand-filling moulds except for the few we stamp. The clay is pressed and cut into bricks. Twelve bricks every eight seconds. Men will need to stand at the ready, to lob them onto the wagons.*

Dat sounds easy work enough.

Those men are called tossers, added Alistair, *and the work is harder than it seems. I've seen tossers with no fingerprints — worn off completely by the rough brick. And keeping up with the machine is no easy.*

The men had many questions; Alistair and Brodie answered them as best they could. They knew the machine would be most effectively powered by steam, but they weren't yet ready for that. More urgent still was the expense of additional horses, and building materials, and more crew. The prospect had already been weighing heavily upon them, but as the men spoke another expense came to the fore: to realize the machine's potential, they would have to install the overhead tramway, the one Admiral Barnes had suggested, for moving the raw materials from the river to the kiln. That was becoming a real necessity, yet they hadn't included it in their planning.

After the men left for home Brodie and Alistair remained at the kitchen table, scribbling down figures and tallying costs, trying to puzzle out how they could manage the additional expense. After all, sales wouldn't cover it—the sale of bricks had slowed right down during the winter months, as no one was building in the cold weather.

We could go to Buffalo, sighed Alistair, *to see if the men will extend our loan for a higher return.*

And give them more o' our profits?

Do you have another idea?

Could we buy more horses?

Alistair sighed again. *The two we have are no so young, and are already hard-worked. And there's the cost of the feed. More horses will be costly. We need to take on more men, besides.*

How many?

Another two men.

And horses?

And building materials.

Bollocks! Is there no other way?

Alistair poured Brodie another glass of whisky and topped up his own glass, downing it quickly. Wiping his hand across his lips, he shook his head. *I dinna think it, Brodie. I've no desire to go, hat in hand, back to Buffalo. But it's necessary. Surely you see that.*

Can we expand more slowly?

If we're too cautious, we willna benefit by the expense of the new machinery, Alistair said stubbornly. *It will take us years to bring production up to where we need it.*

By now they were each staring at the other, both men realizing the impasse they had reached.

More whisky was drunk, more discussion ensued. Alistair had set aside funds to cover payroll for a three-month period and was reluctant to borrow from this amount for the needed infrastructure. Brodie was torn. With the wedding soon to take place, he wanted not to enter married life burdened by large debt. Neither did he want to borrow more funds from their backers in Buffalo. Alistair was frustrated by Brodie's position, and the two men argued.

They broke off for dinner. Alistair made a hash, and Brodie, after serving it out on two plates, took the fry pan and tossed it crossly in the sink. Alistair poured two glasses of milk, slammed them down on the table, and sat down rigidly. Brodie put Alistair's plate on the table but did not sit down to join him. *I'll eat in my room,* he announced, taking his plate and milk upstairs and kicking the bedroom door shut behind him.

Alistair was in a black mood. It wouldn't do to end things in an argument over money just before the wedding. But he couldn't puzzle out how things between them could be resolved. He was not wanting to touch the small capital earmarked for payroll, and besides that amount, there was little enough left to cover expenses.

Borrowing more money was the only thing he could think of, yet here was Brodie, unwilling to pay their silent partners a higher return. Alistair felt boxed in by the dilemma and paced the downstairs floor while he considered their situation. They had an inventory built up from two good firings. Enough brick to construct a large building or several small ones. If they could sell the brick at a discounted price with immediate payment, they might be able to raise enough capital to begin their expansion projects.

Without cash in hand, there was no other way forward. Alistair retrieved the accounts ledger, made some calculations, then called upstairs to Brodie. *Brodie, if we can sell the brick on hand at a discount, we can realize enough operating capital to finance the expansion. Will you come downstairs and look this over?*

Brodie opened his door and padded down, carrying his empty plate and glass. *I'm sorry, Al. I didna want to say something I might regret.*

We're partners in this, Brodie, and we need to calculate how much o' a loss we can take on the brick. Then we need to persuade someone to buy them now and pay us immediately.

Brodie sat at the table, pulling the ledger close to study it. Alistair had scribbled columns of figures on a piece of brown paper; Brodie reviewed these as well. *It's a shame to sell the brick at a loss.*

We need the funds. I'm no happier to do it than you are, and no happier either to borrow more. You ken a little of my history with such things.

Brodie nodded in understanding. *But who will buy brick in the winter?*

Someone who wants a bargain on the price.

Who has that kind of ready coin?

Mr. Colbert at the bank might know. We should ride to Boltyn in the morning and see what he has to suggest. He'll know, if anyone does, who might take them.

It's a good idea, Al, and better than anything I could think o'. We'll start the men at their work and go first thing. Colbert has treated us fair.

I'm sorry, Brodie, that this has come before the wedding.

And I'm sorry for my ill temper, Al. I wasna for telling Charley how things stand.

But she'll need to know that things are no easy when starting a venture.

I mean to provide for her, Al. Brodie hesitated. *I was thinking to take on bridge work to help us out.*

Now it was Alistair's turn to nod in understanding. *The men could look after the sheep. And we've enough men at the brickworks, for now. It might be an answer.*

I'd have to travel again, and be away from home. That's no way to be newly married.

Let us see how we fare at the bank. You dinna have to decide tonight.

In the morning, once they'd conferred with the crew, they saddled their horses and rode to Boltyn. It was a cold winter's day but the sun was shining and the air did not carry with it the chill it sometimes did. They discussed the upcoming plans for the wedding, agreeing that they would grant a day's holiday to the men in honour of the occasion. Brodie wasn't quite as keen on this as Alistair, who insisted that the men would be deeply offended not to be invited.

But Charley said as she wants it small.

Charley willna mind a few friends drinking to your health. The ceremony can be small. You must have a party after.

At the hotel?

Check with Charley to make sure she'll no object. Then we can invite the men and their wives and a few friends.

Just for some punch?

A drink to your health and a dance, and maybe a piece o' cake?

Cake, agreed Brodie. *I'm sure Mr. Ketchum can arrange something. The parlour wedding is at four o'clock, so invite the men to the hotel for seven?*

That sounds right. I'll find someone to fiddle and will pay for the drinks as my wedding gift.

That may be costly if all the lads come.

Och well, how often does such a thing take place?

They had to wait only a few minutes for Mr. Colbert to make himself available. As they sat in his office, Alistair studied the room while Brodie stared openly at the newspaper lying on Mr. Colbert's desk. He picked it up and pointed at the feature story.

FIRE BURNS UNITY BUILDING IN MARTYNDALE
Residents were wakened by the fire bell in the early
hours of Sunday morning while a fire ripped through the

newly completed Unity Building in Martyndale. The Unity Building, modelled after the Simpsons Store in Toronto, was located on the SW corner of Albert Street and Main Street. The fire has devastated local merchants. Gallons of water were poured on the roof by the brave firemen, extinguishing the fire but causing the roof and walls to collapse inwards. All of the building's contents were ruined by the damage. Mr. Bruce Sutton of Sutton's Mercantile, Mr. Matthew Gilbert of the Bakery, and Mr. Walter Musson and Mr. Samuel Roberts, co-owners of the General Hardware Store, were alerted to the fire but arrived too late to salvage anything. The Unity Building was equipped with firewalls but the blaze was intense and carried across the roof. Fortunately, no souls were claimed by this unhappy occurrence.

There's our answer right there, said Brodie, smacking the paper with the back of his hand.

Mr. Colbert walked in just then and sat down behind his desk, swivelling slightly so that he could centre himself in front of the pair who sat before him. Leaning forward, he positioned his elbows on the desk blotter and then joined the fingers of both hands as though he were in prayer.

Gentlemen, gentlemen, delighted to see you on this fine day. I hear your ventures are progressing. Yes, progressing. I hear things are progressing well. You are pleased with your purchase, I think.

Brodie tapped the newspaper article he'd been studying. *Mr. Colbert, we're obliged to sell some bricks quickly—we need the cash for expansion purposes. We've been reading about this fire in Martyndale. Do you think the insurance will pay them in short order? Would they be interested in discounted bricks for rebuilding?*

Mr. Colbert craned his head to read the headline, then reached out and took the paper from Brodie. Settling back into his chair, he adjusted his spectacles and perused the article slowly. *Ah yes, yes, I see. The fire in Martyndale. No souls lost, thank the Almighty. A terrible shame. Terrible shame. A beautiful building it was. I saw it only a couple of months ago when I was visiting in the area.*

Samuel Roberts and his wife, Annie. They stood up with us at our wedding. The wife and me. Thirty-four years ago November. We went to Martyndale to visit them. Good people. Salt of the earth. Couldn't ask for better folk.

Impatient, Brodie snatched the newspaper back and traced his finger along the lines until he reached the list of merchant names. *It says Samuel Roberts was a co-owner of the Hardware. Is that the same Samuel Roberts you know?*

Why, yes. Samuel Roberts and his business partner jointly own the Hardware. Samuel is a good friend to me. Couldn't ask for better folk.

Yes, yes, interrupted Brodie. *Will he be wanting to rebuild quickly?*

Why, I don't rightly know, Mr. Smith.

Now it was Alistair who interrupted. *Mr. Colbert, could you see your way clear to writing us a letter of introduction to your friend? We'd like to sell off some bricks this winter and are prepared to offer them at a reduced price. We have no interest in taking advantage of a man's misfortune, but surely this might be an inducement to someone waiting on an insurance claim. We make a good-quality brick.*

Why yes, Mr. Lamont, a letter of introduction. I could write my good friend such a letter. He might very well appreciate having a letter from me. A reduced offering for the bricks may be just the thing he needs. Insurance never covers everything, you know. No, it never does. Insurance is one of those things we all have and hope to never need. But he needs it now, he does. Insurance is a costly business.

Having agreed to collect the desired letter in an hour's time, Brodie and Alistair headed off down the street to a tearoom, where they ordered sandwiches.

We should strike while we can, suggested Alistair, *and ride to Martyndale next week.*

Have you forgotten that one of us is to be married, Al?

I've no forgotten, Brodie. I thought we could go early in the week.

We'll need an overnight stay. And may be longer if they want time to decide.

Let me go on my own then.

You'll be back for the wedding?

I'll no return until I've shaken hands on the sale. There should be time to spare. I would no miss seeing you tie the knot. Dinna think it.

Chapter Twenty-Six: Martyndale News

Martyndale, Ontario ~ February 3, 1910

The Thursday before the wedding, Alistair was still in Martyndale negotiating the sale of the bricks. Samuel Roberts was every bit as pleasant as Mr. Colbert had described, but his partner, Walter Musson, was not so easily convinced. Alistair had been in Martyndale for four days now. Walter had insisted on shaving another few dollars off the cost of the brick and had refused to pay anything towards cartage, arguing that if he bought bricks locally it would not cost him so dear. Alistair was impatient with the man's parsimony but regulated his responses carefully, not wanting to spoil the transaction. Finally, when the three men had at last agreed to the terms and shaken hands, Alistair sent a telegram to Braemor, informing Brodie that the deal was struck and he was riding back.

He left Martyndale at ten o'clock Friday morning; with fair weather, he anticipated reaching Braemor that night. Then, not two hours outside of town, freezing rain began to fall and Alistair was forced to take shelter in a roadside inn. The little dining room was inviting, with a roaring fire in the fireplace and hot soup at the ready. He settled in comfortably with a stack of old newspapers and began to catch up on his reading. A copy of the *Buffalo Enquirer* dated from December caught his eye. He scanned the advertisements, looking for Callaghan Steel or anything else familiar; then, as he folded the sheets together, the name Lewis drew his attention. The notice was a small one:

The Blaxton Lewis family has returned from Boston, where they were called by the death of the former's mother, Mrs. Nigella Lewis, formerly Nigella Blaxton of Beacon Hill, Boston. They were accompanied on their travels by Mr. William Tremont, a single gentleman and friend of the family.

Alistair folded the pages and placed the paper on the table with the others. He sat thoughtfully, watching the flames in the fire and pondering the announcement. Such things were not printed in the paper, he knew, unless they were deemed of some particular importance. As one of several steel barons in Buffalo, Gibson Lewis's family was newsworthy. Based on his own observations, Violet and her mother seemed to very much enjoy their respective positions in good society. Mr. Tremont was clearly significant also, and must now be, Alistair concluded, engaged to Violet. He would not be travelling with the family to such an event unless he was on the most intimate of terms with them. A business associate would not be admitted to anything so private as a family funeral. Violet must have taken him at his word, and accepted the attentions of Mr. William Tremont. Sighing deeply, Alistair sank back into his chair and closed his eyes.

In Braemor, preparations for the wedding were well in hand. Brodie had made arrangements with Justus Ketchum to host the dance at the hotel, and a flurry of activity was taking place: the rolling up of carpets, the stacking of furniture, and the baking of an immense cake. Lavish swags of white ribbon now decorated the front rooms.

At the Gowan farm, Charley was pressing her new dress—a pale blue wool gown with a pleated bodice and high lace neckline. Instead of a bouquet, she had decided to carry the same small, leatherbound New Testament she had carried on the occasion of her first wedding. This had been a gift from Richard Gowan; she felt to acknowledge him in this way. Johnny had a new suit for the occasion, and she had stayed up late the evening before hemming the trousers.

Brodie was at the brickworks, having packed his trunk with his clothes and books and few personal possessions. At the farm, he'd fed the animals, swept the kitchen, and chopped half a cord of wood before it was fully light. He'd been filled with nervous energy these past few days and did not know whether he should attribute it to the anxiety surrounding Alistair's negotiations or the upcoming ceremony.

Having decided that some hard physical work was what was most required for his equanimity, he'd set out for the river, where the men had continued to hollow out the clay cavern in the steep embankment. The methane gas flame had long since burned itself out, but as a precaution he lit a paper spill with a match, holding it carefully away from his body while checking for other gas leaks. The explosive fire had been traumatizing and Brodie wanted to ensure such an event would not be repeated. He alone among them had seen what such gas could do. Satisfied that no gas was present, Brodie lit the barrel and inspected the plank shoring of the cavern. He wanted to assure himself that all was being done properly.

Brodie was still at the clay excavation when the men arrived, and together they discussed the various jobs that would need doing on this day. Brodie offered to load the sledge in preparation for dragging it to the brickworks.

Ye'll not be helpin' wi' dat, said Kyran. *You needs to be savin' yerself fer te weddin'. We can't have ye shamin' us by not measurin' up.*

Brodie looked stricken by Kyran's little joke. An unfavourable ranking in comparison with Dick Gowan was not something he had previously considered. The men looked at his face and broke out in laughter. *Will you be after needing pointers, Mr. Brodie?* asked Sean.

I'll be fine, thanking you, said Brodie. *There's some things a man doesna need to learn.*

Just te same, piped in Kyran, *if ye put a horseshoe in the bedroom, there's no goin' wrong.*

Much obliged, I'm sure, replied Brodie, grinning.

Mid-morning, a rider came from the post office. The men stood and watched as Brodie read Alistair's telegram. *It's good news!* he shouted, holding up the paper. *Alistair has made a large sale of bricks!*

Jaysus! said Kyran. *I tot it was bad. As sure as te Shannon, I was.*

Brodie patted Kyran heartily on the back. *No, my friend, it's good—and Alistair will be back for the wedding.*

My pipes are at te ready, called Sean. *I've been practisin'.*

Like a dying cat, muttered Patrick. *All night long, screeching and wailing like.*

Hey! said Brodie. *I'm looking forward to it. It's been a long while since I've heard the scurl of pipes.*

I'm fer bringin' drums, said Kyran, *an fiddles. We plan to mark te occasion in style!*

Alistair, meanwhile, was making slow progress. The shaded stretches of road were still deep in ice; his horse had to pick its way slowly across the treacherous surfaces. He was eager to get home and see how Brodie was managing—they'd planned to rehearse a couple of things before the event, and he knew now that there wouldn't be time. With luck he might arrive by midnight, but only if the dropping temperatures didn't further impede his progress.

As he rode on, he thought about the unpleasant argument he and Brodie had worked through, the upcoming wedding, and the surprise they had planned for Charley. Then, inevitably, his thoughts wandered to Miss Violet Lewis and Mr. William Tremont. He supposed another wedding was likely. It was a good thing for Miss Lewis, he told himself; he should be pleased for her good fortune. It was ridiculous to hope she would wait for him, especially given his lack of encouragement. Her father would not look upon him as a suitable candidate, and in truth he had very little to offer in the way of a home or the luxuries to which she was accustomed. Marriage to Mr. Tremont was the best avenue for securing her comfort and happiness and he must accept this. But still, the words of the Psalmist repeated, *How long shall I take counsel in my soul, having sorrow in my heart daily.*

It was near one o'clock in the morning when Alistair finally arrived home. To his surprise, Brodie came rushing from the house when he dismounted. They brushed down the horse together.

I thought you'd be abed, said Alistair, *resting for the big day.*

I can rest easy now you're back. There's stew—I thought you'd be cold through.

I am so. The roads were icy and the wind bitter.

I picked up the rings and our kit in town. Everything else is ready. Tell me about Martyndale.

At just past two o'clock, they agreed it was high time they went upstairs to bed. Alistair, feeling sentimental—this was the last night Brodie would be staying at the farm—proposed a final glass of whisky before retiring. Brodie poured them each a drink. They toasted each other's health. Then they toasted Lamith Bricks, and then the men who worked there. Next they toasted Charley, and also Johnny, and then they remembered to toast Mr. Colbert, and finally they toasted Mr. Samuel Roberts and Mr. Walter Musson. The whisky bottle was emptied in this way, and the men, discovering that the staircase was steep and difficult to climb, slept with their heads upon the kitchen table.

CHAPTER TWENTY-SEVEN: A WEDDING
Braemor, Ontario ~ February 4, 1910

It was after eleven o'clock when Alistair woke. He sat up slowly, blinking against the light. His mouth felt dry; he pumped himself a cold glass of water. Looking around the kitchen, he gradually remembered what day it was and began to panic. He picked up his water glass, approached Brodie, and threw it in his face.

Brodie! Wake up, for the love o' all that's holy!

Brodie sat upright, looking slightly astonished by the chilly splashing.

It's your wedding!

Och, mother of God, Al, lower your voice!

I mean it, Brodie! Today! Alistair was standing at the table, steadying himself with one hand and using the other to shield his eyes from the sunlight.

Brodie looked at him skeptically, still absorbing the message. Suddenly he realized what it was that Alistair was saying. He shot up, knocking over his chair. *Mother of God, Al, she'll kill us!*

Kill us or worse!

Och, Al. I canna see straight.

I'll make tea. You get cleaned up.

With some great effort, both men readied themselves for the ceremony. Then, after managing to harness the horses to the cutter, they arrived at the Gowan farm for two o'clock. Johnny came rushing outside to greet them and take care of the horses. A lethal pot of black tea and adrenaline had supplied the men with courage and, despite their nausea and throbbing heads, they knocked upon the front door feeling satisfied with themselves overall.

Hattie Carruthers, Charley and Johnny's neighbour, stepped backwards to let them inside. Scanning them from head to toe, she shook her head. *Look at the both of you, as drunk as lords on your weddin'. You should be full ashamed, with your skins stinkin' of whisky and your eyes red like you've been up all the night. What have you to say for yurselves?*

It was Alistair's fault? offered Brodie weakly.

I doubt he held yer head and forced it down yer throat, you stupid bampot. Go to the kitchen and drink some tea and straighten yurselves.

Brodie and Alistair slunk down the hall and poured themselves steaming cups.

You're in for it, said Alistair helpfully.

A friend you are.

Dinna be blaming me. You was at the table as sure the devil!

They looked at each other and began to laugh.

Do you think Charley will notice? asked Brodie.

Och no! You look as right as rain.

Hattie Carruthers now appeared in the kitchen doorway and both men stood at attention. She adjusted Brodie's tie and smoothed down his hair with the palm of her hand. Then she smacked Alistair in the stomach and told him to tuck in his shirt properly. Finally she declared that they were presentable enough to go to the parlour.

They looked at each other. It was time. Brodie was about to become a married man.

Johnny was there in the parlour, as were the minister and a half dozen others. Johnny smiled at them happily and ran upstairs to get his mother.

And then there she was: Charlotte, on Johnny's arm, walking slowly and gracefully down the stairs.

Johnny looked proud as he guided her carefully towards Brodie. Charley's cheeks were flushed but she was smiling broadly now. She loosened her grip on Johnny to take Brodie's arm. Then they stood before the minister, exchanged vows simply, and were pronounced husband and wife. When they kissed Alistair sighed loudly, grateful that Charley had not denounced the pair of them.

As congratulations were shared all around, Alistair stepped toward his friends, embracing them both. He and Brodie eyed each other over Charley's shoulder and grimaced slightly, indicating by this that they both still had a thick head.

The afternoon passed easily in the company of their friends. Most ate a light supper before readying themselves for the dance. Alistair and Brodie escaped to sit quietly in the kitchen while the guests talked loudly in the parlour. After six, as they headed upstairs to change from their tweed suits, Charley detained them with a firm hand.

Don't you be thinking I don't know what you two have been up to. There'll be no more whisky drinking this evening or you'll be sleeping in the barn, Brodie Smith. She gave them each a long, steady look, kissed them both on the forehead, and stepped away.

When the men came downstairs a half hour later they were dressed in kilts and fine black Prince Charlie waistcoats—Brodie wearing the Smith tartan, in green and royal blue with a fine yellow thread; Alistair wearing the Lamont tartan, in green and light blue with a fine white line. Both men also sported blue and green socks, garters, fur sporrans, and soft black leather ghillies. They made a handsome pair; the guests exclaimed mightily over their appearance. Despite his pounding head Brodie smiled feebly, hoping their planned entertainment might help to alleviate Charley's displeasure.

Not long after, as the wedding party walked into the hotel, they were greeted by the rest of their friends along with the entire brickworks crew. It seemed as though all of Braemor had turned out to wish them well. Kyran, true to his word, sat in the corner with his assembled musicians, their fiddles and soft Irish drums already filling the room with lively tunes. Next to the players stood a damask-draped table bearing the wedding gifts, among them cut glass, silver, china and ornate picture frames. Charley eyed their proximity to the musicians with some concern.

After the punch was served and the cake cut, Kyran and Patrick stood up to dance an Irish jig. The music grew louder, two more joined them, and the crowd clapped along with the four high-stepping men. A number of couples then stepped onto the floor. A wild reel commenced; the drummers continued to drum; the fiddlers played on; and Brodie held his head discreetly as the music rang out and the dancers spun around the room.

Charley looked at him with faint hope. *I suppose you're not in any shape to dance?*

Brodie, although he was sure this would seal his fate, did not trouble to disagree. He looked over at Alistair. *Help me out, Al?*

Are you sure?

Charley may never forgive us if we dinna do summit.

Can you manage?

If you can.

We'll look right idiots if you blunder.

Helpful!

And so, when the musicians took a pause, Alistair reached into a bag under the table, stepped forward with a pair of swords, and placed them in a cross on the centre of the floor. The crowd grew quiet. Now Sean Maguire came forward and blew a few tentative notes into his pipes. Silence again. Alistair struck a formal pose—fists at his waist, toes pointed out—and waited for Sean. Then, as the first few notes were blown, he bowed forward stiffly and began to dance. The crowd was ebullient, hooting and clapping and whistling as he hopped and stepped over and around the swords, closer and farther away. Higher and higher he jumped until suddenly he finished. He stopped briefly, arms curled in the air, breathing heavily, and looked to his friend.

Brodie bent down to retrieve two more swords from beneath the table, stepping forward to place these, crossed, at some small distance from the others. Brodie and Alistair readied themselves, nodded at each other, and stood in formal position. Then they paused for a moment, eyes closed, before they looked at Sean, who again began to play. Both men began to dance, trading places as they did, so that Brodie danced over his swords and crossed to dance over Alistair's while Alistair likewise crossed to dance over Brodie's. There was some small element of competition between the men as they kicked and jumped and spun over and around the crossed swords. They were both of them panting and perspiring when Sean sounded the last notes and they struck their final position as the music ended. The applause was raucous and sustained.

Brodie and Alistair looked a little unsteady and slightly ill, as though the twirling and hopping had redistributed their whisky intake and they were trying not to be sick. Charley, however, looked charmed and was clapping delightedly.

Brodie leaned towards his friend and mustered a whisper. *Have we managed to redeem ourselves?*

Dinna think it, Alistair laughed. *You'll be spending the night in the barn, for certain.*

Rochester, New York ~ March 11, 1908

Despite the ice underfoot and a bitter wind, Brodie stood on the banks of the Genesee River, scanning the site where a catastrophic flood had washed away the bridge. With Callaghan having given him leave to deviate from the Warren truss, Brodie was completing drawings for a steel camelback truss bridge that would rest on stone abutments fifteen feet above the water, thereby ensuring that spring runoff and high waters wouldn't weaken its moorings and sweep it downriver. It was to be a single-span model, two hundred and forty-six feet long and fourteen feet wide. Additionally, Brodie had decided to strengthen its bottom cord with the use of cables, an innovative feature whose integration presented a stimulating challenge. He'd even sketched a particularly ornate decoration for the portal bracing that incorporated the initials *CS* for Callaghan Steel in a lacy design.

The bridge would take ten months to construct, although the fabrication would be done in Buffalo. For the assembly, Brodie was eager to try out the use of pins instead of the hot riveting method Callaghan typically employed. He hadn't yet discussed this detail with Callaghan, however, and was prepared to let go of the idea if necessary.

The river, he'd noted, had a swift-flowing current that moved inland and north towards a high waterfall. Rock samplings had revealed a heavy bedrock base, with stratifications that indicated some fossil and paleobiological interest. Arrowheads, too, had been unearthed. Brodie was anxious not to disrupt more area than necessary when setting the footings and abutments.

It was a project that excited him as no other had done for some long time. Its engineering drew on all of his training and skill. Callaghan had finally begun to listen to him, and had given him no small degree of creative licence. Brodie was determined to make this bridge one of unassailable safety and of aesthetic distinction.

And yet, even through the long, absorbing hours of work that followed, Brodie found himself primarily looking forward to the bridge's completion—as though simply finishing it meant more to him than any innovation involved in its construction.

February 15, 1909

The little crowd of assembled dignitaries huddled closely together in the biting cold, trying to take shelter by the easterly abutment. Brodie had tied a large red ribbon across the width of the bridge and was standing nearby with an oversized pair of shears, ready for the cutting. A photographer from the local newspaper was attempting to steady his tripod while his assistant nervously held a glass plate. The mayor and his wife waited expectantly, he in a boldly striped suit and no overcoat, puffing vigorously on a cigar, she in an oversized hat, trying valiantly to keep her coat from flapping open to expose her thin dress and stockinged legs.

Daniel Callaghan himself had come for this opening, as the bridge was an important contract and he was anxious to see Brodie's innovations. He'd stumped about the installation the day before, jumping on the deck, grabbing hold of the panels trying to pry them loose from their fastening, scanning the look of the web, running his fingers along the mortar of the abutments— nothing escaped his scrutiny. The cables were of particular concern; Callaghan had many questions concerning their affixing and clasping systems. He'd obtained them from his good friend Lewis—who, along with Brodie, had exerted no small pressure upon him to at least try them.

Brodie surveyed the group and smiled to himself. There were many here today who would boast of their involvement and patronage. They would cut the ribbon and pose for the newspaper photograph and ensure that their names were spelled correctly in the ensuing columns of print. But he, and only he, had designed this magnificent structure. Yes, others had paid for it and had facilitated the business and manufacturing side of it, but he, Brodie Smith, had drawn it, measured for it, planned it down to the tiniest detail and the smallest fastening, and watched over it while it was being assembled, climbing the girders, double-checking calculations and measurements, ensuring that the pieces fitted together perfectly. Despite the *CS* proudly emblazoned in the steel lace, this was *his* bridge, *his* creation. No one would remember to thank him for his work, no one would give him credit in any number of the long speeches to follow, but it was his and would outlive him. It was built to last a hundred years or more. And it was *his*.

Chapter Twenty-Eight: Admiral Barnes's Visit
Braemor, Ontario ~ February 5, 1910

Alistair had just finished his breakfast when an animated series of sharp raps on the door brought him to his feet. Admiral Barnes stood on the porch, silver-topped walking stick in one hand, and a sheaf of rolled-up documents tucked under his arm.

Good morning, m'boy. I thought as how your friend and partner was now married, you might welcome an old man's company this morning. I have the plans here for that overhead tramway. My friend from Wales sent them some time ago, but I thought you'd want to wait until after the big event.

Be seated. There's tea in the pot.

The Admiral shed his outer layers and settled himself with great ceremony at the kitchen table. He placed the sheaf of papers down with care. Then, as he uncurled them, he held them open with his carefully positioned stick. Alistair brought him a cup and went to pour some tea into it.

No need, m'boy. No need. I bring my own you, see.

Reaching into his jacket pocket, the Admiral withdrew a flask and tipped its contents into the cup. He warmed it with the tiniest amount of tea and then sat back in his chair, sipping with great satisfaction. Turning to the papers, he pointed at the detailed illustrations, tapping his finger on various features in turn: the tower assembly, the operating gears, the cable requirements.

We'll have to order the steel from Buffalo, said Alistair. *Brodie can work out what we'll need.*

You could order from the Hamilton steel mills, but shipping would have to route through Toronto.

Except that our backers have interests in Buffalo steel and we have working relationships with them. It makes sense to order from Callaghan's.

Ah, yes, yes. I remember now. You both worked for Callaghan's, isn't that it? Bridges, as I recall. That's how the two of you fell in together. Working on a bridge.

In Welland. I was in charge o' assembly and Brodie the engineering and safety.

Yes, yes, m'boy. I remember now. And you went hunting together. Duck, wasn't it?

Fishing, actually.

Yes, yes, of course, m'boy. Fishing in Lake Ontario. I remember now. Lake char, I believe you said.

Salmon, actually. In the Brae. That's when we spied the clay.

Yes. Yes, I remember now. Salmon. Good salmon in the Brae. There are some that say the water is colder in the Mor and that you catch bigger fish there, but I've never believed that to be true. No, not one bit. I fish in the Brae and I never walk away without a good catch. Big salmon in the Brae. You can be sure of that. Yes, m'boy. Big salmon. Tasty fish, salmon.

Alistair smiled at the Admiral and then pointed to one of the drawings. *These cables may be a difficulty. They look substantial.*

Yes. Woven together and encased in sheathing. Specialized, m'boy. And they need to be. Those buckets will be heavy enough when they're empty, but when filled with wet clay and shale they could easily weigh upwards of a half-ton. And when you string two or three filled buckets on the line, you will need a strong cable. Yes, you will. Very thick indeed. Brodie will know how to judge. He will. He's a clever one, he is. I never met a sheep farmer who was a civil engineer before. No, I haven't. And educated at the best schools. Glasgow and somewhere else, too. Was it Harvard? Yes, I think he said Harvard. One of the best schools.

It was Edinburgh and the Massachusetts Institute.

I don't know about that, m'boy. But he is a well-educated farmer. You are fortunate to have such a partner.

I am indeed. A partner and friend.

One does wonder, though. The Admiral paused theatrically, raising one of his very bushy white eyebrows. *One does wonder.*

Wonder? About what?

The Admiral scrutinized Alistair's face carefully. *Did you never wonder, m'boy? Did you never wonder why a man would spend several years training to be an engineer and then suddenly decide to take up farming?*

It's a joint venture we've started. We're our own masters and can put down roots and no be on the road all the time.

Very well, very well, m'boy. Believe that, if you will. He's a good friend to you, I know. But there is something there, I say. I have determined it.

Admiral, that talk is sheer bollocks! Brodie Smith is near to me as kin and as true a man as they come.

Yes, m'boy. So you say. But even in battle troops have been known to retreat. There comes a time when even the bravest leaders know it's time to withdraw. Sad to tell you, but there it is. Withdrawing is not just the way of the coward. Sometimes it is the only way to save lives. You learn that, m'boy, when you have been to war.

Alistair sat in a quiet temper as the Admiral shook his head solemnly, as though in agreement with the point he himself had just driven home. It wasn't a vehement nodding so much as a subdued acknowledgment of a sobering thought. Slowly he got up from his chair and reached for his stick, then his overcoat, scarf, and gloves. Finally he stood, fully erect with years of naval training.

I will leave the plans with you, m'boy. You can show your friend.

Thanking you, said Alistair stiffly. *I appreciate the trouble you've gone to on our account.*

Yes, m'boy. Happy to do it. Happy to be useful. At my age, you see, there is not much one can do to be of use anymore. That time has passed, you see. The young are not much interested in history, you know. With them it's a matter of the future. History be damned, they say. Ours is the generation that will accomplish things. That's the way it is now with the young. I used to visit the schools, you know, and teach naval history. They don't know about the Napoleonic Wars, or the Opium Wars… No sense of history.

I'm sure that is entirely so.

It is so. It is so. Remember what I have told you, m'boy. Your friend has a past. One day you will remember my words and come to know the true measure of the man you're sailing with.

Alistair walked outside with him to his waiting horse and sleigh. He pulled off the horse's blanket, rolled it up, and handed it to his guest. Admiral Barnes climbed into the sleigh, stood upright for a moment, then saluted Alistair smartly and took his seat. Alistair raised his arm in a farewell wave before returning to the warmth of the kitchen.

The plans were still spread across the table; he perused these distractedly, ruminating on the Admiral's words. They resonated with some truth. When he'd proposed their joint venture, had he asked Brodie to give up too much? Would Brodie become disenchanted and seek other opportunities? Alistair thought about the course of his and Brodie's lives, marvelling at how they had come together at Callaghan's, both of them alone in the world.

He rolled up the plans into a tight scroll and tied them fast with a bit of string. He would show them to Brodie and together they could determine what was needed.

Chapter Twenty-Nine: The Plans
Braemor, Ontario ~ February 5, 1910

Now Alistair was in a bit of a quandary. He wanted to take the plans to Brodie straightaway, but surely such a visit wouldn't be entirely appropriate so soon after the wedding? He was pacing about outside, trying to decide, when he spotted Johnny come to sweep the barn.

Good morning, Johnny! I'm surprised to see you.

Ma said as how you'd be sure to need an extra hand without Brodie this morning. He and my Ma said they had grown-up things to attend and that I best come here and help out for the day. Tonight we're having a family supper. Just the three of us. Unless you join us. Ma said I should ask.

That's fine, Johnny. A family supper should be the three of you.

Did you enjoy the wedding? I thought my Ma looked mighty fine.

She surely did, lad.

I didn't know you and Brodie could dance like that! Would you teach me?

I'd be happy to, lad. It's no so hard as it looks when you know a few basic steps. We improvised a bit.

Are they real swords?

We had them made special. The blades are no sharp, though. Otherwise we'd cut a foot if we stepped the wrong way.

Johnny nodded. *Brodie says when I come of age he'll give me his share of the brickworks.*

Did he now? We'll be partners then.

Mr. Alistair, shall I start feeding the sheep?

Yes. And check the water troughs, please. Make sure they're no froze hard.

Alistair returned indoors to unroll and study the plans once more. It would be difficult, he concluded, to estimate a budget without knowing how much steel was required. Perhaps if he drove Johnny home in the cutter he could steal a minute with his partner. Out he went again to harness the horses. Johnny was just finishing the mucking out and cheerfully accepted the ride.

They set off across the fields, Johnny talking excitedly the entire way. *Did you know, Mr. Alistair, Brodie has said I may call him Brodie, or Father, or anything I choose. He said that if I wanted to choose a name that only I called him, I could do so. I like the idea of having a special name for him that only I can use but I also really like the idea of just calling him Pa. I had a Pa before but he died. I don't remember him. I don't tell my Ma that because it would make her sad. She says I look just like him. My first Pa that is. What do you think, Mr. Alistair? Do you think Brodie would like me calling him Pa?*

Alistair smiled at the question. *Yes, lad. I think he would like it very much. But when you have a chance you should ask your mother first, and make sure it sits well with her.*

They arrived at the Gowan farm in quick time; Alistair brushed down the horse while Johnny ran for the bag of oats, throwing a generous handful into the feedbag. They went inside just as Charley was setting the table.

Hello, Alistair, will you stop for dinner?

No tonight, Charley. I only want Brodie a minute and then I'll leave you.

He's in the parlour, reading.

Al, I thought I heard you, said Brodie as he joined them in the kitchen. *Will you stay for a meal wi' us?*

Dinna think it, Brodie. You've a right to be alone with your family. Admiral Barnes has shown me plans for the aerial ropeway and I wondered when we might take a look together. I'm eager for you to review the specifications.

Take a piece of pie home with you, at least, said Charley.

Without waiting for his response, she cut a fresh pie into quarters and wrapped a wedge of it in a clean cloth. Alistair took the pie, along with a mason jar of hot soup she'd placed in a basket, and bid his friends a good evening. As he was leaving he saw Johnny nuzzle up against Brodie, fitting himself in tightly under his arm. Brodie looked down at him happily and kissed the top of the boy's head. Alistair smiled at the contented scene and left for home.

When Brodie arrived the next morning he brought a cold gust of air and some fresh snow in with him. Once Alistair had cleared the table and spread out the documents that Admiral Barnes had procured, Brodie sat down and pulled the sheaf of papers towards him eagerly. With his finger he traced out the details of the mechanism and the itemized lists of moving parts, frowning from time to time as he reviewed details but nodding his head at other times as though agreeing with some silent muse. Alistair made a pot of tea and sat down quietly to watch his friend carefully review the schematics.

Let me take these back home for a few days, said Brodie, *and I'll draw up a list o' things we'll need.*

Shall we get the steel from Callaghan's?

Of course. You should take the plans wi' you and place an order. They'll be interested to see what we're doing. Did the payment come from Martyndale?

It did. Will the cables be difficult to find?

They'll have to be made. Callaghan or one of his partners will know who to go to.

Is it manageable?

These are good plans. Sinking the towers will be a challenge. And supporting the gears. But it will save hours o' work for the lads. Brodie paused. *Still, it's a large investment.*

We need to do this, Brodie. Any technological advance has its cost. If it's no the money, it's the time in labour, and sometimes it's the cost of men injured while they work. But we canna stand still.

Brodie smiled. *I'll make that list of requirements and you can go over it wi' Callaghan. He'll help locate what's needed. Steel for the towers should come first—I'll write out lengths and weights and quantities. I've plenty o' reasons to stay where I am.*

As Alistair went about his work that morning, he reflected on his friend's good fortune. He was delighted for Brodie and also for Charley and Johnny. How quickly their lives had changed. May was his visit to the art gallery, August their fishing trip to Braemor, and now, in February, Brodie was married and they'd established their brickworks with a flock of sheep besides.

Alistair could not help but wonder about the status of Miss Violet Lewis and Mr. William Tremont. The news item in the society column had put a final damper on any romantic thoughts he had harbored. But still he found that images of Violet kept intruding uninvited—her lovely smiling face, her petite, feminine figure, the teasing manner with which she had previously addressed him. He hoped Tremont fully appreciated her.

Chapter Thirty: The Skating Party

Buffalo, New York ~ February 18, 1910

As the train's jerking and clanking commenced, Alistair settled into his seat to study Brodie's detailed instructions and the lists he had prepared of required purchases. It was important to know which items were to be ordered from Callaghan and which from other suppliers. With a finely sharpened pencil, Alistair made a series of tick marks on the pages so that he could quickly identify the special orders.

He arrived in Buffalo mid-afternoon, whereupon he checked into a hotel, had a late luncheon, and then summoned a cab to Callaghan's. Was it his imagination or had motorcar traffic increased markedly? The roadways were choked with motor vehicles and horse-drawn carriages both, and at the intersections no order seemed to prevail as to which was to be given preference. Perhaps it was the quiet of his country existence that made it all appear so chaotic.

Once inside the familiar building, he was struck anew by its elegance and sophistication. There was nothing half so fine in Braemor, he thought. Johnny and Charley and some of their friends would be astonished to see such luxury on display, and in a factory no less. It struck him that the things he'd taken for granted not so long ago, now seemed excessive and extravagant. At the top of the ornate staircase he was greeted by Mr. Callaghan's secretary; he waited only a moment before the door to the giant office was flung open wide and there Callaghan himself stood, a fat cigar in the corner of his mouth.

Come in, Alistair! I'm eager to hear news of your venture. Cigar?

Alistair declined the cigar but unpacked his valise quickly, anxious to show his benefactor the plans for the ropeway. He spread the papers across the desk and began in an animated manner to itemize its features. Callaghan grasped the significance of the venture immediately, taking up the schematics to review them in detail.

Also packed in Alistair's valise was the little brickmaking catalogue. He showed Callaghan the machine they'd bought, explaining why the timing of the ropeway was now of such particular significance. Callaghan studied the catalogue enthusiastically and seemed much taken with the plans Alistair was outlining.

I am here to order the steel, Alistair continued, *and to request your assistance in locating custom cables and some of the other parts.*

Glad to hear it, son. Always happy to help, you know. Lewis is the man for the cables. Knows all about them. That's his main business interest now. Braided steel cables. He's the man you need to talk to.

Could we see him together?

There's a skating party in Delaware Park this evening. The ladies have arranged it. First there is to be the skating, and afterwards there are refreshments at the Lewis's. You will come and join us this evening. There will be plenty of time to chat with the guests and do a bit of business besides. Gibson will be most interested in this scheme of yours. He'll have an opinion on the cables.

Thank you, sir, but I'm afraid I dinna skate.

As a rule, the men don't skate. We watch the ladies and let them have their fun. Come at eight. I will look for you there.

At that Callaghan stood, and as he ushered Alistair out of his office, the men agreed to meet again on the following day to complete their business transactions. Alistair left the building feeling ebullient. Electing to walk back to the hotel, he crossed the street gingerly, avoiding both horse traffic and motorcars, smiling to think about the response should a motor vehicle ever make its way along the main street of Braemor. Soon, however, the prospect of negotiating a custom cable order with Gibson Lewis began to weigh on him. He suspected that Lewis was a tough negotiator—and that no favour would be shown to an upstart whom his daughter had befriended. Alistair winced to think of it.

That evening, upon arriving at the park, he stood above the lake and watched the activity for some while before descending to the ice. He'd hoped to spy Callaghan and head directly to him, but saw at once that the arrangements were of a haphazard sort. Gentlemen in their bowler hats and long coats stood in throngs along the ice's edge while the skaters glided singly or in couples in the centre of the lake, often darting into groups of bystanders and sending them drifting apart.

Alistair felt anxious and not at all sporting. He'd curled in Peebleshire, but they hadn't worn skates for such a thing. He stepped carefully along the surface, scanning the crowds for a familiar face. Finally, halfway around the perimeter, he spotted Daniel Callaghan. Relieved, he pushed forward eagerly and greeted the men he stood among, most of whom were Callaghan's friends and silent backers of the brickworks. Alistair was pleased to see them, and the feeling was apparently mutual. Gibson Lewis was not among the company. When there was a break in the conversation, Alistair turned to Callaghan. *Is Mr. Lewis here as well?*

Yes, Alistair. He's over there. Daniel pointed vaguely to the other side of the little lake. *I saw him earlier and he said to be certain you came back to the house. He'll talk to us there.*

That is most kind.

Not at all. Are you going to try this foolishness?

No, sir. I like the feel of solid earth under my feet.

I quite agree. But young people do like their entertainments. Callaghan turned to watch the skaters. *Look—there goes Miss Lewis and her beau, Mr. Tremont. Do you see?*

He pointed in the direction of two figures skating together at great speed along the edges of the crowd. Miss Lewis had her hands tucked into a fur muff, but her companion had a firm grasp of her arm and was holding her closely. As they watched, Mr. Tremont let her loose while he spun off in a twirl, stopping abruptly with a deft spray of ice from his blades. He then skated backwards in front of her while she followed him skating forward. He seemed more than adept on skates, and the two of them appeared to be laughing convivially.

They make a handsome couple, observed Alistair wryly.

They do so, agreed Callaghan. *He's a lawyer from Syracuse. Good family. Running for Congress. Has all sorts of ideas. Don't hold with most of them but he is a bright spark.*

And are they engaged?

There may be an understanding but I'm not informed. The ladies keep track of these things.

Mr. Lewis had made his way through the crowd and now greeted Alistair. *We're heading to the house,* he said. *It will soon be too cold for the womenfolk. Be sure to come.*

Alistair accepted a ride with Callaghan in his motorcar, grateful for his friendly companionship. The men all crowded into the Lewis's study, lighting their cigars promptly and pouring whisky into the cut-glass tumblers that lined the top of a nearby table. Alistair enjoyed the burning sensation as the drink went down, warming him. Callaghan drew the men's attention to Alistair and extolled his business prowess and the virtues of the aerial ropeway. The men were interested in the plans, asking a number of questions and offering several suggestions for the scheme. Gibson Lewis was particularly interested in the need for a strong cable, proposing that Alistair visit his showroom to view samples. Things were going far better than he'd anticipated.

After an hour had passed in such pleasant company, Mr. Lewis announced that it was now time to join the others—that he'd be in grave difficulty if they didn't make an appearance before the evening ended. Alistair reluctantly followed the troupe of men into the living room where the ladies had gathered. Seeking a dark corner, he surveyed the room with a view to hiding himself, hoping against hope that he could avoid Miss Lewis altogether.

This was not to be. As he lifted his head to survey the room, he immediately caught the eye of Mr. Tremont. He watched while the gentleman parted from his companion and walked directly towards him. Hand extended, he introduced himself smartly.

William Tremont, sir, at your service.

Alistair Lamont, sir. A pleasure.

The handshake was uneven. Mr. Tremont's was weak and limp, whereas Alistair took pride in applying a great deal of pressure. Alistair noted, with some small degree of pleasure, that Tremont was wearing a large signet ring. He knew as he squeezed that this would create some mild discomfort.

We have not met before, sir, began Mr. Tremont.

I'm here for a few days only.

And are you well acquainted with the Lewis family?

Mr. Lewis and some of the other gentlemen have invested in a business venture with me.

And what business is that, might I inquire? Although Mr. Tremont was demonstrating the politest of behaviours, Alistair did note that he was holding his right hand at his side—and was shaking it almost imperceptibly.

We own a brickworks in Canada. I make bricks.

How very interesting. Tremont deflated markedly, signalling that there was nothing in this that could be of interest to him.

Yes, continued Alistair, warming to the situation, *brickmaking, as you may know, is essential to the development and growth of small communities. Industrialization canna happen wi' out growth and bricks.*

Fascinating, interjected Tremont rather glibly. *I myself am a litigator. Running for Congress.*

Industrialization and advances in modern technology will be of real interest to you then, sir. A government canna run without knowing how the country works. Let me tell you about the aerial tramway we're building...

I'm sure it's quite engaging, Mr. Lamont, but I would not want to detain you. My understanding of such things is, at the moment, quite limited. Please excuse me.

Alistair almost laughed outright at the panicked look of his companion as he backed away. He was about to move towards the table with its decanters when a delicate figure in a soft green dress stood before him.

I see you've met my friend.

I have.

And what has he said that has entertained you so? I saw you smiling as if at some great joke.

Alistair found himself unexpectedly tongue-tied.

Have you been regaling him with tales of bears and wolves?

I havena, Alistair muttered, looking at his feet.

I see you are quite well then, Mr. Lamont, and have not been attacked by the wildlife.

I am well, thanking you. I saw you skating earlier.

It is a great winter entertainment, Mr. Lamont. But you didn't join us. Do you not skate?

No. In Scotland we threw rocks upon the ice and curled for sport.

Is Mr. Smith also well, and your brickworks?

We are managing well.

And will you not ask after my health, Mr. Lamont?

I can see as you look well, and fine.

I was disappointed, Mr. Lamont, not to have had a letter or a card from you at Christmas.

I didna think it proper. Alistair felt his face and neck colouring deeply. The whisky had lessened his reserve but the near presence of Miss Lewis was unsettling. It was proving difficult to keep his head and remember that she was now spoken for. *Mr. Tremont seems an affable gentleman.*

Nothing is decided between us, Mr. Lamont. Although he has made his intentions known. I find that Mr. Tremont is not so interested in broadening his sights as one might wish. He knows nothing of art or music and seems to care only about political subjects and the law. Violet looked up into Alistair's face boldly, seeming to search it for emotion of any kind. He allowed himself to look back at her for only the briefest of moments.

I wish you happy. He bowed and excused himself, taking his leave.

Buffalo, New York ~ April 5, 1909

Brodie wasn't sure when exactly he'd fallen out of love with bridges. It may have been after he missed seeing his mother before she died. Or perhaps it was after the first dozen steel railway bridges had been reassembled like a giant child's puzzle on site. It may have been after a discussion with Callaghan about wanting to increase the use of cables, to move away from the simple truss bridge he'd been drawing and redrawing, site after site. Notwithstanding the concessions Callaghan had made on the Genesee River bridge, in the end he was a practical man and didn't see the wisdom, or the economics, in switching a solid truss approach for something more expensive, more potentially fraught with complications.

However it had come about, somewhere in the process Brodie began to see bridges as merely a means to an end. A way to get from here to there in the most practical manner. No longer did he think safe passage could be secured by a structure that soared through space with a delicate touch of elegance and beauty. There was, he'd learned, no guarantee of safe passage. And Brodie longed for something for which he could not find the words.

Chapter Thirty-One: Devastation

Braemor, Ontario ~ February 18, 1910

It was twilight, the sky a sapphire blue seen only in the cold northern winter. The men were putting away their tools and grousing good-naturedly about the long walk home across the packed snow. A few men were still at the riverside and Brodie was guiding one of the horses to the barn for the night, patting it on its side with abstracted affection. He too would head home shortly, he thought, but with Alistair away he'd first need to tend the livestock. Brodie had almost reached the sheep pasture when a thunderous splashing eruption resounded across the fields. The horse startled; Brodie tightened his grip on the lead as he looked up to see a swelling cloud of smoke and shooting flame by the riverbed. Loud cracking and snapping noises carried through the air, the unmistakable sounds of a fire. Brodie dropped the lead and ran off towards the river.

He gulped down an acrid stench as he ran, sliding across the snow-covered ground with treacherous speed. Propelling himself forward, showers of clay and stone and dirt and snow rained down upon him. Small explosive bursts continued. He stopped abruptly, two hundred feet from the river. Where there had been a steep embankment, there was now an open maw. An enormous crater had blown open, with large and small fires burning everywhere. Even the river was alight with flames. He heard screams and voices shouting around him.

Saints alive!

Sweet Jaysus!

Kyrannnnnnn!

This last was drawn out and resonated pitifully across the devastation as the men rushed to gather near Brodie.

Kyran was after loading te sledge! said Sean.

Where is he?!

The men moved cautiously forward across the ruined ground, avoiding the burning debris as they descended slowly into the ragged opening, calling for their friend.

Over 'ere! yelled Patrick.

Be careful, shouted Brodie. *There could be another explosion.*

Here! yelled Sean.

The men made their way quickly to where Sean stood. At some distance from the crater's centre lay a shapeless bundle. The men crowded near and stared down silently. One after another they solemnly removed their caps. A couple of the men crossed themselves.

Brodie spoke first. *We need to move quickly and get him away from here. Find something to put him on.* They spread out to look. All around them the fires continued to burn, gusts of wind feeding the flames, making them even more alarming.

'ere! yelled Patrick, returning to the site with one of the wide planks that had been used to shore the cave. He laid the wood gently beside the body and tenderly slid it underneath. Sean arrived in time to assist him, and while the two men arranged the corpse, Brodie took off his own coat and gently draped it over Kyran's face so that the melted, disfigured features were covered. All were hushed but for Sean's sharp intakes of breath and Patrick's sobs.

Without speaking, the men divided themselves on both sides of the body. Then they reached down carefully to lift the board and its sad bundle onto their shoulders. Slowly and carefully, they processed across the frozen fields to the village.

As they approached Kyran's house, Brodie spoke. *Let me go first.*

The men stood silently as Brodie advanced and rapped upon the door.

An aproned Mrs. Meacham, heavy with child, opened it promptly with a bright smile on her pleasant face. She hesitated at the sight of Brodie and then looked beyond him to see the men with their burden. Before Brodie could reach out to her she fell to her knees and began to keen and wail in the most heart-wrenching fashion. Brodie took her by the arms and pulled her gently aside so that the men could enter the house. She moved to allow their passage, quaking and shrieking in shock and misery.

The neighbours gathered then and lovingly encircled her, leading her to the kitchen. The men had lain Kyran on the small parlour floor and were arranging the chairs to form an elevated platform for the remains. Sean went to the kitchen and asked one of the women to fetch a sheet; they used it to drape the body once they had it in position.

The Meachams' three children had appeared in the midst of the preparations; they hovered now, terrified, in the narrow space between the parlour and the kitchen. Their mother was surrounded by crying and sobbing women in the kitchen and sad, frightened men surrounded a draped sheet in the parlour. Neither group of constituents was paying the children any mind—and the sheer novelty of that alone made them quiver and cry with fear.

It was near eight o'clock when Brodie returned home. Charley was waiting for him in the kitchen, three places set at the table. She took in the look of him and the smell of fire before rushing forward.

Let me change and wash first, said Brodie, extending a hand to her.

What has happened?!

There's been an explosion. Fire damp, I expect. Kyran Meacham has died. I've just come from there.

And Johnny? Where is Johnny?

Johnny?

Johnny! Brodie, for the love of God, tell me where Johnny is!

I thought he was here.

Haven't you seen him?

No since breakfast.

Dear God... Johnny... Charley collapsed onto a chair and began to rock herself back and forth.

Brodie knelt down quickly beside her and put his arms around her shoulders. *Tell me, Charley! When did you last see him?*

Around five. He said… he said… that he was going to walk to the river and help load the sledge for the last run of the day and then take care of the horses. He said… oh Brodie, do something… he said he wanted to surprise you.

Charley, are you sure?

Oh God, Brodie, do something!

Brodie stood and moved towards the door. *Wait here. I will find him.*

Charley reached for his arm. *Brodie…*

Let me be. I'll come back when I can.

Pushing Charley away from him, Brodie ran from the house and went directly to the Carruthers' farm. He pounded on the door. *I need your horses! Something has happened!*

Mr. Carruthers opened the door. Grasping the situation quickly, he nodded, grabbed his coat, and followed Brodie to the barn. They hitched the sleigh, picked up two lanterns and some blankets, then set off at speed in the direction of the brickworks.

Into town first, directed Brodie. *We'll need more men.* They drove to the hotel where a group of men were smoking on the verandah discussing the explosion and the death of Kyran. When Brodie shouted for help they called back a promise to follow directly with horses. When they arrived at the crater, Mr. Carruthers held up his lamp and was astonished by the devastation. He'd heard an explosion earlier in the evening but had assumed someone was blasting with dynamite.

Fire damp, Brodie said tersely. *Methane gas.*

God in heaven.

Brodie jumped down from the sleigh and began to run around the crater frantically. *Johnny!* he screamed. *Johnny—are you here? JOHNNY!*

Mr. Carruthers followed after Brodie, swinging his lantern high and surveying the destruction. The crater was soon alight with a dozen other men and their lanterns, picking their way through small fires still burning, upturned trees, piles of debris, and the general rubble.

Careful with the lanterns, shouted Brodie. *The heat could trigger another explosion.*

Silhouettes danced menacingly outside the pools of light, and many of the men imagined they saw a boy's shape, which turned out to be a branch or a rock magnified and animated through the shadows. They moved cautiously, aware that another explosion was yet possible. As their search continued, Brodie's panic rose. Two men scouted out the farm and the brickworks to make sure Johnny hadn't taken refuge there. Another man rode back to the Gowan farm to see whether Johnny had yet come home. But most of the men, grim-faced and with lessened expectations, expanded their search to beyond the crater and up and down the hot gashed river bank.

Brodie ran from pile to pile of debris with feverish intensity, kicking mounds, dislodging rocks, turning over planks and tree limbs. The men could hear him desperately calling Johnny's name.

Finally, at first light, the men extinguished their lanterns and congregated sorrowfully. They watched Brodie as he returned to the already searched piles of wreckage, clawing through them on his hands and knees, burning himself in the hot mess. Nodding at one another, the men approached Brodie and pulled him to his feet. He fought against them, screaming Johnny's name, but they overpowered him and dragged him to the sleigh. Thomas held him fast while Mr. Carruthers drove them back to the farm.

When they arrived Brodie hurried inside, momentarily hopeful for good news. Instead he found the house filled with those who'd come to comfort Charley while she waited. Charley ran towards him... and then began to pummel him with her fists before the ladies pulled her off.

A couple of the women saw the state of Brodie's hands and attempted to bathe and bandage them, but he pushed them away and stood woodenly by himself. He was aware that there were people speaking to him but he could not hear what it was they were saying.

Justus Ketchum arrived with Doctor Barrow; they went to see Charley, who'd been taken upstairs. After some time, the doctor called Brodie to the kitchen and made him sit down so that he could dress the burns. Brodie submitted to this treatment but could not understand what it was the doctor was telling him. When both hands had been wrapped in layers of gauze so thick that they resembled padded mittens, and after the doctor had held a glass of whisky to his mouth and made him drink, the shock began to wear off and Brodie wept.

The Carruthers stayed at the Gowan farm throughout the day, and then overnight, and then again for a second day. They tended to Charley, who remained upstairs, and to Brodie, who remained in the kitchen.

The rest of the men, meanwhile, had rested and then returned to the crater to continue their efforts. On the second day, determining that Johnny did not weigh as much as an adult male, they wondered if he might have been thrown farther by the blast, and widened their search area to include the opposite bank of the river. The river was deep and had a fast-flowing current that ran down the middle. The centre of the river wasn't iced over solid, although ice shelves extended twenty feet on either side, ice that was thick at the edge and tapered to a thin crust near the rushing water. The surface of the ice was now littered with matter from the explosion. One of the men found a plaid woollen cap that they recognized as belonging to Johnny. Patrick Lynch was seen raising the cap to his lips before carefully folding it into his jacket pocket.

As they made their way downstream, in the bright glare of the sun, they saw a dark shadow bobbing gently under the ice. Tying a rope around his waist, Sean crawled out onto the frozen shelf with an axe and began to chop a hole in the thick barrier. Patrick and the others held the rope in the event that Sean's icy perch broke and sent him into the frigid water. After some exertion, Sean smashed through and was able to throw a second rope around the drowned boy.

He shimmied backwards off the ice while the men began to tug at the rope. As they pulled the boy free, they saw that one leg had been torn off in the explosion. A few of the men retched at the sight. The others carefully spread a blanket on the snow and laid the boy in its centre. They swaddled him tenderly and carried him as though he were yet a sleeping child.

Chapter Thirty-Two: Aftermath

The ladies of the village had divided themselves into two groups and begun the process of providing care and succour to the Meachams and the Smiths. Pies and stews and biscuits and soup were prepared daily and delivered to both households. Some ladies took the Meacham children home to be with their own; others took turns sitting with Charley while she stared vacantly around her bedroom. Doctor Barrow visited both women and supplied powders to help them sleep.

The employees of Lamith Bricks did not return to work. With Alistair in Buffalo and Brodie in no state to make decisions, they decided to halt production until at least one of their masters was able to provide direction. Patrick offered to tend the livestock but the rest of the crew were dispirited and felt unable to continue with their routines.

Justus Ketchum and Admiral Barnes knew the men felt rudderless and discussed the situation at length, believing that no good would come of such moroseness. They visited Brodie in an attempt to elicit some instruction from him, but he seemed unable to focus on their words and did not respond in a sentient way to any of their pointed inquiries. Finally, after much debate, they sent a telegram to Callaghan Steel in Buffalo.

ALISTAIR LAMONT STOP EXPLOSION AT BRICKWORKS STOP RETURN HOME STOP

Alistair was meeting with Daniel Callaghan to review the ropeway schematics when a secretary knocked on the door. Walking into the room, she said, *Excuse me, sir, there's a telegram for Mr. Lamont.* Alistair stood and reached for the extended piece of paper. He read the message twice before passing it to Callaghan.

Callaghan looked at him. *Are you all right?*

I wonder what has happened.

Were they blasting?

No. But there was some trouble with methane a while back.

You should go, son. Send me word when you can.

Alistair swept up the papers and stuffed them into his valise. *I'll come back, sir, when I have a chance, to finish our business.*

Of course, I understand. Go.

There should be a train this evening.

I'll give your regrets to the ladies.

Alistair hesitated briefly. *Yes. I had forgotten about this evening. Please extend my apologies.*

Alistair returned to the hotel, threw his belongings into his bag, then strode to the post office to sent a telegram to Justus Ketchum.

RETURNING TONIGHT STOP

He did not know what else to say. Why hadn't Brodie telephoned directly? A telephone had recently been installed at the mercantile and one at the hotel. He imagined a hundred things that could have happened. A kiln explosion. A barn fire. He cursed his friend for not having sent more details. Perhaps someone had been hurt in the explosion? Maybe one of the workers? Maybe several of the workers? Maybe the animals? Had they lost their buildings? The not-knowing was unbearable for Alistair, who found himself walking at a furious pace up the street and towards the art gallery.

The train wouldn't be leaving for several hours yet and he needed to find a way to occupy himself. He resolved to walk through the building slowly, to look at the art itself, not merely the structure. An unbidden thought came to him: Violet would be pleased. Under entirely different circumstances he'd have been happy to report his visit to her.

As it was, he found the gallery empty and cold. His footsteps echoed sharply. He stared at paintings but the colours seemed to blur into one another until everything became shapeless and unrecognizable. He was sure he was missing some key to understanding, but he couldn't fathom what it was. Resigned to feeling frustrated and inadequate, he sank down on a bench and stared gloomily out the window to the park.

Alistair heard her laughter before anyone entered the gallery. He stood and prepared to greet Miss Lewis and whomever else was escorting her. The day could not get any worse, he thought. The very person he felt least capable of facing was now approaching.

Mr. Lamont! How lovely to see you. An unexpected pleasure. Violet walked towards him with her hand extended. He held it lightly and bowed.

She was wearing one of her grown-up outfits, in softly coloured pink with fragile-looking material and lace, her hair pinned up neatly in tiny curls and twists. Alistair preferred her as he'd first seen her, with her hair dishevelled and in plain, comfortable-looking clothes. He supposed that this more adult and sophisticated appearance must be attributable to Mr. William Tremont. Her manner was, as always, warm and intimate.

My goodness, Mr. Lamont. I believed you were to be in meetings all week with my father and his friends. I heard that you and Mr. Smith have been planning something of vast interest and that the men are anticipating great things.

You flatter me, Miss Lewis. I assure you it is no so grand as you have imagined.

Taking his arm, she led him back to a seat on the bench. *Then will you not tell me about it yourself? I will listen and not interrupt.*

Alistair waited for her to be seated and then bowed formally. *You must excuse me, Miss Lewis, I've had a telegram and must now depart.*

Miss Lewis stood at his words. *Herbert has driven me in the motorcar. I can't ride my bicycle in this weather, you see. He's waiting right outside. Let us drive you to your hotel. It will save you time.*

I wouldna wish to impose. You have only just arrived. I must take my leave.

Mr. Lamont, that is nonsense! Surely you wouldn't insult a friend by refusing such an offer. She came closer and linked her arm in his, looking up into his troubled face. *I insist upon it. I will be affronted if you refuse.*

Alistair nodded and docilely submitted to her lead. Since arriving in Buffalo, he'd found that merely being in the same city with her had unsettled him. He knew she was all but betrothed, and yet some part of him couldn't be reconciled to the knowledge. As they were being driven to the hotel, she reached across the seat and took his hand. *Mr. Lamont,* she said, *I understand from Father that Mr. Smith has been married.*

Yes. They are well suited.

Is Mrs. Smith someone I might know?

No. She's a widow from the area. You wouldna have met her.

I see. Violet was quiet.

Alistair coloured afresh. His breathing began to feel constricted. He looked out the window of the automobile, hoping they were nearing the hotel. *And where is Mr. Tremont today?*

We're to meet again this evening at Delaware Park. He's visiting some gentlemen on a matter related to the Congress. I am sorry that you won't be joining us skating.

I am no much for skating, Miss Lewis, as you know. He handed her the telegram. *This is my business. I'm anxious to hear that my friends are safe, and to see what damage has occurred.*

She read the paper and returned it to him. *I am sorry for your troubles, Mr. Lamont.*

I wish you and Mr. Tremont every good fortune. At this he knocked on the window glass and asked the driver to stop. *I will walk to my hotel from here. Thank you for the ride.*

Alistair stumbled from the motorcar and tipped his hat as it pulled away. His last glimpse of Miss Lewis was her astonished face peering at him from the back window. He felt despondent, and yet was somehow strangely elated as well.

Chapter Thirty-Three: Alistair's Return
Braemor, Ontario ~ February 22, 1910

Alistair stepped onto the little platform at Braemor and looked around expectantly. Despite the late hour, it was unlike Brodie not to greet him when he arrived back from a journey. Alistair tried to convince himself that this was not a particularly bad omen. *The man's just been married,* he said to himself. *He's as like tucked up in bed with his pretty wife and will see me in the morning.* But still, the feeling lingered that all was not as it should be. Gathering his overnight bag and valise, Alistair began the short walk to the village. He would borrow a horse from the hotel, he thought.

Justus Ketchum was easily aroused—he'd been snoozing comfortably by the fire but stood immediately when he heard the door. As Alistair moved forward to greet him he was struck straight away by Justus's solemn look.

Do you know what has happened? asked Alistair. *I received a telegram.*

It was I that sent it, Alistair. And Admiral Barnes. We thought it right that you should know.

Have we lost the brickworks? Was Brodie injured? He didna meet me at the train.

Sit down.

Alistair threw himself into a chair, impatient to hear the tale. Justus Ketchum walked to the sideboard, filled a glass with whisky, and brought it to him.

Drink this first. It will warm you.

Alistair downed the drink in one long swig. *Tell me.*

It happened down by the river. It seems that Kyran Meacham had been using a pick to loosen the clay and he must have hit a methane pocket. He was killed in the explosion. So too was Johnny Gowan.

Kyran killed?!

And Johnny.

Both of them?!

Yes.

Alistair groaned, standing up directly and walking across the room. *Anyone else?*

No.

And Brodie?

Beside himself with grief. And Charlotte. And Kyran's wife. The doctor has seen to them.

And the rest o' the men?

They are at loose ends with no work to do and no will to do it.

Do they blame us?

There has been no talk of it. Brodie takes on all the blame for himself.

What's to be done?

Justus sat down heavily. *I can't say that I know, Alistair. It will all take time.*

Can I borrow a horse?

Stay the night. There's a room ready upstairs. Everyone will be in their beds. I'll get you a horse in the morning.

Alistair, suddenly very weary, reluctantly accepted the offer. Once upstairs, he sank down heavily upon the bed. The news was far worse than anything he could have imagined. Without undressing, he stretched out flat and thought about what he'd been told. He thought, too, about the aerial tramway, and his visit to Buffalo, and Miss Lewis, and custom cables, and Mr. Tremont, and the awfulness of everything overwhelmed him until finally he closed his eyes to shut out the grief and simply lay there waiting for daybreak.

In the morning, Alistair swallowed down several pieces of toast and tea. He borrowed a horse as soon as Justus had one readied, and rode straight to the Gowan farm. When Brodie opened the door Alistair was taken aback by the look of him. He embraced his friend and the two men held each other briefly without speaking.

Alistair stepped back and said, *You look loused and you reek.* Brodie turned then and walked slowly towards the kitchen, Alistair right behind him. Brodie sat down at the table and shrugged.

Where's Charley?

Upstairs, Brodie said woodenly.

Brodie, we would change things if we could but we canna. I'm as sorry as can be.

Aye.

Have you been to the Meachams'?

We carried him back home.

I should go.

Aye.

Will you tell Charley I was here?

Aye. Brodie's eyes were red-rimmed and filled with tears just waiting to spill over.

Brodie, you must try to hold yourself together. Charley will have need of you.

Yes.

I'll be back once I've seen to some things. Alistair left Brodie sitting morosely at the table, awkwardly holding a cold pipe in his gauze-wrapped hands. He had never seen his friend so passive. It was unnerving. Brodie sat quietly after his friend left, remembering the voices that had taunted him in childhood. *Murtherer.*

Alistair's visit to the Meacham house was equally difficult. Unlike the stillness of the Smith household, the Meacham's was filled with women and children of all sizes and description, talking and crying and shushing one another in desperate pandemonium. Alistair could not tell which of them belonged to Kyran and which were merely stopping in. Kyran's wife was seated, apron over her face, in the front room, where a crudely made casket was now positioned on two rows of facing chairs. When she removed the apron Alistair saw that she was yet young and still very pretty, despite her forlorn expression and tear-swollen face.

I am sorry for your loss. Kyran was a good man. We will miss him.

Mrs. Meacham looked up at Alistair sorrowfully. *Thank you for coming. He was partial to you and Mr. Brodie.*

When the burying is at an end, I'll come back and we can say what is to be done.

I don't know how we'll manage.

The brickworks will take care of the funeral expense. We can talk further another time.

Thank you, Mr. Alistair, I'm grateful to be sure.

Alistair bowed and excused himself hastily. He could not bear to remain a moment longer in Kyran's house with his lovely wife and the swarms of children. The grief and the overwhelming sense of responsibility weighed upon him.

It was a mild day and he rode home briskly; his first thought had been to check on the livestock, unsure whether anyone had remembered to care for them. He saw when he arrived that he need not have worried—the sheep and horses were well tended. After depositing his valise and bag in the house, he started up the woodstove to warm himself before taking a walk to the river.

The snowy field heavily littered with debris was marked by many footsteps and signs of great activity. As Alistair neared the gentle hill leading to the embankment, he got his first glimpse of the destruction. The crater was at least a hundred feet wide and the explosion had blown away a large section of the natural riverbank. The convergence of the Brae River and the River Mor now pooled inland before continuing a rapid coursing to the south. Cautiously, Alistair made his way closer and stared in horror at the upturned trees, the mass of wreckage, the gritty mixture of earth and stone that covered everything in a dirty thick powdering. The strong acrid smell of fire lingered, and as Alistair nudged objects with his boot he made out the remains of charred branches and planks and other materials he could not recognize. He found himself wondering how safe it would be to continue excavating for clay. Was this the end of their venture? Would any of the men even agree to return to work?

The devastation he saw brought home what had happened and filled Alistair with deep despair. Kyran had been a favourite, always ready with a joke or a smile, always willing to give something a go. He'd been with them since early on. And Alistair himself had hired Johnny; he'd held his small hands in his own and declared they were not yet ready for a man's work. And their trip to Toronto—Johnny had been so taken with the hotel and the train ride and the motorcars on the street. He'd spoken of it for weeks until everyone in Braemor knew every detail.

How would Charley recover? How would Brodie? He'd never seen his friend in such a state. And how to even begin to repair the damage? And what of the tramway? Should they abandon their plans or forge ahead? Alistair turned and made his way slowly back to the house. He would need to sort these things. In time, he thought, everything in its time.

When he walked in the front door he encountered an unexpected sight: Brodie, seated in his regular chair at the table. He looked as he had earlier in the day, unshaven and unkempt and completely miserable.

Brodie. I am surprised to see you.

I thought as I might come and pass the time wi' you.

How's Charley?

Above stairs. She willna come down. The ladies are with her.

Have you eaten?

A whisky.

Will you have tea? I will put the kettle on.

Something stronger?

I'll no begrudge you a wee dram, Brodie, but I think you've already had more than what's good for you. It willna fix what's been broke, or replace what's been lost. Alistair poured him a finger, put it down before him, then sat down at the table across from his friend. *We've work to do, Brodie. And I can set out on my own to do what's needing done, or you can help. But I'd no be a friend of your'n if I left you bladdered when Charley needs you and the men are looking to us.*

Brodie had already emptied the glass. *It's my fault, Al. Do you see?* He sank his head into his hands and began to cry. Alistair waited uncomfortably until the sobs had abated.

You think it. But no one blames you.

Charley does.

No! I dinna believe it. Did she say?

It's true, Alistair. She doesna say but I can tell by the way she looks at me. She blames me. She blames me, and I blame me.

Dinna talk pish.

I should have protected him. Brodie began to choke down more sobs. The sound of it pained Alistair.

Alistair got up from the table and paced the small kitchen. *It's no your fault, Brodie. It's no your fault. But your duty now is to comfort his Ma. You need go home and bide your time with her. There's grieving to be done, and you best be doing it together.*

Brodie poured himself another whisky and drank it down in one desperate gulp. Placing the glass carefully on the table, he repositioned it with his forefinger as though aligning it to some invisible demarcation on the surface.

Alistair, the truth is, I'm cursed. And my father before me was cursed. They called me murtherer at school. And now it has come to pass.

Brodie, you're talking shite, and if you were no half so bladdered you would know it.

Al, I tell you true. It wakes me up nights and I walk the floor. I canna sleep and the nerves take over. There's the feeling of bugs on my skin and I have trouble breathing, and I'm drenched all over.

Everyone has trouble in the night a time or two. I've seen you pacing here in this very room. But it's no a curse or a blight you bring.

No, Al? Then tell me what it is. Tell me why Kyran and Johnny died. They died because I didna protect them. I should have seen to the gas and stopped the digging. And I canna rest easy for knowing it. And Charley, she doesna want me, Al. The sight of me makes her sorrow fresh.

Momentarily confounded, Alistair sat down across from his friend. *Brodie, I dinna know a thing about being married but I do ken this. A man has to keep his word. And you made a vow to stand by her. You must help her get the grieving out.*

She canna stand the look of me, Al, I can see it.

Hate you or love you, you're joined together before the Almighty. She as like hates the world now but that will come right again.

Moving to the door, Alistair collected Brodie's coat and brought it to him. *The Bard says, Love is not love which alters when it alteration finds. You best be away home, my friend. That's the only advice I can give and it's no for lack of caring. God knows.*

Chapter Thirty-Four: After the Funerals

Braemor, Ontario ~ March 7, 1910

The weeks following the explosion passed in a haze of sadness and the unpleasant business of death. Kyran's wake lasted three days. The removal preceding the funeral was cause for another unhappy occasion, followed by the funeral itself, and then the burial, and then another series of long visits at the Meacham house. Alistair attended every one of these events, ensuring that the whisky flowed freely and the priest was paid.

The visitation for Johnny was informal, with neighbours and friends merely dropping in to check on the couple and to pay their respects. Johnny's funeral was held at the white church. School had been dismissed for the afternoon so that his friends could attend. Johnny was buried in the small churchyard beside his father's grave. It was decided that Charley was too unwell to have people back to the house, and so Alistair arranged for the hotel to provide refreshments for the mourners.

Brodie was unusually tender and demonstrative with his friend—thanking him profusely for everything, weeping in his arms at the slightest provocation. Alistair began to worry that Johnny's death had broken him in a way that might not be healed. And so he endeavoured, however clumsily and whenever possible, to engage Brodie in discussions about the tramway, the spur line, and whatever else he could think of, hoping in this manner to rekindle a spark of interest in something. He noted with concern that Charley and Brodie continued to seem distant and disconnected. Brodie's appearance was also much altered. His face, normally clean-shaven, now sported a beard that was patchy and unkempt. Most alarming was the way his clothes hung upon him and the broad streak of white that had suddenly appeared in his hair.

Alistair had lately remembered to send a letter to Daniel Callaghan informing him as to the details of the explosion. In it, he enclosed Brodie's lists of materials and asked that Daniel, take it upon himself to procure all that was needed for the towers and to ship the materials by train. He had since received a telegram in reply:

REQUEST STOP UNDERTAKING DETAILS ON YOUR BEHALF STOP EXTREMELY SORRY FOR YOUR LOSS STOP WILL COM-MUNICATE FURTHER LATER STOP

Alistair was relieved. Even as he sorted out what next needed to happen, the tramway could progress. And despite his fears, the men, bless them all, had returned to the brickworks. He set them to work on the new building for the manufacture of bricks, not daring to ask that they return to the river. He worried that come spring, when brickmaking would recommence, the river might not be seen as a source of safe material. He could not share this worry with anyone, especially not Brodie, but neither did he want to alarm the crew, many of whom he suspected were mor-bidly superstitious.

The dilemma of the Meacham family, too, weighed heavily upon Alistair. With three children to care for and a fourth com-ing soon, the widow was in a sorry way. He had since arranged with the landlord to pay for two months' rent but he knew he could not undertake to do this in perpetuity. One evening he called on Mrs. Meacham, handing her an envelope filled with what he said was Kyran's outstanding wages. She slipped it, with her thanks, into an apron pocket.

Broaching the subject awkwardly, Alistair began. *Have you any family about?*

Mrs. Meacham looked up at him shyly. *I do. A brother in Barrie. He works on the steamboat.*

And is he a family man?

His wife, Mary, passed last year.

Would he welcome you and the little ones, do you think? You could may be keep house for him?

Mrs. Meacham looked only slightly startled by the suggestion. *I been thinking. Paddy was always kind. I never been to visit. Tis a long way.*

Does he know about Kyran?

She shook her head faintly and became once more tremulous, her pale skin suddenly blotched, tears beginning to fall.

Shall I write him for you?

How would we git away?

Dinna worry. I'll see to the details. Give me his name and address and I will write.

Mrs. Meacham excused herself and went upstairs, stopping along the way to scoop up and embrace the smallest of her three children who was sitting on the floor. She returned carrying a letter from her brother with his address on the envelope. Alistair promised to return it later in the week. He was greatly relieved to know that there was family. Had she been without any relatives he would have been sore put to know best how to help. As it was, the letter was soon written and posted; Alistair hoped for a good result.

That evening, as he did every evening, Alistair rode over to the Smith farm. It was, as had become usual, a glum visit. Charley was yet above stairs and Brodie was in the kitchen, brooding by himself.

I thought you might like to know that Mrs. Meacham has a brother in Barrie, Alistair said. *I've written to see whether he'll accept protection of her and the brood. He's a widower—so I'm hopeful that he may agree to having her keep house.*

Brodie looked up with a blank stare. *Why is that good news?*

She'll be cared for and protected, and the little ones will have a home.

But he'll have the expense o' a family not his own.

Family does that for family. I imagine they all eat like little birds.

Still. It's an expense.

I've offered to drive them myself in the wagon. Then I can be certain they're in a good situation. Kyran would like that.

You canna Al. You're unmarried. It wouldna be proper travelling so far on the road with a widow.

How else can we get her there with all her belongings and the progeny?

Ask one of the men.

Och, aye, they would do it. And be glad too. How are you today?

Charley is still upstairs. She lies in bed or sits in Johnny's room. She'll no come down and eats nary a thing.

That canna go on, Brodie. What does the doctor say?

Only that grief takes time.

And are you looking after yourself?

The women have made us soup and biscuits. I had pie for lunch. There's a piece left. Do you want some?

You look rough, Brodie, and I'm concerned.

Calm yourself. I'm fine. Better than I deserve.

You must no blame yourself.

I knew there was methane in the area and I should have hammered in more pipes and run more tests. And Johnny, do you know, only the week before, he asked if he could call me Pa? What kind of Pa lets his boy get blown up and leaves him in the river two days? It's no wonder Charley hates me. I hate me.

Brodie, that's pish. No one could have been more careful than you about the gas. You showed us how to test for it. And had the bank shored with planks, and were clear with the men many times about safety. No one blames you.

I'm no better than my father before me.

You're no meaning the Tay Bridge, are you?

Brodie nodded. *I was ashamed o' my father. I dinna even use his name, Al.*

It was no the fault o' one man, as you yourself have said.

Aye. There were problems with the steel fabrication. And they hadn't compensated for wind force, and the footings weren't sunk on bedrock... There were a host of problems. But it was my father drove that train into the Tay and that's what people remember.

Brodie, the Tay Bridge has naught to do with the explosion and you are no to blame for either of them.

I'm an engineer. It has to be someone's responsibility. Someone has to say, Look at me, I'll take the blame. That's the way of it.

It's progress, Brodie. With every advance, there is always a cost. Sometimes it's jobs, and sometimes it's a way of life, and sometimes it's

people. *That is the price we pay for advancement. We have spoken o'
this before.*

That was afore we lost both Kyran and Johnny.

Chapter Thirty-Five: Working Machinery
Braemor, Ontario ~ March 16, 1910

While Brodie remained at home, Alistair and the men had followed his plans in the construction of the two-storey manufacturing building, with its two wide earthen ramps. They took advantage of the frozen ground to create a polished icy surface leading to the lower level; that way, with the use of ropes and with some effort, they were able to slide the new machinery into place. Despite recent losses, they felt a little celebratory. Alistair passed around his flask and the men shared it out, each partaking in a small swallow.

I see where te clay and shale goes in, said Sean, *but those knives will break if te stone hits te blade.*

The others murmured in agreement.

Alistair saw what Sean was concerned about but did not have a ready answer.

Will Brodie know how to replace te blades?

If anyone can figure it, Mr. Brodie will.

Do we start using et now or keep wi' te old ways?

I say we do both an see which is the faster.

I bet on Sean. The men chuckled at this, for Sean was always moving and jumping from one thing to another, with the men calling out such things to him as *Yer like a blue-arsed fly, never settlin'.*

Now, said Alistair, *I have something to say. I've heard from Mrs. Meacham's brother in Barrie. He is willing to have his sister and the children come to him. He's a widower and will be glad to have her keep house. But he's no a wealthy man and canna spare time away to come for her. Brodie and I have spoken, and we are proposing to pay one o' you to drive her. It will be a hard two-day journey on the road.* He paused briefly. *Kyran would like that we do this, I think.*

The men talked softly among themselves, agreeing with Alistair about Kyran and remembering afresh the upset of the explosion. The consensus was that their employers were being kind.

I can do it, said Thomas. *I reckon a couple of nights from 'ome will do te missus good. She'll be waiting for me when I get back, if ya know what I'm saying.*

A few of the men chortled. *Jaysus, yer a mad bastard.*

She's already got four tied to her apron. Your time has long passed, mate.

Well, lad, if it's a man she's needin', I offer me services, said Patrick, thrusting his hips forward suggestively.

Wat do ya mean by that? snapped an indignant Thomas.

I'm only saying she's a pretty miss, an I will step up te oblige her, like.

Thomas threw himself at Patrick and the two set to fighting angrily, the others looking on in surprise. Thomas got in a heavy blow to Patrick's face—they all heard the crack as his nose broke and blood began to stream out.

Enough, lads! shouted Alistair. *It was only meant in fun.* He forced himself between the two combatants while the other men held back the still swinging Thomas.

Patrick slumped to the floor. *'e broke me nose,* he said incredulously. *Te fecken eejit 'as broke me nose.*

It was an inauspicious way to end the day's proceedings. Alistair, feeling suddenly like a schoolmarm from his youth, insisted that the two shake hands. Then he sent the entire lot home early. He was exhausted from the drama and could not thole the thought of making one more decision. It was at times like this when he most missed Brodie.

Alistair trudged back to the farm and tended to his duties there. Without Johnny to carry out the simple barn chores, he found his days had been lengthened. He would need to reassign the men's duties or hire someone else—he couldn't continue to do all of Brodie's work and Johnny's both. He felt sore exhausted by the time he was finished.

He placed an open tin of baked beans in a pot of boiling water, buttering a couple of thick slices of bread and readying a mug of hot sweet tea as he waited for the beans to warm up. Then, tipping the beans onto his plate, he sat down at the table thoughtfully, reflecting on the events of the day and trying to steel himself for his evening visit to the Smiths. He was just tucking in when the door swung open and Brodie himself walked in.

Alistair greeted him and reached for another plate. Having divided his portion neatly into two, he sat down with his friend to share his dinner. Brodie began to shovel in the food. *It's good,* he said. *I've missed your cooking.*

Alistair nodded. *I'll make more.* He opened another tin, plunked it into the pot of still boiling water, cut more slices of bread, and began to regale Brodie with the events of the day, concluding with the punch-up between Thomas and Patrick. He wasted no detail in the telling and was delighted to see the faint whisper of a smile on Brodie's lips. Alistair left unasked his many concerns. Instead he talked on merrily as though nothing had wearied him and all was well. He and Brodie finished the beans and then ate an entire loaf of bread, slathered in butter and brown sugar.

If you have a mind, said Alistair, *we could take lamps and have a look at the machine. The men are eager to see it working.*

Brodie nodded. *It needs power, though. We canna try it tonight.*

No, but we can may be check that everything is as it should be, and try it tomorrow.

You want to make bricks in this weather?

No. But the men would like to see the machine up and running, Brodie. It would give them a lift.

They took up lanterns and traversed the distance to the new building, where they opened the lower-level doors. Placing his lantern on the floor, Brodie walked slowly around the brickmaking machine, now and then thrusting his shoulder into the side of it to see if it would budge with his weight. Running his hands up and down the apparatus, he checked that all the joints were flush and the fittings tight.

I didna bring the manual, he said. *We need to check this in the daylight and make certain all the pieces are in place. A steam engine is what is really needed.*

But it will work with horse power.

Aye, but steam is the thing.

Brodie tilted his head from side to side, as though considering something serious. *And I think we should fasten it down. Once it's filled with clay it may jump around a bit even though it feels solid now. We dinna want it to work loose.*

Alistair nodded.

It looks good, Al. We can try it tomorrow. I'll come by at noon.

The men will be pleased to see you.

I need to turn my hand to summit.

They returned to the house but at the front door Brodie stopped and handed Alistair his lantern. *I won't come in. I should get back.*

Will Charley mind you coming out tomorrow?

She willna notice.

Brodie led his horse from the barn, hitched it to the cutter and climbed in, raising his hand in a cursory wave.

As Alistair readied himself for bed he thought about the morning to come. Tomorrow was the Meachams' moving day. The ladies in town had been packing the household, and he'd promised to help Thomas load the wagon early. Anticipating much emotion and confusion, he was not looking forward to the upset. The words to a Psalm came to him, *What is man, that thou art mindful of him?*

Although the *Almanac* had promised fair weather, a fine snow was falling when Alistair awoke. He cursed the sight—he'd need more tarps and ropes and blankets for the wagon than he thought, and now he'd have to make another visit to the mercantile. He dressed rapidly and harnessed the wagon; two horses would be needed to draw it.

Just as he'd predicted, the Meacham house was bedlam. Children wrapped in layers of clothing sat bundled together on the stairs. Half-filled crates spilled pots and pans and bedding.

Pieces of furniture were everywhere. Chairs and trunks lined the street in front of the house. Meanwhile, baskets of baked buns and pies were being carried in and deposited on every surface. Alistair was ready to howl with frustration. When Thomas arrived—neither man making reference to his two black eyes and the cut on his cheek—the two attempted to create some order in the chaos but were subverted at every turn. Finally Alistair stomped down the street to the mercantile, grateful for the relative quiet of the shop and the opportunity to air his grievances to Admiral Barnes, who listened sympathetically, then offered up a solution.

Send them to the hotel for breakfast, he said. *Get rid of the lot of them. Then you and Thomas can do what needs doing without the others underfoot.*

After purchasing some additional tarps and rope, Alistair ran back to the Meachams. He and Thomas herded all and sundry out the door and down the street to the hotel. *Tell Justus Ketchum, I'll pay. And stay there warm until we come for you!*

Assessing the mess, the two men seized control and loaded the wagon as efficiently as they could, leaving room for the travellers and baskets of ready foodstuffs. Without interference, the work was soon done; next they drove the wagon the short piece to the hotel to collect the passengers. There were many tears as the Meachams climbed aboard with Thomas. Once Alistair had passed him a small roll of notes to cover expenses, he and Justus Ketchum and Admiral Barnes and the assembled neighbours stood by to wave them on their journey. Alistair returned once more to the hotel to settle the bill, but Justus wouldn't take his money.

It's well you have done, Alistair. I will cover the breakfast.

Alistair, embarrassed, thanked him all the same. Finally he made his way back to the brickworks, where Patrick, his face bruised and swollen, feigned a lack of interest in the departing travellers. Brodie had been there some time already—for by now, at his direction, the men had bolted the machine to a raised wooden crib to house the footings, thus making it impossible to shift or dislodge it. Alistair thought Brodie looked slightly calmer and tidier this day. He was relieved to see his friend making an effort.

Braemor, Ontario ~ March 19, 1910

Brodie was having difficulty breathing. Another in a succession of nervous attacks had woken him from a deep sleep. He sat upright on the uncomfortable pallet, perspiring, gulping air, trying to focus. He was never sure what contributed to such events, but when he experienced them they felt so encompassing that he was sure he would suffocate from lack of breath. He had suffered from these episodes since adolescence.

A doctor he once consulted told him they came from deep-rooted fears. This made sense to Brodie; he found that identifying their source was some help. Over the years he had discovered that worry made them far worse.

He got up and looked in on Charley. Sleeping soundly, he saw, with deep, even breaths. Brodie shut the door, crept downstairs, and began to pace the hallway between the kitchen and the parlour, attempting to regulate his breathing and to calm himself.

When he lived with Alistair he'd taken great comfort in staying up through the night talking out their troubles and worries. These talks were frequently accompanied by whisky, a combination that had contributed to his eventual sleep. He felt the need of a drink now but did not want to upset Charley should she discover it.

Instead, Brodie returned to the box room he'd claimed as his own and tried to settle. Beside him on the floor was the wooden case his uncle Hamish had sent after his mother's death. Inside was the arrowhead from the Genesee River, pieces of his mother's jewellery, and a sheaf of yellowed newspaper clippings about the Tay Bridge disaster. The papers were old and frail, and curled limply in his hands when he held them.

Also inside, kept in secret, was Johnny's plaid woollen cap. Patrick had passed it to him after they'd brought Johnny home. Brodie had instinctively placed the cap inside his vest, not wanting to distress Charley with it. It had rested there, a sad talisman, for two days; Brodie had not the heart to remove it. When Alistair told him he reeked, he knew he needed fresh clothes and a bath. And so for some reason, not fully understood, he had hidden it in the box, keeping it entirely for himself.

Five days later Thomas returned from Barrie; Mrs. Meacham and the children, he told Alistair, were now safely established in her brother's house. On his return journey, though, Thomas had been caught in a surprise snowstorm with no shelter in sight and had lost his way. Having decided to wait out the storm, he tied the horses to a tree and slept beneath the wagon with a small fire to keep himself warm. He allowed that several wagon boards would need replacing as there was no other kindling to be found.

Alistair reassured Thomas that he'd done well, that his life was likely worth the price of a broken wagon. *As long as it's no too badly broken,* he added. The men all laughed at this and resumed their work.

Alistair was relieved that Mrs. Meacham's plight had been so readily addressed. He'd wondered what they would have done had she not had family. This troubled him—he felt responsible for his workers, and wanted to emulate Callaghan's model as a kind employer. When he walked home at the end of that day and came within sight of his squat farmhouse nestled snugly in the winter fields, he thought to himself that housing really was the challenge for the poor. If there had been a house for the Meachams to live in rent-free, her living expenses would have been modest and easily covered by some part-time occupation. The thought took hold, and as he prepared his evening meal, Alistair considered its implications.

He was washing up the plates when Brodie walked in.

I've just finished dinner. Can I make you some oatmeal?

Well, I am hungry. I dinna think I've eaten today.

What have you been doing with yourself? I thought we might see you at the site.

No. I stayed in with Charley. She's still abed. Doctor Barrow came. He said it was low spirits.

Is she eating?

Hattie Carruthers comes over every day and tries to feed her but she hasna had much success. A spoonful o' broth. A forkful o' pudding.

It's early days yet.

It's a month, Al. She's no been downstairs.

Alistair poured milk into the pot and tipped in some oatmeal. He stirred this with a wooden spoon then left it to sit while he cut slabs of bread and, in deference to Brodie's sweet tooth, put the cream jug and a small pot of brown sugar on the table.

Is she trying to starve herself?

She doesna care. She just sleeps and lies abed.

Alistair was now stirring the oatmeal.

You're going to have to shake her out o' it, Brodie. Give her a reason to get up. It canna be good for her to lie still.

What can I do?

Pick her up and carry her downstairs and make her talk to you. Let her cry and scream at you if she still has that in her. Let her get it all out and not poison herself with the grief all stoppered inside.

D'ya ken?

I do. She's no getting better lying above stairs. Now's the time for you to help her, Brodie.

Alistair tipped the oatmeal into a large bowl and served his friend. *Now eat up and have a visit, and then go home and set a new routine. She's no made of glass, Brodie, and willna break if you move her. It's hert-sair, she is.*

Brodie dug into the meal, *you're right, Al. Something has to change.*

I've been thinking on something else, Brodie. About what we would have done for Mrs. Meacham if her brother hadna agreed to take her.

Is Thomas back?

Yes. This afternoon. He was caught in a storm and had to sleep one night under the wagon.

He's well?

Yes, but no so much the wagon. He burned some o' the planks and it will need repair.

Brodie nodded. *And Mrs. Meacham?*

Thomas says that the brother pulled her down from the wagon with a great embrace. They seemed very fond of one another and he feels they'll make out well.

What were you thinking?

Well, only that we would have had a situation if her brother had no taken her. I was thinking about houses for our workers. What if we took the piece of land north o' the sheep pasture and built a short row of cottages? We could rent them for a small amount to anyone who works for us or is widowed or disabled and has anything to do with Lamith Bricks. Then, if there is another accident, God forbid it, we could establish them here on the property and look after them at very little expense.

So, we are to become landlords?

Benefactors, more like. There would be more charity than profit involved.

It's a good idea, Al. Let's think on it. Timing may be the thing. We've the new machine to get geared up and the tramway to build. And I've no done anything to help for a month. We should be out there getting more orders for bricks.

You need to focus on Charley. That is your priority. Callaghan is sending the steel for the towers. When that comes you'll need to direct the men.

And orders for bricks?

Why not hire a salesman? We could send him around with samples and he could take orders for us. Then we can be freed up to stay here and do what's already on our plates.

How can we take on more men? There's been no money coming in since the sale to Martyndale. And there's the steel to pay for.

We've enough to cover the next three months. And if we hired a salesman we wouldna need to worry about sales.

How much would we pay him?

A small commission.

Ah.

Not long afterwards, once Brodie had left, Alistair went out to do a last check on the sheep, to ensure that everything was fastened tightly and that their trough still held open water. It had been a full moon, and the wolves and coyotes had been howling and yipping with especial vigour the last few nights.

There were no lights on in the house when Brodie arrived home. Entering the kitchen, he lit some lamps and carried one upstairs to check on Charley. She was in the dark, lying awake in bed.

Charley?

No response.

Charley? Can you hear me?

Yes.

I think it's time you came downstairs.

No response.

Charley?

No response.

Charley, I'm begging you. Talk to me.

Nothing.

Charley, I'm going to put the lantern down and I'm going to pick you up and carry you downstairs.

No response. Brodie set the lantern on a table.

Then he went over to the bed and pulled back the quilts. He was shocked by the emaciated look of her. She had the form of a much older woman. Bending down, he scooped her in his arms. She hung there limply and he sobbed as he felt her bones sharp against him. Gently he carried her downstairs and lowered her into a chair beside the stove. Then he wrapped her carefully in quilts so that only her face was uncovered.

She was utterly placid, staring blankly ahead.

There's some soup in the pot, he said. *I'm going to warm it up and feed you some.*

She shook her head.

I am. I will warm it up and you will eat it. I'll be damned if I let you starve.

Brodie lit the stove and set the pot in place. He readied a bowl and spoon and stirred the soup. He concentrated on his task, praying that Alistair's approach was the right course of action. Nothing else seemed to be working, he reasoned. Even the doctor had more or less given up. Kept saying it would take time. Bloody hell, there'd be nothing left of her.

When the soup was ready, Brodie ladled a small portion into the bowl. Then he carried an armchair through from the parlour. Moving this chair very close to the table, he lifted Charley and all her covers and sat down in the armchair with her on his lap. In this way she was secure and snug against him, and he began to spoon the soup into her mouth. She parted her lips obediently and swallowed slowly. Brodie said not a word. He just kept feeding her soup until the bowl was emptied.

He put down the spoon and she rested her head against his shoulder. He kept her there, pressed against him quietly, for some long time. Finally, afraid she may be growing uncomfortable, he asked, *Would you like to go back upstairs now?*

She nodded, and so he carried her back to the room they had only briefly shared. Brodie pulled up a chair beside Charley's bed and sat with her until she closed her eyes. He didn't know whether she was sleeping or simply too weary to keep her eyes open. He stayed watching her for several minutes and then, kissing her lightly on the forehead, blew out the lantern and left the room.

Not wanting to disturb her, he'd been sleeping on a pallet of folded quilts in the box room. He supposed he should ask Alistair to bring him his bed from the farm but was not yet willing to accept that this arrangement might become a permanent one. Without undressing, he lay down on the pallet and pulled his coat and a thin blanket over himself. Lying there, he reflected on the last few months and wondered how it was that life could hold such extreme happiness and good fortune in the one moment and be so utterly wretched in the next. His life with Charley and Johnny had been so happy, so flush with promise, and then it had all vanished.

Alistair was the only one in his life whom Brodie felt he could completely rely on. He was shouldering their shared responsibilities at the brickworks, and was thinking about ways to be helpful to people in the community with his housing scheme, and had given him the only advice that had worked, so far, with Charley. He was a rare friend. Brodie clung to the thought of him as he rolled over and tried to sleep.

CHAPTER THIRTY-SEVEN: RAILWAY LINES
Braemor, Ontario ~ March 21, 1910

Alistair sat up long after Brodie had left. Despite the assurances he'd given him, their finances were troubling. He'd seen his father's house and brickyards disappear at public auction—something that had left him with a lasting fear of debts and loans and mortgages. So much of their venture depended on their working together, and with one man down he worried he was missing something or not attending to things in their proper order of importance. Spring lambing was about to start, according to Patrick, and there would likely be all manner of sheep jobs needing attention. Patrick had asked him to order sheep dip a while back, along with two pairs of shears, and in the confusion he had forgotten to do so. He would need to remember to place the order in the morning.

Mr. Tulliver from the railway company had recently sent a letter specifying the requirements for the spur line. Two chains on each side of the track needed to be clear of all obstacles, whether trees, bushes, or buildings. Necessary permissions from adjacent landholders were needed in writing. Aggregate was required in large quantity to build up a solid base, and ties had to be prepared with at least two flat sides, preferably using hardwood timber. Seasoned oak was specified as the preferred wood. If hardwoods were not available for the ties, then softwoods could be used but only if treated with creosote or other preservative such as chromated copper arsenate.

The specifications for the spikes alone filled half a sheet. *Five and one half inch spikes are required, made with strong high carbon. The width of the shank must be nine-sixteenth of an inch, with a T-shaped head. The bottom of the head must be sloped to match the flange of the rail. The tip is to be wedge-shaped and not pointed so that it can easily pierce the wood without splitting it.*

The rails, he'd read, needed to be *flexible enough to withstand a curve of three to four degrees. Curves greater than that would require manual bending or short sections of pre-bent rails could be ordered directly from the steel manufacturer.*

All materials and labourers needed to be assembled at the point of connection to the main railway line before work was scheduled to commence. As the spur line would require one short length of track, it had been determined that the actual laying of the track should take only one day, assuming that all preparations were in place and subject to inspection by Mr. Tulliver or his designate.

Alistair had carefully calculated the number of rails and spikes needed and had sent a telegram to Daniel Callaghan two weeks before with the specifications. Clearing the land, ordering aggregate, and preparing the ties required immediate attention. He could not fathom how this was to be done without hiring more workers. If he paid eight dollars a month to each new hire and kept them on for only one month, he would be dipping into the payroll and operating monies set aside for the brickworks. He didn't want to risk the payroll, and he didn't want to worry Brodie with the details. Settling Mrs. Meacham had also been costly and Alistair had depleted his own savings for that.

At least five men would be required for the month's work: three to work on clearing the land, one to build up the base, and one to prepare the ties. On the day when the line was to be laid, the entire brickworks crew would assist. Additionally, he had just encouraged Brodie to advertise for a salesman. Puzzling this out was putting Alistair in a black mood. Determined to resolve the conundrum, he drew up a list of employees:

LYNCH, Patrick—experienced with sheep, tends sheep, helps with building ($8 mo)

JOBSON, Thomas—experienced brickmaker, manages brickworks and kiln ($8.75 mo)

MEACHAM, Kyran—($8 mo)

MAGUIRE, Sean—builds, excavates clay and shale ($8 mo)

SALESMAN—commission only

TWO EXTRA MEN—one month only ($7.75 each)

He had automatically added Kyran's name but then crossed it out heavily. A man could be hired to replace Kyran at no additional expense, he reasoned. If he left Patrick and Sean and Thomas to finish the buildings and begin those preparations for work in the spring, he could put Sean, and Kyran's replacement, to work on the spur line. He himself could lend a hand, and with luck and good weather they might be able to meet the deadline set by Mr. Tulliver.

They would need a strong replacement for Kyran hired at once, and two further men for clearing brush. Only then could they reorganize responsibilities and fulfill their commitments. Alistair felt encouraged by this plan and looked forward to sharing its details with his partner. If Brodie was able, he might agree to help with some of the physical labour and the work would progress even more quickly. Satisfied with his calculations, Alistair prepared to retire for the evening. He was just about to go upstairs when he heard a tentative knocking. Holding his oil lamp high, he went to the door and opened it to a tall, craggy man, his hat and shoulders thickly powdered in snow, his face reddened by the cold.

I've come from the east and am looking for honest work. The snow makes for heavy travel and I wondered if I could shelter in your barn for the night. I'll be gone in the morning.

Alistair sized him up quickly. His manner was polite and deferential. His clothing looked not badly worn. His accent was unfamiliar but not unpleasant. *Warm up by the stove,* he said. *Come away in.* He opened the door further.

The man kicked his boots against the side of the house, shaking off the snow. Then he stepped inside and nodded at Alistair. *Thank you.*

Alistair reached for the man's coat and placed it on a chair by the woodstove. He then flattened some newspaper in front of the stove and placed the man's boots there to warm. *Have you been long on the road?*

Since first light.

What type of work are you wanting?

Any honest work.

I'm Alistair Lamont. I may have work for you.

Piet Schmidt.

They shook hands.

Where have you come from?

I've been logging at an estate in King. Stone masons were hired to build enormous but first there were trees needing cutting down. My share of the work is complete and so I'm looking for other employment.

Alistair nodded thoughtfully. *Some tea?*

I wouldn't say no.

Alistair poured a mug for his guest. *Have you eaten?*

I had a bun with cheese a while back.

It's a long, cold walk you've had. Sit and I'll fry some eggs and potato.

Danke.

We run a brickworks and I'm in need of men no afraid of hard labour. Using a pick to loosen shale and clay, clearing trees, leading horses—there willna be just one type of work, and all of it will be hard and honest. The pay is fair, seven dollars, twenty-five cents for the month. There's good rooms to be rented in town for a dollar and a half.

I accept.

A week's trial, mind. Alistair scraped the egg and potato mixture onto a plate and served his guest, observing him carefully. He was well-mannered and used his cutlery in a genteel way, without shovelling in the fare as others might. Still, Alistair reasoned, it wouldn't do to let his guard down. He'd give the man blankets and let him sleep with the animals. There was hay out there for bedding and he should manage nicely for the night. When he'd finished his meal, Piet took the offered blankets and slipped into his warmed coat and boots. Thanking Alistair, he prepared to leave for the barn.

Come inside for breakfast, Alistair said. *I eat at five. We work six to six.* He fastened the door, went upstairs to his room, undressed, and climbed into bed. Propped up like a small tent on the bedside table was the Christmas card he'd received from Violet. As he lay down and pulled up the covers he thought back to his last glimpse of her astonished face when the car pulled away. He supposed that by now she was formally engaged. It would be a society wedding of some note, he thought. She would look charming in whatever she wore, and Tremont would look proper and stiff in his morning coat or tails. He supposed there must be some affinity or affection between them.

It was strange thing, thought Alistair, that one could feel so completely captivated by another human being, so welded to them, only to discover that they were capable of forging a bond with someone else entirely. Connections and money did enter the equation, no matter how romantic one might wish to be. Miss Lewis had clearly chosen a husband from the correct station and rank and would likely be contented. In the end, despite whatever convictions and ideals she may have expressed, she had chosen the sure and comfortable life.

He slept uneasily, dreaming of Buffalo and with everyone all in the wrong places—Charley in the art gallery, Mr. Tremont buying fishing gear in the mercantile, Thomas at Callaghan's, and he watching for Mrs. Meacham and Kyran at the Institute of Music—everything in a horrible muddle. He woke feeling provoked, and thumped downstairs grumpily when he heard a rapping at the door. Piet was standing outside, holding the folded blankets and waiting calmly for Alistair. Glancing at his pocket watch, Alistair saw that he'd overslept: it was almost five-thirty.

Come. We have to eat fast. I've been busy this morning. There's bread and molasses and I'll put the kettle on. Alistair threw some split wood in the stove and blew at the burning embers.

I can tend the fire, offered Piet. He scooped up the newspaper on the floor and twisted it into a tight spiral, using this to shift the burning embers close to the logs and then leaving it in place to wick the fire.

You'll come with me to the brickworks first. We're just starting to use a press. Then you and I will head out to the railway track, where we have to clear brush on both sides. We'll make a start today.

Alistair looked at Piet to gauge his reaction. Piet was sitting at the table now with hands folded, waiting patiently for Alistair to join him, looking not at all intimidated by the work Alistair described. Then, when Alistair finally sat down, Piet nodded contentedly. The two ate quickly. Brodie was at the brickworks when they arrived, shovelling clay into the press with Thomas, while Sean and Patrick pushed the giant cog.

We can get the horses to do that, said Alistair.

We thought to go slow at first—make sure everything is working.

As the two men pushed, the clay could be heard churning in the machine. Loud thudding and clunking noises resounded off the sides when the knives connected with the material and spun it downwards in their splicing, spiral movement. When small stones or pieces of shale connected with the blades, the metal sounded out dissonantly with unpleasant, worrying tones. After several minutes they heard something else: Thomas, who'd been standing sentry on the lower level, suddenly shouted, *Tey dropping out, lads! Te bricks is jumping faster den salmon. Come look!*

They all rushed downstairs to see what Thomas had described. Sure enough, the pressed bricks lay on the table in a small jumble. Alistair grabbed one up and smacked it with his palm. Satisfied with the slapping sound it made, he grinned broadly. Their experiment was a success.

Chapter Thirty-Eight: A Setback

Braemor, Ontario ~ March 22, 1910

It was mid-afternoon and the timbering was not going well. Piet and Alistair were hard at work but had to alternate between chopping at a gigantic trunk and wiping the wet snow off their faces so they could see. What had begun as a light flurry was fast becoming thicker and heavier, accumulating on the ground and making secure footing difficult as they swung their long-handled axes with vigour. Finally Alistair nodded at Piet and the two shouldered the axes and walked back towards the brickworks. *The snow is too heavy for safety,* said Alistair when they arrived. *You canna see your hand in front of your face and canna be sure where the axe is going to land.*

He asked the crew to find a job for Piet. Then he turned to Brodie. *I'll go to town and post a notice for more men.*

Brodie looked at him. *More men?*

Yes. When you have time, I'll go over the requirements from the railway company. We have four weeks to prepare the site or we'll miss our chance. Alistair nodded, indicating the doorway. Brodie followed him outside.

Can we afford two more on the payroll?

We canna afford not to, Brodie. We've had no production this winter and have to prepare for a good spring. We need the line for shipping. If we dinna do it now, we'll have to wait a full year.

The two men walked slowly to the farmhouse. The snow was yet falling steadily and they proceeded cautiously, careful not to twist their ankles in the deep drifts. *I havena been much help of late, Al. Are we still solvent?*

Barely.

Brodie turned sharply to eye his friend. *How bad is it?*

We need to get the kiln firing by the end of the week, and we need to sell some bricks, and we need to be paid, and if all that can happen by the end of the month we'll be fine.

Or?

Alistair paused. *Or if no, we'll be forced to borrow more money or lay off the men. I emptied my own account to see to Kyran's family.*

Och, Al, and I was no help.

You have your own worries.

I've money still in my account. Let me help.

I will manage, Brodie. It's the payroll I worry about. We canna let the men down. They have others counting on them.

Brodie shook his head thoughtfully. *If it's ready cash we need, I could take a bridge job. We've spoken of this, Al. And there's work to be had in Quebec—a project that's in mid-construction. An old acquaintance wrote recently, offering me a job there wi' his crew. It pays well. The salary could be plowed back into the brickworks.*

And Charley?

Charley willna care. She still takes no notice o' me most days.

Just the same, Brodie, you canna leave her.

It may be just the thing, Al. We clearly need the income.

Dinna rush. Let us see how far we can go before you take it on. You'd be away for months.

I need to do something to help.

You are doing something. When you come to work, it helps with the men and it helps to have another pair of hands. You could help with the timbering, too, if you wanted. It would make the work go faster.

Brodie was silent for a moment. *Did we expect too much? The press and the tramway and the spur line at the once?*

Likely.

Where did you find Piet?

He came to the door last night, having walked from over King way. I hired him on trial—I knew I could find the money for a week's pay at the least.

Och, Al. Let me take on work. It's a railway bridge in LaSalle. There's a bridge already there but they want a new one.

Would you take Charley?

We live in tents.

Have you asked her?

She's very quiet.

I have to go to the mercantile. When it's six, why not try to pick her up and take her to the hotel for dinner?

She hasna left the house, Al.

May be if we appear together and ask, she'll change her mind.

Later that day, after Alistair had completed his town errands and Brodie had supervised the men working the press, they hitched the wagon and headed to the Smith farm. When they passed their men—who were now walking home—Alistair slowed the wagon so that they could jump onboard. Alistair was pleased to see Piet enter easily into the camaraderie. Patrick was in especially good form and kept them laughing with his ready quips and jokes.

If you stay on, said Alistair to Piet, *speak to me. Brodie's room is vacant and I'd be glad for the company.*

Brodie looked over at him quizzically.

The cooking woan be much, said Patrick, *nor te 'ousekeeping. It's camping indoors ye be doing, like.*

When the men were deposited at the edge of town, the partners turned the wagon around again and drove to the farm. *Are you keen to take in a boarder?* asked Brodie.

If I can deduct lodging from a week's pay, we'll be further ahead with very little trouble or expense. We need at least two more men to help clear cut in the next month, and I'll offer them rooms as well. Of those five wee rooms above stairs, I need only the one.

Brodie nodded.

There'll be the added expense o' food, but I dinna eat like a laird. Alistair pulled up at the end of the drive.

Let me go and see how things are. Brodie sprang down from the seat and headed towards the kitchen door. Alistair waited patiently in the chilly damp for many long minutes. He was about to relinquish hope when the front door opened and Charley, wrapped up snugly for the weather, stepped out tentatively. He jumped down, embraced her in a hearty hug, and led her back to the wagon. Brodie followed and lifted her up onto the seat between them.

It's good to see you, Alistair ventured. *It's been a trying day and I'm glad for some merry company.*

Charley looked at him gravely. *If it's merry company you seek, Alistair, you may have come to the wrong farm.*

Och, don't say so! Alistair's voice projected a good humour that he didn't actually feel. He'd choked down his own sense of grief in the effort.

Chapter Thirty-Nine: New Beginnings
Braemor, Ontario ~ March 22, 1910

Justus Ketchum seated them at the table closest to the fireplace. Apple wood was just then blazing, the room redolent with its fragrance. Charley smiled timidly when Justus took her coat and said again how glad he was to see her. Alistair was shocked by the look of her without the coat. Her dress seemed overlarge; she'd lost a great deal of weight. There were dark circles under her eyes and a lethargy to her movements. Yet Charley looked so pleased by Justus's attentions that both Brodie and Alistair relaxed to see her making an effort.

I think I shall have the rabbit stew, she announced. *I've not had rabbit in such a long time.*

And I will have the oyster soup, said Alistair, *and the chicken.*

I would like the oyster soup followed by the stew, added Brodie.

Justus left the three of them with a basket of bread and a dish of butter.

The bread is still warm, said Brodie, reaching for the basket. *Who will join me?*

To his delight, Charley picked up a shiny dinner roll. All three of them solemnly proceeded to butter their rolls.

So good, said Brodie, having devoured two big rolls and reaching for a third.

It's because they're warm, agreed Alistair.

Charley smiled faintly at the men. *It's because you have hollow legs. I've never seen you two turn down bread or potatoes or pie or anything sweet.*

Brodie grinned. *I just think it's a shame to disappoint the cook by no enjoying food when offered. I only eat like that for fear o' offending the cook.*

That's correct, said Alistair. *We wouldna choose to give offence when we can easily pay a compliment and eat the evidence.*

Besides, Brodie added, *Alistair is no a very good cook and any opportunity for a meal properly prepared is important for his civilization. It keeps him in trim for society.*

I see, responded Charley, *and so your ravenous ways are intended for the greater benefit of others only.*

Exactly! said Brodie, buttering his third roll. *Our habits are in all ways benevolent.*

After Justus had served their dinner he remained hovering nervously by the table. *Charlotte, I'm afraid the chicken may be dry and the soup too salty. Do not be hard on me. Mrs. Babcock does the best she can but everything she makes comes out like pasteboard and salty so as you think it was preserved in a barrel before she boiled away any remaining flavour.*

The three dinner guests looked at Justus askance and did not pick up their cutlery.

It canna be so bad, surely, said Alistair. The others watched as he seized his spoon and supped heartily on a first taste of soup. His lips puckered and he reached quickly for a tumbler of water.

Brodie was next; grimacing, he took first one and then two spoonfuls of the broth. *Perhaps,* he said, putting aside his spoon, *we should eat our main course first.*

Justus picked up the bowls, shaking his head sorrowfully. *You are missed, my dear, and would be welcome any time you felt well enough to come in.* Then, addressing the men, *Enjoy your meal.*

Charley winced as she tasted the rabbit stew. *The meat was soaked too long in brine and not properly rinsed. The sauce is fine but the meat and vegetables are overcooked.*

Well, it's cooked and it's hot, Alistair replied. *It will do.*

Nowhere near as good as yours, Charley. I can see why Justus is missing you. He must be losing business.

Charley began to look fatigued from the outing and picked at her food, eating only small morsels. The effort to be sociable was clearly exhausting her. Justus appeared then, asking whether they required dessert. *There are pies,* he said, *made by Mrs. Babcock, but none with so light a crust as yourn.* He directed his remarks to Charley.

Well, I'm willing to assess the difference, enthused Brodie. *Bring me a slice of what you think is best.*

Justus nodded his head thoughtfully. *The apple is made with fresh apples from the barrel in the cellar, and the peach from tinned peaches, but the custard pie is not worth sampling as I believe she scorched the custard while attacking the lumps. I will bring you the apple without recommending it but will not charge you, as the pastry cannot easily be cut.* The delivery of this message was subdued, as though Justus had resigned himself to further complaints and disappointment. Brodie barked out a laugh and Charley smiled the tiniest of smiles.

Then Justus delivered three generous wedges of apple pie entirely covered by mounds of fresh whipped cream. On each plate he had delicately set a small fork and a serrated knife. This further omen did not pass unnoticed. Charley giggled.

Brodie looked at Alistair and grinned happily. Then he undid his cuffs, rolled up his sleeves theatrically, picked up the knife, and with exaggerated movements attempted to saw off a piece.

You are only spoilt, said Alistair. He picked up his own knife, pushed aside the whipped cream, and assessed the crust in an elaborate manner, attempting to locate a structural weakness that would act as an entry point. At this Charley began to giggle afresh. The men looked at her with great affection and a deep sense of relief.

I shall cover this, said Brodie, signalling Justus for the bill.

Let me help, offered Alistair.

Al, I know how things stand.

Charley looked from one to the other but said nothing.

Let me walk home, said Alistair. *You keep the wagon and horses until morning. The walk will be good for my digestion.* The friends laughed and said their goodbyes.

Once in the wagon and on their way, it was Charley who spoke first. *What did you mean when you said, I know how things stand?*

Brodie considered carefully before responding. *Only that we've expanded quickly and there has been no income this winter.*

Is the brickworks in trouble?

Money is tight, but our plans are solid and we shall be fine again when we can run the kiln and sell bricks.

Will you lay off the men?

We need them now more than ever. They're cutting wood for the kiln fires, and clearing brush for the spur line, and working on the buildings. There's much to do, and it all needs doing now.

But can you pay them?

Alistair is very good with accounts, and he says the payroll is secure. We need an infusion of cash and are hoping to hold on. It's no a thing for you to fuss yourself with, Charley. We've had a pleasant evening. I trust Alistair.

But is there nothing that can be done? Will the bank give you credit?

Brodie hesitated. *Our backers in Buffalo would advance funds if we asked, but we dinna want to give away more o' the business. They require payment with interest for each amount they lend us, plus a percentage of our sales.*

What will you do?

Brodie reached across and put his arm about Charley, pulling her close to him on the wagon seat. *We willna worry about it this evening, my love. All will be well.* Charley did not pull away from his embrace. Brodie found himself wishing that the drive home was a further distance. To sit with her this way was like the best of times.

Chapter Forty: Another Bridge
Braemor, Ontario ~ March 22, 1910

Brodie checked the woodstove in the kitchen, carefully banking more ash around the hot embers. Resting on top of the stove were two Lamith bricks, and these he wrapped in flannel and carried upstairs. He saw that Charley was already abed, and lifted the quilts by her feet to insert the hot bricks.

Thank you. The night is yet damp.

Brodie smiled and bent over to kiss her forehead.

To his surprise, Charley reached up and caressed the side of his face. *I've had a lovely evening.*

He sat down on the edge of the bed. *Yes. It was good fun.*

Brodie?

Yes?

Why do you not stay? There's no need for you to sleep down the hall.

Are you certain?

Charley pulled back the covers and shifted herself so that he could slide in beside her. Brodie undressed hastily and joined his wife, being careful not to crowd her. But Charley lay tightly against him and closed her eyes, sighing deeply. Brodie lay still, watching her in repose, cautious not to disturb her or make her in any way uncomfortable.

Come morning, when Brodie woke he saw at once that she was lying on her side, watching him. *I've been wondering,* she said, *what you and Alistair are planning.* Brodie rubbed his eyes and looked at her scrutinizing him. When he extended his arm, she resettled herself close against him. *Tell me,* she prompted.

We need cash, and would like to secure it without incurring more debt. He paused. *I've been offered some bridge work in LaSalle. The money would be helpful. Alistair would continue to run things here. I could go to Quebec and send the money back for you and Al. I'd need to be away for a while—I'm not certain how far along they are.*

And would I continue here, alone?

You could visit. We live in tents and the conditions are primitive. And I could come home for short intervals. Or you could move to the hotel—stay with the Ketchums, and maybe help out there, if you choose. Or, if you want, I'll stay here and hope for something else to come along.

Charley began tapping her fingers nervously on Brodie's chest. After a moment he clasped her hand raised it to his lips for a kiss. *It's as you wish, Charley. I'll do what you consider best for all o' us.*

She remained silent, and when Brodie looked at her he saw that she was quietly crying. He pulled her in close, kissing her hair and her forehead and her cheeks. *I willna go if you dinna wish it, Charley. I'll stay here with you and we'll find another way.*

There is no other way, Brodie. You must.

At this she pulled away and clambered out of bed.

Brodie reached for her arm and held onto her. *Charley, dinna distance yourself again, please God. You will break my heart. Stay here wi' me and talk this through.*

She shook her head, pulled away again, and lifted a dress off the peg on the wall. *It's late. You're expected at work.*

Brodie stood hurriedly and moved towards her, encircling her waist with his hands.

Dinna leave like this, Charley. It's more than I can bear.

She hesitated. *You are as well to go. I am no good to you.* With that she left the room.

Brodie shouted after her, *what do you mean by that?* Pulling on his clothes from the night before, he rushed out, only to find that she'd locked herself in Johnny's room. He heard sobbing from within.

For God's sake, Charley, open the door and talk wi' me.

Go away.

I insist you open this door. Brodie pounded on it impatiently to emphasize his point. *If you dinna open this door, Charlotte, I will break it down.*

He heard her footsteps and the sound of the key being turned, and now Charley stood before him, looking down. Tenderly, he reached his finger to her chin and tilted her face upwards. She was the picture of abject misery. Brodie clasped her to his chest and held on to her tightly while they both wept. Finally Brodie led her back to their room, laid her down in the bed, and covered her tenderly. *You must tell me your worries, and explain what you meant. We're intended to share our sorrows and worries. It's what we have pledged to do.*

I did not think it would be this hard.

Brodie reached for her hand and held it tightly. *Tell me what you meant.*

Only that I'm no good for you. Everyone I love dies. First Dick and then Johnny. I promised to protect Johnny and raise him to be a fine man, as near to his father as I could manage. And I have failed. I've let them both down.

Oh, Charley…

Brodie bent his head against her body and began to sob. *I thought you blamed me. I was the one who should have protected Johnny. All this time… I thought you blamed me…*

After a time, Brodie felt her hands stroking his back. He sat up and saw that she'd stopped crying. He cupped his hands around her face and looked at her intently. *You must never shut me out like that again, Charley. It was an accident. A horrible, awful accident.*

I can't help feeling responsible.

That willna bring him back.

Charley sighed deeply. *But what shall we do? How will we bear it?*

Brodie stretched out beside her on the bed. Then he leaned across, resting on his elbow, and kissed her lightly. *Like this. We will bear it together. We'll hold on to each other and comfort each other. It's the only way.*

He felt her hands embracing him and altered his position to pull her in close. They lay together breathing evenly, hands clasped together tightly, both as fully at peace as they'd been since the explosion. After an hour Charley murmured that she should prepare something for them to eat. Brodie stood up along with her, saying that he should ready himself for the brickworks.

Will you go to Quebec?

Will you countenance it?

If you deem it necessary.

And what will you do? Will you go to the hotel?

Yes. And rescue the town from Mrs. Babcock's cooking. My small salary might also be useful. The little I earn can help.

Brodie walked over to where she was standing and took the slackened corset laces from her hands. He kissed her neck tenderly. *And I will come home to you as ever often as I may.*

Will you pull this tight? asked Charley, indicating the corset.

I would much rather be loosening it, teased Brodie.

They finished dressing above stairs and ate a hasty breakfast of cold biscuits and jam. Brodie was in a hurry to meet with Alistair and tell him of the decision. He knew that a small advance on his wages could be arranged and might be just enough to satisfy their immediate obligations.

Alistair was relieved by the news. *Are you sure it's wise to leave her?*

I'm certain.

She seemed in good spirits at dinner.

She greatly enjoyed herself. It was good, Al.

Alistair slapped Brodie on the back in half manly pat, half congratulatory clout. *I'm glad to hear it.*

You will look in on her?

I will.

Every night?

I'll make certain she is no in need of anything.

She may become depressed again and you should watch for signs.

You must think a great deal o' your importance to her, if you believe the loss o' your company will create a depression. She may well skip around the hotel, glad o' a reprieve from your ugly mug.

Alistair, be serious. She's fragile yet.

I know, but I wouldna want you to get a swelled head.

I'll send a telegram this afternoon and should hear back tomorrow. If all goes well, I should leave in a few days.

Alistair nodded. *It willna be easy, this parting.*

Brodie reached out and shook Alistair's hand, pumping it firmly. *Never met—or never parted—we had never been broken-hearted.*

Burns?

It seemed fitting. You're always the one wi' a quote at the ready.

Chapter Forty-One: Brodie's Sacrifice
Braemor, Ontario ~ March 27, 1910

When Alistair attended church that Sunday—he hadn't been for weeks and thought it was time—he was surprised to see Charley and Brodie walk in together, arms linked tightly. He slid sideways in the rough pew to make room.

When do you leave? he asked Brodie.

In the morning. I'll help Charley move some o' her things to the hotel this afternoon. I'll write once I've arrived.

Are you certain that Charley has accepted this?

Brodie smiled at him then glanced at his wife. *I am a fortunate man.*

In his relief, Alistair began to meditate on what he supposed were the great advantages of marriage. Having someone with whom to face your future cares seemed tremendously attractive. He'd felt, in these last months, the want of close companionship. By now Piet had moved in, but he wasn't someone Alistair could confide in, and the difference in their stations meant he didn't feel free to do more than have meals with him and some limited conversation. In any case, Piet would usually retreat to his bedchamber after dinner, not to be seen again until morning. Alistair was quite lonely.

Sometimes in the evening, when he was reading by the woodstove, he would have conversations with Miss Lewis in his head. These were often exchanges that had actually transpired, but sometimes he would embellish them, engaging her in spirited debates about the brickworks, improvements to the house, and whether they would have four children or five.

He had, once or twice, imagined excuses to travel to Buffalo so that he might confirm for himself her engagement. But this would be both frivolous and expensive, and could only lead to further disappointment. And so he would manfully collect his thoughts, rein in his emotions, and undertake the tasks that filled his days. He'd throw himself especially into those labours that required brute strength, in the evenings rubbing liniment into his sore arms and shoulders before retiring to the cold of the upstairs.

After the service he stood in the tiny church hall with the others, fortifying himself with two cups of weak tea. He did not often linger for these socials, but on this day Alistair felt a need for company. Several matrons in the community struck up conversations, two or three making a point of introducing him to their daughters. These were, he considered, healthy-looking young girls, plain and simple but good-natured, if not a little too anxious to appear so. One in particular, Dorothy Millar, seemed especially obliging; it was she who refilled his tea and brought him a scone.

You may call me Dot, she said after a few moments of stilted talk. *Everyone does.*

Alistair attempted to smile, but with his mouth full of scone at that moment, he thought it might seem a bit lopsided.

I work at the mercantile, she continued. *I've seen you in there, Mr. Lamont, buying things for the brickworks, as I imagine.*

Yes, I shop there. I dinna think I have seen you.

I work in the section with the personals and fabrics.

Well, perhaps I'll see you when I'm in next.

Will you really? I should like that ever so much. Dot's face broke into a wide smile and she beamed at Alistair with an enthusiasm that frightened him. It wasn't that she was unattractive, he thought, but that she seemed to assume a level of promise he hadn't intended. He swallowed the last of his tea and excused himself, striding so hastily towards his horse that one might suppose he was fleeing the scene.

The next several days were spent in a flurry of logging and brush clearing. Piet was a strong worker, demonstrating repeatedly his determination and physical tenacity. Alistair sometimes struggled to keep up with him. They worked long hours, most often accompanied by the others but sometimes needing to labour on their own. As they cleared the area the other men set brush fires and compacted the aggregate into a tightly packed bed for the railway tracks. Sean and Thomas remained behind at the brickworks, where they measured and cut the heavy ties and coated them thickly with creosote. One afternoon Sean was notably absent when Alistair stopped in; Thomas obligingly explained that Sean hadn't been particularly careful about not splashing the creosote that morning, and that when he went to relieve himself he'd forgotten that his hands were covered with the stuff and had touched his privates. *'e did 'imself a harm,* Thomas concluded gravely, trying to smother his grin.

Alistair marvelled at the many projects they had undertaken and at how well all the pieces were now coming together. The fly in the ointment was the worrying state of their finances. He brooded about this non-stop, and so was relieved to hear from Brodie that a bank transfer would be forthcoming.

Alistair felt keenly the sacrifice Brodie had made in leaving behind a warm bed for a camp cot to earn the capital they so desperately needed. Alistair had kept his word and had stopped by the hotel every evening to visit with Charley after the evening rush. She seemed to be enjoying the accolades her cookery was receiving. Yet she was not altogether merry; Alistair often saw that a sad stillness had settled upon her.

LaSalle, Quebec ~ April 4, 1910

It was hard to reconcile. He'd not been away from Braemor a week and yet he felt entirely dislocated. Brodie chided himself for growing soft, for becoming too accustomed to the comforts of life indoors. The tent was damned cold, his wool sleeping rug scant consolation. The cook was trying his best but the results were no better than Alistair's crude cookery. He missed them both: Charley and Alistair.

Charley was yet fragile, he knew. He wanted to be with her in the evening, to slip under the covers and hold her hand while they whispered their goodnights. And he wanted to see her beautiful face in the morning when she smoothed her hair down with a wet comb and fastened it tightly into a knot at the nape of her neck. And he wanted to hold her when she was sad, and help the pain of their loss ebb away.

The sheep would soon be lambing; he'd looked forward to seeing the first of them bouncing in the pasture as only the newly born do. And Alistair was left looking after everything. Such a good, faithful friend. More of a brother, really, all things considered. And while yet feeling homesick, and unmoored, Brodie wrote letters home filled only with news and happy events.

April 14, 1910

An idea had begun to take hold, one that Brodie turned over and over again in his mind. He and Charley had never taken a wedding trip; he wondered now if it might be a good thing to do once the brickworks and farm were established. She'd been struggling with low spirits, and despite putting on a brave face, he knew there were days when the sadness gripped her.

What he had in mind was a trip to Scotland. A change of scene, he thought, might be just the thing. He had business to finish with his uncle's estate, and they could take a leisurely tour around the country after those transactions were concluded.

In fact, if she was so inclined, they could use the sale of his uncle's house to purchase a small holding of their own... and not return to Braemor at all. It was an idea he had harboured for some time without even quite realizing it. He would miss Alistair and the others, of course he would, but together he and Charley could make a new life. Away from the farm, perhaps the loss of Johnny and the earlier grief of losing her husband, might not seem as bitter.

He felt disloyal in thinking these things, but the prospect of a new start, far from the reminders of loss, was tempting. He and Alistair had fought hard to carve out a place for themselves in Braemor, but surely this meant he could do so again? Or was he fooling himself? Was the life they had constructed meant to be the only life he should embrace? How many chances was one given to make amends?

CHAPTER FORTY-TWO: THE SPUR LINE
Braemor, Ontario ~ April 18, 1910

I've been thinking to visit him, Charley told Alistair after Brodie had been gone for a while. *Do you think I should? I've never been to Quebec.*

Yes! said Alistair. *He will be delighted to see you.*

I shall do it then. Do you have news for him?

Only this. The brush has been cleared and the railway bed shaped and tamped and rolled. We've begun to set down the ties and have only a day's work to ready ourselves for the railway lines. And the lambing has begun—eleven born yesterday and another five today. Patrick stayed through the night and is managing. There are more to come, he says. I will take you to see them if you like.

Thank you, Alistair, but now I have things to prepare before the morning. Meanwhile I have two apple pies I set aside, one to take and one to send home with you. Mrs. Babcock is engaged to fill in and I know you're not well disposed to her baking.

You're right, said Alistair, getting to his feet. *I shall fend for myself until you return.*

Wait here a moment. Charley disappeared into the kitchen and returned with a warm apple pie lightly covered in a linen cloth. Alistair took it from her carefully. *You've been a good friend,* she said, standing on her tiptoes and kissing Alistair's cheek. *I shall report to Brodie that you have been a faithful watchdog.*

Upon Alistair's return to the farm, his first care was to secure the pie safely in the kitchen and then to check on the lambing. Another two lambs had since been born; he stood at the pen with Patrick, gazing down at the new arrivals.

Dat's a runt, said Patrick, pointing, *'e'll be kilt, like.*

What should we do?

Let nature do 'er ting.

Brodie would be sorry to lose one. Can we bottle feed it?

Patrick shook his head.

Alistair looked at him. *There's fresh pie in the kitchen. Come away in and have a slice.*

Patrick followed him to the house, wiping his boots carefully at the door and sitting down at the kitchen table. As Alistair set about making the tea, he called up to Piet to join them. The three men made short work of the pie, then sat together nursing their tea.

Is there news of Master Brodie? asked Piet.

Mrs. Smith is to visit him tomorrow. We should have news when she returns. At that he slapped his hands against his thighs. *I should to bed, gents, as there is one hard day's labour left before the railway men come. I will say good night.*

Alistair went upstairs and left the two talking quietly together in the kitchen.

The railway crew, when they arrived two days later, consisted of five men and two heavy wagonloads of equipment. They set up camp on the farm and proceeded directly to the site of the spur line to inspect the work that had been done. The foreman, Mr. Alfred Bellis, was a portly man who huffed and puffed as he navigated the aggregate bed. Finally, he looked up at Alistair. *The work is satisfactory. We'll lay the tracks tomorrow.*

Alistair let go of the breath he'd been holding. *Well done!* he exclaimed to the crew who had gathered round. *Well done, indeed!*

At the end of the day, the railway men prepared to go into town for a hot meal at the hotel. *I must warn you,* said Alistair, *that their regular cook is away.*

The men turned to look at Alistair skeptically. *There's tinned beans at the farm,* he continued, *and you're welcome to join me.*

Mr. Bellis smiled at this. *I'm sure the hotel food will be satisfactory.*

All right then, but dinna say you weren't cautioned! Alistair and his men chuckled, and several remarks were heard regarding the unfavourable taste of pasteboard.

Alistair checked on the lambing before entering the farm-house. *How many today?*

Nodder four, replied Patrick, *but te runt be dead now. Kilt by 'is Ma, like.*

I see.

Is te way o' t'ings.

At six the next morning, the brickworks crew and the rail-way men met at the work site. The materials had been neatly stacked in readiness, and now the assembled waited for Mr. Bellis to issue instructions. *Good morning, men,* he began. *May I state, firstly, how pleased I am to see the preparatory work that has been com-pleted. The foundation for all such engineering projects is of the utmost importance, and you have followed our instructions with great attention to detail.* The men all relaxed and smiled at one another.

But secondly, I must state that your offer of hospitality last evening, should it be extended to us again, would be most welcome. Our evening meal consisted of what was advertised as Beef Tripe, which I must say is a delicacy of which I personally am most fond, but what appeared seemed only to be a mixture of onions and flour and beef fat, heavily salted and served in bowls floating with an unknown substance. We are none of us feeling the better for having eaten such fare. Mr. Bellis huffed emphat-ically, his face bearing the unmistakable look of someone whose internal system was roiling uncomfortably.

By this point, and along with the rest of his crew, Alistair was laughing so hard that he couldn't help doubling over. Once he was able to compose himself he again extended an offer of, *better grub to be had at the farm when they were done.*

As Alistair's men took on the heavy carrying and lifting jobs, the railway crew scuttled about, heaving and shifting and driving spikes into place—and were so experienced at measuring and lay-ing down tracks that it took only part of the morning to nail into place an entire section. Alistair would have fully enjoyed the process had it not been for his day-long swatting away of black-flies and mosquitoes, their swarms so thick and so persistent that the men were driven half mad with the irritation. They couldn't open their mouths to speak lest they swallowed a mouthful.

Alistair felt his eyelids swell and saw that many others had welts on their faces and necks and hands.

Finally, and to general relief, Mr. Bellis declared that they'd save the switch and final rails for the morning. The two crews gathered their tools and headed to the farmhouse, where Alistair served them ginger beer. The railway men were now milling about in the kitchen and beyond, waiting for supper.

By God, Alistair remarked to the room at large, *there was a plague after us today!* He and Piet had just put the potatoes on to boil. Patrick and Thomas looked over at him sympathetically.

Have you no been attacked? he asked.

Bear grease, said Thomas. *Coats te skin. As ye see, te bugs keep away. It's te only t'ing wot works.*

Where do I get some?

Careful, chimed in Patrick, *te people will stay away from ye as well.*

At te mercantile. In a small pot. Te 'unters render bear fat to sell. Goes quick.

Does it smell?

Reeks like te bear et comes from.

Ye should put it on yer 'ead, te locals say, as it prevents 'air loss, added Patrick.

Alistair put his hand to the back of his head and felt the thick hair there. *There's naught wrong with my hair.*

Ooooh, said Patrick, *looks like a bit tin on top. Bear grease would fix ye.*

There is no bald spot!

Friends will tell ye wot tothers woan, teased Patrick. The men laughed while Alistair continued to run his fingers through the hair at the top and back of his head.

Et's also good for aches, said Thomas. *Te rheumatiz will begin shortly.*

I dinna have the rheumatiz, said Alistair indignantly. He'd been cracking eggs into a big bowl, and turned now to Piet. *Do you think I'm getting a bald spot?*

Piet had cut thick slices of bacon and was frying them on the stove. *I did not know you when you were young, so I cannot say.* He kept his eyes down as he pushed the slices about. *You may have always had a certain thinning,* he added. *Some men do.*

Alistair grunted and busied himself with a fork, rapidly beating the eggs with milk and butter.

The following morning he would gladly have ridden over to the mercantile for bear grease but for a certain delicate reluctance concerning Miss Dot Millar. So when he arrived at the switching point, he was relieved to see the men wiping grease around their faces and necks. Despite the revolting odour of the stuff, he took the pot and coated himself liberally.

Mr. Bellis showed the crew how the parallel rails were to be laid and how the switches were manoeuvred. Although the mechanism itself was quite simple, the placement and angling of the rails required much finessing and adjustment. Were the calculations not correctly implemented, the result would be certain derailment. It took the entire day to position and install the switching points at either end of the spur line, but Alistair was thrilled at its completion, as was Mr. Bellis, who'd been in much better spirits owing to Alistair and Piet's not elegant, but infinitely preferable meal, the night before.

That night, Alistair had offered to stand Piet to a drink at the hotel, where Justus Ketchum told him that Charley had arrived safely home. *Let me just run upstairs,* said Alistair, *and ascertain that she is well.* He knocked quietly on the door. Charley opened it at once, stepped into the hallway to greet Alistair, then stepped right back.

What do you reek of?

Alistair laughed. *Bear grease, to keep the bugs away.*

It will keep more than the bugs away!

Alistair moved down the hall about twenty feet. *Does this help?*

Only slightly.

And how is our Brodie?

Brodie is fine. He made short work of his pie, so I knew his appetite was unharmed.

Alistair laughed. *I'll no keep you if you're weary—I only wanted to check that all was well.*

Charley smiled at him. *You are a worrier, Mr. Lamont. I wish you had someone of your own to worry about.*

He flinched at her words, *I'll see you tomorrow. I'm glad you're home safely.* Alistair walked back downstairs to meet with Piet. Her words had wounded him unexpectedly and despite the great accomplishments of the past week, he felt deflated. It would be good, he thought, filled with a sudden longing, to return to Buffalo again.

CHAPTER FORTY-THREE: SANDER COOMBS
Braemor, Ontario ~ April 20, 1910

The letter from Brodie arrived Wednesday afternoon, and Mr. Sander Coombs arrived on the train from Montreal Thursday. That night Charley greeted Alistair hurriedly and pointed out Mr. Coombs dining fastidiously by the fire. Alistair looked on askance as a fancy man dabbed delicately at the corners of his mouth after every spoonful of soup—as though fearful that traces of the hot broth would stain his lips and spoil his expensive-looking ensemble.

That's our new salesman? What in the blazes was Brodie thinking? He looks more fit to be a catalogue model than fit for tramping around the country selling bricks.

You may be right, Alistair, but as Brodie has recommended him, we should at least be civil. He's travelled a distance, and at some expense.

I'll be civil. But selling bricks is taxing work and no trade for a fancy man.

Striding to the table, he stood before the gentleman, planting his feet forcefully in a stance that suggested aggression rather than good manners.

Alistair Lamont! he boomed, startling the other guests and surprising even himself. *Friend and partner to Brodie Smith. You are acquainted, I am told.*

Sanders laid down his spoon in a much affected manner and made further pretense to carefully fold and set aside his napkin. He stood finally to extend his hand, and Alistair crushed the fine fingers heartily in his calloused mitts. Then, aware that Charley was watching, he bid the man sit and finish his meal.

We start at six, he blurted. *And anyone in town will tell you how to find us. Spend a day wi' us in the works and then we'll settle the terms.*

I assure you, Mr. Lamont, Sander responded in a thin, quavering voice, *that I've had experience in sales and can represent myself and your brickworks with an effective presence.*

Alistair nodded, bowed briefly in the politest of courtesies, and excused himself, taking a seat in a quiet corner with his back to the room.

Charley brought over a tray laden with two dinners.

I ordered for you, she said, *as it seemed you were much employed in the intimidation of your new salesman.*

Alistair stood at once and took the tray, setting it down and pulling out a chair for her. *I did no such thing. I simply introduced myself and told him be sharp in the morning.*

Just the same, Alistair, you seemed fierce.

What in blazes was Brodie thinking?

He may yet surprise you.

Alistair harrumphed and turned his attention to the shepherd's pie, eyeing the dish approvingly. *The town will be glad you're back in the kitchen.* He couldn't help noticing the small shy smile that crossed her face.

A bit later, as they were finishing their dinner, Charley said, *There was something Brodie said to tell you. He's made the acquaintance of a gentleman from New York who sells steam turbines. He'll be displaying one at the fair in Glen Mor. Brodie was encouraging us to go. He says that this type of engine will save on the men and horses; that the two of you have discussed it.*

Alistair nodded at this, then suggested an after-dinner stroll along the main thoroughfare. As they walked, he realized that Charley was directing him gently towards the church yard.

There's fireflies about, Alistair. Do you see them?

I do.

Johnny loved fireflies. He'd catch them in mason jars and bring them inside for me to see. We let them go again quickly, but he loved them so much. He said it was a wonder how God put all that light into such a little thing.

Alistair held his breath, thinking she would begin to weep and that he didn't know how to respond to a woman's tears.

Let's go, she said suddenly, tightening her grip on his arm. *He's with his maker now, and his father. Maybe they will show him how the light gets inside.*

Alistair let out his breath and steered her back in the direction of town. A shadow had fallen over them and was lingering unbidden, their mutual silence now a considered attempt to protect the other from the rawness of sorrow. Only when they were alone would they take out the hurt and examine it carefully, reliving precious memories and letting loose restraint. The wounds had only begun to heal and would not withstand the sharing of emotion. Instead they walked briskly back to the hotel, watching the spots of light darting ahead through the gloaming.

Chapter Forty-Four: Fire in Zion's Corner
Braemor, Ontario ~ April 21, 1910

The next morning Alistair arrived early at the brickworks, anxious to make sure all was prepared for Sander's visit so that he might show him the operation at its best. He wanted to impress upon Sander their imminent technical advancements—the brick press, the aerial tramway, and possibly even a steam turbine. That last had been put into his head by Brodie's message. Where they would find the funds was a worry, but the idea of effortless power hung in Alistair's mind as a matter of consequence.

Alistair thought of his own Da, and felt he could now understand how a man became harnessed by debt and mortgages and the expectations of others. As a young man he'd swallowed down his disgust for the lack of financial acumen his Da's debt represented. But as he and Brodie struggled to establish their business he came to appreciate how such a thing could have taken hold. It was now to him a cautionary tale.

The crew arrived at a few minutes shy of six in their customary flurry of jibes and jests. Alistair smiled broadly as he greeted them. Then, with a piercing whistle, he stood upon a stool and announced that they would shortly have a visitor.

Brodie has hired a salesman. He'll spend the day wi' us and then undertake the sale o' our bricks, meaning that I'll have more time to work on our projects here. Also, I'm told there's to be a fair at Glen Mor, and that they'll have a steam turbine on display. I'm going to view it, and have decided to give you a paid day Saturday so that you can all go as well. Bring your families and fill our wagons and we'll make a pleasant day of it!

Hear, hear! shouted a few. *Great news! Hurrah!* shouted others. Alistair stepped down as the men talked excitedly about the steam turbine and the pleasure their families would have at the fair.

It's always a good one, said Sean.

A fair distance te go, Thomas remarked, *but no end of interesting displays and such.*

Te wife and little uns will be merry when I goes 'ome and says to 'em that we are te 'ave 'alf a day for te visit te fair, added Patrick.

As the men drifted off to their stations Alistair walked towards the kiln to check on the current firing, looking about for Sander Coombs as he went. Thomas was there before him; he'd already begun the delicate work of chipping away the hardened clay from the kiln door and dismantling the brick wall used to seal it. A small pile of bricks lay discarded on the grass, ready to be cleaned and set aside to use again. Alistair had just picked up a chisel when Sander Coombs arrived.

He turned at Sander's greeting, stood up slowly, and barked, *You're late! We start at six.*

Sander looked flushed and a little tremulous. *Mr. Lamont, I assure you, I intended to arrive on time but the breakfast was late, and the water for shaving was cold, and there were many obstacles on my path this morning.*

That's no apology, man. We keep our time and we keep our word. If you're to sell bricks for us you will do well to remember it.

Of course.

Remembering Charley's rebuke, Alistair stuck out his hand, grasped Sander's firmly, then squeezed it gently. Sander did not return the pressure; in fact, his fingers folded together like a wet piece of paper.

Alistair withdrew his hand directly. *Sorry,* he muttered.

Sander was just then shaking his hand daintily.

I learned early in life that there was honour in a man's grip.

Sander attempted a smile but managed only a thin grimace with a slightly menacing look to it.

Alistair studied him carefully. *These bricks need cleaning so we can use them again to close in the kiln door when we fire. You can help me clean them or I can send you to Thomas and he'll give you a tour o' the works and introduce you to the men.*

Sander looked down at the jumble of bricks with jagged pieces of mortar stuck to them. He stepped back from the pile and carefully replaced his yellow glove, smoothing the leather over his fingers. *I'll be of more use to you in sales than I will in your drudgery. If you would be so good as to direct me to Thomas, I'll amass the information I require and be on my way.*

Alistair was astounded by the man's effrontery. Had he not been clear that a day must be spent at the brickworks before terms were decided? He was about to send him on his way to the devil when Thomas appeared.

Alistair, called Thomas, *is this the salesman?*

It is.

Shall I take him around?

If you do the honours, I'll continue my drudgery.

Thomas approached and shook Sander's hand. Alistair nodded at the two men and with some vigour set to the cleaning of bricks. He was just finishing the pile an hour later when Thomas returned.

That's a fine gentleman you an Mr. Brodie 'ired.

Fine is one word for him.

Do you think 'e'll manage?

He's to be on straight commission, so he canna hurt us.

I gave 'im samples and the price list.

Thanking you, Thomas. I havena the patience today.

The balance of the day was spent in agreeable labour. The men were pleased to have Alistair working alongside them. The heaviest and dirtiest jobs were the ones he took on first, and he was always the last to sit down.

Alistair was visiting with Charley at the hotel the next evening when the story went around of a fire in nearby Zion's Corner. It had broken out at the bank in the night, and with no fire brigade organized, the entire building had gone down in a blaze as the locals stood helplessly by. The bank's safe was fireproof and so was left standing, along with some grillwork and steel doors—everything else was a blackened pile. People marvelled that no one had been hurt. The mystery of it was that the bank was long closed for the day when the fire started; no one could understand how it had begun in the dead of night.

Alistair and Charley discussed the blaze with the others and said how glad they were that Braemor had both a fire brigade and a siren at the train station that was to be used for such emergencies. They congratulated one another on their community's foresight and planning, and felt confident that they were as secure against the ravages of fire as they could be. Charley was in good spirits, as Brodie had written to say he would be coming home for a short stay to visit the Glen Mor Fair, intent on viewing the steam turbine with Alistair.

As the date of the fair grew closer, the men peppered Alistair with questions about the steam turbine. He had to admit that, although he'd seen ones in Buffalo, it was Brodie who had the real knowledge of them.

Meanwhile work on the aerial tramway had begun. Admiral Barnes had, it seemed, taken up residence on the site, supervising Piet and Patrick in assembling its towers; eight of the fourteen had now been built. These were yet lying on the ground awaiting the massive piers to hold them steady. Portland cement had been ordered from Grey & Bruce in Owen Sound for the purpose. In the interim, Piet and Patrick were busily pickaxing and digging deep holes for the foundations. It was heavy work, and the incessant chirping of the Admiral, who had erected an awning for himself and was ensconced comfortably in a camp chair with a canteen and sandwiches, proved no small source of irritation.

Alistair was pitching in with the backbreaking work of removing a boulder from a deep hole when the Admiral approached, waving his canteen invitingly. Alistair, hot and thirsty, climbed out of the hole, took the canteen from him, and drank liberally before realizing that it wasn't cold water he'd just guzzled down but a potent alcoholic mix of some kind.

Bathtub gin, said the Admiral, beaming. *Bought it from Harold Rogers. The last of his inventory.*

Alistair wiped his arm across his mouth to remove the burning sensation on his lips. *Whewee! That's strong.*

Indeed it is. The still is smashed now. The pigs got into his mash and were lying all across his field as drunk as lords when the mayor rode by and deduced how things stood. He summoned McGary, who went around on official police business to check for a permit. *The still was found out back of the convenience and all the pieces broken and taken away. Rogers was some put out. And his old wife, Anna, she's hollerin' the whole time, telling Rogers it was the devil's drink. Have you ever seen that woman at haying? Tosses a fork of hay like as if it be a feather pillow. Nothing too fine or ladylike about her.*

Alistair grinned and wiped his brow. *I best be getting back to this rock and see if I can get my pick under it.*

Before you do, the Admiral said, *another swig?* He passed Alistair the canteen. *Last of the inventory!*

Alistair was still at work a couple of hours later, possibly a little worse for wear, when a messenger from the post office brought him a telegram. Alistair climbed out of the hole once more and gave the messenger boy some coins for his trouble. He held the telegram with a sense of foreboding. His first thought was that something had happened to Brodie. His second thought was of Miss Lewis's wedding in Buffalo. With trembling fingers he peeled open the thin flap of the envelope and read the message.

SOLD 24 THOUSAND BRICKS STOP BANK IN ZIONS CORNER
STOP NEEDED QUICKLY STOP

Well, I'll be damned! Maybe that little skiver knows what he's about after all. Holding the telegram above his head, he waved at Piet and Patrick and shouted the news. Then he strode across the field to the brickworks, where he sought out Sean and Thomas and showed them the telegram. It was a big order, but after some rapid calculations Thomas assured him that they had more than enough bricks.

Call in at the hotel this evening and see if you can hire some lads to drive them out, instructed Alistair. *We canna do without all our men just now. If there are more orders like this to come, we'll need all hands at the ready.*

Alistair proceeded to the matchbox of an office he shared with Brodie. Sitting down in his swivel chair, he turned it around slowly, leaning back to reflect on the sequence of events. Sander had wasted no time in arriving at Zion's Corner to sell the bricks, he thought. Something nagged at Alistair as he sat there but he couldn't quite puzzle out what.

Saturday morning, as arranged, Alistair drove to the Smith farm to collect Charley and Brodie, who'd arrived back only the night before. The two men grinned hello as Brodie swung the picnic basket merrily into the back of the wagon. It was the fairest of early summer days—the sky a gentle blue, the clouds softly drifting—as the three set off for Glen Mor. They descended into the shallow bowl of the village, crossed the Mor River, then drove up the long, gradual hill to the fairgrounds.

The Burke brothers had donated one of their vast pasture fields for the event. At one end stood a wooden grandstand, gaily painted white and green, for viewing horse pulls; off to its side was a long shed for showing livestock; and a little further on, another larger building had been constructed for the competitions, among them the domestic and fine arts but also shining examples of all the latest equipment on show. A row of fencing had been erected for the wagons and carriages, and water-filled troughs had been set about for the horses. Situated at one side of the field were a series of booths and stands where popped corn and cotton candy, balloons and squawkers could be purchased, with games to test your skill, and where a man tried to guess your weight. Crowds of excited people, young and old, clustered everywhere, eager to try their hand or buy a treat. Blankets marked out a picnic area near the tree line where families with small children sat at their afternoon meal. A pleasanter scene could not be imagined.

Brodie and Alistair and Charley stood at the edge of it all, taking in the views and enjoying the gentle breeze. Looking down into the village, they could see the mill and the granaries, the general store, the small farms dotting its outskirts. There was no movement in the village itself—everyone was above the ridge at the fair.

So peaceful, said Charley. *It looks a picture.*

It does, agreed Alistair.

The only thing that would make it better, Brodie added, *would be some fresh berry pie.*

Charley and Alistair followed him to a shady spot under a tree where Alistair spread the blanket and Charley began to unpack their picnic, including the pie Brodie had seen her bake early that morning.

Where do you think the turbine is? mused Brodie.

Inside with the displays? suggested Alistair. *Or maybe out back?*

This pie is sooo good, said Brodie, forking a generous amount into his mouth. *You should have entered it in the baking competition.*

If I'd done that, Mr. Smith, you would not be eating it!

Alistair smiled at their nonsense. It was a relief to see them once more getting on. He'd worried that their grief would break them apart, and so to see them again like this filled him with equanimity. There were still many times when low spirits brought tears to Charley's eyes, he knew. It was the way of things, he understood, but the spark that had once illuminated her was gone and he doubted it would ever really return.

The steam turbine, when they found it, was outside behind the livestock. A group of men were watching the salesman demonstrate it. At one end giant pinwheels had been planted in the ground some distance away, and at the other end stood a large tank of water. The steam slowly gathered and began to spin the pinwheels until they were a blur of colour. The crowd clapped appreciatively.

Gentlemen, do you see that merry-go-round being turned by those men over there? The crowd followed the direction of the sales-man's arm to see two men straining against a wooden bar as they walked around a circular platform. A steel pole stood in its centre, supporting a disc from which were suspended eight wooden swings. The whole contraption was swung into a spinning motion by the men leaning into the bar and forcing the upper-most disc to slowly revolve, creating a gentle swaying motion for the children seated on the swings. *That merry-go-round could be easily powered by steam, my friends, with no effort required from our good labourers hard at work there. Buyers tell me that it uses less wood and water than other models and does the work of ten horses. There are many applications for this beauty—wood sawing and threshing among them. And she can be yours on very easy terms. Entire satisfaction guaranteed.*

Brodie, entranced, moved up close, watching the gears and pistons moving and at work. The sound the turbine made was thunderous; some of the ladies and children covered their ears. Alistair meanwhile, wondered about its cost, its weight, its maintenance. He wondered how much water it would take and how often the tanks would need filling. But when he saw the excitement on Brodie's face he knew that the answers to such questions would come later. They'd just have to find the means to buy it.

Patrick and Thomas came crowding to the front along with their families and hearty hellos were exchanged all around.

I see that you're to be congratulated, said Brodie, nodding at Patrick's wife. *You're expecting another member of your family.*

We are so, said Patrick, patting his wife's stomach. *But I 'ave to tell ye, Mr. Brodie, dat dey are a sight more fun puttin' in den dey are takin' out. My missus is none pleased te be facing dat again, are ye mother?*

Patrick's wife swatted his hand away and blushed deeply. *Paddy! Do not be speakin' so in front of t'others.*

As Charley quickly inquired after her health, Brodie and Alistair looked away, both much amused. Patrick stood, legs apart, hands in his trouser pockets, as happy as a man could be. The group turned back to the pinwheels, once again spinning furiously in the steam. But soon Brodie and Alistair saw that tears marked Charley's face. Brodie put his arm about her shoulder protectively and whispered something in her ear. Alistair followed as Brodie led her away to the grandstand.

I'm sorry, Charley began, *it's just that this time last year Johnny won the blue ribbon for a drawing of the farm. Being here made me remember afresh. I'm sorry. I don't mean to ruin our day. The ribbon is pinned in his room.*

Shhh, said Brodie, pulling her close beside him.

It's no matter. We can leave, Alistair offered.

Charley shook her head and clenched her jaw. *No. Leaving or staying won't alter things.*

Together they moved towards the building with the displays. Brodie and Alistair accompanied Charley through the fine arts section, feigning interest in the painted china and coloured pencil drawings and rows of vases arranged with cut flowers. They were indulging her and she knew it, teasing them by asking for their opinion on a particular drawing of violets, then on a cup and saucer, finely decorated with a painting of a cow. The three of them passed a pleasant half hour quietly congratulating themselves on having moved past an emotional moment.

They were slowly progressing through the butter, honey, and maple sugar displays—Brodie and Alistair eagerly anticipating the end of the ladies' exhibitions so they could proceed to the plows, mowers, potato planters, and threshers—when a great cry was heard outdoors. The crowd stopped moving. Everyone strained to hear the words.

FIRE, BY GOD, AT THE MILL!

Other voices were heard in the crushing scramble. *SHITE! COME QUICK!*

SHE'S AFIRE!

RUN!

Brodie grabbed Charley's left hand and Alistair grabbed her right. Moving away from the throng pressing towards the nearest doorway, Brodie led them to the furthest exit and up to the crest of the hill where they had stood not long before. There they saw the devastation that was in full fury. Flames had engulfed the mill—and even at this distance the roar of the burning could be heard. Men were tearing down the hill towards the conflagration. A few women, their skirts flapping, could be seen following behind. Shouts of *STAY HERE!* were heard as more and more men left their wives and children and ran to join the others.

Alistair and Brodie tore off their jackets, tossed them on the ground, and set off running. Charley watched them go, scanning the crowd for others she knew. She thought she saw Patrick and Sean and looked behind her to locate their wives. She saw knots of women clinging to one another, holding their children close, sobbing. The mill wasn't their only worry—they were frightened of the falling debris, frightened for their men who might be reckless in stemming the spread of it. It had been weeks since the last rainfall; if the flames caught hold the fields and crops would burn like tinder. The entire village could be lost.

Charley sank down on the edge of the hill and watched the drama as it unfolded below. She saw the line of men passing buckets of water from the dam along a human chain, saw them tossing what seemed thimbles of water onto the snarling flames. Smoke billowed upwards; gusts of it caught in the northward breeze; women and children coughed. Charley did not take her eyes from the scene, straining to identify first Brodie and then Alistair among the sticklike figures rushing to and fro. Soon a great cracking roar was heard on the hill and the men ran for the river. The mill crumpled in on itself with resounding explosions and rumbling crashes. The men yelled out, grabbing at each other, pulling one another to safety. Charred timbers bounced in the air, clouds of ash and smoke billowed in bursts of grey-black haze. Deep intakes of breath were heard on the hillside while the families watched it all.

The bucket brigade was soon at work again, dampening the surrounding area with water. Screams rang out and the men turned to the sound. Several rushed to a fallen corner of the mill and could be seen pulling at beams and timbers; a couple of women joined the small throng and began to shriek and keen in the most pitiable fashion. At least one of the party must be badly injured, if not worse. Everyone waited to learn who.

The men laboured on as some of the watchers wept and others crooned rhythmically as they held children close. Charley sat rigid, lightly stroking the wool jackets spread neatly across her lap. If only, she thought, she had allowed the men to take her home; they would have been safely away.

The air about the hillside stung now with smoke and fumes. Many mothers took their children indoors while others left theirs in someone else's charge and scurried down the hill to help. Charley was soon left alone, still searching for glimpses of Brodie and Alistair. Twilight had set in and with it the damp chill of evening air, when the first of the men began to climb the hill. Before long, a steady parade was on the ascent. Charley scrutinized the blackened figures as they wearily approached. She was standing now, and when she recognized the set of Brodie's shoulders she ran towards him crying his name.

Were you worried about me? he teased, reaching for her.

I was frightened you'd be the hero and do something foolish, she answered, pulling back and examining her now ruined dress front.

No, said Alistair, *he was ordering us about and kept clear o' the worst of it.*

Is there any trace of the cause? asked Charley as they walked towards their horse and wagon.

No that we ken now, said Alistair, *but when the ashes are cool they may search for the source.*

Who was hurt?

A lad from Glen Mor. No yet whiskered. He lost his footing and fell into the blaze. His father and mother not twenty feet away.

The poor woman, said Charley quietly, *to lose a son in such a way.*

The men let her words linger as they quietly led their horse to the wagon for the road home.

Glen Mor, Ontario ~ May 14, 1910

Brodie felt rather than saw the impact of the collapse. The earth beneath his feet shuddered with the crash just as he heard the sound of it. He felt sure that only a miracle would prevent further calamity. Too many people were trying to stanch the fire, colliding with one another as they ran to and fro with buckets. Order was needed. He shouted instructions to the crowd. A few listened, and they in turn grabbed at others, slowing them down so that soon a line was formed and the buckets themselves, not the men carrying them, were passed from the river to the mill.

He, Alistair, and a contingent of others were at the front of the line, taking the filled buckets and dousing the blaze as well as they might. He heard the shrieks and keening, saw the boy's body pulled out, but did not stop. He was needed at the front of the line, damping the spoiled mill and any remaining embers. There were others who could attend the grieving.

Only later, when he and Alistair began their ascent up the hill in search of Charley, did he allow himself to dwell on the human loss. He imagined the faces of those who loved the boy, the burns on their hands as they handled the timbers to reach him, the punishing grief as they endeavoured to salvage enough of their lives to continue.

Chapter Forty-Six: A Stabbing

Alistair waited outside in the wagon while Brodie ran indoors to wash himself and collect his valise. There was no time for supper, so Charley prepared him something to eat on the train. The three of them drove glumly to the train station.

Will they rebuild, do you think? asked Brodie finally.

If they're insured they will. Wi' out, they'll be hard-pressed to finance it. Anyone would, said Alistair dourly.

Be days afore they can sort out what's what.

Alistair nodded. Then, after a pause: *Did I say that the tramway is coming along? Some of the towers are assembled and the bases are ready to be installed.*

Is the Admiral helping?

He thinks he is. Patrick and Thomas have had no end of his advice.

Brodie laughed. *I gather it's only advice he offers.*

Well he is in possession of some very nasty gin. Burned my insides out.

The arrival of the train cut their conversation short. Brodie embraced Charley before climbing the metal stairs onboard. He and Alistair shook hands vigorously. *I'll write,* said Brodie, *as soon as I can.*

The train pulled away slowly from the platform, then gathered speed as it puffed its way along the line towards Montreal. *I'll take you to the hotel,* Alistair told Charley, *and see you in.* After leaving her, Alistair drove home at a leisurely pace, savouring the fresh evening air, the stars out full and clear. It was very dry, he thought; rain would surely be welcome. Two fires inside of two weeks could be an omen of sorts. Grass fires might be next. He'd seen such a fire catch once and take out several hundred acres before the weather turned and a rain came. These arid conditions could well be dangerous.

Alistair unhitched the wagon, brushed down the horse, and checked on the lambs. A reservoir of water was what the town needed, he thought. He'd seen them in his travels, close by train stations. One of the men in Buffalo was sure to know someone who had knowledge of these. He would write to inquire.

When the cement shipment arrived Monday morning, the men all stopped to help unload it. Alistair insisted on stowing it in the barn even though it was a fair distance from where it was needed.

If it rains, he said, *it will ruin.*

Patrick looked up dramatically, striking a pose as he squinted his eyes and pointed to the blue sky. *Tis dry as a fart,* he finally said.

Well, it may no stay so, responded Alistair, smiling. *We have need of rain, and when it comes it may be a deluge all at the once.*

The Admiral arrived just as they'd finished heaving the heavy bags into place. *Yes sir, yes sir, that will do the trick! Just the thing! Portland cement. Nothing better.* Whacking his walking stick on the pile of bags, he beamed at the men. *Nothing for it now. If we begin mixing we can pour by nightfall and let it set overnight. In the morning we can tip in the base structures and leave them to cure before assembling the tops. We can get at least four holes filled today if we start at once.*

With the men out of puff from their labours, such eagerness was not met with a great deal of enthusiasm. Alistair intervened. *After lunch, Admiral. We'll leave off everything else and all set to.*

An dat's te reason why, whispered Patrick to no one in particular, *we likes workin' fer Mr. Brodie and Mr. Alistair an not te ol' Sassenach.*

As the men tucked into their lunch Alistair rolled out the barrel he'd been saving for this express purpose. Tipping half a bag of cement into it, he added buckets of water and began to work the mixture with a long-handled spade. As it thickened, it grew harder and heavier to manipulate.

The men were speculating about the source of the fire and who it was that spotted it first.

Did I tell ya that I spied our salesman at te fair? said Thomas.

Sander? queried Sean.

Te very one. I was sure it was 'im. Outside te exhibition building, as wot.

I dint see him, said Sean.

Nor me, to be sure, said Patrick.

Well I did, said Thomas. *No mistaking 'is fancy ways.*

Last we heard he was in Zion's Corner. Why would he criss-cross the country?

Makes no sense.

'e is a fine one.

That's one way of sayin' it.

The Admiral, meanwhile, was supervising Alistair's efforts closely. *Almost there, m'boy, almost there!* The trouble was, as Thomas pointed out, one barrel of cement wasn't nearly enough for even one hole, let alone four. At this, the others began to scout around for shovels and barrels; soon everyone was busy mixing cement and ferrying it to the holes. It was hard going but they worked steadily, understanding how important it was to get the mix just right and to tamp the holes tightly with the wet mixture.

In this way the holes were filled and covered with wet canvas tarps for the evening. When the men, and even the Admiral, had left for the night, Alistair looked inquiringly at Thomas, who alone remained. *What is it, Thomas? Why are you no off home wi' the lads?*

Thomas flushed. *Mr. Alistair, sir, I doan mean to speak bad…*

Go on.

I doan mean to speak bad but doan ye find it queer there been two fires inside tree weeks?

It's been very dry, Thomas. These things happen when there's no rain.

But…

Yes?

But it's been tree weeks since we 'ad a salesman.

What?

I mean no disrespect.

A dozen thoughts flitted through Alistair's mind. The big brick order. His unease with something he couldn't quite put his finger on. His instant dislike of the man. The disaster at Glen Mor. The possibility of grass fires and worse. *Do you have reason to suspect Sander of something?*

Thomas hesitated. *It seems queer, doan it?*

Alistair did not know how to respond. Thomas was hard-working and honest and loyal. He'd waited until the men were gone to share his thoughts. He wasn't trying to work anyone up. But surely the suggestion was ludicrous.

I'll thank you to keep this to yourself, Thomas. I know you mean well. But what you say is out o' the question. No decent man would do such a thing.

Mister Alistair, I just tot to say. In case it mattered.

Thank you, Thomas. Now get home to your wife. She'll have dinner on the hob and not be pleased if you keep her waiting.

Thomas left quickly. Alistair stood and watched him cross the fields, hearing the faint sound of Thomas's whistling as the good man walked further and further away. Alistair moved slowly. He was bone weary from the day and troubled by Thomas's suggestion. He went to the house and sat down at the kitchen table, rubbing his hands through his hair. This was a conundrum. He had no reason to fault Thomas's suspicions, but still, he couldn't fathom how anyone would be so cold-hearted as to set fires for personal gain. If it were true, Lamith Bricks might easily be ruined if word went round that an employee of theirs had done this.

He closed his eyes and tried to wish the trouble away by summoning a more pleasant meditation. He willed a picture of Miss Lewis to come to him as she was on the night of the Beethoven concert. Leaning back in his chair, he tried to focus on that tender memory, but Sander Coombs and William Tremont kept appearing and ruining his reveries.

He was still sitting there, rubbing his hands through his hair, when Piet called to him.

I can put on some potatoes.

Please, said Alistair, *I'm too knackered to do anything.*

The next two days were spent mixing yet more cement and setting the platforms for the towers into the partly cured mix.

The shovels needed cleaning regularly, as the cement clung to them and made them heavy to use. The work required that all the men pitch in together, and despite the onerous work, Alistair was enjoying the camaraderie of the crew. The Admiral would regularly appear to check in on them, and then hours later, in great state, leave them to their labour. In this manner he continued to feel very much a part of the project without in any way exerting himself. And since Alistair was amused by his proprietary air, the others too took it in stride.

On Thursday afternoon they were manoeuvring the final platform into place when they spied a figure coming towards them.

Is it the Admiral?

No. He's already been.

Who then?

They stood watching as the figure drew near. It was Sander Coombs. *Good afternoon,* he called. *A fine day it is.*

A few of the men called out a less effusive greeting in return, but most ignored him and resumed their work. Alistair wiped his hands on his pant legs and moved slowly towards Sander. *Where have you been?*

I've been in Zion's Corner, and sent you that order, and have just now come from Glen Mor. You may have heard, Mr. Lamont, they had a fire recently. A terrible blow. The mill burned completely down. But it was insured, and they're wanting to rebuild with bricks. Lamith Bricks! He said this last triumphantly, smiling at Alistair. *I have the order in my vest pocket.*

Alistair did not return his smile. *When were you in Glen Mor?*

Just yesterday. I was in Zion's Corner, staying at the inn there, when word came about the fire. Not having another destination in mind, I engaged a horse and rode there directly.

So you arrived in Glen Mor on Wednesday?

As I said.

And not on Saturday?

No. Sander flushed just slightly at the question. Alistair noticed Sander's right hand. It had begun to twitch almost imperceptibly. The middle finger was stroking the thumb in a self-calming gesture. The speed with which the thumb and middle finger moved was so rapid that it looked as though the entire hand was tremoring just slightly. Alistair glanced at the hand, and glanced back at Sander's face.

Tell me again. Where were you on Saturday? Alistair took two steps closer.

At the inn in Zion's Corner. Sander moved back a step.

And you were no where near the fair at Glen Mor? Alistair took three steps closer.

No.

And will the innkeepers verify this? By now the tone and timbre of Alistair's voice had drawn the others' attention. They stopped their work and came and stood behind him in a half circle.

Sander looked flustered. *Why would they?* His hand was still twitching but his voice remained steady, even as it was thin and quivery.

I have a man says he saw you on Saturday in Glen Mor! Alistair boomed. *A man I trust. He saw you midday and didna see you again.*

There was mumbling and the sound of angry voices murmuring behind Alistair. Patrick broke free from the group and stepped towards Sander with his fists drawn. Alistair reached out and grabbed Patrick by the shoulder. *Easy now. We'll write to the inn at Zion's Corner and see if what he says is truth. There may be a mistake.*

Nodding at Piet and Thomas, Alistair continued. *Take him to the farm and tie him to a chair. He'll stay wi' me till we hear from the inn. If the news bears out what he's said, he'll have my apology. If he's lying, we'll turn him over to McGary and let the law deal with him.*

Piet grabbed one of Sander's arms and Thomas the other. At this Patrick ran forward and butted him in the chest with his head, knocking him flat on the ground. Jumping on top of him, Patrick administered some heavy blows. Sander wrestled free and stood up with a growl. Then he reached into his right boot, pulled out a knife, and waved it menacingly at the group. His posture was hunched, his feet planted apart, his knees bent. The men were amazed by the sudden transformation of the thin-voiced fancy man into a furious knife-wielding figure poised to fight.

His voice, now deeper and throaty, swore and taunted them. Patrick was the initial focus of his ire; he lunged at him, knife extended, intending to do him a serious harm. Patrick was taken off guard and stepped back, tripped over the uneven earth, and fell heavily, arms extended. Sander moved quickly, jumping down astride Patrick's torso with his right arm raised and the knife held high. He was about to plunge the knife into Patrick's chest when Alistair leapt towards him in a flying tackle, grabbing Sander's arm and wrestling it to the ground. The knife was kicked from Sander's grasp by one of the men but not before it plunged into Alistair. Piet and the others piled on top of Sander and took a firm grasp of him. Sander continued to writhe and struggle violently, the curses and profanity that came from his mouth shocking even the roughest of the men.

Alistair stood up slowly. The others saw that blood was seeping through his shirt and vest.

Thomas said, *I'll take a 'orse and ride to Glen Mor.*

Never mind that, said Alistair, *go for McGary. Tie him tight, men, and stay wi' him.*

Ye saved me life, Mr. Alistair. Saved me life. He's not what we thought at all, said Patrick.

Bind him tight, said Sean tersely, *but put him in te wagon. Check his pockets and boots.*

Thomas walked over to where Patrick and Sean and Piet were holding Sander and reached into his jacket pocket. His fingers found something hard; he pulled it out and held it up for the others to see. *Brass knuckles,* said Alistair in disgust.

Sander spit in Thomas's face and cursed him and the others, and their mothers, in the foulest of language. Patrick looked over at Alistair, who was now holding his side. *We need te get ye to te doctor.*

Let's go, said Thomas. *We can find McGary and the doctor both.*

By the time the men had bound Sander and put he and Alistair in the wagon, Alistair was feeling light-headed. The blood had seeped down his pant leg and was steadily dripping onto the wagon boards, forming a small puddle. He was attempting to press the wound but felt that he wasn't applying enough pressure. There were pins and needles in his hand, and he wondered why it was acting so strangely. The men drove directly to the blacksmith's shop, where they had Sander fastened with a chain to a post. Sitting propped up in the wagon, Alistair could hear Sander's new voice, shouting insults and threats and cursing at the men. Alistair pondered this while he waited, wondering how Sander had managed to transform into such a thug. When the men returned to the wagon, they found Alistair slumped over and unconscious.

What Alistair next remembered was Miss Lewis soothing his brow with a cold cloth and murmuring something soft and sweet. He couldn't see her yet, as he felt unnaturally tired, but he could make out her slight form and feel her gentle hands.

You came, he said, smiling. *I'm glad you came.*

Of course I came, ye big pillock, said the voice. *Why wouldn't I come? Someone has te see after ye. Jumping onto a knife like ye was Brian Boru his self.*

Dinna be cross, I love you so much.

Well then, Alistair Lamont, we loves ye too but enough of yer nonsense.

Say you'll marry me?

Marry ye?! Yer a daft lummox.

Alistair closed his eyes again, smiling. Miss Lewis had come. And she would marry him. What could be better. When Alistair woke again he saw that Charley was asleep in an armchair at the end of his bed. Thomas and Patrick and McGary were standing in a corner of the room conferring quietly. Struggling to sit up, Alistair saw that he was in a room at the hotel. *What day is it?*

The group came over to the bed. *It's Saturday now. You been asleep three days. The apothecary has sewn your wound and given you laudanum.*

Ye saved me life, Mr. Alistair. Do ye remember?

Where is Coombs?

McGary spoke. *On the train to Montreal with a couple of escorts. I took his coat to Glen Mor, and there were many who said they saw him. With his fine clothes, he stood out. Then, when I searched his room, I found a pistol and a notebook with a record of payments. I telegraphed Montreal—it seems he's wanted there. Apparently he's in the persuasion business. Persuading people to pay him for burning down buildings and keeping quiet about insurance fraud, and blackmailing those who've had encounters with undesirable ladies. There are a number of people in his little book who are very unhappy with him.*

When he met Mr. Smith, he was needing to get out of Montreal for a while. He thought brick sales would be easy enough to manage if he used his expertise to burn down a building or two first. He's a nasty one.

I knew I disliked the snivelling little skiver!

Easy now, said Charley, who'd risen from her chair and gently touched Alistair's shoulder. *The doctor says you're to be careful yet. You've lost a great deal of blood. You need some red meat and bed rest before you can get up. I have written Brodie.*

Alistair had a vague memory of Miss Lewis being there and looked around the room. *Was there no one else about?*

A lady perhaps? smiled Charley.

Did you see her?

No. I'm afraid I've been the only lady here. But you did make Patrick an offer of marriage.

Alistair groaned, and the men snickered quietly. *I apologize…*

No need, Charley laughed. *It was very sweet.*

Turning to the men, she said, *Gentlemen, now that you know he'll live to see another day, we should leave him rest.*

Obediently, the small group prepared to leave, with Patrick first clasping Alistair by the hand and saying, *I owes ye me life, Mr. Alistair.*

Chapter Forty-Seven: News

Braemor, Ontario ~ May 25, 1910

Alistair was confined to bed for several more days before Doctor Barrow changed the dressing and examined the stitches. As they appeared to be healing, he said that Alistair was able to go home but only if he did not exert himself in any way. With some difficulty, Alistair was able to get up and dressed. Charley had laundered his shirt and sponged the blood from his trousers and vest as best she could. He walked downstairs slowly, still feeling weak, and arranged for a messenger to run to the brickworks for someone to come.

As he waited, he had lunch in the dining room and then walked, somewhat unsteadily, to the post office to collect the mail. To his delight a thick packet of letters was waiting, including two from Brodie and one from Daniel Callaghan. He stuffed the lot into his jacket pocket and joined Piet, who was now waiting patiently by the wagon.

Time to get home, Piet.

Piet nodded obligingly.

We need to check on the lambs. See if Patrick needs any help.

Again Piet nodded.

You're pretty quiet, Piet. Is everything in order?

Piet nodded.

What is it, Piet, is there something amiss?

I was waiting in the wagon, and— Piet seemed to need to collect himself before continuing. *And someone walked by and asked me how the Kaiser was. Germans are not welcome here.* He looked down at his boots.

Alistair paused. *People are always afraid of those things they dinna understand.*

Piet nodded his head but did not look convinced. He was quiet and broody for the ride home and made himself scarce while Alistair checked on the sheep. Later the men ate together companionably, but Piet excused himself after the washing up and went directly to his room. Alistair was not entirely sorry for the solitude; his wound was paining him. He sat down at the kitchen table to read the mail.

The letter from Brodie was light-hearted, filled with descriptions of the bridge project and some of the engineering challenges he'd puzzled out with the others in his group. It seemed he was enjoying the work, although he heartily missed being home for the lambing and the installation of the spur line. The chief engineer—Brodie's acquaintance, the man who had originally told him about the job—had been welcoming and complimentary both. The new bridge was a complex structure, one that integrated space for both train and automobile travel.

Brodie was excited by some of these new solutions and detailed, at length, the calculations for tension, sheer, compression, and torsion he had undertaken and that now were in their final stages. The bridge, thought Alistair, sounded as though it would withstand a herd of elephants crossing during a winter ice storm. He was both amused and reassured by his friend's meticulous detail. As an aside, scribbled on the bottom, was a postscript saying that Brodie had just received Charley's letter about Sander and the fire and encouraging Alistair to take his time in recovery.

The next letter was from Daniel Callaghan. It seemed that he and his friends were thinking to do some salmon fishing in the middle of June. They would travel by train, he wrote. Would Alistair kindly book accommodations at the hotel for twelve guests needing a minimum of eight rooms? The party would include mostly gentlemen, but some of their wives had decided to accompany. The letter proposed that Callaghan and the other investors tour the brickworks for part of one day, spending the remainder of the week fishing and at their leisure. He added a note about a letter Brodie had sent him regarding a certain steam turbine—an intriguing proposition, he wrote, one that he and his men were eager to look into. Meanwhile, he hoped that Alistair would make all necessary arrangements and join them for some of their sport.

Alistair read and reread the letter carefully. Normally he would have been elated by the proposed visit—especially the promise it held for the brickworks' future—but without Brodie there as reinforcement he wasn't certain he could manage facing Mr. Tremont, should he be included in the party. His jealousy for this man rose from deep down in his system and lodged itself in his throat so that he felt he couldn't swallow or speak. He poured himself a whisky and read the letter again, trying to determine whether he'd missed any indication of who would make up the party. He had not. Alistair crushed the letter in his hand and flung it to the floor.

News from Buffalo had the effect upon him that it always did. Visions of Miss Lewis entered his mind unbidden and he sat motionless, remembering her, feeling his anger subside as he became once more subdued by longing, and by emotions he could not name. After another stiffening drink, Alistair seized a fountain pen and some paper. He wrote Brodie a response to his letter that was perhaps more affectionate and effusive than he might have ordinarily done, had he not imbibed quite so much whisky. He assured his friend that all was well—with the lambs, the bricks, and Charley—unfortunately in that order—and that he was pleased to hear that the bridge work was so infinitely interesting and satisfying. He included a cryptic aside about elephants. The final, rather frantically scribbled lines contained an earnest and most impassioned plea that his good friend take a short holiday from the bridge during the middle of June so that he could be present when the steel barons, as well as the noxious dandy Mr. Tremont, were visiting. Having concluded the letter and satisfied his need to communicate, Alistair fell promptly asleep with his face upon the kitchen table.

When Piet found him there the next morning, he shook him gently. Alistair was disoriented at first, but when he spied the completed letter the events of the evening broke upon him.

I have to get this to the post office, he muttered, standing upright and then steadying himself by placing both hands on the table. *Brodie must come home and he has to receive this letter quickly.*

Let me go—you look like you could use some time to yourself.

Alistair nodded and handed Piet coins for postage. *My thanks. I'll see you at the brickworks after.*

The men were already at work when Alistair arrived, Sean having already organized the roster and assigned jobs. Alistair thanked him for his good management then asked what he might do; he was given the task of driving the horses back and forth across the farm with some clay and shale. The clay pile had been treated with lime before winter had set in, and Thomas was eager to see how pliable it was after having had the cold months in which to break down.

A couple of the men had geared up the brick press; it was thunking away as the first clay and shale deposits were cut and mixed into a medium soft enough for pressing. Alistair, pleased to have an outdoor job—one soon to be made redundant, what with the tramway about to be completed—walked the horse slowly to the riverbank, giving it a light respite before the hard pulling began.

He was partway across the fields when he saw Piet walking towards the house with an unusual lean to his body. Alistair veered off in his direction; as he drew closer he saw that Piet was hobbling and supporting his right arm with his left hand.

Drawing to a standstill, Alistair called out, *What has happened, Piet?*

Piet seemed to have trouble meeting Alistair's gaze. *Men attacked me outside of town. They followed from the post office. There were three of them. I think they have broken my arm.*

Alistair eased himself carefully down from the wagon. *Bloody cowards. Who were they? Tell me their names and I will deal with them.*

I don't know them.

We must make a sling.

The arm is not straight.

There's whisky inside. Have a glass and I'll ride for the apothecary.

Alistair drove the wagon to the barn, unhitched it, and carefully saddled one of the horses, cautious of his sore side and the stitches. Before he headed to town he rode back quickly to the brickworks to tell Thomas what had happened. Alistair was taken aback by Thomas's lack of surprise.

Tere's plenty o' anti-German tinking, Thomas said.

Alistair was annoyed by this. *Has he no proven himself as good a worker as any o' the rest?* he railed. *Has he done anyone here a harm? He's as much a part o' this crew as any.*

Alistair was still thinking about this as Piet's arm was being set. The apothecary left Piet some powders for the pain. After they were left alone, Alistair looked around the kitchen uncomfortably. *Is there anything I can get you?*

Piet shook his head. *The man said this will take six weeks to heal. I'm no use with a broken arm. I will leave in the morning.*

Stay here, Piet, and let us find something.

No. You are having a hard enough time without a cripple.

You could drive the horses and help with the sheep.

I have no way with animals.

It's no hard.

Thank you, Alistair, but I have overstayed and must move on. Piet drew himself stiffly erect and walked over to extend his left hand. *You have treated me fair, but I will leave in the morning.*

Alistair shook the man's hand and Piet excused himself to go upstairs. Alistair stood in the kitchen for a moment contemplating the sudden decision. As he went outside he thought once more about the shifts and changes taking place all around him, and how dear was the human cost.

LaSalle, Quebec ~ June 2, 1910

Charley's recent letter had filled Brodie with concern. Sander Coombs a refugee from the law? Alistair stabbed? He must return to Braemor, and he must do so quickly.

He'd also received a puzzling letter from Alistair himself. Perhaps he'd been at the whisky? For it sounded shoogly, with

much to-do about elephants and bridges and all manner of sentimental nonsense.

It was time to return home.

June 3, 1910
Messrs. Sorley & Still
Darley Lane
Edinburgh, Scotland

Dear Sirs,

This letter is to inform you that I will be in Scotland on
the 30th of July and hope to attend you in your cham-
bers. It is my intention to list my property for sale and
desire that you would conduct all necessary transactions.
In particular, please advise the tenants so that they might
make arrangements to vacate the property. I will take
possession of some personal effects and small items of
furnishings upon my arrival. Please arrange for the dis-
posal or sale of the remaining furnishings.

I thank you for your kind attentions and will wait
upon your response.

I remain,

Brodie Smith

Chapter Forty-Eight: Visitors from Buffalo

Braemor, Ontario ~ June 20, 1910

When Charley told Alistair of Brodie's imminent return, his relief was palpable. He'd since made the arrangements Callaghan had asked for and instructed his crew that important visitors from Buffalo were coming.

Still, Alistair woke on Monday morning with a sense of unease. Today was the day his guests were expected. He had already confirmed with Justus and Charley the hotel's preparedness for the party of twelve. He had smartened up the downstairs of the farmhouse in case a visit was warranted, and had carefully selected his nearly best tweed suit and a new woollen tie for the occasion. His shoes were polished, his hair combed down, and his nerves on edge as he set out for the brickworks.

Thomas had arrived early; the men were in full production. All around them haying was taking place on neighbouring farms, its sweet, freshly-cut aroma wafting occasionally towards them on the breeze. Tiny figures could be seen in the distance, bending over with their scythes and cradles. The bricks had been drying for over a week, and today was the day when they would once more begin loading the kiln. Alistair instructed Thomas to keep the loading light lest their visitors be interested in viewing the inside dimensions of the kiln itself. Thomas lifted his cap in acquiescence. Alistair smiled at this, knowing full well what his silence implied: that he'd rather not be held back by waiting upon toffs.

Three trains were scheduled that day, and Alistair found himself listening for their whistles at the crossing. He deliberated riding to the station but decided that would appear overeager. His guests would expect to meet him at the hotel in the evening, and not before.

At four o'clock Alistair heard a familiar voice greeting the men and asking after him. He stepped outside to meet his friend.

Brodie!

Is all well here?

Indeed. We're loading for another firing.

You've left our guests unattended at the hotel.

Have they come so soon?

Yes. On the noon train. Justus has welcomed them and seen them to their rooms. The ladies have rather a lot of luggage and are resting after their journey. The men, it seems, are eager for their sport and have already taken a walk to the river.

I thought for certain they'd arrive later and that I'd see them at the hotel.

Och well, they're looked after.

I should go meet them.

I'll come. I directed them to the Brae. They'll likely want to fish when the sun goes down. It's still too high.

Shall I stop for my gear?

There'll be time for that tomorrow. I have Charley's trap close by.

Alistair swept dust from his trouser legs and reached for his jacket. Shrugging himself into it, he grimaced at Brodie. *Is Mr. Tremont with the party?*

I canna say. I was no introduced to everyone.

How was your journey?

It was well. I met a chap from outside Ottawa who was on his way to a farm implement show in Toronto. We passed the time together and I found the trip went quickly. He was a clever fellow, I think.

Brodie, I'm glad you're back, that is certain. I couldna have managed this as well without you. Alistair clapped Brodie on the back as they climbed up into the pony trap.

And I'm glad to be home. I'm sorry about Coombs. A bad job. Brodie directed the pony towards the river; they travelled companionably until the path ran out. The two hopped down from the bench and fastened the reins to a tree.

Let's walk down the embankment to see if we can spy them. Brodie paused. *There's something I need to discuss, Al. Charley is still no well. She's trying, but the sadness overwhelms her.*

I know, Brodie, I've been watching her in your absence.

I think she needs a change of place. Everything here reminds her o' Johnny. The house, the farm, the town, the people. Her loss is writ large everywhere she looks.

Alistair stopped walking and looked at Brodie curiously. *What are you thinking?*

A long holiday. It would be good for her.

Where would you go?

My uncle's house is let for the time being. I'll take her to Edinburgh and see to the property. We could visit the Highlands and spend some time touring. There are places I would show her.

Alistair listened, his stomach sinking at the thought of losing his friends. *But you will come back?*

After a time. When she's ready.

Alistair nodded. *It willna be the same wi' out your ugly mug.*

The men laughed awkwardly. *Shall we?* Brodie asked, gesturing towards the river.

They set off down the steep incline, picking their way through the brush until they were able to step among the river rock and scan the banks in either direction. To their surprise they saw the group, thigh-deep in the river, a few hundred feet away, already at sport although it was yet bright.

Callaghan spotted them at the same time. As they waved at one another he waded out of the water and along the bank towards them. Amid enthusiastic greetings, they shook hands with firm grasps.

It's early yet for fishing, Brodie remarked.

Callaghan smiled. *We're not fishing so much as trying our casts. There are some among us who were determined to get in some practice.*

Who's fishing? asked Alistair. *Do I recognize Mr. Lewis and Mr. Carmel?*

You do.

Alistair couldn't help himself. *And is that slight young man Mr. Tremont?*

Not Mr. Tremont, said Callaghan. *He's returned to New York, as I understand it.*

Och… that is a surprise, said Alistair, attempting to suppress a grin, *I thought he and Miss Lewis were keeping company.*

We thought so too. The ladies in particular. But Gibson couldn't stand the chap's politics. He was a Taft booster. Always going on about the damned reciprocity agreement and free trade.

Alistair took a step back.

No offence meant, son. You're not so much a Canadian yet that I might speak freely. The agreement provides infinite advantage to the Canadians and is not good for American steel. All his talk of such trade made him unpopular.

I see.

The ladies said something about an offer, Callaghan continued blithely, *but I understand he was refused. Miss Lewis could fill you in. You became acquainted during your time in Buffalo, I think.*

Alistair flushed deeply at this.

I wouldn't worry, Alistair. We are all of us men guilty of having fallen prey to their charms. And she is spirited.

Alistair cleared his throat. *So, she has no become attached?*

Mr. Callaghan looked at Alistair indulgently. *Not that I know. Gibson Lewis hasn't indicated otherwise.* Despite himself, Alistair broke into a wide smile. He kept on smiling at Callaghan as a dozen thoughts raced through his mind.

She's not so bad with a rod either. She can cast as well as most of us. Not having a son, Gibson has taken her with him on many of his fishing trips.

Alistair looked at his companion quizzically.

It was Callaghan's turn to smile. *Look, over there.* Gesturing with his head, he indicated the slight boy who was just now tossing the most elegant of casts above the river, the lengthy line looping gracefully as it fell.

Alistair looked from Callaghan to the boy and saw, for the first time, that wisps of long curling hair were trailing down from under the hat, and that the figure was indeed girlish.

Is that…

Callaghan nodded. *It is. That's why some of the ladies have come. To keep things proper. That girl loves to fish.*

Without responding, Alistair plunged into the Brae and took giant sloshing steps towards her. He moved rapidly until he was perhaps eight feet away and then stopped to look at her. She smiled at him as she pulled off her hat and shook out her long hair. And then she laughed, the gay, tinkling laugh that he'd remembered so many times. Alistair stood still for a moment, taking in the sight and the sound of her.

Later she would joke that since the salmon weren't yet biting, she'd decided to catch herself a husband instead. But Alistair didn't mind how she put it. She was in Braemor. And while he knew that trouble and change would come to challenge them, he was, for now, content.

Dundee, Scotland ~ September 21, 1910

Brodie had looked forward to this stop on their excursion. The day before, when he and Charley had wandered through the city, he'd pointed out the school, the tiny row house, and the Firth that formed the three touchstones of his earliest memories. The day had been a fair one, and so they had left the area around Dundee's port and walked out into the country, passing orchards and the manor house where he and his mother had trekked carrying a wicker basket between them, filled with starched and mended linens. He did not point out the house to Charley but reminisced inwardly instead, conjuring the memory of his mother slipping mason jars into lace cuffs and daubing them all over with a fine starch made from sugar and a little potato.

When, after a distance Charley grew weary, Brodie spread his jacket on lush grass near an apple tree. She lay down and was soon deeply asleep. Brodie sat beside her and studied her restful face. She looked particularly well, he thought. The trip had done wonders for her. She'd gained a little weight and her face and figure were looking fuller and softer than they had done. He'd noted a thickness to her waist when she was dressing, and had seen her loosening the laces on her corset.

After an hour of lazing roadside, they returned to their rented rooms. For their evening meal the landlady had prepared a simple fare of bangers and tatties. Charley had suddenly pushed her plate aside, saying quietly that the sausages must have gone off. Brodie lifted her plate to his nose and sniffed it delicately, assuring her that all was well. *No matter,* she said. *I've no appetite.*

Later that evening she had again been sick, insisting once more that the food hadn't been well prepared and had upset her stomach. Lying abed, she told Brodie that the smell of baked salmon was drifting upstairs and making her gag. Could he please go downstairs and find whoever was eating fish so late at night and bid them please stop? This last request seemed particularly ludicrous but Brodie obligingly did as asked. To his relief, he discovered that there was no one eating fish or anything else that might be mistaken for fish. He returned upstairs to find Charley once more retching violently.

And now they were standing on a hill, studying the curve of the bridge expanse away from the bank, stretching boldly through the Firth of Tay. Brodie eyed the piers and riveted girders appraisingly. Much work was represented in this assembly, he knew. A crew of near forty men had laboured five years to construct it. Besides that were the more than twenty directors who had financed the undertaking and provided oversight. The stumps of the old bridge piers were still visible. Under the water, Brodie knew, lay some of the ironwork and detritus from the first bridge. Although pieces of the original trusses had been salvaged and incorporated into the new structure, the new bridge was far larger and more carefully built.

Charley watched him as he studied the scene, her arm tucked securely into his. He looked alert, his gaze piercing; he was clearly deep in thought. This was a side of him she had not often witnessed. With her he was typically attentive and light-hearted, setting aside his work concerns and interests.

Will you tell me, she finally said, *what has you so in thrall?*

Brodie startled at the sound of her voice. *It's seeing these waters again that brings it all back. How when the first bridge went down my father had the blame of it. How our name was tarnished, and I... well. You know all this. How it was that bridge-making took hold of me. How to make them safe. How beautiful they could be.* He stopped and shook his head. *I was gazing at this great construction, you see, and thinking on't.*

And did you never think, said Charley shyly, *that you might make something besides a bridge?*

Like bricks? laughed Brodie. *No, but I met Alistair and we set out together to see what we could do.*

I meant something smaller, perhaps, like a baby?

Brodie was about to retort, to say something foolish and laugh off her question, when he saw that she was looking at him anxiously, her free hand resting at her waist. And then he realized what it was she was saying and he pulled her to him in the tightest of embraces and squeezed her close.

It will atone, he whispered. *It will atone.*

Acknowledgements

I wish to respectfully acknowledge the unfortunate souls who lost their lives in the *Tay Bridge Disaster*. An event of this scale leaves its mark on families and also on a community. This work is no way intended to accurately document the disaster nor the lives of persons involved in the actual tragedy. My apologies for any inadvertent inaccuracies, omissions, errors or misrepresentations I may have committed in the text. My thanks to Chris Needham and the team at Now Or Never Publishing for their belief in this book and for their support. My thanks also to Karen Alliston who edited a final version of the manuscript. I am particularly indebted to Daniel Weinrub for his suggestions about the engineering of bridges and the importance of rivets. I appreciate the expertise of Jack and Lois Taylor who answered questions about brickmaking in Beaverton, Ontario. Paul and Isabel Arculus and Marilyn Black were keen enthusiasts and early readers of the manuscript. Al Playter's historic photographs of the *Don Valley Brickworks* were also inspiring, as was my childhood visit there when it was still in operation. Andrew Black's suggestion about fire-setters was a timely and significant addition to the story. Kay Notman's assistance with the language and dialect was valuable although any missteps in this regard are my own. *The Claybank Brick Plant National Historic Site* in Claybank, Saskatchewan is an interactive museum providing a glimpse of brickmaking and early twentieth century industrialization. My research there has greatly informed this work. Similarly, published papers from ASI Heritage were also instructive. *Verdant Works* in Dundee, Scotland is a restored jute mill that celebrates the importance of the textile industry to the local economy. My visit was both inspiring and informative. With thanks also to my family and many friends who continue to encourage and indulge me. In particular I must thank Donna Morrissey, Angie Littlefield and Shelley Macbeth for their ongoing and faithful support. My writing sisters, Crystal Fletcher, Hollay Ghadery, Laura Francis, Anna Liza Kozma, and Hejsa Christensen are a tremendous gift in my life and I love and appreciate them. And finally, with thanks to Michael Black, my partner in all things.

"*Stella's Carpet* is a treat—a multinational, multigenerational gem of a novel about family, loss and the ties that bind. Lucy Black writes with heart, verve... and oodles of talent."

~Brad Smith, award-winning author of *Copperhead Road, The Return of Kid Cooper* and *Cactus Jack*

"*The Brickworks* is an entertaining glimpse of life in the burgeoning industrial age of late 19th century Ontario and New York. As an archaeologist who has studied 19th century brickmaking sites in Ontario, I was delighted by Lucy E.M. Black's detailed descriptions and accurate portrayal of the industrial brick-making process, the innovative machinery for mass production, and its impact on the people who toiled to turn clay into building material. The hardships of such entrepreneurial endeavors, the passion and drive to make them happen, and the engineering know-how are all vividly and meticulously depicted in this enchanting read."

~ Gregory Pugh, MA, Senior Archaeologist, ASI Heritage

"At a time when so many writers are venturing into the genre of historical fiction while displaying so little effort applied to historical research, it is refreshing to encounter a novel that is meticulously researched while being so entertainingly presented. In *The Brickworks* Lucy E.M. Black has presented us with characters, their personalities, their language and technology and the events that surround them, all flawlessly accurate and plausibly set in the late nineteenth and early twentieth century. As the setting weaves seamlessly from Scotland, to Ontario and then New York State, the development of the story and characters is contextually and chronologically accurate and highly entertaining. With this novel, Black has placed herself firmly among the most capable of Canadian writers of historical fiction. I am anxiously waiting to read more of her work."

~ Paul Arculus, writer and historian

"Lucy E.M. Black arrives into the world of CanLit with this compilation of beautifully written short stories that speak to the heartfelt intimacies of both her characters and her readers."

~ Donna Morrissey, author of *Kit's Law* and *Downhill Chance* on Black's *The Marzipan Fruit Basket*